# Citadels of Mystery

*Atlantis – Troy – the Pyramids – Ma'rib – Tikal – Stonehenge – Zimbabwe – Tintagel Castle – Machu Picchu – Rapa Nui – Angkor Wat – Nan Matol . . .*

For hundreds of years, scholars and poets alike have been caught in the spell of these citadels of mystery. Men through the ages have become obsessed with them, and volumes have been written on each; yet in many cases the truth lies hidden in the darkness of unrecorded history. The emergence of archaeology as a science has forced the past to yield up many of its secrets, but often the advance of knowledge gives rise to riddles even more perplexing and fascinating than the myths and legends that haunt these sites.

With consummate mastery the authors of *Citadels of Mystery* describe each site, review its factual and legendary history, and evaluate contemporary theories and controversies and they never exploit the mystery at the expense of scientific accuracy or sound judgment.

L. SPRAGUE DE CAMP has been engineer, patent expert, naval officer, editor, lecturer and well-known science fiction writer. He is the author of *The Floating Continent* and *A Planet Called Krishna*. CATHERINE C. DE CAMP, formerly a teacher, has long assisted her husband in editing and writing.

# Citadels of Mystery

L. SPRAGUE DE CAMP AND
CATHERINE C. DE CAMP

Fontana/Collins

First published in Great Britain by Souvenir Press Ltd 1965
First issued in Fontana Books 1972
Second Impression September 1972
Third Impression February 1973
Fourth Impression June 1973
Fifth Impression May 1974

Printed in Great Britain
Collins Clear-Type Press London and Glasgow

*This book is dedicated to our old friend and collaborator,
P. Schuyler Miller, who is what we have often secretly
wished to be: a real archaeologist.*

# Contents

*Introduction*

| | | |
|---|---|---|
| I | Atlantis and the City of Silver | 1 |
| II | Pyramid Hill and the Claustrophobic King | 27 |
| III | Stonehenge and the Giants' Dance | 43 |
| IV | Troy and the Nine Cities | 67 |
| V | Ma'rib and the Queen of Sheba | 95 |
| VI | Zimbabwe and King Solomon's Mines | 111 |
| VII | Tintagel and the Table Round | 139 |
| VIII | Angkor and the Golden Window | 161 |
| IX | Tikal and the Feathered Elephants | 179 |
| X | Machu Picchu and the Unwalled Fortress | 203 |
| XI | Nan Matol and the Sacred Turtle | 221 |
| XII | Rapa Nui and the Eyeless Watchers | 237 |

*Postscript* 262
*Notes* 264
*Bibliography* 271
*Index* 283

# Plates

1. The Sphinx and the Great Pyramid of Cheops (*J. Allan Cash*)
2. Stonehenge (*photographed by Donald McLeish, Popperfoto*)
3. The walls of Troy (*Turkish Tourism Information Office*)
4. Zimbabwe ruins (*J. Allan Cash*)
5. Tintagel Castle (*Aerofilms Ltd*)
6. Merlin's Cave, near Tintagel Castle (*Aerofilms Ltd*)
7. Angkor (*Popperfoto*)
8. Mayan pyramid, Tikal (*Mike Andrews*)
9. Statues outside the crater of Rano Raraku, Easter Island (*Popperfoto*)

# Illustrations in Text

1. City of Atlantis — 5
2. Landa's "Mayan Alphabet." — 9
3. Symbols from the Troano Codex — 10
4. Map of Atlantis — 12
5. Inscription on a ring found at Tartessos — 22
6. Cross-section of Khufu's Great Pyramid — 35
7. Plan of Stonehenge — 53
8. Plan of Troy VI and VIIa — 87
9. Ma'rib region of Yemen — 101
10. Map of the Ma'rib Dam — 103
11. Tribal map of South-east Africa — 122
12. Drawings of a Mayan glyph — 184
13. Top of Stela B at Copán — 185
14. Map of Tikal — 189
15. Map of Nan Matol — 225
16. Writing on a Pascuan rongorongo board — 255

# Acknowledgements

Several short sections of this book have appeared as articles in *Astounding Science Fiction, Fate, Frontiers, Natural History Magazine, Other Worlds Science Stories, Science Fiction Quarterly,* and *Travel,* for which permission to use is gratefully acknowledged. Permission is also gratefully acknowledged for the use of drawings as follows: to the American Foundation for the Study of Man for the maps of the Ma'rib Dam (from Bowen & Albright: *Archaeological Discoveries in South Arabia,* © 1958 by the American Foundation for the Study of Man); and to the American Philosophical Society for the map of Angkor (from Briggs: *The Ancient Khmer Empire,* © 1951 by the American Philosophical Society). Photographs are acknowledged in the list of plates.

Grateful acknowledgement is made to the following for permission to include the following copyrighted selections included in this book:

*Dodd, Mead & Company* and *Miss D. E. Collins* for the excerpt from "Lepanto," from THE COLLECTED POEMS OF G. K. CHESTERTON. Copyright 1932 by Dodd, Mead & Company. Reprinted by permission of the publisher and Miss D. E. Collins.

*Travel* Magazine for "Lost Cities" by L. Sprague de Camp, which appeared in *Travel* Magazine in the December 1957 issue.

Thanks also to the following for the use of quotations: To Arkham House for the quotations from Lin Carter's poem *Carcosa,* Robert E. Howard's poem *Easter Island,* H. P. Lovecraft's poem *To Clark Ashton Smith,* and Clark Ashton Smith's poem *Revenant;* to Lin Carter for the quotations from his poems *Carcosa* and *Black Zimbabwe;* to Stanton A. Coblentz for the quotation from his poem *Atlantis;* and to the Dowager Lady Dunsany for the twelve lines from Lord Dunsany's story "The Lord of Cities," in *A Dreamer's Tales,* John W. Luce & Co., 1910, pp. 205ff.

The sources of the quotations used as chapter headings are: Chapter I, from Stanton A. Coblentz: *Atlantis,* in *Weird Tales,*

Nov. 1947, © 1947 by Weird Tales, Inc.; and in *Fire and Sleet and Candlelight*, edited by August Derleth, Arkham House, 1961. Chapter II, from H. P. Lovecraft: "Robert Ervin Howard: A Memoriam," in *Fantasy Magazine*, Sep. 1936, © 1936 by Julius Schwartz; and in Robert E. Howard: *Skull-Face and Others*, Arkham House, 1946. Chapter III, from George Gordon, Lord Byron: *Childe Harold's Pilgrimage*, Canto IV. Chapter IV, from the Byzantine historian Georgios Kedrinos, in Edwyn Bevan: *Later Greek Religion*, Lon.: Dent, 1927, p. 234. Chapter V, from Edward Fitzgerald: *Rubáiyát of Omar Khayyám*, Stanza xviii. Chapter VI, from an unpublished poem by Lin Carter: *Black Zimbabwe*. Chapter VII, from Alfred Tennyson, Lord Tennyson: *The Holy Grail*. Chapter VIII, from Robert E. Howard: "Black Colossus," in *Weird Tales*, June, 1933, © 1933 by Popular Fiction Publishing Co.; and in *Conan the Barbarian*, Gnome Press, 1954. Chapter IX, from H. P. Lovecraft: *To Clark Ashton Smith*, in *Weird Tales*, April, 1938, © 1938 by Popular Fiction Publishing Co.; and in *Beyond the Wall of Sleep*, Arkham House, 1943. Chapter X, from Percy Bysshe Shelley: *The Revolt of Islam*, Canto XIII, Stanza xxxv. Chapter XI, from Lin Carter: *Carcosa*, in *Fire and Sleet and Candlelight*, Arkham House, © 1961 by August Derleth. Chapter XII, Robert E. Howard: *Easter Island*, in *Weird Tales*, Dec. 1928; © 1928 by Popular Fiction Publishing Co.; and in Robert E. Howard: *Always Comes Evening*, Arkham House, 1957. Clark Ashton Smith's poem *Revenant*, quoted in the Introduction, was published in *The Dark Chateau*, Arkham House, © 1951 by Clark Ashton Smith.

For various helping hands—obtaining books and pictures for us, answering questions, speeding us on our travels to visit some of the sites, reading parts or all of the manuscript, and making suggestions and criticisms—we are grateful to William Boney, François Bordes, C. Gordon Bulloch, John L. Caskey, Ray L. Cleveland, Roy Creeth, August Derleth, Senator Thomas J. Dodd, Caroline Gordon Dosker, Mohamed Ezzat Abdel Wahab, Samuel Freiha, Bernard Groslier, Mary Virginia Harris, Josephine Henry, Alex Inglesby, Ibrahim Kazanjian, Alfred Kidder II, Willy Ley, J. Alden Mason, P. Schuyler Miller, Denys L. Page, Roger C. Ravel, John H. Rowe, James Sax, Walter Scott-Elliot, Catherine Pearce Shoeffler, Mohamed Sobeih, Robert C. Suggs, Robert Wauchope, Donald N. Wilber, Howard H. Williams, Richard H. Wilmer, and Conway Zirkle.

*L. Sprague de Camp*
*Catherine C. de Camp*

# Introduction

Many people are romantics at heart. Ancient ruins and lost cities fascinate them. Every year they swarm abroad to seek the glamour of the old, the faraway, the mysterious. Standing in the shadow of a moonlit pyramid, gazing across the battlements of a timeworn castle, or watching the sunset redden the marble columns of a Doric temple, they dream of a heroic past in which all men were mighty, all women beautiful, all life adventurous, and all problems simple.

Of course, we really know better. No demon-king Thevatat ever spun deadly spells of malignant magic in his jeweled lair in the Atlantean City of the Golden Gates. No Conan of Cimmeria ever strode through "Zamora with its dark-haired women and towers of spider-haunted mystery" or "Stygia with its shadow-guarded tombs." The real Carthage, as revealed by the archaeologist's gingerly shovel and whisk, is not Flaubert's fantastic fictional metropolis, with its somber magnificence and sinister glitter; instead, it is more or less "a prosaic city of shopkeepers."[1]

Nevertheless, the old glamour still clings to these ancient buildings,

> As the ghost of Homer clings
> Round Scamander's wasting springs . . [2]

And many of the facts that science has turned up concerning them are not prosaic at all, but very curious indeed. Even the legends and fictions that waft about such places are delightful in themselves. Moreover, many of the ideas, discoveries, and arts of the people who built these structures are woven into the fabric of our own civilization.

This book will describe a dozen of these ruins, widely scattered about the globe, in which the shards of history lie waiting to be sifted out of the dust heaps of myth and ignorance. We will tell of the discovery of these ruins, the controversies over them, the fictional and pseudo-scientific uses to which they have been put, and the progress of archaeology towards solving the enigmas they present. We have visited as many of these sites as circumstances allowed. If we have not included all the latest discoveries and speculations about all twelve places, the reason is that new facts are unearthed every year. Had we waited for the final, definitive theories to take shape, this book would never have been written.

So come with us, and

> . . . search, in cryptic galleries,
> The void sarcophagi, the broken urns
> Of many a vanished avatar;
> Or haunt the gloom of crumbling pylons vast
> In temples that enshrine the shadowy past.[8]

We have used the same system of indicating dates as that employed in *The Ancient Engineers*. Dates B.C. and A.D. are indicated by the signs — and + respectively. Years are in Arabic and centuries in Roman numerals; hence —II means the second century B.C., while +50 means A.D. 50. The plus sign is omitted from dates after +1000.

# I

# Atlantis and the
# City of Silver

Legend has sunk it where the shoreless foam
Goes scudding over unplumbed leagues of sea.
But I have seen it glittering, dome on dome,
Spire on spire, in castled sovereignty . . .
                                        *Coblentz*

A ruin strikes a romantic chord in all of us. Do its lines of crumbling brick or mossy stone trace out the streets of a city? Our fancy rebuilds its broken masonry, piece upon piece. Imagination peoples the site with garrulous throngs that anciently jostled, squabbled, haggled, and laughed along the avenues, where now all is still save for a whirring bird, a scuttling scorpion, or a wandering goat.

Even though we scoff at magic, a ruin rouses the awesome feeling that everything that ever happened in a place somehow lingers on there, that the very stones could whisper the secrets of centuries if they would. "The battlefields where the dice of world history have been thrown can never be ordinary fields again and no god from a vanished civilization is so dead that he does not live on in his ruined temple."[1]

We sense that the ruin and we ourselves are parts of the same vast stream of history. We fancy that by our mere presence we draw upon the strength and craft of mighty men, whose very names are now forgotten but who strove and schemed here long ago. So strong is this surge of feeling that nineteenth-century romantics sometimes built synthetic ruins on their estates, where they could sit and brood like Shelley's Prince Athanase upon his Alp.

In the thousands of years since men began to build them, many splendid cities have raised their shining towers against the stars. Of those in which men still dwell, Jericho is perhaps the oldest, because the site (or one close by) has been occupied for at least seven thousand years. Arbela in northern Iraq has stood nearly as long; Damascus, Tyre, and Cádiz were all founded over three thousand years ago. But scores of other cities have flowered for a few centuries and then vanished from the earth, save for such skeletal remains as still project above the desert sands, or lie askew and tumbled beneath the jungle's groping grip, or maintain their existence only as a whisper in a dubious legend.

How have they vanished? Conquerors have leveled some, while burning buildings cast a lurid light on piles of human heads, reflected redly in streams of blood that gurgled in the gutters. The shift of a trade route, the drying-up of a river, or the removal of a seat of government has caused others to wither like girdled trees.

Angkor in the Cambodian jungle, Sijilmassa in the Moroccan waste, and Nineveh in the Assyrian hills all fell to foes. Rose-red Petra dwindled when the Romans ousted its Nabataean dynasty and the caravan routes removed to Tadmor. An earthquake leveled Knossos, while Crustumius sank beneath the sea.

Some ruins, though vast, are not the remains of true cities at all. Some like Persepolis, Hadrian's Villa, and the Escorial were oversized palace compounds, whence a mighty monarch sent his orders speeding to the corners of his far-flung realm. Others were temples, like Stonehenge, where the Elder Gods were adored with solemn or sanguinary rites. A few, like the City of the Dead across the Nile from Luxor, were nought but huge necropoleis, on which their builders lavished more thought and effort than they did upon the dwellings of living men.

Much of human history has vanished forever down the voracious gullet of time. Much can only be guessed from worn coins, mute shards, and cryptic literary hints. Yet around a number of ruins, like swarms of bats, swirl clouds of rumors, legends, theories, controversies, and outright hoaxes. This book tells of some of the more enigmatic of these ruins, of the disputes that have raged about them, and of the progress that has been made towards unlocking their crypts of mystery.

In history and archaeology there are several kinds of mystery. Sometimes the information exists, it is hoped, but has not yet been dug up or deciphered; examples are the archaeology of the Pacific islands and the Indus Valley script. Sometimes the information existed but was accidentally or purposely destroyed, as when the Christian missionaries burned the writings of the Mayas. And sometimes it is a synthetic mystery; there is nothing really very cryptic about the ruins, but enthusiasts—pseudo-scientists, occultists, crackpots, and otherwise sober men with an *idée fixe*—have striven to make it mysterious. We shall come across mysteries of all three kinds in the course of this book.

Perhaps the grandest and most colorful mystery of all is that of the lost continent of Atlantis. The name "Atlantis" conjures up visions of something wonderful, a shining land of beauty and plenty, where peace and justice reigned; a country lying far off in golden splendor in the midst of the wide blue sea; a land, alas, now gone forever beneath the ocean waves.

Nearly two thousand books and articles have been written about Atlantis. Scores of novels and short stories and several motion pictures have been based upon the idea. The Catalan poet Jacinto Verdaguer composed an epic poem, *La Atlántida*, on the theme; Manuel de Falla based an unfinished opera upon the epic. The name has been used for ships, periodicals, hotels, restaurants, book shops, theatrical acts, an engineering firm, a publishing company, a real-estate development, and a region of the planet Mars.

The concept of Atlantis has given rise to speculations from the soberest science to the wildest fantasy. Learned men have spent years running down the sources of the idea of a sunken continent in the Atlantic Ocean. They have thumbed old manuscripts, dug for vanished civilizations, and lowered searchlights and cameras to the bottom of the sea.

Where did this idea of a sunken Atlantic continent come from? And what scientific basis, if any, is there for it?

The answer to the first question is simple. Atlantis came from the teeming brain of the Greek philosopher Plato.[2] In all ages there have been men who, disappointed in the world as it was, consoled themselves by composing imaginary Edens, Utopias, and Golden Ages. Of these builders of Cloud-Cuckoo-Lands, Plato was the most successful.

About —355, when Plato was in his seventies, he wrote two dialogues, *Timaios* and *Kritias*. These are little plays in which Plato's old teacher, Sokrates, sits talking with his friends, one of whom tells the basic story of Atlantis. These two dialogues are the sole source of today's huge mass of lost-continent theory, legend, and literature. Except for Plato's tale and the comments upon it by his successors, there is not another word about Atlantis in all the ancient literature that has come down to us.

In *Timaios*, Plato's older kinsman Kritias (in real life a talented historian and a rascally politician) explains that he got the story from his grandfather, who got it from *his* father, who got it from the statesman Solon. According to Kritias, when Solon visited Egypt about —590, a priest of Saïs told him the following tale:

Nine thousand years before, there had existed a great Athenian nation, a prehistoric precursor of Solon's Athens. There had also been, in the Atlantic Ocean, a mighty empire of Atlantis, set on a rugged island or continent larger than North Africa and Asia Minor combined and rich in plants and minerals. Atlantis tried to conquer the Mediterranean world but was beaten off by the brave Athenians. Then a fearful earthquake ruined Athens, engulfed the Athenian army, and sank Atlantis beneath the sea. One could no longer sail westward from the Pillars of Herakles—the Strait of Gibraltar—because of the shoals of mud left by the continent when it settled.

In *Kritias*, wherein the same group of characters carries on the dialogue, Plato goes into more detail. When, after the Creation, the gods divided up the world, Athena acquired Greece. There the goddess of wisdom set up the first Athenian state. This state was organized according to a plan, which Plato (by quaint coincidence) was to set forth nine thousand-odd years later in his earlier dialogue *The Republic*, and which the Spartans of Plato's time were to realize in actual fact. The realm was ruled by a communistic military caste. Everybody was brave, handsome, and virtuous (just like the Red Army as described in *Pravda*).

Poseidon, the sea god, got Atlantis for his share. Here he mated with a mortal maid, Kleito. A fertile fellow like all the gods, Poseidon begat ten sons. He divided the island up amongst these sons to rule as a confederacy of kings. The eldest, Atlas, was to be the high king.

These kings and their descendants built the city of Atlantis. Like the Caliph al-Manṣûr's Baghdad, Atlantis was a perfectly circular metropolis. It was fifteen miles across with a canal through the middle, connecting the sea with a great oblong irrigated plain, about 230 miles wide by 340 miles long.

4

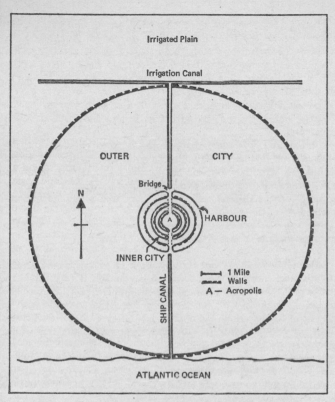

*Fig. 1  The city of Atlantis, as described in Plato's Kritias.*

In the center of the city, on the site of Poseidon's love nest, stood the citadel, also circular and about three miles in diameter. It consisted of concentric rings of land and water, interconnected by bridges and tunnels. Here were palaces, temples, racetracks, and other public structures. The palaces and temples were lavishly decorated with gold, silver, bronze, ivory (from Atlantean elephants), and the mysterious metal *oreichalkos*, literally "mountain copper," which "glowed like fire." By this "orichalc" Plato probably meant either brass or some other yellow alloy of copper.

There is, however, no word of explosives, searchlights, or airplanes, despite the fact that imaginative modern Atlantists have credited the Atlanteans with these and other advanced devices. The only ship mentioned is the trireme (*triērē*), the standard battleship of Plato's own time. Plato described no technics not known to his own Mediterranean world of —IV.

The ten Atlantean kings met every fifth or sixth year to discuss affairs of state. This they did after sacrificing a bull with elaborate ceremonies.

For hundreds of years, the Atlanteans were virtuous like the Athenians of that elder day. But in time they suffered a moral decline. In fact, they became so greedy, corrupt, and ambitious that Zeus decided to punish them. He called the gods to a meeting in his palace to discuss the matter, ". . . and when he had assembled them, he spoke thus: . . ."

Here the dialogue ends in mid-sentence. We never do learn the promised details of the Atheno-Atlantean war.

Although several ancient writers after Plato mentioned Plato's Atlantis story, none of them seems to have taken it very seriously. Plato's pupil Aristotle, Strabon the geographer, and Plinius the Roman encyclopedist all took it for granted that Atlantis was an allegorical fiction, which Plato had made up to set forth his theories about the perfect state. From what we know of Plato, this would have been quite in character.

In the later Roman Empire, however, critical standards, which had never been high according to modern ideas, declined still further. As a result, writers like Proklos the Neoplatonist began to take the Atlantis tale seriously.

After +VI, Atlantis was neglected and almost forgotten for almost a thousand years. But, when the Age of Exploration began in late +XV with the voyages of Columbus and Vasco da Gama, interest in Atlantis came to life. Some scholars identified Atlantis with America, even though Atlantis was supposed to have sunk.

At this time, rumors of new lands ran riot, and the Italian and Iberian explorers were far from exact in their reports. Maps were covered with geographical fictions. The Atlantic in particular was spotted with nonexistent islands, sometimes including Atlantis, raised again from the deep for the cartographer's purposes.

One such geographic ghost, not exorcized from the maps until

+XIX, was an island supposed to lie about a hundred miles west of Ireland. It was known as Brazil or Hi-Brazil. In 1674 a Captain Nisbet arrived in Scotland with some "castaways" whom he claimed to have rescued from Hi-Brazil. He said the island was inhabited by gigantic black rabbits and by a magician who had been keeping the castaways captive in his castle until the gallant captain broke the spell that bound them. Alas for romance! There never was any such island near Ireland, although the legend may have grown from some pre-Columbian voyage that reached Newfoundland.

At this time, also, several thinkers wrote fanciful accounts of ideal commonwealths. Sir Thomas More composed his celebrated *Utopia* (Greek for "nowhere") and was disconcerted when people wrote him urging that missionaries be sent to Christianize the Utopians. Later, Sir Francis Bacon wrote *The New Atlantis,* drawing upon both More and Plato. His narrator tells of discovering a South Sea island inhabited by Atlanteans. These people had fled thither from the original Atlantis, in the Americas, when a great flood devastated it.

The writing of utopias was already an old and well-developed art. The Hellenistic writer Iamboulos, shortly after Plato's time, had written about an island in the Indian Ocean, where the people— who had flexible bones and forked tongues, with which they could carry on two conversations at once—lived according to the rules of Stoic philosophy.

The discovery of America loosed a flood of pseudo-scientific speculation about the origin of the redskinned natives. People who met the Amerinds for the first time rashly concluded that they were speaking Welsh and hence were the descendants of the half-legendary medieval Welsh Prince Madoc and his band; or that they were practicing Hebrew religious rites and were therefore the Lost Ten Tribes of Israel. Because anthropology and linguistics hardly existed, such assertions could not easily be disproved. Although none of them was true, some people have adhered to them even to this day. They believe them in spite of the fact that science has shown, as conclusively as such a thing can be proved, that the Amerinds belong to the Mongoloid race of mankind and came over from Asia via Alaska in a trickle of migrations lasting thousands of years.

One sixteenth-century invader of the New World was Diego de

7

Landa, a Spanish monk who came in with the conquistadores and rose to be bishop of Yucatán. The Mayan Indians over whom he presided had a considerable native literature, written on books made of long strips of tree-bark paper folded zigzag and bound between a pair of wooden covers. From 1562 onwards, Landa, determined to wipe out "heathen" culture and substitute Christian European civilization, burned all of these books he could find. He explained:

"We found a large number of books in these characters and, as they contained nothing in which there were not to be seen superstition and lies of the devil, we burned them all, which they regretted to an amazing degree, and which caused them much affliction."[3] Landa could not read the books, but that did not stop him from condemning them. For this vandalism the fanatical priest was criticized by some of his own Spanish colleagues and has been consigned to his Christian Hell by scholars ever since.

Subsequently, Landa became interested in the Mayan culture and undertook to learn the Mayan writing. He assumed that the Mayas wrote with a phonetic alphabet like that of Spanish and Latin, whereas they really had an ideographic system of picture writing, something like the systems of early Egyptian and modern Chinese writing. Apparently, Landa's method of research was to drag in some literate Maya, explain what he wanted, and bark:

"*¿Qué es A?*"

The poor Indian, no doubt shivering in his sandals for fear of being burned as a heretic, thought the terrible old man wanted the sign for *aac*, "turtle." So he drew it—a turtle's head.

"*¿Qué es B?*"

Now, *be* in Mayan means "road," so the Maya drew the glyph for "road"—a pair of parallel lines representing a path, and between them the outline of a human footprint. And so on through the alphabet, until Landa had twenty-seven signs and a few compounds, which did not mean at all what he thought they did. He did, however, take down a correct explanation of the Mayan numerals.

In the 1560s Landa was recalled to Spain on charges of exceeding his authority. In preparing his defense (a successful one, we are sorry to say) he wrote a great treatise on the Mayan civilization: *Relación de las Cosas de Yucatán*, or *Account of the Affairs of Yucatán*. Therein he set forth his "Mayan alphabet."

8

In this work, Landa also helped to spread the theory that the American Indians were of Jewish origin. This hypothesis—launched a few years earlier by the Spanish historian Francisco López de Gómara—led an active life for over two centuries. Even William Penn adopted it. Some believers suggested that the Amerinds ought to go back to Palestine, but luckily for the peace of the world they showed no interest in doing so.

After Landa's time, knowledge of Mayan writing was lost, because the Catholic priests continued their campaign against Mayan literature and because the Mayas themselves dropped their cumbersome ideographic writing for the easier Latin alphabet. Even Landa's treatise disappeared. Only three Mayan books survive. These are the Dresden Codex (damaged in the Second World War), the Codex Perezianus in Paris, and the Tro-Cortesianus Codex in two sections (since reunited) in Madrid.

Mayan writing remained unreadable until in 1864 a diligent but erratic French scholar, Abbé Charles-Étienne Brasseur de Bourbourg, found an abridgment of Landa's *Relación* in the library of.

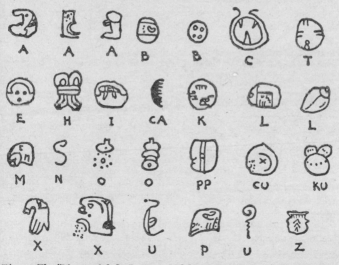

*Fig. 2 The "Mayan alphabet" transcribed by Bishop de Landa for his Relación de las Cosas de Yucatán.*

the Historical Academy of Madrid. When Brasseur saw Landa's "Mayan alphabet" he was overjoyed, thinking that he had the key to Mayan writing. Eagerly he undertook to translate the Troano Codex, one of the halves of the Tro-Cortesianus, using this alphabet and an unfettered imagination.

What Brasseur got was a rambling account of a volcanic catastrophe, beginning: "The master is he of the upheaved earth, the master of the calabash, the earth upheaved of the tawny beast (at the place engulfed beneath the floods); it is he, the master of the upheaved earth, of the swollen earth, beyond measure, he the master . . . of the basin of water."[4]

In this manuscript, Brasseur came upon a pair of symbols:

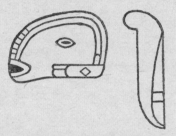

*Fig. 3  Symbols from the Troano Codex, identified by Brasseur de Bourbourg with the M and U of Landa's "Mayan alphabet."*

which he could not otherwise account for. Noting that they looked a little like Landa's M and U, he inferred that the land destroyed by this convulsion was called "Mu." That is where the name "Mu" came from.

Other scholars who tried to use this "key" got only gibberish. Now that Mayan writing has been partly deciphered, we know that Brasseur's translation was completely wrong. The Troano Codex, it turns out, is not the story of an eruption but a treatise on Mayan astrology.

Despite the downfall of Brasseur's translation, his theories were further developed by two remarkable pseudo-scientific Atlantists, Donnelly and Le Plongeon. That versatile American writer, scholar, and politician Ignatius Donnelly (1831–1901) made Atlantism into a popular cult.

Donnelly was a Philadelphia lawyer who, as a young man, moved to Minnesota and there embarked upon an active political career. At twenty-eight he was elected lieutenant governor of Minnesota. Later, during eight years in the House of Representatives in Washington, he spent much of his time in the Library of Congress, soaking up information and becoming perhaps the most erudite man ever to sit in the House. He helped to found the Populist Party and as its candidate twice ran for Vice-President of the United States.

Donnelly's *Atlantis: The Antediluvian World* appeared in 1882 and went through at least fifty printings, the last in 1963. It became the Bible of Atlantism, despite the fact that it consisted almost entirely of misstatements of fact and errors of interpretation.

Donnelly argued that if small islands can vanish in earthquakes and eruptions, why not a continent? He cited resemblances between the cultures of the peoples of New and Old Worlds and argued from these resemblances that civilization began in Atlantis. He noted, for instance, that both Amerinds and Europeans practiced marriage and divorce, that both used spears and sails, and that both believed in ghosts and flood legends. Such arguments merely show that all these people were human beings, with customs and techniques found all over the world.

Donnelly also thought he saw likenesses between Landa's "Mayan alphabet," as published by Brasseur, and Egyptian hieroglyphics. He lined up the Egyptian signs, and the Mayan symbols according to the values that Landa had assigned them, and concocted "intermediate forms" to reconcile their glaring differences.

Moreover, Donnelly claimed to detect similarities between the languages of the Chinese and of the Otomi Indians of Mexico. But, when he compiled comparative tables of Chinese and Otomi words, he succeeded in getting the Chinese words for "head," "night," "tooth," "man," and "I" dead wrong.[5]

Donnelly also popularized the equally baseless theories that Sir Francis Bacon wrote Shakespeare's plays and (long before Velikovsky) that the earth had been devastated at the dawn of history by running into a comet. When his Baconian treatise, *The Great Cryptogram*, appeared, an unkind cryptographer pointed out that by Donnelly's loose methods one could just as easily prove that Shakespeare wrote the Forty-sixth Psalm. The forty-sixth word from the beginning of this psalm is "shake"; the forty-sixth word from the end is "spear"; Q.E.D.!

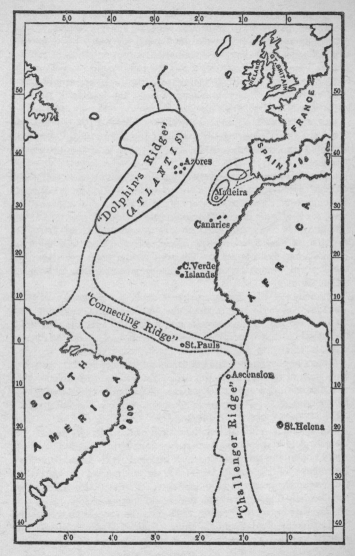

Fig. 4 Map of Atlantis, according to Ignatius Donnelly.

Donnelly's contemporary, Augustus Le Plongeon (1826–1908), was the first to excavate Mayan ruins in Yucatán, where he lived for many years. A sad-eyed, fiery-tempered French physician with a magnificent beard of patriarchal length, an apparently self-conferred medical degree, and a fiercely loyal young American wife, Le Plongeon was familiar at firsthand with the customs and speech of the Mayas. Otherwise he was no more scientific than Donnelly. He deemed Egyptian hieroglyphics to be like the Mayan and claimed to read the latter, using a modification of Brasseur's version of Landa's alphabet. But, as with the original Landa alphabet, other people who tried to read Mayan with the help of this key got nowhere.

From Brasseur's "translation" of the Troano Codex and some pictures he found on the walls of Chichén Itzá in Yucatán, Le Plongeon wove a romantic tale of Móo, queen of Atlantis or Mu, whose hand was sought by her brothers Coh ("Puma") and Aac ("Turtle"). Coh won Móo but was murdered by Aac. Then the land sank. Móo fled to Egypt where, as Isis, she founded Egyptian civilization; but at last the vengeful Aac tracked her down and killed her. Meanwhile other Muvians went to Yucatán and became the Mayas.

In the 1880s Le Plongeon and his wife settled in Brooklyn for their remaining years. They both wrote books, denouncing with ever increasing bitterness the scientists who would not take seriously their weird assertions, like the claim that Christ spoke Mayan on the cross.

The next prophet of Atlantis was Dr. Paul Schliemann, grandson of Heinrich Schliemann the archaeologist. In 1912 the younger Schliemann, apparently getting tired of being a little man with a big name, sold the New York *American* an article entitled *How I Discovered Atlantis, the Source of All Civilization.*

Schliemann said that his grandfather had left him a batch of archaeological papers and an ancient owl-headed vase. The envelope containing the papers warned that it must be opened only by a member of Schliemann's family willing to swear to devote his life to research into the matters discussed in the papers inside. Paul Schliemann took the pledge and opened the envelope.

The first instruction was to break open the vase. Inside, he found square coins of platinum-aluminum-silver alloy and a metal plate inscribed, in Phoenician: "Issued in the Temple of Transparent

Walls." Among his grandfather's notes, quoth Paul Schliemann, he came across an account of finding at Troy a large bronze vase inscribed: FROM THE KING CRONOS OF ATLANTIS.

Schliemann borrowed—without credit—the arguments of Donnelly and Le Plongeon for the common origin, in Atlantis, of the New and Old World cultures. He claimed to have read the Troano Codex. He confirmed the story of the sinking of Mu by reference to an imaginary 4,000-year-old Chaldean manuscript from a Buddhist temple in Tibet, of all places. He claimed this manuscript told how the Land of the Seven Cities was destroyed by earthquake and eruption after the star Bel fell, while Mu, the priest of Ra, told the terrified people that he had warned them of their fate.

Schliemann promised further revelations, but they never came. Nor did the owl-headed vase and its contents ever see the light of public display. The patent fact that the whole thing was a hoax has not stopped Atlantists from quoting Paul Schliemann as an authority, sometimes confusing him with his grandfather.

Following Schliemann came James Churchward, a small, wraithlike Anglo-American who called himself "colonel" and claimed to have traveled widely in Asia and Central America, where he was once attacked by a flying snake. In the 1920s and 30s Churchward broke into print with a series of books on Mu, beginning with *The Lost Continent of Mu* (1926). He averred that his main source was the mysterious "Naacal tablets." These, he said, had been shown and translated to him by a Hindu temple priest. To be exact, according to one book he saw the tablets in India, but according to another he saw them in Tibet.

Churchward's facts, like his assertion that the Otomi and Japanese languages are akin, were mostly wrong. His authorities were Le Plongeon and Paul Schliemann. However, he improved upon their hypotheses. Instead of one sunken continent, he offered his readers *two*: Atlantis in the Atlantic and Mu (corresponding to the Lemuria of the occultists) in the Pacific.

Churchward claimed to be able to read the symbols of ancient peoples by preternatural intuition. The rectangle, he said, was the letter M in the Muvian alphabet; therefore any decorative use of a rectangle was evidence of Muvian influence. As the ordinary brick is entirely bounded by rectangles, Churchward easily derived everybody and everything from Mu. He misquoted Plato and printed nonsensical footnotes reading: "4. Greek record." or "6. Various records." He rejected the "monkey theories" of evolution, holding that man was created fully civilized in the Pliocene Epoch; also, that continents sank beneath the sea when great gas-filled chambers ("gas belts") collapsed beneath them.

Interest in Atlantis has continued all through this century. It is lively enough to encourage the publication of a new book on the subject every few years. Most of these books merely repeat, with variations, the long-exploded arguments of Donnelly, Le Plongeon, Paul Schliemann, and Churchward.

Perhaps the prize specimen of such books was *Atlantis: die Urheimat der Arier (Atlantis: the Original Home of the Aryans,* 1922) by Karl Georg Zschaetzsch.[6] According to Zschaetzsch, the Atlanteans were the original Aryans: blond, virtuous vegetarians and teetotalers.

Like Donnelly, Velikovsky, and several others, Zschaetzsch claimed that the collision of the earth with a comet destroyed Atlantis. The only survivors of the sinking of this land, after the collision, were Wotan, his daughter, and his pregnant sister, who took refuge in a mainland cave among the roots of a giant tree beside a cold geyser. Wotan's sister died in childbirth, but a she-wolf suckled her infant. The blood of these splendid Nordics became mixed with that of the non-Aryans of the mainland, and their degenerate descendants resorted to eating meat and to drinking fermented liquors. This last loathsome practice was invented by a non-Aryan girl witch named Heid, like Wotan from Norse mythology.

By "racial memory" the author "proved" that these events underlay the legends of the Christmas star, the world-ash Yggdrasill and the spring of Mimir beside it, Romulus and Remus, and almost any other myth you care to mention. The Greeks were an Atlantean colony, and Zeus one of their early chiefs. All of which proved that Herr Zschaetzsch was himself a descendant of Zeus, as you can easily see from his name!

This kind of amphigory explains why historians and scientists often see red at the mere mention of Atlantis—particularly when one of them gives a popular lecture, at the end of which somebody stand up and starts an argument about Atlantis, waving a copy of Churchward to prove his points. In fact, Atlantist arguments have been circulated so long and loudly that many intelligent peo-

ple cannot separate fact from fiction. Acquaintances often ask us:
"Was there *really* ever a continent of Atlantis?"

Geology gives the answer. Whole continents do not sink out of
sight overnight as the result of a few earthquakes. There are good
reasons for saying this. The evidence is that, while small areas of a
few square miles have been suddenly submerged, much larger areas
—hundreds or thousands of square miles—never are. Large areas,
such as the Baltic region or the east coast of North America, *do*
rise and fall; but the average rate of rise or fall is never more than
an inch or so a year and is usually only a fraction of an inch.
Therefore, a continent would take thousands or millions of years to
sink from sight. Likewise, the sea level has fallen as much as three
hundred feet during glacial periods and has risen again with the
melting of the ice. But this, too, is a slow process, measured in
millimeters a year.

When a continent sinks, the material beneath it has to go somewhere. This process takes millions of years. Great gas-filled chambers deep in the earth would violate the laws of physics, because at
such depths the rock is rendered plastic by heat and pressure, and
such a chamber would soon close up. Permanent changes in parts
of the earth's crust during earthquakes are measured in inches or
feet. The severe San Francisco quake of 1906 caused relative movements of up to 22 feet, but only over a small area.

Geologists also know that certain kinds of rock, especially granite,
always occur in continents. Hence there is no use looking for
sunken lands where these rocks do not exist. There are places in
the Southwest Pacific around Australia and New Zealand, and in
the western Indian Ocean, where lands may conceivably have sunk.
But there is no sign of lost lands in the middle of the North Atlantic
and Pacific oceans, where Atlantists put their continents. And, since
any real sunken lands must have disappeared millions of years ago,
when our forebears were running naked through the woods and
turning over flat stones for their dinner, these places could not have
harbored civilizations.

The enthusiasts of the Atlantist cult have not only asserted that
the Atlanteans lived on this alleged continent, but even—something
that Plato never said—that they were superscientists. Now, several
forgotten civilizations, such as the Harappâ culture of the Indus
Valley and the kingdom of Arzawa in Asia Minor, have been dug
up in the last century. But none of these old cultures had the

modern inventions that cultists have claimed for Atlantis. Radio-carbon dating shows that man first rose above the hunting and food-gathering stage of culture in Syria and Iraq about eight to ten thousand years ago. This was long after Atlantis, according to Plato, had vanished.

Atlantists make much of the myths of ancient and primitive peoples. They assert, for example, that Noah's Flood and the various American flood legends are all disguised traditions of the sinking of Atlantis.

It is one thing to admit that myths, like all fiction, have a basis in fact, and quite another to think that one can reconstruct the fact from the fiction. Sinclair Lewis' novel *It Can't Happen Here* (1935), about an imagined Fascist dictatorship in the United States, is based upon certain facts. But a future historian, who knew nothing else about the twentieth century and tried to reconstruct the history of the United States from that novel, might conclude that Windrip the dictator was a real man while Franklin D. Roosevelt was a myth like Osiris. In short, myths often distort out of all recognition the reality on which they are based.

Myths are not handed down to posterity for simple love of historical fact. This is a rare quality even in our advanced culture. They are passed on because they are entertaining and so provide a living for storytellers, or because they are useful in answering children's questions, serving as librettos for rites, and persuading the common people to respect and obey their priests and support them in the style to which they would like to become accustomed.

Nor is there any sound reason to think, as nearly all Atlantists do, that the civilizations of the New and Old Worlds had a common origin. The differences between the culture of the Mayas, for instance, and that of the ancient Egyptians are even deeper than likenesses. The two had in common no food plants, no domestic animals except the dog, and no epidemic diseases. The Mayas lacked the plow, wheeled vehicles, and metal tools. If they sprang from a common civilized center, the Egyptians and the Mayas ought to have shared such things as maize and smallpox. Most decisive of all, Mayan civilization arose only about the time of Christ. At that date, Egypt was already thousands of years old and had become a Roman province.

Other Atlantists argue that there must have been an Atlantis because certain New World languages resemble Old World tongues.

They find two words in the two languages having similar sounds and meanings, and from this they conclude that the two languages must be related.

But this is not necessarily so, except in the sense that all human languages are probably descended from the grunts of some wandering clan of early-Pleistocene ape-men. The study of the relations among languages is more complicated than that. There are sure to be a few seeming similarities between *any* pair of tongues. Thus "ten" is *dix* in French and *disi* in Hottentot; "search" is *examine* in English and *eggâmen* in Tuareg; among the Yuki of California, "go" and "come" are *ko* and *kom* respectively; and so forth. The reason for these resemblances is that most languages have but twenty to fifty phonemes, or significant sound units, and at least several thousand words. Therefore some such resemblances are bound to occur by chance.

To find real relationships among languages, one must consider *all* the words in certain classes, such as numbers, colors, family relationships, parts of the body, and so on. Let us compare, for instance, the words for the first ten numbers in several New and Old World languages, bearing in mind that Le Plongeon has claimed that Mayan is fully one third Greek, and that other Atlantists assert that Otomi is a form of Old Japanese:[7]

| English | Greek | Arabic | Chinese | Japanese | Mayan | Otomi |
|---------|-------|--------|---------|----------|-------|-------|
| one | hen | wâhid | yi | hitotsu | hun | da |
| two | dyo | ithnên | êr | futatsu | ca | yojo |
| three | tria | thalâtha | san | mitsu | ox | tiu |
| four | tettara | arba'a | sz | yotsu | can | coojo |
| five | pente | khamsa | wu | itsutsu | ho | guitta |
| six | hex | sitta | lu | mutsu | uac | dato |
| seven | hepta | sab'a | tsi | nanatsu | uuc | yoto |
| eight | oktô | thamânya | ba | yatsu | uaxac | giato |
| nine | ennea | tis'a | giu | kokonotsu | bolon | guito |
| ten | deka | 'ashara | shï | tô | lahun | detda |

As you can see, English and Greek are obviously related; but the other languages show no clear resemblances. For a real linguistic analysis, of course, a much larger list would be needed, as well as a study of phonology, inflection, and syntax.

When the American languages are studied this way, it transpires that Eskimo is related to the languages of eastern Siberia, which is natural enough. The Amerindian languages, however, show a wide diversity among themselves and *no* clear relationship to any Old World language. This is what we should expect if the ancestors of the Amerinds had come to the Americas many thousands of years ago and had had little or no further contact with the peoples of the Old World until the Age of Exploration.

Some Atlantists say that many inscriptions in Old World languages have been found in the Americas. When these "Phoenician inscriptions" are investigated, however, they turn out to be something quite different. Dighton Rock in Massachusetts, for example, bears scratches that have been attributed to Phoenicians, Druids, Hebrews, Chinese, and Atlanteans. At last, in the 1920s, Professor E. B. Delabarre, with black filling material and a camera, disclosed the name of Miguel Cortereal, a Portuguese explorer who sailed for Newfoundland in 1502 and never returned. Presumably Cortereal survived a shipwreck and lived the rest of his life with the Narragansett Indians.

It is now plain that there never was a continent of Atlantis inhabited by supermen. When, then, *is* the origin of Plato's romantic tale? Was it all just a flight of fancy?

Not at all. With a little sleuthing, we can discover the sources of practically all the main ideas that Plato set forth in *Timaios* and *Kritias.* There is nothing in Plato's story that he could not have derived from the knowledge and beliefs of his time.

For instance, the general theme of the defeat by heroic Athens of the barbarian invaders was inspired by the Greco-Persian Wars of —492 to —448. When Plato wrote, every Greek was as conscious of this as we today are of the Second World War.

Poseidon and the other elder gods, of course, come from the general corpus of Greek myth. Although some educated men of Plato's time looked skeptically upon these deities, they were still celebrated by literary men and worshiped by the masses. The Atlantean ceremonial may have been suggested by Orphism, a Greek mystical cult.

The idea expounded by Plato's Egyptian priest, that the earth is visited by periodic catastrophes, originated in Babylonian astrology. This pseudo-science had just begun to infect Greece in Plato's time.

The concept of a land submerged by the sea comes from the earthquake wave that inundated the little Greek island of Atalantê in —426, the year after Plato was born. The name "Atlantis" is derived from the same source. Plato combined the flooding of the real Atalantê with the myth of the demigod Atlas and the mountain into which Atlas was transformed, somewhere at the western end of the Mediterranean. And Plato's Atlantean elephants are derived from the real African elephants that, in Plato's day, roamed the valleys of the Atlas Mountains.

People who have written about Atlantis have located it in all parts of the world. Besides accepting Plato's statement that it was in the North Atlantic Ocean, they have inferred that it was "really" in North Africa, South Africa, Iceland, Ceylon, Palestine, Crete, Mongolia, Malta, France, Nigeria, Brazil, the Caucasus, the Arctic, the Netherlands, East Prussia, the Pacific, the Sahara, Greenland, Iran, Mexico, Iraq, the Crimea, Cambodia, the West Indies, Sweden, and the British Isles.

If Plato's city of Atlantis is based upon any real place, however, the likeliest location is in southwestern Spain. Here, at the mouth of the Guadalquivir River, for many centuries flourished a rich city-state called Tartessos, the Tarshish of the Bible. Tartessos—the first strong national state of western Europe—stood about twenty miles northwest of Cádiz, the ancient Gades. Although the origin of its people is not certain, they may have been Karians from southwestern Asia Minor; or if not Karians, one of the neighboring Anatolian peoples with a similar language. All these peoples were united for a while in the late second millennium B.C. under the kingdom of Arzawa, which ruled southwestern Anatolia. The Karians were active seafarers and colonizers in the early centuries of the first millennium B.C., and they liked to give their towns names ending in *-assos* or *-essos*, as in Halikarnassos and Salmydessos.

The first king of Tartessos is said by the ancient historian Justinus to have been Gargoris, who was succeeded by his grandson Habis, famous as an improver and lawgiver. Whether or not these kings were real men, Tartessos certainly long flourished as a trading and mining center. To the Phoenicians it must have seemed like a city of silver. They found the metal so common that the Tartessians' hogs ate from silver troughs. In order to carry away as much silver as they could in return for olive oil and other wares, the clever Phoenicians cast anchors of silver and used them on the homeward voyage in place of their anchors of wood and lead.

It is open to question just when the Phoenicians first reached

Tartessos. During —X, when King Solomon and King Hiram of Tyre had their profitable partnership, their joint fleet used to make a round trip to "Tarshish" every three years, returning with "gold, and silver, ivory, and apes, and peacocks."[8] If, as is often supposed, Tarshish was Tartessos, the Phoenicians must have arrived there about —1000.

On the other hand, the archaeological remains of the Phoenicians in the western Mediterranean seem to show that the Phoenicians did not reach that part of the world until two or three centuries later. In fact, they may not even have preceded the Greeks. In that case, Tarshish would have to be sought somewhere else: possibly at Tarsus in Cilicia (although it would not take three years to travel from Tyre to Tarsus and back, even in a rowboat!); possibly at some port in the Red Sea or the Indian Ocean.

The Greeks learned of Tartessos about —631, when a Samian merchant ship under Kolaios, bound for Egypt, was blown far out of its course by an easterly gale and made land at Tartessos. The delighted Samians sold their wares for six talents. This is about four hundred pounds of silver, an enormous fortune for that time, equivalent to hundreds of thousands of dollars.

Next came men from Phokaia in Ionia, who found Tartessos ruled by the hospitable King Arganthonios ("Silverlocks"), although we need not believe with Herodotos that he lived 120 years and reigned for 80 of them. The Phokaians used, not the tubby merchantman of the time, but the swift fifty-oared pentakonter. If such a galley had less room for cargo, it had a better chance of escaping when a Carthaginian trireme came crawling like a giant centipede over the horizon with the intention of making the interlopers walk the plank.

In its heyday, Tartessos was the leading city of southwestern Spain; the people of that region, the Turduli,[9] were deemed the most civilized Spaniards. They had a caste system and their own alphabet, in which their poems, laws, and history were written. The Turduli were probably among the peoples who lived in Iberia before the Celts from Gaul overran it at the beginning of recorded Iberian history. The unclassifiable Basque language is a legacy from these pre-Indo-European Iberians.

Perhaps the Turduli were the same as the Beaker Folk of the archaeologists: a tall, powerfully built, broad-headed, trading and cattle-herding people who, starting out from Iberia about —2000, spread widely over western Europe. Everywhere they bartered bronze for local products—northern Europe was still in the Stone Age—after softening up their customers with beer; hence the numerous pottery beakers for which these people have been named. They bore one-piece bronze daggers, fastened garments of woven wool and linen with buttons, flaunted golden ornaments, and for archery used a bracer or wrist guard of stone.

Tartessos stood at the mouth of the Guadalquivir River.[10] The region is flat and sandy, bordered by a sea dangerous for strong tides and a heavy surf, and inhabited by a dark people taller and broader-headed than most Spaniards. In ancient times the river ended in a great bay, which once reached inland as far as Hispalis (Seville). But in historical times the bay had partly silted up, so that islands grew in it, reminding us of the legendary shoals left by the sinking of Atlantis. Tartessos stood on the main island, between the two mouths of the Guadalquivir.

Today the bay has become a great marsh, Las Marismas, where herds of half-wild longhorned cattle roam. The northern arm of the river is dry land. On the south side of the remaining arm, across the stream from Tartessos, stands the port of Sanlúcar de Barrameda, whence Columbus set out on his third voyage to the New World. Part of Las Marismas is a privately owned game preserve, swarming with beasts and birds that have become rare or extinct elsewhere in Europe.

In the 1920s Professor Adolf Schulten of Erlangen dug up the site of Tartessos. He found a copper ring inscribed with the following characters:

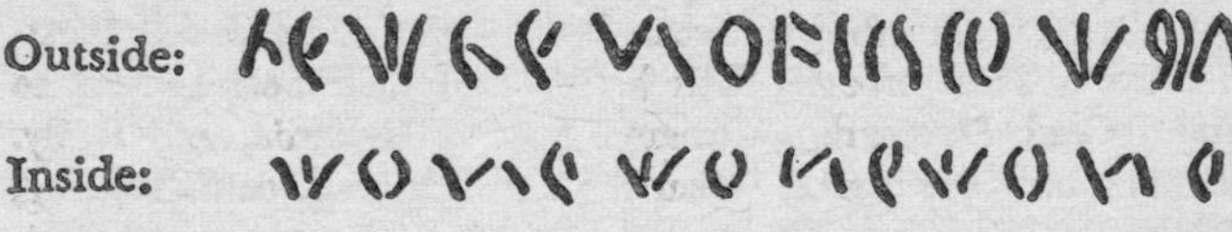

Fig. 5 *Inscription on the ring found by Schulten on the site of Tartessos.*

According to Schulten, this is an inscription in an old form of Greek, reading: OWNER, BE FORTUNATE! and GUARD THE RING WELL! Besides the ring, Schulten found the ruins of a fishing village of

Roman times and concluded that this village had been built of stones taken from the ruins of Tartessos. But the high water table prevented digging far down. For aught anyone knows, the remains of Tartessos still lie buried in the mud of the Guadalquivir estuary. With modern electrical prospecting equipment, some enterprising archaeologist may find it yet.

In fact, another set of relics, probably Tartessian, were found in 1959 near Seville. Workmen digging on the premises of the Royal Pigeon Shooting Society, on a hill called El Carambolo, struck gold and, being honest Spaniards, reported the find. The Carambolo treasure consisted of twenty-one pieces of pure gold, weighing altogether over ninety-four troy ounces. There were a necklace with seven (originally eight) pendants that look like little baskets but are actually signets; two bracelets; two breastplates; and sixteen rectangular plates, designed to be threaded on belts, crowns, and the like and ranging from 2 by 3½ inches up to 2⅜ by 4⅝ inches. All the larger pieces are densely decorated with alternate rows of hemispherical knobs and rosettes. The makers used inserts of tin and other metals but no jewels. All this lavish decoration is purely geometrical, without pictures or reliefs. Many pottery fragments were found, decorated in a similar geometric style, unlike anything found before. Spanish archaeologists tentatively ascribe the Carambolo treasure to the Tartessians and date it from about −600. Several smaller golden treasures found in southwestern Spain, notably at Aliseda, show a similar style of decoration, which Spanish archaeologists consider as native Iberian with some eastern Mediterranean influence.

In any case, we now have enough information to make a reasonable guess about the origin of Tartessos. During the second millennium B.C., the Turdulians became active as traders all over western Europe. They brought their bronze and their beer beakers to Britain, Gaul, Denmark, Germany, Austria, Sardinia, and Sicily. This was also the period when the horse-driving, cattle-herding, battle-ax-wielding Indo-Europeans or Aryans were swarming westward across Europe from their native Russian and Polish steppes, subduing tribe after tribe in their path and setting themselves up as a ruling class over those they vanquished.

Around −1000, during the great folk-wandering that wrought havoc among the old kingdoms of the eastern Mediterranean, the Karians, sending out colonies from their home in southwestern Asia

Minor, established Tartessos. They were able to do this whether the native Turdulians liked it or not because the Karians were a warlike people, who served as mercenaries in the armies of the Pharaohs. The details of the Karians' conflicts and alliances with the Spaniards are forever lost. But, at the dawn of trustworthy Greek history in —VII, Tartessos had become the richest city of the West, with a mixed Anatolian-Turdulian population and far-spreading tentacles of trade.

After flourishing for at least five or six centuries, Tartessos disappeared about —500. Nobody knows what befell it; it simply ceased to be mentioned as a living place. Perhaps the Carthaginians destroyed it, to abate competition with their own colony of Gades; or the Celts, who overran Iberia in —VI, sacked it. Maybe the silting up of its harbors ruined its trade, so that people drifted away. Or perhaps, like Plato's Atlantis, it was devastated by an earthquake and never recovered.

The resemblances between Tartessos and Atlantis are many: its western location, its site at the mouth of a large river, its wealth and active trade, the large plain in back of it, and finally its mysterious disappearance.

Plato may not have been the only writer to draw inspiration from travelers' tales of Tartessos. In Homer's *Odyssey*, Odysseus is cast ashore near Scheria, the capital of the Phaiakes or Phaeacians. Odysseus spends Books IX to XII telling the story of his adventures to the kindly King Alkinoös, who then loads him with gifts and sends him home to Ithaka in a magical ship.

The resemblances between Tartessos and Scheria are equally striking. Perhaps Plato got his accounts of Tartessos directly from sailors. Perhaps he got them indirectly, through Homer's Scheria. Or perhaps he used both sources.

There is not much question as to what sort of tale Plato's Atlantis story is. It is a kind of pioneer science-fiction story, which he wrote to set forth his political doctrines. He even hints that this is the case. In *Timaios*, Kritias says: "And the city with its citizens which you described to us yesterday" (in *The Republic*) "we will now transport hither into the realm of fact; for we will assume that the city is that ancient city of yours, and declare that the citizens you conceived are in truth those actual progenitors of ours, of whom the priest told."[11]

Like all fictions, Plato's allegory is based upon certain facts. But

24

Plato would be astonished to learn that some people in later ages insisted on taking his yarn far more literally than he ever intended. Moreover, he would be distressed to find that they ignored his earnest arguments for authoritarian government—to him the important part of the work—in favor of the melodrama of the sinking of Atlantis, which he meant merely as the icing on the cake.

The curious ending of *Kritias,* in the middle of a sentence, is also significant. Perhaps old Plato lost interest, but it is even more likely that he ran into plot trouble. He started out to show how his *Republic* would work out in practice. But, since his story started with the Creation, he had to bring in the gods, and these involved him in difficulties about free will and divine justice.

It was easy enough to argue that the gods had destroyed Atlantis for its sins; but why should they destroy virtuous Athens along with wicked Atlantis? That did not square with divine justice. Yet Plato had to get rid of his imaginary prehistoric Athens somehow, to account for the historical gap between it and the real Athens. So perhaps he puzzled for a while and gave up.

Although it is fiction, not history, the story of Atlantis has been kept alive by its beauty and charm, by Plato's fame as a thinker, and by our longing to believe that somewhere, somewhen, there *could* be a land of beauty and plenty, where peace and justice reigns and where we poor mortals could be happy. In this sense Atlantis—whether we call it the Kingdom of God, the Classless Society, or Utopia—will always be with us.

# II
# Pyramid Hill and the
# Claustrophobic King

*. . . vast megalithic cities of the elder world, around whose dark towers and labyrinthine nether vaults lingers an aura of pre-human fear and necromancy . . .*

*Lovecraft*

The best-known graveyard in the world stands five miles west of the River Nile, a little above Cairo on the east bank. This is Pyramid Hill: a rocky plateau, a little less than a square mile in area, rising out of the flat alluvium where the Nile Valley slopes up sharply to meet the Libyan Desert. The structures that stand upon it are not only the most celebrated monuments in the world; they are also the most controversial.

Of all these buildings, the most famous is the Great Pyramid of King Khufu, the Cheops of Greek writers. It alone, of the Seven Wonders of the World listed by these authors, survives more or less intact. Because you have heard this pyramid called "the Great Pyramid of Giza," you might expect it to stand at Giza; but this is not so. Giza is a suburb of Cairo, across the river from the metropolis. Whereas Giza clings to the river bank, the pyramids rise from the edge of the desert to the west.

Until recently you could reach the pyramids by taking a Number 8 streetcar from downtown Cairo. You rattled across the Nile on the Abbas II drawbridge and out into the country to the end of the line. Now the tram has given way to a bus line, and the suburbs crowd close to the desert sands. For Cairo, like most ancient places, has been caught up in the fever of progress. Across the placid Nile at sunset, you still hear the Muslim call to prayer; but the minarets have been fitted with electrical public-address systems, and the call is made from a recording.

Suppose we follow the tourist track in visiting the pyramids. Our car drives out to the village of Kafr es-Sammân. Probably we stop for refreshment at the gracious old Mena House Hotel. Then we climb the curving road up to the top of the plateau.

At some stage we are bundled on the backs of camels. Although the camel drivers cluster around, anxiously clutching our arms and legs lest we fall off when the camel gets up, there is no danger if we remember firmly to grip the horns before and behind the saddle. A camel has an easy gait so long as it does not break into a gallop, and the camel driver walks ahead holding the halter to see that this shall not happen.

As soon as the caravan is on its way, your camel driver starts pressing you to pay him his tip in advance. Don't; it will only cause you trouble. Find out from the guide what the going rate is and pay it—no more—at the end of the journey. Your *gammâl* is likely to be especially persistent on the trek across the desert between monuments. He hopes that the tourist will be so terrified of being abandoned in the wilderness that he will pay up without protest.

At the edge of the plateau, looming over Kafr es-Sammân, stands the Sphinx. Behind the Sphinx you see the geometric forms of the three great pyramids and eight small ones, some of the latter pretty much in ruins. The sandy, lunar landscape is speckled by a multitude of small graves and tombs, and nearby yawns the newly-opened trench that once held Khufu's solar boat.

Everybody has seen photographs of the Sphinx with the pyramids rising majestically behind it. Few visitors shoot the Sphinx from the rear, showing its tail wrapped around its body like that of a crouching pussycat, and the houses of Kafr es-Sammân lying just beyond it at the foot of the slope.

Seen close up, your first impressions are that the pyramids are fully as large as you expected, but that they are much browner and much more dilapidated. The courses of stones form a steep, rough, irregular stairway with risers over a yard high. Formerly a trio of husky Egyptians boosted brave travelers to the top of Khufu's Pyramid and down again. After several tourists had been injured or killed in the process, the government stopped this strenuous enterprise.

For forty-five centuries and more, men have gaped at the pyramids and have wondered how and why such vast piles were raised. Some have made the wildest guesses. It has been said that the pyramids were built as displays of royal power (Aristotle), vaults wherein the sages of old stored their archives (Ammianus), Joseph's granaries against the Seven Lean Years (Benjamin of Tudela), models of Noah's ark, astronomical observatories, irrigation pumps, phallic symbols, Masonic halls, standards of measurement, and nuclear reactors.

These notions can easily be disproved. For instance, the passages inside the pyramids were blocked off as soon as the kings were laid to rest, so they could not have been used for granaries, star-gazing, or Masonic meetings. Also, it is unlikely that the builders, had they planned the pyramids as standards of measure, would have furnished them with temples and other elaborate accessories, which once surrounded them.

The modern cult of Pyramidology began in the 1830s, when Colonel Howard Vyse blasted his way into Khufu's and Menkaura's pyramids with gunpowder. From Vyse's measurements, a London publisher named John Taylor evolved the remarkable theory that Khufu's Pyramid had been built by Noah and his sons under divine guidance, and that it incorporated in its structure such cosmic wisdom as the true value of $\pi$ (the ratio of the circumference of a circle to its diameter). Taylor converted to his theory a Scottish astronomer, Charles Piazzi Smyth.

This Smyth was an able astronomer who did notable work in spectroscopy. He was also a religious fanatic whose strongest passion was to discredit ancient Egyptian "idolatry." Like any proper pseudo-scientist, Smyth first published a book, *Our Inheritance in the Great Pyramid* (1864), and then went to Egypt to confirm the opinions he had set forth. He spent four months measuring the pyramid by means of extremely accurate instruments, made specially for the purpose, with the help of a gang of temperamental *badawîn*.

However, Smyth neglected to measure the most important dimension of all—the length of the base side—perhaps for fear of upsetting his theories. Upon his return to England, Smyth sent the Royal Society a paper on some of the occult wisdom he had uncovered. When they refused it a reading, he haughtily resigned his fellowship.

Wilson and Smyth claimed, among other things, that the sides of the Great Pyramid were perfect equilateral triangles; that the distance around the base was 36,524 "pyramid inches," or 100 times the number of inches that there are days in the year; that the height of the pyramid was 1/270,000 of the earth's circumference, or one billionth of the distance to the sun; that its mass was one trillionth that of the earth.

They averred that the sarcophagus was a standard of measurement, like the Standard Meter in Paris. This standard, however, worked in a fantastically complicated and illogical way. The unit of volume, they thought, was the original capacity of the tub; and this volume was one tenth of a cube whose edge was twice the Pyramidological unit of length, multiplied by the earth's specific gravity. This system of measuring they alleged to be the ancestor of the English system of measures.

Scores of such marvels are listed in the books of the Pyramidologists. But, like a badly preserved mummy, they crumble at the touch. For example, the "pyramid inch" is an imaginary unit, invented by Smyth. The original height and mass of the pyramid are not known because of the dilapidation it has suffered; estimates of the original height vary by more than 30 feet. Therefore nobody can say what ratios these quantities bear to the size of the earth and the solar system.

There is no reason to think that Fourth Dynasty Egyptians suspected the earth to be round and therefore to have a circumference, let alone a specific gravity, the very idea of which was unknown until Archimedes discovered it thousands of years after Khufu. The Egyptians, like the early Sumerians, thought of the universe as shaped like the inside of a shoe box, with us crawling around like ants on the bottom. Although the Egyptians developed a crude astronomy, with their own system of constellations, they never got beyond the shoe-box stage until the Greeks taught them better.

As for the idea that the sarcophagus was a measure of volume, nobody but a lunatic would take as a volumetric standard a vessel holding the awkward amount of a ton and a quarter of water and then shut it up in an artificial mountain so that it could not be used.

Smyth believed that the Great Pyramid had been built by the Old Testament patriarch Melchizedek, who was Jesus Christ in an earlier incarnation. Hence the system of weights and measures incorporated in the structure possessed divine approval. So, naturally, did the irrational English system he supposed to be derived from it. Pyramidologists used this argument against the metric system, which they denounced as "atheistic" because it was adopted in France during the French Revolution.

Smyth also embraced the vagary of a Scot named Robert Menzies, that measurements in the Grand Gallery, which leads to the Pharaoh's burial chamber, symbolize in advance the future history of man. Smyth inferred from these measurements that a great miracle, comparable to the Second Coming of Christ, or the Millennium, would occur in 1881.

When no miracle took place in 1881, the Egyptologist W. M. Flinders Petrie made the definitive survey of the Great Pyramid. Because Petrie's father, a prominent engineer, had adhered to Smyth's theories, Petrie himself leaned at first in that direction. Once on the actual ground, however, he was soon disillusioned. He found that most of Smyth's measurements had been grossly inaccurate despite his expensive instruments. Ever since Smyth's time, Pyramidologists have haunted the pyramids with tapes and transits. Petrie even found one of these cultists trying to file down a granite boss in the vestibule of the burial chamber to the size that his theory demanded.

It has often been shown that, with enough figures to juggle, one can readily extract cosmic results from unlikely material. Borchardt, as an anti-Pyramidological joke, derived the base $e$ of natural logarithms from the slope of Sahura's pyramid. Barnard, by juggling the dimensions of the Temple of Artemis at Ephesos, got the moon's diameter, the length of the lunar month, and the date of the building.

However, the cult mind is proof alike against the arguments of science and the lessons of experience. David Davidson, using Petrie's figures instead of Smyth's and adding in the lengths of the reigns in the king-lists of the Egyptian historian Manetho, came up with a new body of prophecy. According to this, a great war would break out in 1928 and the Second Coming of Christ would occur in 1936. Most Pyramidologists followed Davidson until these events failed to come to pass. Then they reshuffled the numbers to make other predictions. The last was that the world would end in 1953

As engineering achievements, the pyramids are wonderful enough without bedizening them with such occult absurdities. Considering when they were built and the tools and materials the Egyptians worked with, they are among the greatest and most difficult constructions ever conceived by man.

To be sure, one of our huge concrete dams or steel suspension bridges is a more advanced and—to our way of thinking—a more useful structure. But our engineers, able and conscientious though they be, deserve less credit than the pyramid builders, because they have powered machinery, concrete, and structural steel to work with. Give one of them the task of duplicating Khufu's Pyramid with no metal tools but copper saws and chisels; no surveying instruments but strings, bits of charcoal, and the stars; and no means of moving heavy stones but wedges, levers, sleds, palm-fiber ropes, and rafts; and they might not do nearly so well as their ancient colleagues.

To understand how the pyramids were built, we must see how the custom of pyramid building arose.

The capital of the Pharaohs of the Old Kingdom was Memphis,[1] across the Nile from modern Cairo and twelve miles upstream. About —2700, in the reign of King Joṣer[2] of the Third Dynasty, lived the world's first known engineer and architect, Imhotep.[3] He it was who built the first pyramid for his king. Although hardly any details of Imhotep's life are known, he was famous in later ages as a physician, architect, writer, magician, statesman, and all-around sage. From the monuments that Imhotep and Joṣer built, we can tell something of how Imhotep came to invent the pyramid.

Most peoples believe in life after death—a belief that probably arose in prehistoric times in consequence of the fact that people sometimes dream of meeting other persons whom they know to be dead. Although most ancient folk did not make much of this belief, holding the afterlife to be—like a dream—a dim and shadowy affair, the Egyptians developed elaborate doctrines about the hereafter. One of these ideas was that the afterlife could be enjoyed only so long as the body was kept intact, because only so long as the body was preserved could the soul of the dead man enter the body to commune with the living and enjoy their offerings. Therefore, the Egyptians mummified corpses and built massive tombs designed to thwart the thieves attracted by the hoards of jewels, precious metals, and other valuables buried with kings and nobles.

These lords thought that in the afterworld the spirit of a dead man needed the spirits of the things he used in life to keep him happy.

Before King Joṣer, Egyptian kings and nobles were buried in tombs called mastabas.[4] These were rectangular structures of brick, with inward-sloping walls, set over an underground chamber. Kings of the Third Dynasty built larger mastabas and began to use stone instead of brick.

When Joṣer came to the throne, he and Imhotep built a stone mastaba of unusual size and shape west of Memphis at Ṣaqqâra. It was square instead of oblong and measured over 200 feet on a side and 26 feet high.

Not yet satisfied, Joṣer and Imhotep twice enlarged this mastaba by adding stone to the sides. While the second of these enlargements was in progress, the king changed his mind again. He decided not only to enlarge the structure still further but also to make it into a step pyramid—four square mastabas of decreasing size piled one atop the other.

Then Joṣer changed his mind once more. The tomb ended as a step pyramid of six stages, 200 feet high on a base 358 by 411 feet. The bulk of the pyramid was made of blocks of limestone from local outcrops. Imhotep finished his tomb with a facing of high-grade limestone from quarries across the Nile at Troyu.[5]

Under the pyramid lay its burial chamber. From this chamber many corridors branched out, probably to hold the wealth that Joṣer hoped to take with him. A walled inclosure, about 885 by 1,470 feet, surrounded the pyramid. This contained Joṣer's mortuary temple, where priests of a permanent staff were supposed to perform rites forever to strengthen the king's spirit. The temple compound included living quarters for these priests, tombs for royal relatives, and other structures, all of gleaming golden-buff limestone.

Joṣer's successors began step pyramids like his, but these were either abandoned at an early stage or so plundered for stone that little is left of them. A few decades after Joṣer, however, three large pyramids arose: two at Dahshûr, a few miles south of Ṣaqqâra, and one at Maydûm, about twenty-five miles farther south.

The Maydûm Pyramid was begun as a step pyramid of the Ṣaqqâra type, with seven steps, later enlarged to eight steps. In the end, the steps were filled in and the structure was converted to a true, smooth-sided pyramid. Now the last addition has fallen away, leaving the top of the second stepped stage projecting out of a pile of débris.

The southernmost of the two pyramids at Dahshûr was begun as a true pyramid. But, about halfway to the top, the angle of inclination of the sides decreases sharply, so that the sides appear folded in like the top of a carton. Hence this pyramid is called the Bent or Blunted Pyramid. Perhaps the king for whom the pyramid was built expired before its completion, and his successor hastily finished the dead king's tomb.

The other pyramid at Dahshûr, usually ascribed to King Seneferu, was the first large true pyramid to reach completion as planned. It still stands—huge, silent, and solitary—above the undulating sands of the desert, near the modern road from Cairo to the Fayyûm. It is as impressive in its isolation as is the Great Pyramid on the crowded hill at Kafr es-Sammân.

On Pyramid Hill, the second king of the Fourth Dynasty, Khufu, built the largest pyramid of all. Khufu called his masterpiece Khuit-Khufu, "Khufu's Horizon." Although some cultists have denied that Khufu was the builder, there is no question but that he was. The ancient historians Herodotos and Manetho said so, and moreover Khufu's name was found painted in red on some of the inner stones.

This enormous pyramid measures 756 feet square. It originally rose to a skyscraper height of about 480 feet, although the topmost thirty feet are now missing because masses of stone have been plundered from the outside. It is made of about 2,300,000 blocks, weighing an average of two and a half tons apiece. At least, this is the closest estimate that we can make without taking the pyramid apart to count and weigh the stones. Except for the Great Wall of China, it was the largest single ancient structure.

Khufu's Great Pyramid is not only the largest of the pyramids but is also in many ways the best constructed. The sides of the base come to within 7 inches of forming a perfect square. They are oriented to within less than 6 minutes of arc—one tenth of a degree—of the true north-south and east-west directions, and the south side is within 2 minutes of the true east-west direction. This was no accident; such accuracy demanded the most meticulous care. None of the other pyramids is oriented so closely, although some come nigh the Great Pyramid in this respect.

Like his predecessors, Khufu used limestone from local outcrops for the bulk of his pyramid, while for casing he used fine limestone from quarries across the Nile. The capstone was probably gilded. But nearly all the fine stone was removed by medieval Muslim rulers of Egypt to build bridges and houses in Cairo.

Khufu changed his mind twice during the construction. Perhaps the real secret of the Great Pyramid is that King Khufu was a claustrophobe. After the building began, the king may have called in his architect (either Prince Hemiunu or Prince Wepemnofret, both of whom bore the title of Royal Architect under Khufu) and told him that the thought of all those tons of stone lying on top of his final resting place gave him the horrors.

Anyway, Khufu decided not to be buried in the usual underground chamber dug out of solid rock. This chamber was therefore abandoned, and a large room, wrongly called the "Queen's Chamber," was built into the structure. This Queen's Chamber had been roofed but not completely floored when Khufu decided to go higher yet. Therefore work was stopped on the Queen's Chamber, and the plans were changed to include a third and higher room, the so-called "King's Chamber."

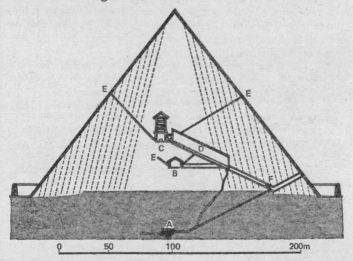

*Fig. 6  A cross section of the Great Pyramid of King Khufu. A. Underground burial chamber; B. "Queen's Chamber"; C. "King's Chamber"; D. Grand Gallery; E. Ventilation shafts; F. Granite plugs. (After Borchardt)*

Because the construction had already risen above the level of the Queen's Chamber, the passage to the new chamber was partly bored through existing masonry. Moreover, lest an earthquake cause the King's Chamber to collapse, several small rooms, one above the other, were built into the structure above this chamber to lessen the weight on its roof.

Actually, the queens and other womenfolk of the three kings whose pyramids stand at Kafr es-Sammân were buried in the eight small pyramids scattered about the plateau. Scores of other graves on the hill held the remains of nobles and members of the court, who hoped to benefit from the magical aura that radiated from the resting places of the divine kings.

In the Great Pyramid, the passage from the outside first slopes downwards towards the underground chamber. Then this passage forks. One branch continues down to the underground chamber, while the other, the Ascending Corridor, slopes up on its way to the Queen's Chamber. Nowadays the Ascending Corridor is floored with planks crossed by iron cleats, while fluorescent tubes run along the ceiling. No longer must visitors grope their way about these passages by candlelight; progress has caught up with the pyramids, too. However, the roof of the Ascending Corridor is so low that we go up it bent nearly double. In returning, we have to back down to avoid cracking our heads on the ceiling.

The Ascending Corridor forks in its turn. One branch runs horizontally to the Queen's Chamber. The other, still rising, opens out into the Grand Gallery. This is a high, narrow, sloping tunnel in the form of a corbeled vault, leading to the vestibule of the King's Chamber.

The King's Chamber is a big room, 16 by 33½ feet and 18 feet high. Nine huge granite slabs, weighing about thirty tons each, form its roof. The chamber is empty save for a much-battered sarcophagus. The walls remain dark even in the pallid light of the fluorescent tubes, as if loath to yield their secrets to modern men.

As we entered the pyramid, our guide picked up a local man—an elder in flowing galabiyya and skullcap—who lectures us on pyramid lore while we are inside. His voice reverberates hollowly in the King's Chamber. His information is fifty years out of date and inaccurate to begin with, but there is no use questioning him on doubtful points. If we interrupt his well-rehearsed speech, which is all he really knows, he gets confused and has to go back to the beginning and start over like a phonograph record.

Around the base of the Great Pyramid, Khufu built the usual inclosure. This included mortuary temples and a great stone causeway leading down to the Nile. Herodotos, who in —V saw these structures well preserved, thought them as impressive as the Great Pyramid itself. Now, however, they are almost all gone.

Herodotos also reported the stories told him by his guides. They said, for instance, that Khufu had prostituted his own daughter to help to pay for the Great Pyramid, that it took a hundred thousand laborers working in three-month shifts twenty years to build this pyramid, that Khufu's sarcophagus lay on an island in an underground lake beneath the pyramid, and that the hieroglyphics carved on the outer casing of the pyramid recorded the food consumed by the workers. All of these tales were untrue. But the guides, like some of their modern descendants, told whatever tales they thought would please the tourist.

When Khufu died, attendants put his mummy into a wooden coffin. They carried this coffin up the Ascending Corridor and the Grand Gallery to the King's Chamber. Here they placed the coffin in a plain granite sarcophagus, which must have been installed during the building of the pyramid because it is a little too wide to go through the narrow passage to the King's Chamber. The sarcophagus had a heavy stone lid. When this lid slid into place, stone bolts dropped into recesses in the trough and secured the lid—it was hoped—for all time.

On their way out, the workmen knocked loose a set of props in the vestibule of the King's Chamber. This allowed three huge portcullis blocks to fall to the floor of the vestibule, blocking it. Removal of more props in the Grand Gallery permitted three granite plugs to slide from the Grand Gallery down into the Ascending Corridor, blocking it as well.

Khufu's son and successor, Dedefra, began a pyramid at Abu Roâsh, five miles north of Khufu's pyramid. Of Dedefra's pyramid, only the base remains.

Dedefra was succeeded by Khafra (Greek, Chephren), probably another son of Khufu. On Pyramid Hill, Khafra built the Sphinx, a colossal lion with Khafra's head. It was partly carved from an outcrop and partly built up of limestone blocks. The rest of the outcrop was quarried away for pyramid stones, so that the Sphinx lies in a hollow. This basin tends to fill up with sand blown in from the desert until all of the Sphinx is buried except its head. Thothmes IV (reigned —XV) had it dug out while he was still a prince and recorded his deed on an inscribed stone. In classical times, some tourist scratched on one of the toes of the Sphinx a distich from an otherwise unknown Greek poem:

> . . . they are perished also,
> Those walls of Thebes which the Muses built . . .

Then the quarry filled up again. About the year 1400, a Muslim fanatic battered off the nose of the Sphinx. British archaeologists dug the sand out of the quarry in 1818, 1886, and 1926. The last time they did this, they found that sand had eroded away the statue's neck until the Sphinx was in danger of losing its head. So they applied a collar of reinforced concrete to its neck.

Like the Great Pyramid, the Sphinx was long a citadel of mystery. Mystics and fiction writers have woven endless legends, theories, and stories around these relics of a distant age.

For instance, Sax Rohmer's early novel *Brood of the Witch Queen*, a fine old creepycrawly full of bats, scorpions, and deadly fire elementals, tells of dark supernatural doings around Khufu's Pyramid. Houdini once collaborated with H. P. Lovecraft, the Providence recluse and twentieth-century master of the Gothic horror tale, on a short story called *Imprisoned with the Pharaohs*. The narrator (supposedly Houdini himself) tells of being seized by a gang of Arabs at night near the Sphinx and lowered by a rope an immense distance down a burial shaft. At the bottom he finds a horde of indescribable monstrosities performing unspeakable obscenities.[6]

Besides the Sphinx, Khafra built a pyramid slightly smaller than Khufu's. It looks even taller than the Great Pyramid, however, because it stands on a higher part of the plateau. This pyramid lacks the complex interior corridors and chambers of the Great Pyramid, having but a single underground burial chamber with a passage leading down to it.

Khafra's successor Menkaura[7] built a smaller pyramid on Pyramid Hill, and other kings continued the custom down to the Twelfth Dynasty. The last Egyptian pyramids were built around —1600. By this time, about seventy pyramids dotted the land of Khem.

Most of the later ones, however, were filled with rubble instead of good cut stone. Hence they wore away to mere mounds after builders stole their limestone facings.

Robbers broke into all the Egyptian pyramids, despite the granite plugs, false passages, and other precautions of their builders. The Great Pyramid held out until the Caliph al-Ma'mûn (+IX) got past the granite plugs by boring through the softer limestone around them. Caring nothing for relics of the Days of Ignorance, as Muslims call the ages before Muhammad, he smashed the lid of the sarcophagus and tore Khufu's mummy to bits for its gold.[8]

Some claim that the ancient Egyptians must have used powered machines of modern types to build the pyramids, or even that they called upon occult powers whose secret has been lost. Herodotos is to blame for the idea that the pyramids were built by construction machinery like ours. He wrote:

The pyramid was built in steps, battlement-wise, as it is called, or, according to others, altar-wise. After laying the stones for the base, they raised the remaining stones to their places by means of machines formed of short wooden planks. The first machine raised them from the ground to the top of the first step. On this there was another machine, which received the stone upon its arrival, and conveyed it to the second step, whence a third machine advanced it still higher.[9]

Nobody has found any trace in Egyptian art, architecture, or literature of anything like these wooden hoisting machines. Therefore they were probably the fantasy of some guide or priest, recounted to the eminent Greek tourist in hope of getting an extra obolos from him.

From various sources—tool marks on stone, quarries with blocks half detached, ancient tools found in modern times, remains of ramps up which the workers hauled their stones, and tomb paintings that show Egyptians working—we know quite a lot about how the Egyptians built their pyramids. From these sources we learn that the Egyptians of Khufu's time used very simple methods. They had no tongs or pulleys and no tools of any metal but copper. They made but little use of the wheel.

The true secrets of the ancients' engineering triumphs were three: first, the intensive and painstaking use of such simple instruments and devices as they had; second, unlimited manpower; and lastly, willingness to take their time. Most important of these was the last—the infinite patience they applied to their projects.

The pyramids and other Egyptian monuments were not, as is often thought, built by hordes of slaves. Although Egypt was a land of vast class differences, slavery in the strict sense never played much part in its history. On the other hand, forced labor was common. It was the usual method by which all ancient empires built roads, canals, temples, and other public works, because tax-gathering machinery was not yet efficient enough to make it practical to hire voluntary workers.

Simple calculations show that Herodotos' tale of the building of the Great Pyramid by 100,000 men working for twenty years is much exaggerated. Even with the simple methods of the time, the pyramid could have been built with a fraction of that labor. Probably there was a small permanent staff of skilled workmen. A set of barracks of rough stone and dried mud, whose ruins lie west of Khafra's Pyramid, may have housed this permanent staff. These barracks are thought to have harbored about 4,000 men.

In addition, the king conscripted tens of thousands of peasants to help with the heavy work during the season when the Nile was in flood and these farmers would otherwise have been idle. They were probably paid in food, because money did not yet exist. They were organized in gangs with such heartening names as "Vigorous Gang" and "Enduring Gang." The kings also freely pressed their soldiers into service for work on such a monument.

Although it is unlikely that the workers were constantly flogged, as the legendary slaves are supposed to have been, such a project was not all sweetness and light, either. Egyptian paintings show foremen carrying yard-long rods, and an occasional whack with a stick has been usual in bossing a gang of Egyptian workers from ancient times almost to the present day. The inscription on the tomb of the architect Nekhebu, in boasting of Nekhebu's virtues, asserts that he never struck a workman hard enough to knock him down.

Most of the stone for the pyramids, quarried from local outcrops like that of which the Sphinx is a remnant, could be dragged directly to the site on sleds. Fine limestone from Troyu had to be rafted across the Nile. Granite for the linings of chambers was floated down the Nile on barges from distant Swenet (modern

Aswân). For pyramids built on low ground, the kings commanded that canals be dug from the Nile part way to the pyramid, so that the stones could be brought near the site by water before being dragged overland.

The Egyptians had divers methods of quarrying. One was to cut notches in the rock along the line of fracture, drive wooden wedges into these notches, and wet the wedges. Little walls of clay around each notch held the water in contact with the wood. When the wood swelled, the block split off. Another method was to drive copper wedges between thin copper "feathers" on the sides of the notches.

The stones were moved by the lavish use of levers, ropes, and ramps, first to get the stones on their sleds, then to bring the sleds to the places where the stones were to be set. The Egyptians made enormous ropes of palm fiber or reed. If, as Lord Dehutihotep's[10] tomb painting indicates, 172 men could move a sixty-ton statue, eight men should have been able to drag an ordinary 2.5-ton pyramid block on the level. Sometimes oxen did the pulling.

While some men quarried the stones for the pyramid, others cleared and leveled the site of the tomb. The sides of the base were measured off with cords to form a square. There were several ways to check the trueness of the square, as by measuring the diagonals. For leveling, a long, narrow trough of clay, into which water was poured, served as well as a modern spirit level.

It is not known for sure how the Egyptians found the true north so accurately. A possible method is to build an artificial horizon— that is, a circular wall, high enough so that a person seated in the center cannot see any earthly objects over the top of the wall. The seated observer, with his head at the center of the circle, watches a star rise (any bright northerly star would do) and directs another surveyor to mark the place on the wall where the star appeared. When that same star sets, he causes another mark to be made. By lowering a plumb bob from the marks on the wall, the surveyors find the places at the foot of the wall, inside, and directly below the marks. They then draw lines to the center of the circle. By bisecting the angle between these lines with cords and markings, they determine the true north.

In building a pyramid, the stones were sledded to the site, levered off their sleds, and shoved into place. For a lubricant, the masons probably spread a layer of mud on the rock over which the stone was to be slid.

We can imagine these gangs of swart, sweating, sturdy, breech-clouted men, moving their stones to a rhythmic chant in gutteral Egyptian. Once in a long while the straw-boss takes a cut with his stick at a loafer, who yelps. A crackle of jokes at the victim's expense runs down the line, for Egyptians can make a joke of almost anything. The victim grins shamefacedly and grunts:

"Huh! He didn't hurt *me!*"

The boss glowers. "Want me to try again?"

This brings another outburst of jokes, until the boss himself has to smile. Thus have Egyptians behaved in recent times, and thus they probably behaved in the days of Khufu and Khafra.

As the pyramid rose, the builders raised a mound of earth on all sides of it, with long ramps for hauling up the stones. As each course was laid, mound and ramp were raised to another level. The core stones of common limestone were only roughly fitted together, but the fine limestone blocks of the casing were fitted so carefully that a knife blade could hardly be thrust between them. The joints between adjacent blocks were all more or less askew, showing that each row of casing stones was lined up on the ground, and the stones were trimmed to fit one another before being hauled up the ramp and pushed into place. When the job was done and the gilded capstone had been set in place, this whole vast mass of earth had to be hauled away in baskets.

During the removal of the mound and the earthen ramp, masons trimmed away any irregularities left in the stone facing. At last the earth was gone, and one more pyramid stood pointing to the desert stars, to awe and puzzle men of many lands and tongues through all the ages to come.

# III

# Stonehenge and the Giants' Dance

Chaos of ruins! who shall trace the void,
O'er the dim fragments cast a lunar light,
   And say, "Here was, or is," where all is doubly night?
                                                        *Byron*

Salisbury Plain rolls gently away towards a flat horizon, hazy in the moist British air. In ancient times the land was covered with grass and scrub, broken by scattered stands of trees and a few shepherds' huts. Crowning a swell of this lonely plain, the cluster of massive megaliths that we call Stonehenge has loomed in silence for nearly four thousand years.

Salisbury Plain forms part of the Western Downs, in the county of Wiltshire. The Downs, despite their name, are plateaus which, rising several hundred feet above sea level, stretch across southern England. The gently undulating land is today divided by hedgerows into squares of farm and meadow, except where modern men have planted wood lots.

You may read that the Downs were anciently treeless, like the hills of the Pennine Chain to the north. Having seen what vigorous trees can grow on the Downs when given a chance, we do not believe this. Still, the subsoil of the Downs region is chalk: a soft, whitish rock made up of the skeletons of millions of tiny marine animals. Since a chalk formation gives a thin, infertile soil, the growth of trees that such a soil can support is sparse compared to the dense oaken forests of the prehistoric British lowlands. Over the centuries, men have largely destroyed this original growth of trees to make plow and pasture land, for the Downs have been used for sheep and cattle-raising ever since Neolithic times.

Alone on the wet, windy Downs stands Stonehenge. Two miles to eastward, the roofs of the village of Amesbury and a nearby military camp can be seen, lying in a slight hollow; but in all other directions the vista is almost as empty as it was in primeval times. Travelers, sighting Stonehenge for the first time across Salisbury Plain, often exclaim at its smallness. Compared to the Pyramids or the Roman temples at Ba'albakk, Stonehenge is indeed small; but when you walk into the midst of its mystic circles you find its huge stone pylons impressive enough.

Stonehenge is the best-known ancient monument in Britain and, after the pyramids of Egypt, one of the most famous in the world. It comprises a circular area 320 feet in diameter, surrounded by a low bank, around which in turn runs a shallow, discontinuous ditch or moat.

Within these outer circles, in compact array, abide a multitude of thirty-foot, brick-shaped, elephant-colored, lichen-spotted, rough-hewn monumental stones. Some stand erect; some lie fallen; others rest horizontally atop the standing stones to form lintels. It looks as if a giant's child, playing dominoes with the megaliths, had set them up in a complicated pattern and then, with a careless gesture, knocked half of them over. Among the giant stones, a number of smaller, slightly darker stones stand or lie about in even more chaotic disarray.

Stonehenge never had to be "discovered." It has brooded there, in the midst of teeming England, for thousands of years. But only lately have the diggers begun to unravel the tangled threads of its history.

After a brief mention in Henry of Huntington's *History of the English* (written about 1130), Stonehenge next appeared in literature a decade later in Geoffrey of Monmouth's *History of the Kings of Britain*. Geoffrey was a monk, probably Welsh. His book is not a true history at all, but a historical novel written in imitation of the epics of Homer and Virgil. Although it sometimes touches on historical events like Caesar's invasion of Britain, most of it is the purest fiction. Nevertheless, Geoffrey's book is the main source for the host of legends, stories, and poems that have been woven about King Arthur and his Knights of the Table Round.

According to Geoffrey's pseudo-history, after the Roman Army left Britain in +V, the Saxon chief, Hengist, warred against the usurping British king, Vortigern. The Saxons, by a treacherous attack during a parley, slew 460 British nobles. Soon afterwards, the rightful heir to the British throne, Aurelius Ambrosius, and his brother, Uther Pendragon, returned from Brittany, where they had been reared in exile. The brothers slew the wicked Vortigern and captured Hengist, who was beheaded by the Bishop of Gloucester. Bishops were made of stern stuff in those days.

Aurelius wished to raise a monument to the 460 slain nobles. To design the monument and execute the work he was advised to hire Merlin, seer and wizard to the late King Vortigern. When the king consulted with him, Merlin said:

> If thou be fain to grace the burial-place of these men with a work that shall endure forever, send for the Dance of the Giants that is in Killaraus [Kildare?], a mountain in Ireland. For a structure of stones is there that none of this age could arise save his wit were strong enough to carry his art. For the stones be big, nor is there stone anywhere of more virtue, and, so they be set up round this plot in a circle, even as they be now there set up, here shall they stand for ever . . . For in these stones is a mystery, and a healing virtue against many ailments. Giants of old did carry them from the furthest ends of Africa and did set them up in Ireland what time they did inhabit therein. And unto this end they did it, that they might make them baths therein whensoever they ailed of any malady, for they did wash the stones and pour forth the water into the baths, whereby they that were sick were made whole.[1]

Delighted, Aurelius sent his brother Uther with an army to Ireland to steal the Giants' Dance. After defeating the Irish army, the warriors tried in vain to haul the stones away. Then Merlin set up devices, or perhaps cast a magical spell, by which the stones were easily moved to the coast, loaded on shipboard, brought to the site of Stonehenge, and set up. Aurelius was buried there when he died. So was Uther, who succeeded his brother, and so was Constantine, the cousin of Uther's son, Arthur, after he had reigned in his turn.

Most people who thought about Stonehenge at all accepted Geoffrey's tale, until in 1624 Edmund Bolton suggested that Stonehenge was the tomb of Boudicca, the British queen who led a fierce revolt against the Romans in +61. In 1620, King James I sent the architect Inigo Jones to inspect Stonehenge. Jones had come back from the Continent full of the Roman revival that was taking place among Renaissance architects. In his report on Stonehenge, *The Most Notable Antiquity of Great Britain . . .* (1655) Jones allowed that the ruin could be of Druidic origin but concluded that it was the remains of a Roman temple.

The rise of the public stagecoach in late +XVII brought more and more tourists to see Stonehenge. John Evelyn, the diarist and civil servant, noted:

> Now we were arrived at Stone-henge, indeed a stupendous monument, appearing at a distance like a castle; how so many and huge pillars of stone should have been brought together, some erect, others transverse on the tops of them, in a circular area as rudely representing a cloister or heathen and more natural temple, is wonderful. To number them exactly is very difficult, they lie in such variety of positions and confusion, though they seem not to exceed 100; we counted only 95. As to their being brought thither, there being no navigable river near, is by some admired; but for the stone, there seems to be the same kind about 20 miles distant, some of which appear above ground. About the same hills, are divers mounds raised, conceived to be ancient entrenchments, or places of burial, after bloody fights.[2]

Samuel Pepys noted more briefly that he found the stones "as prodigious as any tales I ever heard tell of them, and worth going this journey to see. God knows what their use was . . ."[3]

The next investigator was John Aubrey (1626-97), whose gossipy notes provide us with much of the information we have on the private lives of Shakespeare and other literary men of Stuart England. Aubrey was a man of a new kind: an antiquary, one whose greatest pleasure in life was to find, collect, study, and report on the relics of antiquity.

Not really new, this kind of man—Nabuna'id, the last Chaldean king of Babylon, had been an antiquary with a collection of ancient Sumerian inscriptions. But such interests had lapsed until the Renaissance revived them. An English antiquarian society was formed in 1572 and flourished until James I abolished it in 1604 for fear its members might harbor political ambitions. A successor society appeared in early +XVIII, and antiquarianism soon spread to other lands.

The antiquary was the predecessor of the archaeologist. His methods make a modern archaeologist shudder; for much priceless evidence was ruined in the antiquary's awkward eagerness to dig out some handsome statue or vase for his collection, with no regard for stratigraphy or any other meticulous modern technique.

An archaeological site is to an archaeologist what the scene of a crime is to a detective. To solve the problem—whether it be the lives of ancient men or the identity of a murderer—every little fact, no matter how trivial, must be noted down before anything is moved. Once the site has been tampered with, the evidence is gone forever. That is why "pot hunter" is, among archaeologists, a term of opprobrium and insult. It refers to the kind of person who, even when he claims to be a scientist, amateurishly messes up a site in his hunt for trophies instead of patiently extracting from it every possible scrap of information.

Still, antiquarianism was an infancy through which archaeology had to pass. At least the antiquary, unlike most people of his time, was trying in his blundering way to preserve the relics of the past, instead of regarding them as useless things to be melted down or broken up for practical purposes. From the antiquary's interest in ancient things grew the whole huge structure of modern archaeology, with its world-spanning expeditions, its vast museum collections, its lavishly illustrated tomes, and its incredibly refined and meticulous techniques.

Aubrey eagerly followed Jones's suggestion that Stonehenge might be of Druidic origin. He noticed one unremarked feature: a circle of pits, concentric with the outer rampart and 30 feet inside it, which are now in his honor called the Aubrey Holes. He also discovered that at Avebury,[4] seventeen miles north of Stonehenge, there was a much larger circular rampart and ditch, with concentric circles of standing stones inside it. Nobody had paid this site much heed because the village of Avebury stood right in the center of the main circles, spoiling the effect.

In +XVIII another antiquary, William Stukeley, carried on further researches and indulged in wilder speculations. A friend of Isaac Newton in his youth, Stukeley practiced medicine and later went into the Anglican priesthood. He not only attributed Stonehenge and Avebury to the Druids but also assigned all the many barrows or megalithic graves in the neighborhood to various ranks in the Druidic hierarchy. Such was his obsession with Druidism—

which he hoped to reconcile with Christianity—that people called him the Arch-Druid. In fact, he sometimes signed himself "Chyndonax, Arch-Druid," after a name inscribed on an ancient coffer dug up in France in 1598.

Stukeley did not dream up the Druids. The Druids were priests of the Celtic peoples, who once ruled much of Europe and who arrived in Britain from Gaul about —IV, over a thousand years after Stonehenge reached its definitive form. Since the Druids had no writing, none of their doctrines has come down intact. Our knowledge of them has been pieced together from a few brief paragraphs by such classical writers as Diogenes Laërtius, Julius Caesar, Strabon, Tacitus, and the elder Plinius. A few facts about the Druids can also be gleaned from the lives of saints, Welsh and Irish legends, survivals of pagan customs, and archaeological remains. Because we know so little about them, mystery-makers have attributed to the Druids virtues never found in any real barbarian priesthood.

We do know that the Druids worshiped a multitude of gods, mostly incarnations of local mountains, rivers, and animals. They built very few temples (only one was ever described) and usually met in sacred oakenshaws or groves. They carried bits of club moss as amulets and venerated the mistletoe as a fertility charm. One of their ceremonies was to climb an oak on the sixth day of the moon, cut off a mistletoe with a golden sickle, and catch it in a white cloth as it fell. Ancient writers speak of them as expounding "Pythagoreanism," by which they probably meant that the Druids taught reincarnation and made much of sacred numbers like three.

The Druids served the Celtic tribes as judges and provided the fiercely quarrelsome Celts with a rudiment of intertribal organization. They regularly resorted to human sacrifice. Reporting on their festivals, Caesar wrote:

They have, besides, colossal images, the limbs of which, made of wicker-work, they fill with living men and set on fire; and the victims perish, encompassed by the flames. They regard it as more acceptable to the gods to punish those who are caught in the commission of theft, robbery, or any other crime; but in default of criminals, they actually resort to the sacrifice of the innocent.[5]

The Romans, who had done the same sort of thing a few centuries earlier and who were at that time forcing gladiators to kill each other by the thousands in the arena, professed to be shocked by these sacrifices. They suppressed Druidism, perhaps less because of its human sacrifices than because the Druids stubbornly refused to be regulated by the Roman bureaucracy.

During the Roman occupation of Britain, the general Suetonius Paulinus led an expedition against a Druidic stronghold on the island of Mona. The Druids' armed supporters lined the shore, while "the Druids, lifting up their hands to heaven, and pouring forth dreadful imprecations, scared our soldiers by the unfamiliar sight."[6] The Romans soon recovered their nerve, routed the British warriors, and burned the Druids in their own groves. So persecuted, Druidism declined under Roman rule and was finished off as a major religion by the triumph of Christianity.

Traces of Druidism still survive in many of our customs, such as those relating to Hallowe'en. Down to the last century, Belgian towns kept wicker giants like those used for human sacrifices, to be harmlessly wheeled about in yearly parades. It was also customary in parts of Europe in recent centuries to burn animals alive in wicker cages: cats in the Ardennes, for instance, and snakes in the Pyrenees.

Some modern Celtophiles like the late Talbot Mundy have tried to whitewash the Druids by denying that they practiced human sacrifice. But the evidence is so strong, and the parallels among other peoples at a similar stage of culture so many, that the effort is wasted. In fact, the Celts went in not only for human sacrifice but also for head-hunting and cannibalism. Among the ancient Irish in particular, "They count it an honorable thing, when their fathers die, to devour them . . ."[7]

The writings of Aubrey and Stukeley stimulated an interest in Celtic antiquity that soon reached the pitch of Celtomania. This cult began with eighteenth-century antiquaries like John Toland, who expanded classical allusions to the Druids' white robes and golden ornaments into an account of an occult brotherhood preserving the arcane wisdom of the ages. Around 1700 Toland, it must be said to his credit, started the serious study of old Irish manuscripts that might shed light on conditions in pre-Christian Ireland. Other Celtomaniacs formed occult societies. The Ancient Order of Druids, founded in 1781, is a British fraternity on the Masonic model, which calls its meeting-places Groves.

Neo-Druids perpetrated a remarkable series of literary forgeries, such as the "Ossianic poems" of James Macpherson in the 1760s and the *Barzaz-Breiz*, or songs of the Breton Bards, of the Vicomte Hersart de la Villemarqué, in 1839. In late +XVIII, Macpherson's fellow Scot, the Gaelic scholar John Smith, published a series of supposedly ancient Gaelic poems alluding to Druids. It turned out that "he had himself first written the poems in English, and after translating them into Gaelic, he then published the translations as originals, and the originals as translations."[8] At the same time Edward Williams, writing as "Iolo Morganwg," rendered similar assistance to the Druidic bards of ancient Wales, of whom he represented himself as one of only two survivors.

Others composed whole shelves of books and articles linking the Druids with the Persian Magi or Zoroastrian priesthood, with the original monotheistic patriarchal religion of Noah and Abraham, and with the Hyperboreans of Greek legend. Leading British writers from Milton to Blake took a hand in the game.

In the long run, however, Neo-Druidism lost out in competition with occultisms based upon oriental traditions of Egypt, India, and Tibet. But, on certain days of the year, British Neo-Druids still gather at Stonehenge to perform their rites. A journalist has written:

> . . . I joined a few dozen tourists the next morning to await the sunrise and watch the Druid celebration. The predawn darkness was like an eerie twilight, and a ground fog chilled us and defied our raincoats.
>
> But there was excitement and speculation in the mist-filled air. We waited for the sun as if it had never risen before and might not again. We scanned the cloudy, murky sky pessimistically.
>
> Beside the altar stone, the modern Druids made final preparations for their rites. Dressed in a ceremonial robe of white and gold, the Chief Bard whispered and gestured to the solemn-faced lesser bards.
>
> As the sky began to lighten, our impatience heightened. Sunrise, according to Greenwich, would be at 4:48 A.M. But there was no sun at 4:48 A.M.
>
> "The sun is late," a bystander remarked.
>
> Then suddenly at 4:55 ½ the clouds parted and the sun rolled over the horizon. The shadow of the Hele Stone fell in a direct line across the altar.
>
> Now the Druids kindled great fires with long torches, and in

solemn procession, their long robes billowing, they marched around the ovoid chanting rituals. The flickering torches swayed and made the boulders look larger and seem to quiver and bob . . .⁹

The services planned by the Ancient Order of Druids for sunrise on Midsummer Day (June 21), 1959, were spoiled by the presence of two thousand boisterous youths who had spent the night there in revelry, littering the holy fane of ancient Britain with bottles.

Serious archaeological investigation of Stonehenge began in 1801, when William Cunnington dug under the Slaughter Stone near the northeastern gap in the bank. Cunnington found nothing conclusive but thoughtfully put a sealed bottle of port under the stone for the benefit of future diggers.

During +XIX, the volume of books and articles on Stonehenge reached an imposing size. Most of them backed the now completely discredited theory that the Druids built the monument. Others attributed the work to Phoenicians, Romans, Saxons, Danes, or Atlanteans. In 1901, Professor Gowland made six excavations and straightened up a sarsen that had begun to lean. In his diggings, he passed through layers that yielded a few coins ranging from the time of George III back to that of the Romans. Below the Roman level he came upon eighty-odd stone axes and hammers weighing altogether several hundred pounds. This showed that Stonehenge was built with stone tools by Stone Age men, although a trace of copper oxide on the base of one sarsen showed that this metal was just beginning to come into use at that time.

In 1915 Cecil Chubb, the owner of the tract, presented Stonehenge to the nation. King George V appropriately rewarded Chubb by making him First Baronet of Stonehenge. A committee raised money to buy up the surrounding lands, demolish the modern houses on them, and turn the area into a national park.

In 1920, Hawley and Newhall made further excavations. They rediscovered the Aubrey Holes and discovered the Y and Z Holes. They also found Cunnington's bottle of port; unfortunately the cork had disintegrated. Also unfortunately, Colonel Hawley's work was not up to first-class archaeological standards, so that much evidence was destroyed without being recorded in sufficiently meticulous detail.

In the 1950s, Professors Atkinson, Piggott, and Stone dug some more, deliberately leaving half the monument alone for future archaeologists with even more advanced methods and instruments. Their investigations resulted in the radiocarbon dating of the Aubrey Holes, the discovery of the Q and R Holes, and most of the other details from which the history of the monument has been pieced together.

Stonehenge is now about half in ruins, and a third of the stones are missing. In spite of the disheveled appearance of the monument, however, we can discern a fairly simple plan.

Stonehenge consists of three kinds of structure: (a) the surrounding circular bank and its ditch; (b) a multitude of holes, dug within the circle of the bank and later allowed to fill up with airborne soil and rubbish; and (c) the stones. Of the holes, some seem to have been dug to receive the cremated remains of the dead; some were evidently holes for wooden posts; and some may have been meant for upright stones.

The stones are of two different kinds. The larger stones, weighing up to forty-five tons, are all of a kind of hard sandstone that occurs in huge boulders at Marlborough Downs, twenty miles north of Stonehenge. The large stones are called sarsens. The word comes from "Saracen stones," a name that medieval English countrymen applied to the stones in the belief that Saracens—meaning any kind of foreign unbelievers—must have erected them.

The small stones, standing up to five and a half feet tall and weighing about four tons apiece, are with one exception of another kind. They are of dolerite and rhyolite, igneous rocks of a faintly bluish color; hence they are called bluestones. The odd thing is that Stonehenge stands amidst an area of sedimentary rocks. No igneous rocks occur in any direction for nearly a hundred miles.

In 1923, the geologist H. H. Thomas showed by petrographic analysis that the bluestones came from Mynydd Prescelly.[10] This is a small mountain range in the southwest corner of Wales, where outcroppings of igneous rocks occur. Mynydd Prescelly is 135 miles from Stonehenge in a straight line; the roundabout sea-and-land route, which the builders probably used, is 240 miles long.

To understand the plan of the prehistoric builders of Stonehenge, we must separately consider the bank and ditch, the holes, and the stones. The bank that surrounds the monument has a gap at the

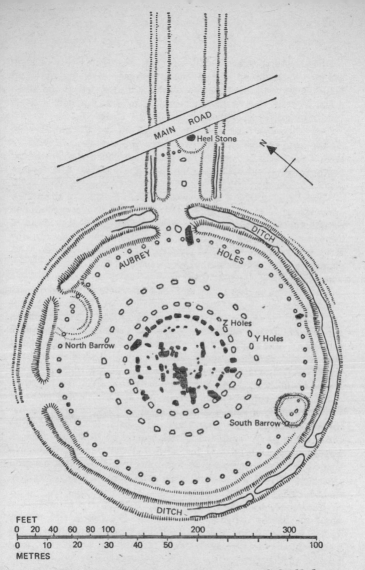

Fig. 7 Plan of Stonehenge; the surviving stones are marked in black.
(After Atkinson)

northeast side, which we call the Causeway. From this opening a wide, banked road, the Avenue, anciently extended northeast before it curved around to the southeast and ended at the River Avon. The entire Avenue was about a mile and a half long. A smaller causeway breaks the bank on the south side.

Just inside the bank are two shallow circular ditches forming circles 40 to 50 feet in diameter. Since these circles are more or less on the north and south sides, they are called the North and South Barrows, although they are not real barrows—that is, prehistoric grave mounds.

Now the holes. There are several concentric circles of them. The outermost is a circle of fifty-six Aubrey Holes. Some contained burned human bones; other cremation burials have been found in the surrounding bank and ditch. The real purpose of the Aubrey Holes is not known. Perhaps they were dug—as the Greeks dug pits many centuries later—as part of a ceremony to open communication with the gods of the underworld.

Between the Aubrey Holes and the main circle of stones, diggers in the 1920s discovered two more concentric circles of holes. The outer circle, called the Y Holes, comprises thirty holes; the inner, the Z Holes, twenty-nine. One Z Hole is beneath a fallen sarsen; another on the southeast side would have been under another fallen sarsen—but this one was never dug. It appears that the latter sarsen fell before the circle of holes was completed, and the people who dug the holes could not figure how to reërect the megalith.

Inside the main circle of sarsens lies another double circle of holes—or rather a single circle of dumbbell-shaped trenches, arranged radically. These are called the Q and R Holes, the latter being closer to the center. They are spaced about 6 feet apart. A large gap on the west side indicates that the circle of dumbbell-shaped holes was never completed; moreover, their positions have been obscured by the present circle of bluestones, which stand on the handgrips of the dumbbells.

In addition, there are many holes for wooden posts. There is one large cluster on the south side between the Y and Aubrey Holes; another inside the stone circles; and still another in the Causeway. As the first two clusters of postholes seem to have no relation to the plan of the whole monument, they may indicate houses erected there after Stonehenge had gone out of use for religious purposes.

Lastly, the stones. They are arranged in four main groups. From the outside moving inward, there stand a circle of sarsens, then a circle of undressed bluestones, then a horseshoe of sarsens, and lastly a horseshoe of dressed bluestones.

The circle of sarsens once consisted of thirty uprights weighing twenty-five to thirty tons and tapered upward. Their tops were joined by thirty curved seven-ton lintels to form a closed circle. Inside this main circle stood a circle of sixty bluestone uprights.

The sarsen horseshoe consisted of five *trilithons*—that is, sets of three stones. Each trilithon was made up of a pair of forty-five-ton uprights capped by a huge lintel, the whole forming a kind of gateway. The horseshoe opens towards the Avenue. Inside this horseshoe is another, smaller horseshoe of nineteen bluestones; these stones may once have formed a complete ellipse.

Thus, as you walk towards the center of Stonehenge, you cross, one after another, these eleven circles:

1. The Ditch.
2. The Bank.
3. The Aubrey Holes.
4. The Y Holes.
5. The Z Holes.
6. The Sarsen Circle.
7. The Q Holes.
8. The Bluestone Circle
9. The R Holes.
10. The Sarsen Horseshoe.
11. The Bluestone Horseshoe.

Besides the circles, there were also several isolated stones. A stone lying inside the tip of the Bluestone Horseshoe is called the Altar Stone. It is of sandstone, but not the Marlborough Downs variety. Instead, it seems to have come from Milford Haven, the harbor in southwestern Wales whence those who transported the bluestones set out in their dugouts.

Four sarsens were also spaced around the outer rim of the circle, on the line of the Aubrey Holes. Two of these "Station Stones" survive; the other two, which stood on the North and South Barrows, have disappeared.

A sarsen lying flat on the Causeway, just inside the bank, has been called the Slaughter Stone. This name conjures up a splendidly macabre picture of pagan priests, their white robes soaked with blood, cutting the throats of shrieking victims. But it seems more likely that this stone originally stood upright and formed one of a pair that served as a gateway to the monument.

On the Avenue, a hundred feet outside the Bank, rises an un-shaped, phallic-looking sarsen called the Heel (or Hele) Stone. The Causeway, the Avenue, and the Heel Stone are all in the same general northeasterly direction from the center of the circles. From the center, the centerline of the Causeway is about five degrees to the left of the centerline of the Avenue, and the Heel Stone is about one degree to the right of it.

In 1901 the Astronomer Royal, Sir Norman Lockyer, measured and calculated the positions of these stones. Lockyer claimed that if one stood on the center of the Altar Stone at dawn on Midsummer Day, one would see the sun rise (if one saw it at all in British weather) almost exactly over the tip of the Heel Stone.

Lockyer, who believed that Stonehenge was built by sun-worshiping Druids, calculated that, at the time Stonehenge was built, the sun rose exactly over the point of the Heel Stone. But the slight periodic increase and decrease in the obliquity of the ecliptic (the angle between the plane of the earth's equator and that of its orbit) had spoiled this alignment. However, knowing the rate of change in the obliquity of the ecliptic (which goes through a complete cycle in 40,000 years) Sir Norman figured back to the date of construction: between −1900 and −1500.

More recent study has shown Lockyer's reasoning to be wrong on several counts. For one thing, the sun now rises to the left of the Heel Stone on June 21, and in ancient times it rose even farther to the left. It will not rise directly over the Heel Stone for another thousand years. For another thing, the Heel Stone cannot cast a shadow on the altar stone, because one of the uprights of the Sarsen Circle stands between them. For still another, the Altar Stone is now thought to be not an altar at all but another fallen upright. Finally, even if the stones were originally aligned as exactly as Lockyer supposed, this orientation cannot now be exactly determined because of the leaning or fall of several of the stones by which this orientation would be measured.

Nevertheless, when W. F. Libby, discoverer of the radiocarbon method of dating, analyzed a sample of charcoal from one of the

Aubrey Holes, it gave a date of —1848, with a possible error of 275 years either way. As this date falls neatly into the interval calculated by Lockyer, the astronomer must have reached the right destination by the wrong route.

Even if the builders of Stonehenge were not sun worshipers—a question that cannot now be settled—the fact that the horseshoes face in the general direction of the rising midsummer sun probably indicates that the monument did have the practical purpose of keeping track of the time of year. This was a serious matter to Neolithic farmers, who had no calendars. By facing in the direction opposite to that of midsummer sunrise, you face the direction of midwinter sunset and thus have a date from which to count the days to spring planting. The monument may as well have been oriented towards one as towards the other.

Aside from their minor function as timekeepers, and despite all the argument over and research into Stonehenge, we still do not know the true meaning of these stone circles. It is not known whether the stones comprised a magical fence, or a dwelling place for ancestral spirits, or what. Barbarian peoples have erected stones for many different supernatural reasons.

It is logical to ask: Is Stonehenge unique, or are there other monuments like it in Europe? Well, there are many monuments somewhat like it but none so ambitious. It surpasses the other pre-historic monuments of western Europe somewhat as Khufu's Great Pyramid excels the other Egyptian pyramids.

Half a mile north of Stonehenge, for example, is the Cursus: a bank-and-ditch system forming a long narrow ellipse, 1¾ miles long and 100 yards wide. Stukeley gave it the Roman name for a chariot racecourse, thinking that it was actually used for this purpose. More likely, it was a processional avenue employed for religious ceremonies in connection with the long barrow or multiple grave at the east end.

Avebury likewise was surrounded by a bank and a ditch, much larger than those of Stonehenge. The circle was nearly a third of a mile across, and the top of the bank rose 50 feet above the bottom of the ditch. One large circle of standing stones lay close against the bank. Within the 28.5-acre inclosure were two smaller stone circles, side by side; one of them had a smaller ellipse inside it. The stones, weighing up to 40 tons, were all undressed sarsens; this

57

suggests that they are older than the sarsens of Stonehenge. More than half the stones have now disappeared, and the town cuts off the view, so that Avebury is much less spectacular to look at today than Stonehenge. Nevertheless, Avebury represents a tremendous investment of primitive labor.

Two miles northeast of Stonehenge are the remains of another circular bank with a ditch inside it, called Woodhenge. The temple here seems, as well as one can tell from the postholes, to have been a ring-shaped wooden building, something like a long barn bent around to form a circle. Since nothing of the structure survives, the existence of Woodhenge was unknown until the circular bank was discovered from an airplane.

A mile south of Avebury is Silbury Hill: an artificial conical mound 130 feet high and covering 5½ acres. Could it be that the king who built Stonehenge sleeps under this mound? Tunneling into the hill has failed to settle the question.

Several other, less notable circular structures exist elsewhere in Britain. Stonehenge, then, is but one of a number of sacred circles. Such a circle might have had no structures inside the bank; or the magic of the circular bank might have been reinforced by inner circles of holes, wooden posts, standing stones, or a covered circular building.

Nor are such structures confined to Britain. Brittany, across the channel, is famous for megalithic monuments. There are many large standing stones called menhirs, sometimes roughly trimmed to shape. The biggest of all, the "fairy stone" of Locmaricquer, was over 60 feet high and weighed over 380 tons. It was broken into several pieces in ancient times, possibly while being erected.

The menhir of Île-Melon, blown up in the Second World War, weighed around ninety tons. Of those still standing, that of Kerloas stands 37 feet tall, and at least twenty-five others exceed 20 feet. Some rows of standing stones form circles, semicircles, or rectangles. Other stones stand in long parallel rows, the "alignments." There are sometimes as many as ten or eleven parallel rows over half a mile long; the best-known are those of Carnac in Brittany, which has nothing to do with Karnak in Egypt.

In addition, hundreds of megalithic graves are scattered over western Europe, from Scotland to Sardinia and from Denmark to Portugal. They are variously called cists, cromlechs, dolmens, and dysser.[11]

These graves come in many shapes and sizes. Some are built on the surface, some in trenches, and some in artificial caves. While some are made of small stones, most are constructed of large slabs of rock or of a mixture of small and large stones. Usually a number of large slabs stand on end in a row, forming an inclosure with a small stone-flanked entrance. Often a larger slab, weighing several tons, lies on top of the uprights like a lid, and a mound of earth may be (some think always was) piled up over the whole structure. If the mound is missing today, it has probably been eroded away by weather or dug away by treasure seekers, leaving the supporting stones exposed. Such "howe-breaking" was, next to robbery, murder, and arson, a favorite sport of the Vikings.

The largest multiple graves are found in Ireland; the circular mound at New Grange is 265 feet in diameter and 45 feet high. Although arguments are endless as to which people built which tomb, and when, most megalithic graves fall into the general period of Stonehenge: the second millennium B.C. It is a common archeological opinion that there never was any "megalithic race." Instead, the spread of these monuments in the second millennium B.C. represents the spread of a new religion, which probably originated in the eastern Mediterranean and was based upon worship of ancestors and of the mother goddess. This cult was carried to the western Mediterranean, perhaps before —3000, by traders and colonists (Cretans, Mycenaeans, or Karians?) and thence spread far and wide over Europe.

And then there are the megalithic temples of Malta and the prehistoric castles of Sardinia . . . One wonders: if western European men of this period were kept so busy sledding huge stones around the country, how did they find time to raise their crops?

Little by little, during the past seventy years, the history of Stonehenge has come to light. It transpires that Stonehenge was built, not all at once, but slowly over several centuries. We can divide its history into three phases, Stonehenge I, II, and III.

Stonehenge I consisted of the Bank, the Aubrey Holes, the Causeway, and the Heel Stone. (The Ditch was incidental, being merely the place from which earth was taken to build the Bank.)

About —XIX, the Bank and the Aubrey Holes were laid out in accurate circles from the center, probably by driving a stake into the ground and tracing out circles around it with a rope at least

160 feet long. We can be sure that the standing stones in the middle of the circle had not yet been erected, because such stones would have interfered with the laying out of the outer circles.

The builders of Stonehenge I were Neolithic peasants, living at a time when head-hunting and cannibalism were practiced in Britain. Wild cattle roamed the forests and wild horses the Downs. Stonehenge was built shortly after the first farmers (known as the Windmill Hill people) arrived in Britain, about —2000. Since they practiced intensive cattle-raising, they quickly settled the grassy Downs. The circular inclosures they built—aside from religious centers like the Henges—are often called "causewayed camps" but may really have been cattle corrals.

The actual builders of Stonehenge I, however, may have been what British archaeologists call Secondary Neolithic people. These were descendants of the hunters and food-gatherers who dwelt in Britain before the arrival of the farmers and who had begun to learn the rudiments of agriculture from these immigrants.

The Stonehenge II period began when the beer-swilling, metal-bearing, trading Beaker Folk, who preferred single to multiple graves, arrived from Spain about —1700. This is perhaps an oversimplified statement. But, as archaeology advances, the story of prehistoric European migrations, conquests, and cultural borrowings becomes more and more complex, until the popularizer despairs of presenting it in detail.

Furthermore, we must not think of the Mesolithic, Neolithic, Copper, Bronze, and Iron ages as taking place everywhere in the same order at the same time. When Stonehenge I was under construction, the First Dynasty of Babylon was coming to an end, and the Asian war-band called the Hyksôs[12] was overrunning Egypt. The Near and Middle East and the eastern Mediterranean were in the Bronze Age. Central and southeastern Europe had reached the Copper Age. Northern and western Europeans were still mostly Stone Age Neolithic peoples. And in the remoter parts of the North, Mesolithic hunting bands still plied their ancient trade.

The Beaker Folk, taking advantage of their possession of metal, seem to have made themselves rulers of Britain and to have set their subjects to hauling huge stones for religious structures. Such monuments require a government sufficiently strong and centralized, and on a large enough scale, to compel great numbers of men to work together. The techniques of such organization had already begun to be worked out, for some megalithic graves of western Europe antedate the expansion of the Beaker Folk.

About —1650, the Britons began to fetch eighty-odd bluestones from Wales. Probably the Welsh stones had already been erected to form an outdoor temple, of—we can guess—extraordinary holiness. News of the extreme sanctity and wonder-working powers of these stones must have reached the ears of some covetous chieftain on Salisbury Plain. This lordling set out to possess himself of them, on the good old barbarian principle that what's mine is mine and what's yours is mine, too, if I'm strong enough to take it. Perhaps if the bluestones could speak, they could tell a turbulent tale of bloodshed and rapine.

In any case, the bluestones were probably sledded down to Milford Haven, loaded aboard craft made of two or more dugout canoes lashed together, sailed and paddled along the rocky Welsh coast and up Bristol Channel, and then sledded overland to the site of Stonehenge. On arrival, they were erected in a double circle in the Q and R Holes. Each pair of uprights may have been capped by a lintel. At least some of the bluestones were furnished with tenons and mortise holes, the former on the uprights and the latter in the lintels.

Some sort of bluestone structure seems also to have been erected at the west end of the nearby Cursus, judging from the bluestone chips found in the ditch of that structure. This temple and the Avenue were built at the same time as Stonehenge I.

To judge by the gap in the holes on the west side of the Q and R circles, this phase of the monument, Stonehenge II, was never completed. About —1500, a century to a century and a half after Stonehenge II was begun, some ruler commanded a new and different plan, using the much larger sarsens of Marlborough Downs. The people of the region now belonged to what archaeologists call the Wessex Culture, combining traits of the Beaker Folk with those of the first waves of the Aryan Battle-ax People. The ruler who ordered the building of Stonehenge III must have reigned over most of southern Britain, to command the manpower needed for so pretentious a structure.

So the hardworking peasants of the Downs country set out with their sleds and their ropes of braided thongs, their timber balks and stone mauls, to shape and haul and erect the stones, until the Sarsen Circle and the Sarsen Horseshoe arose in all their glory. It probably took over a thousand men to haul one stone. The general plan of this part of the work followed that of the previous erections of bluestones, but with more refinement. Technical advances and larger governmental units made it possible to move and erect larger stones, for the glory of the chieftain and the pleasure of the gods.

For example, the uprights were furnished with tenons and the lintels with mortises, as had been done with the bluestones; but the stones were more thoroughly shaped. The tops of the uprights were slightly dished to provide a more secure resting place for the lintels, and adjacent lintel stones were fitted together by hewing tongues and grooves in the alternate ends. Because of the difficulties of accurate measurement, the Sarsen Circle is not quite concentric with the Bank and the Aubrey Holes.

The Beaker Era was a time of widespread travel and commerce in western Europe. Objects imported from or made in imitation of Mediterranean models turn up in British graves. One evening in June, 1953, the setting sun struck slantwise across the face of one of the sarsens. Professor Atkinson, photographing a seventeenth-century inscription, noticed that the light cast peculiar shadows on the face of the stone. These turned out to be carvings in the shape of axheads and a dagger, which nobody had noticed in the three centuries since antiquaries had begun to peer at the megaliths. The axheads are of a typical Bronze Age shape, like the axes then made in Ireland and imported to Britain.

The dagger, however, was of a kind found nowhere (except for one imported specimen from a grave in Dorsetshire) nearer than Mycenaean Greece. From this the archaeologists infer that there was definite Mediterranean influence in the building of Stonehenge III. Another reason for suspecting Mediterranean influence is the fact that the closest architectural kin of Stonehenge are the megalithic temples of Malta. But whether, as some suggest, the local ruler hired a Cretan, Mycenaean, or Maltese architect is a matter of guesswork.

So much for Stonehenge III in its first stage—Stonehenge IIIa. There were still the bluestones to dispose of. If less impressive than the sarsens, they were too sacred to throw away.

The events of the next few centuries are obscure. We know that the bluestones of the Cursus were removed. Some bluestones, possibly from the Cursus, were set up in an ellipse inside the Sarsen Horseshoe (Stonehenge IIIb, about −1450). The Y and Z Holes were dug, perhaps to hold the remaining bluestones. These circles are less regular than the outer ones. They could not be measured from the center of the area, because the sarsens were in the way. But at last this plan was given up and the bluestones arranged in the circle and horseshoe that obtained in historic times (Stonehenge IIIc, about −1400).

Stonehenge thus reached the climax of its glory. We do not know what sort of rites were celebrated in this temple, for temple it undoubtedly was. The pantheon of these ancient Britons was probably like that of other peoples in that cultural stage, with departmental deities of the sun, the sea, the forest, war, crops, and motherhood. There is some evidence of human sacrifice in the Britain of this time—the builders of Woodhenge split the skull of an infant at the dedication of the temple—although such sacrifices seem to have been uncommon.

Then Stonehenge declined. At least one sarsen is thought to have fallen over before the Y and Z Holes were dug, and it was not reërected. Perhaps a later and more barbarous wave of Aryans or Battle-ax People reached Britain at this time, bringing their horses, their bronze swords, their sky gods, and their Indo-European language, and causing the culture of the island to backslide towards their own more primitive level.

The pseudo-scientific doctrine of a pure and noble Aryan race has been debunked so often that we do not think we need demolish it here once more. But, if you wonder why Indo-European languages are spoken today by peoples as different in appearance as Swedes, Armenians, and Hindis, remember that in such a conquest the conquered far outnumbered their conquerors. Because Bronze Age farmers were not efficient enough to produce large surpluses of food to feed non-farmers, the migrating, conquering warrior class could be only a small fraction of the whole population. So, when the Aryans spread over an area from Portugal to Bengal, they spread themselves so thinly that in a few generations their original racial type—whatever it was—disappeared by intermarriage with the natives.

Then came a later Indo-European wave, the head-hunting Celts. The Celts invaded Britain about −IV, with their iron weapons, their scythe-wheeled chariots, their two-ox plows, and their white-robed Druids. Perhaps the Druids put Stonehenge back into use as a center of worship, although there is no positive evidence that they did so.

Some archaeologists think that the Y and Z Holes were dug by the Celts, though others disagree.

Britain's next invaders were the Belgae, who dwelt in the Low Countries and whose culture combined Celtic and German traits. They were extremely warlike, did highly skilled metal work, minted their own coins, and used the heavy colter plow (with wheels and a knife in front of the share to slit the turf), which made their farming more productive than that of most peoples of their time. The Belgae landed early in —I; but they had conquered only the southeastern corner of Britain when the Romans arrived. Julius Caesar's probing expeditions of —55 and —54 failed to subdue the Britons or to stop the growth of Belgic power. However, in +43— nearly a century later—the emperor Claudius mounted a full-sized invasion, with 50,000 of the world's most efficient soldiers; and Britain became a Roman province for four centuries.

Nothing is heard of Stonehenge during the Roman period and the Dark Ages. In medieval times the stones began to disappear. The Romans may have begun this destruction as an anti-Druidic measure. Later, some stones were probably broken up or taken away and buried by Christian fanatics, to whom the outdoor temple was a work of devils and a heritage of detested paganism.

Spoliation of all the prehistoric monuments of Britain became severe in +XVII and +XVIII, when increasing population pressure incited farmers to turn every patch of ground into plowland and increased the demand for stone for houses and millstones. The rise of tourism also encouraged damage. Visitors to Stonehenge rented sledge hammers in Amesbury, two miles away, wherewith to knock chips off the stones for souvenirs.

Stukeley described a campaign at Avebury to get rid of the stones there because they interfered with plowing and the building of houses. The people dug pits beside the stones, kindled fires in them, upset the stones into the pits, and, when the stones had been weakened by heat, battered them to pieces. Unfortunately, all these people are dead and so cannot be boiled in oil as they deserve. It is some consolation to learn that one of the destroyers of Avebury, a speculative builder named Robinson, was ruined when his houses burned. Perhaps the Elder Gods are not to be affronted with impunity, after all.

In the last century, the damage to these monuments has been stopped and some repair and restoration done; several fallen stones have been put back on their bases. So Stonehenge will long continue to brood over Salisbury Plain. In fact, it may still stand there when there are no more men to gape at it.

Although the main questions about the origin and development of Stonehenge seem to have been answered, one nagging little mystery remains. Do you remember Geoffrey's fanciful tale of King Aurelius' expedition to fetch the Giants' Dance from Ireland, with the help of Merlin's wonder-working powers? This story shows a surprising parallel to the tale that archaeology unfolds about the source of the bluestones.

True, Geoffrey got the details wrong. The stones fetched from afar were the bluestones, not the sarsens; they came from Wales, not from Ireland; and they were brought to Stonehenge in −XVII, not in +V. But Geoffrey's story and the facts are so much alike in outline that it is hard to believe that Geoffrey, by pure happenstance, hit upon the idea of an expedition to the West to rape away a whole temple whose stones possessed special magical virtues.

Oh yes, we know, coincidence ought to be the true answer. It is incredible that the tale should be handed down for 2,700 years, during which time Britain was overrun by Battle-ax People, Celts, Belgae, Romans, Saxons, Danes, and Normans. Moreover, during most of this time there were no written records to preserve the story. But it is equally incredible that Geoffrey should have come so close to the truth by pure guess . . .

# IV
# Troy and the
# Nine Cities

Tell ye the King: It is fallen,
   the temple of wondrous adornment;
Gone are the booths of Apollo,
   the green oracular laurel;
Dumb the streams; dry, dry
   is the garrulous water for ever.
                    *Kedrinos,*
                    tr. *Bevan*

According to the Poet, it was the tenth year of the Siege of Troy.
Among the well-greaved Achaians, fleet-footed Achilles[1] had quar-
relled with King Agamemnon, lord of Mykenê and leader of the host,
over one of the women whom Achilles had captured in his great raid
on the southern Troad. Therefore, Achilles retired to his hut, refus-
ing to fight any longer.

The next day, while Achilles still sulked, the armies drew up for
battle. Among the Trojans was godlike Paris, also called Alexandros,
a son of King Priamos. Paris had brought on the war by stealing
Helen, the wife of Agamemnon's brother Menelaos, king of Sparta.
Chided by his brother Hector, Paris proposed that the strife be
settled by a single combat between himself and Menelaos.

So they fought. Menelaos of the loud war cry was having the
better of it when the goddess Aphroditê snatched Paris away from
the battlefield. The charming but light-minded Paris was a favorite
of hers, since in return for the promise of Helen he had given her
the golden apple of Discord in the beauty contest amongst herself,
Hera, and Athena. Meanwhile Athena persuaded the Trojan Pan-
daros to shoot an arrow at fair-haired Menelaos, wounding him

and breaking the truce. Soon the armies were hard at it again, drenching the plain of Troy with the blood of heroes.

The gods were always interfering on one side or the other, so that success depended less on the might and valor of the warriors than on the power of the gods each army happened to have on its side. This was how the men of old explained the capricious, unpredictable, irrational element in life and luck. This explanation had another advantage: when somebody acted discreditably, he and his friends blamed the act on one of the meddlesome deities. As Priamos says to Helen: "I hold not thee to blame; nay, I hold the gods to blame who brought on me the dolorous war of the Achaians . . ."² Nowadays we say, instead, that the culprit is maladjusted.

After several days of fighting, the Trojans, led by Hector of the flashing helm, drove the Achaians back within the wall they had built around their ships. Hector broke down the gate of this wall by casting a huge stone against it. The Trojans and their allies poured into the inclosure, meaning to burn the hollow ships of the Achaians. While grim Achilles, who really took pleasure in nothing but killing, was preparing to sail for home, his friend Patroklos borrowed his armor to go forth, pretending to be Achilles, and hearten the flowing-haired Achaians. Thus clad, Patroklos drove the Trojans out of the inclosure. However, in the fighting on the plain, Hector slew Patroklos and robbed the corpse of Achilles' armor.

Now Achilles was roused to fight once more; but he had no armor. His mother, the sea nymph Thetis, persuaded Hephaistos, smith of the gods, to forge a new suit for her son. In his flashing new armor, fierce Achilles rushed upon the Trojans and scattered them everywhere, slaying right and left. Only Hector stood against him. Panic seized even bold Hector and made him run thrice around the walls of Troy, pursued by Achilles. Then bright-eyed Athena, who (like Hera) hated the Trojans because Paris had not given her the apple, intervened. By a trick she persuaded Hector to stand fast, while she helped Achilles in the fight. Achilles slew Hector, tied the corpse to his chariot, and dragged it back to the Achaian camp.

Achilles then staged a fine funeral for his friend Patroklos. He erected a huge pyre and slew and placed upon it many sheep and oxen, two of Patroklos' dogs, and twelve Trojan prisoners of noble blood. The Achaians held a chariot race, a boxing tournament, wrestling matches, and other games to celebrate the funeral. The gods persuaded Achilles to allow King Priamos to ransom the body of horse-taming Hector, which the Trojans in their turn cremated and buried.

Thus Homer's *Iliad*,[3] a long narrative poem about the Siege of Troy. When translated into English it runs to about 150,000 words, the equivalent of a long novel. People who have never read the *Iliad* sometimes think that it tells the entire story of the Trojan War, but this is not so. It merely recounts one episode, the Wrath of Achilles, padded out with long speeches and minor incidents like the raid of Diomedes and Odysseus on the Trojan camp. However, there exists a large body of Greek legend outside the *Iliad*, from which we can piece together the rest of the tale.

According to these stories, after the death of Hector, new allies appeared to help the Trojans: the Ethiopians and the Amazons, the latter a race of warrior women. Achilles slew Memnon, king of the Ethiopians, and Queen Penthesilea of the Amazons. Then Paris slew Achilles, only soon to be mortally wounded himself by a poisoned Greek arrow.

Homer says nothing about the legend that Achilles' mother made her infant practically invulnerable by dipping him in the river Styx, and that Paris' arrow struck Achilles in the heel by which his mother had held him. If Homer had used this idea, Achilles would have needed no armor at all. Since much of the plot of the *Iliad* turns on Achilles' armor, Homer would have had to change his whole tale. Far from being invulnerable, Homer's Achilles is actually wounded in the elbow in one combat,[4] so that his red blood flows.

According to Homer and other mythographers, the Trojans held out until crafty Odysseus,[5] king of Ithaka, devised a plan. This was to build a huge wooden horse, hide a band of warriors inside, and pretend to sail away for good. This they did, leaving behind a man named Sinon. Sinon gave himself up to the Trojans, to whom he told the following story: Athena, he said, had commanded the Achaians to build the horse as an offering to her, and if the Trojans took it within their wall it would act as a talisman to protect their city. So the Trojans moved the horse into the city, although they had to break down the wall to do so.

The next night, when the Trojans were sleeping off their victory revel, the Achaian volunteers came out of the horse, opened the gates of Troy, and admitted the returning Achaian army. The Achaians captured and sacked the city, slew all the men, and enslaved the women. (If the Trojans had really broken down their wall, there would have been no need to open the gate. But such inconsistencies are to be expected in epics.)

Among the few Trojan survivors was Priamos' nephew Aineias. Homer implies that Aineias rebuilt and ruled Troy after the Trojan War.[6] Later mythographers, however, alleged that Aineias led his followers to various places in Greece and Italy and that his descendants founded Rome.

When Menelaos had been reconciled with Helen, the Achaians set out for home across the wine-dark sea with their captives and loot. So many had offended one god or another, however, that many perished on the way, or were delayed for years, or were murdered on their arrival. The *Iliad*'s companion poem, the *Odyssey*,[7] tells of the adventures of Odysseus on his ten-year homecoming voyage. Although many modern scholars consider the *Iliad* the more artistic of the two epics, the general reader is likely to find the *Odyssey* the more entertaining.

There is also a Greek legend, alluded to by Homer, of an earlier destruction of Troy. This story tells that the gods Apollo and Poseidon built the walls of Troy, but then King Laomedon (an ancestor of King Priamos) refused to pay them. In revenge they sent a sea monster to ravage the coast. An oracle told the king that the monster could be appeased only by sacrificing a maiden to it every year.

The sixth such maiden, Laomedon's daughter Hesionê, was rescued by Herakles on her father's promise to reward the hero with some supernatural horses. But perfidious Laomedon never learned. Once the girl was safe, he refused to hand over the immortal mares, so Herakles gathered his gang and sacked the city.

Most classical Greeks and Romans considered the Homeric poems to be true history. Moreover, a small town in the northwestern corner of Asia Minor, facing the Gallipoli Peninsula across the Hellespont, was called by the ancient names of Troia, Ilion, and Ilios.

Still, there were always doubts and arguments as to whether there ever was such a person as Homer and whether the tale he told was true. For over two thousand years, these arguments have raged. What says archaeology about this citadel of controversy?

Before going into the "Homeric question," we should take a deep breath. Except for the Bible, no other works of ancient literature have been reissued so many times in the original as Homer's two great poems have been. They have been translated over and over, wholly and in part, in prose and in rhyme, in hexameters like the original and in free verse, into all the important and some of the unimportant languages of today.

The translations alone would fill the bookshelves of a room, and the commentary would require a whole library. The works of Homer have furnished the English language with many words and figures of speech such as "odyssey," "Trojan horse," "lotus eater," and "Achilles' heel." Names from them have been freely bestowed upon modern people and things: "Ulysses Grant," "Troy, New York," and "H.M.S. *Achilles*," not to mention several hundred minor planets, a few craters on the moon, and some surface features of Mars.

Students of history, literature, philology, mythology, and archaeology have argued endlessly as to whether Homer really lived, whether he was one man or a dozen, whether he was an original poet or a mere compiler, where he came from, how much he knew, how widely he had traveled, what Greek dialect he used, and whether he was literate or composed from memory. They have asserted that the Trojan War took place at Troy, or in Greece, or in Egypt, or not at all. They have speculated that perhaps the Trojans really won it. They have averred that it was in revenge for the theft of a woman (as Homer said), or a buccaneering raid, or a war for the rule of trade routes. They have wrangled over the course of the Trojan rivers and the contour of the Trojan coast in ancient times.

Pausanias (+II), who wrote a travel guide to Greece 1,700 years before Karl Baedeker, said that the Trojan horse was "a contrivance to make a breach in the Trojan wall."[8] This is an ingenious idea, although it is doubtful if such a device—a battering-ram hung by chains inside a wheeled shed—was in use as early as the Siege of Troy. Homerists have claimed that Homer's characters were real people, or humanized gods, or natural forces like the sun, or personifications of tribes. Nor do the countless disputes over Homer's poems show any signs of dying down.

In classical times, most people took it for granted that the *Iliad* and the *Odyssey* had been composed by a blind poet from Ionia (the west coast of Asia Minor) named Homêros, who had wandered about the blue Aegean Sea singing lays to the tune of his lyre. They attributed his birth to a dozen different cities and dated it anywhere from —1159 to —685. In Hellenistic and Roman times, several biographies of Homer circulated, all probably written about or after the time of Aristotle in response to the demand for nonexistent information, and based mainly on conjecture from the poems themselves and on sheer fabrication. From genealogies and other traditions, classical scholars reckoned various dates for the fall of Troy. That of —1184, computed by the all-around Alexandrian genius Eratosthenes of Kyrenê, was the most widely accepted.

Opinions varied, even in ancient times, from extreme skepticism to an idolatrous reverence of Homer's truthfulness and accuracy. Strabon the geographer boiled with rage whenever some skeptic like Eratosthenes cast doubt upon Homer's accuracy by remarking that poets are paid to please, not to teach.

There was also a small school of "separatists," who asserted that the two poems were by two different authors. But few took these people seriously, especially after the grammarian Aristarchos of Samothrace, who was Librarian of Alexandria in —II, squelched them.

Serious study of Homer revived with other classical studies in the Renaissance. A seventeenth-century French Homerist, the Abbé d'Aubignac, theorized that there had not been any *Iliad* or *Odyssey* until the time of Peisistratos, a *tyrannos* or dictator of Athens in —VI. There had been instead a multitude of shorter Homeric lays. According to Cicero (—I) and later writers, Peisistratos gathered a group of poets to edit this mass of material, choosing certain lays and combining them to make the two Homeric poems we have.

In early +XVIII an English scholar, Richard Bentley, made a discovery that became important in reconstructing the history of Troy. Scholars had long been puzzled by the fact that many lines of Homer refused to scan. Bentley discovered that the Greek of Homer's time had a sound represented by the letter digamma, resembling our F. (It was called "digamma" because it looked like two gammas, one above the other.) The sound represented was either a *v*, or a *w*, or something in between. Between the time of Homer and that of Peisistratos, both sound and letter disappeared from the Attic dialect, which became the standard literary form of the language, although the sound long survived in other dialects and the letter appears in some old inscriptions. With the restoration of the lost digammas, Homer scanned perfectly.

In 1795, Friederich August Wolf of Halle and Berlin startled the academic world by proclaiming that there had not even been any real Homer; or rather, that "Homer" was not one man or two, but many. "Homer," he said, was a collective name adopted by or applied to a group or school of poets, who composed the series of heroic lays combined into the *Iliad* and *Odyssey* under the supervision of Peisistratos.

The uproar caused by this pronouncement still resounds, with no decision in sight. Among modern Homerists, some believe in one Homer and some in many. Quite a few believe in two Homers. Of these, some take the old "separatist" view, holding that the *Odyssey* was composed several decades after the *Iliad* and must therefore have been by another poet. Some believe in two Homers but divide the work differently between the two authors, for instance by assigning the *Catalogue of Ships* in the second book of the *Iliad* to one author and all the rest of the two poems to the other.

A view that most modern Homerists could agree upon would run somewhat as follows: The Homeric poems deal with events supposed to have taken place in —XIII and —XII. Many of these events are plainly fictional, such as the interference of the gods in human affairs and reports of private conversations that could never have been recorded. Nor is it likely that any siege of that era lasted any ten years; an army of Bronze Age barbarians could probably not have been held together more than a few months at a time. Outside of such patent fictions, however, the rest of the poems probably contain some historical facts, although it is often impossible to separate the fact from the fiction.

Parts of the poems go back to —X or even earlier. The poems took roughly their present shape in —VIII. Although more than one man had a hand in the work of combining older materials and recasting them into their present form, the greater part of this composition was performed by one (or possibly two) poets of outstanding genius, and this man (or the first of these two men) was very likely named Homer. Some further revisions and additions were performed by later poets, until the poems were stabilized around —530 on the orders of Peisistratos. Occasional extra lines continued to be added, however, as late as —IV.

Hence the poems contain many anachronisms. With Homer in

73

—VIII recomposing shorter poems from —X and —IX about events of —XIII and —XII, and with other would-be improvers putting in their two cents' worth after Homer, the stories display a mixture of the costumes and customs of different centuries, like those medieval tapestries that show Achilles and Hector, clad in fifteenth-century steel plate-armor, whaling away at each other.

However, Homer was not unaware of the problem of anachronism. His allusions to the great leather figure-eight shield, almost as tall as a man, and the leather helmet armored with rows of boar's tusks refer to defenses that went out of use before —1200.[9] Furthermore, while he was familiar with iron, he was careful to describe his warriors as using weapons of bronze only, as men actually did in —XIII.

The *Iliad* and the *Odyssey* were not the only ancient Greek epics. Eight or more epics, including such poems as the *Cypria*, the *Sack of Ilion*, and the *Homecomings* as well as the *Iliad* and the *Odyssey*, made up the Trojan cycle. There were, besides, several other whole cycles like the *Argonautika*, which told of the adventures of Jason and his Argonauts; and the *Herakleia*, which recounted the life and labors of Herakles. Of these many epics, only the *Iliad* and the *Odyssey* have come down complete, and they probably survived because in —V they were chosen for yearly public recitation at the festival of the Panathenaia in Athens. The other epics, some attributed to Homer and some to other more or less legendary bards like Stasinos, are known only from fragments, which have come down to us as quotations. We also know something of their plots from the many later Greek and Roman plays, poems, and mythological treatises based upon them.

Until the middle of +XIX, all that men knew about Troy and the Trojan War was based upon the *Iliad* and the *Odyssey* and such inferences as could be drawn from them. Few Westerners had visited the actual site of Troy. Travel in that region became particularly uninviting during +XVIII and +XIX, when the Turkish Empire was in decline, and the suspicious Turks blamed all their troubles on the hated European infidel. It was also dangerous because of banditry. During Schliemann's excavations, a battle at a nearby village between the peasants and a band of Circassian robbers left two dead on each side.

The few visitors to deep-soiled Troyland located Troy in either of two places. One site was on a low hill, which the Turks called Hisarlık[10] ("citadel"), about 2.5 miles from the sea at the northwest corner of a peninsula. The other site was atop a higher peak named Ballı Dağ, four miles south of Hisarlık near the village of Bunarbashi.

The man who brought the real, palpable city of Troy back into the light of day was Heinrich Schliemann (1822–90). Schliemann was not, as some have said, the founder of archaeology. When Schliemann began digging, men like Rich, Layard, and Botta had been working for years in Mesopotamia; Rhind and Mariette were excavating in Egypt; and Stephens had begun the rediscovery of the Mayan cities of Central America. Nevertheless, Schliemann's spectacular finds and his dramatic personal history combined to make him the most famous single archaeologist of his century.

Schliemann, the son of a poor Lutheran pastor, was born in a village in Mecklenburg, a small German state on the Baltic Sea. His education was cut short by his mother's death and a feud between his father and his father's parishioners. Schliemann became a grocer's apprentice at Fürstenberg until, in lifting a heavy cask, he strained himself and began spitting blood. Next he worked as an office boy and bookkeeper in Hamburg, then as a cabin boy on a brig bound for Venezuela. When the ship was wrecked on the Dutch coast, Schliemann got a job in a counting house in Amsterdam.

Tales that his father and others had told him of Homer and Troy had already fired Schliemann with a passion for the Homeric Age. In order to study these matters at first hand, he determined to make a fortune, so that he could do as he liked without having to worry about money. For five years he lived a Spartan life in Amsterdam, studying commercially useful languages. Having unusual energy, determination, and a powerful memory, he mastered not only correct High German (instead of his native Plattdeutsch) but also Dutch, English, French, Spanish, Italian, Portuguese, and Russian. To this formidable assortment he later added Norwegian, Danish, Swedish, Polish, Slovenian, Latin, ancient and modern Greek, Arabic, and Turkish. The years that most youths pass in the search for a good time, Schliemann spent in a grim pursuit of self-improvement. He lived in small furnished rooms, spent all his spare money on language lessons, and indulged in no vices save lots of tea with sugar.

In 1846 the house of B. H. Schröder, importer and exporter, sent Schliemann to St. Petersburg as its commercial agent. For seventeen years he made his home in Russia, except for long trips to other parts of the world. He began to represent other foreign firms as well and at last set up in business for himself. He dealt in indigo, profiteered in the Crimean War, and smuggled tea—an activity which had much the same status in Tsarist Russia that bootlegging had in the United States in the 1920s. By application of superhuman intensity, a natural nose for business, and good luck, he was rich at thirty. When he retired at forty-two, he was worth—in modern terms—several million dollars.

In Russia he married the daughter of a business acquaintance, a coldly mercenary young woman who soon discovered that she really detested Schliemann. After several years of prosperous misery, he left Russia in 1864, made a leisurely tour around the world, lived in Paris, and wrote a couple of books. When his wife refused to join him, he went to the United States (in which he had already traveled widely), settled in Indianapolis, took out American citizenship, and applied for a divorce from the termagant.

While waiting for his divorce, he found time to visit the Greece of his dreams. In 1868, after a tentative dig on the island of Thiaki —Odysseus' Ithaka[11]—he made his way to Troyland.

Here Schliemann met two Englishmen, the brothers Calvert. Frank Calvert, who acted as American vice-consul at the Dardanelles, owned half the hill of Hisarlık. A believer in the Troy-at-Hisarlık theory, he had excavated there with the Austrian consul, J. G. von Hahn. On the other hand, Frederick Calvert, who owned a tract near Bunarbashi, thought that Troy had stood on Ballı Dağ, near Bunarbashi.

Frank Calvert had hoped that a British archaeological expedition would settle the question. When none forthcame, the Calverts cordially welcomed Schliemann and helped him to get started. As Schliemann impetuously wanted to start digging at once, Frank Calvert gently suggested that, since summer was already gone, it would be better to wait until the following spring.

Schliemann was not idle in the meantime. Although almost entirely self-educated, he was becoming known not only as a successful merchant and globe-trotting millionaire but also as a minor man of letters and an able, if amateur, classical scholar. Now he obtained a doctor's degree from the University of Rostock by the extraordinary method of submitting as his thesis an autobiography in classical Greek.

A quick trip to Indianapolis gained him his divorce. Then he wrote an old friend, a Greek Orthodox bishop, asking help in finding a new wife. The bishop obliged. In September 1869, Schliemann married seventeen-year-old Sophia Engastromenos, the darkly handsome daughter of an Athenian draper.

Despite his great abilities, Schliemann at forty-seven was not the sort of man whom most young girls would find prepossessing. He was short and slight, with a droopy mustache and a large nose flanked by small brown eyes. Lank, graying hair receded from his high-domed forehead. Gold-rimmed eyeglasses gave him an owlish look. He dressed shabbily, and his manner combined a cold reserve with an apprehensive nervousness. A superficial polish of manners, gained in the world of high finance, thinly concealed a volcanic temper, an immense egotism, a pompous boastfulness, and an avid thirst for fame and recognition. Sensitive to any slight, he indifferently trampled on others' feelings. Despite his fame, in his later years he had only two close friends: his assistant Wilhelm Dörpfeld, and Rudolf Virchow, the suave and versatile German pathologist-politician.

Not exactly an attractive personality. But then, in these days of winning friends, getting along with everybody, and practicing life adjustment, perhaps we overvalue charm and amiability and undervalue sheer intelligence, ability, and force of character.

Nevertheless, against all probabilities, the marriage proved a happy one. When the Schliemanns' children, Andromache and Agamemnon, were born, Schliemann, instead of having them baptized, read verses from Homer over the infants.

The Troad is a stubby peninsula, shaped like a badly battered square about sixty miles across, which lies at the northwest corner of Asia Minor. Troyland proper projects as a right-angled promontory from the western side of this peninsula. The Plain of Troy is a flat, placid-looking, undramatic stretch of low, gently rolling country. Scattered stands of the small valonia oak, whose bark and green acorns are used in tanning, lightly cover the plain. Elms, willows, tamarisks, and rushes grow along the streams, just as they did in Homer's day.[12]

In spring the plain is purpled with poppies. In autumn some of

77

the streams dry up; in winter they swell and make parts of the plain into a swamp, which in Schliemann's time fostered malaria. In this country of hot, dry summers, cold, wet winters, and lots of wind and dust at all times, Schliemann found the Greek and Turkish peasants building houses much like those of their predecessors three thousand years before.

The two principal streams are the Mendere-su (Homer's Skamandros) and the smaller Dumbrek-su (Homer's Simoeis). Today they enter the Hellespont separately. In ancient times, however, they seem to have flowed together near the city:

> Now, when they came to Troy and the two rushing rivers,
> Where the Simoeis and Skamandros mingle their currents . . .[18]

Homerists argue whether the Skamandros has changed its course; if so, whether it flowed between Troy and the Achaian camp; and which of the swales in the plain is its former bed.

Several gentle ridges cross the plain. The largest of the ridges, a little over four miles long, rises at its western end to a hillock 30 feet high. From the top of this knoll, looking southeast, one sees, thirty-odd miles away beyond tier after tier of low ridges, the snowy crest of Mount Gargaros, the topmost peak of the Ida range.

When one looks northwest, the plain gleams here and there with the silvery streaks of winding watercourses. Beyond lies the Hellespont. On the right, the rugged Gallipoli Peninsula rises against the skyline. On the left stretch the hills of Cape Sigeion, on which an ancient town was once built of stones taken from the ruins of Troy; and beyond them stands the rocky isle of Imbros. Over Imbros looms Mount Saokê, the main peak of holy Samothrace, and to the west on a clear day one can glimpse the cone of Mount Athos on the Greek mainland.

Schliemann soon decided that Troy was at Hisarlık. For one thing, Bunarbashi was too far from the sea to permit the Homeric heroes to run back and forth between Troy and the Greek camp in the time allotted by Homer. For another, no Achilles could have chased Hector around the walls of a city on Ballı Dağ, because that would have meant climbing up and down steep slopes on hands and knees. Whether by luck or by genius, or by the help of the gods of ancient Ilion, the former grocer's boy hit the bull's-eye on his first attempt.

In August of 1870, Schliemann began digging into Hisarlık. The part that interested him, however, was not the eastern half, which Frank Calvert owned, but the western half, owned by two Turks. The Turks arrived a few days later, astonished to find a horde of workmen shoveling away at their property. Schliemann persuaded the Turks to let him continue digging, since they could use for a bridge some of the stones he had uncovered. As soon as they had all the stones they needed, however, the Turks ordered him off.

It took Schliemann a year to get going again. He haggled with the Turkish owners. He pestered officials in Istanbul. He appealed to the learned and influential of Europe to bring pressure to bear on the Turks.

Like most oriental officials, the Turkish Minister of Public Instruction, Safvet Pasha, did not understand why any man in his right mind would waste time on relics of the Days of Ignorance. Hence he was convinced that Schliemann was treasure-hunting. He kept Schliemann dangling by promises while he made a deal to buy the western half of Hisarlik for himself.

Schliemann, however, was not so easily brushed off. He spent much of the rest of his life in battles with officials. By wheedling, blustering, intriguing, bribing, flattering, threatening, wire-pulling, and sheer persistence, he usually got his way. He promised to give Safvet Pasha any treasure he found and thus obtained permission to resume digging. He had no intention of keeping his promise, however. Since the Turks had dealt craftily with him, he planned to use them likewise.

His turn came in 1873, on a hot May morning. The Schliemanns had passed a wretched winter, frozen by icy winds, which whistled through the walls of their little house, and almost roasted when the house caught fire one night. Now in spring they were plagued by swarms of small but venomous adders, were kept awake all night by the croaking of frogs and the screeching of owls, and were hard put to it to prevent the workmen from stealing their finds and carrying off the ancient stones for their own use.

On this particular morning, while digging at the base of one of the fortification walls, Schliemann came upon a copper cauldron packed with other metallic objects. Not wanting the Turks to know of his find, he told his wife:

"You must go at once and shout, 'Paidos [rest period]!'"

"Now, at seven o'clock?" replied the astonished Sophia.

"Yes, now! Tell them it is my birthday, and I have only just remembered it! Tell them they will get their wages today without working. See that they go to their villages, and see that the overseer does not come here . . ."[14]

Sophia dismissed the workmen and fetched her large red shawl from the Schliemanns' house. Ignoring the fact that the wall might topple over on him, Schliemann dug out the whole mass with a pocket knife, dumped it into the shawl, and carried it back to the house.

When spread out, the find proved astonishingly large, because many of the objects had been packed one inside the other. There were forty-one large pieces: six of gold, eleven of silver, twenty-three of copper, and one of electrum. They included a shield, a cauldron, vases, a bottle, cups, daggers, knife blades, spearheads, a fillet, and two diadems. There were nearly nine thousand small pieces of gold, mostly rings and buttons. The diadems were elaborate golden headdresses made up of linked chains and pendants in the form of leaves and flowers.

Schliemann packed his find into six baskets and a bag and smuggled them to the house of Frederick Calvert, whence they were taken to Greece. The following month, Schliemann paid off his workmen and returned to Athens, where he announced his find. Such was his fundamentalist faith in Homer that everything he uncovered at Troy he named for something in the *Iliad*. Thus one building became the "temple of Athena," another "Priam's palace," and his metallic hoard "Priam's treasure."

Learning how Schliemann had duped Safvet Pasha, the Turkish Government sued Schliemann in the Greek courts for the return of the treasure, which he had illegally taken out of the country. The court ordered Schliemann to pay 50,000 francs, a fraction of the value of the treasure. Schliemann further bewildered the Turks by sending them five times this amount as a gift to the Imperial Museum at Istanbul.

Meanwhile, Schliemann moved his operations to Greece, to dig at Mykenê, Agamemnon's capital. He quarreled furiously with Stamatakes, the Greek Government's representative, when Stamatakes tried to slow down Schliemann's hammer-and-tongs approach to ancient ruins.

Sites like Troy and Mykenê consist not of single cities but of whole series of cities, each built on the ruins of the previous one.

To get at the older remains, one must often demolish the more recent ones on top of them. This fact often places the archaeologist in a painful dilemma. Shall he leave a particular ruin *in situ* and never learn what is underneath? or shall he remove it and perhaps find nothing at all below it?

There is no simple rule. If a building is imposing, historically important, or well preserved, it is usually better to leave it. But there is room for a difference of opinion on the importance of a particular ruin. One archaeologist inclines towards ruthless destruction of the overlying layers, while another is unduly timid about touching them.

Schliemann belonged to the ruthless school. At Troy he drove a huge trench into the northern side of Hisarlik. This trench, together with his other diggings, removed half the hill. Ever since Schliemann's time, archaeologists have ruefully written that this or that piece of construction at Troy would be very interesting if Schliemann had not destroyed it in his haste to reach the Troy of Homer.

Another fault of Schliemann's approach was his passion for the Homeric Age. In later Greek and Roman ruins he had little or no interest. This bias caused his feud with Stamatakes, who wished to preserve the later ruins.

A well-trained modern archaeologist tries to keep himself above such prejudices. A Greek enthusiast may have no interest in remains of Roman date; a Roman specialist may care nought for Byzantine ruins; and a Byzantine authority may feel only contempt for Turkish relics. Nevertheless, each should be as meticulous in collecting, measuring, recording, photographing, and preserving remains of one period as those of another. Otherwise, when a digger interested in a later period comes along, he will find that the remains of his pet period have been destroyed without a proper record.

In those days, archaeology was still in its infancy, and to berate Schliemann for not using the techniques of today is like blaming Columbus for not installing a Diesel engine in the *Santa Maria*. Archaeologists of Schliemann's generation could learn only by doing; hence mistakes were inevitable.

The modern standards of archaeology—including the careful recording of the exact location of every find—were worked out in the last years of +XIX. This was largely the achievement of a retired British general, A. H. Lane Fox, who took the name of Pitt-Rivers in accordance with the terms of an estate he inherited. Pitt-Rivers excavated Neolithic barrows on his estate, published reports that were models of meticulous detail, and told the archaeological world without any false modesty that by Gad, sir, this was how that sort of thing should be done! He was right, too.

At Mykenê, in a cluster of royal graves, Schliemann found another treasure, comprising a mass of golden objects even greater than the treasure of Troy. There were golden disks, plates, breastplates, masks, crowns, and cups. There were narrow, rapierlike swords with bronze blades and golden hilts. There were many objects of silver and copper. Schliemann announced that he had found the remains of Agamemnon himself.

The treasure at Mykenê was Schliemann's last spectacular find, although he had several years of useful archaeological work left. He dug some more at Troy, until he had put in nine seasons there. He investigated the site of Knossos in Crete but could not come to terms with the owner for purchase of the place. He wrote big, authoritative tomes on his researches.

Schliemann's methods improved under the advice of learned colleagues. He also became more cautious about identifying everything he found with some place or person in the *Iliad*. In fact, on his last Trojan dig of 1890, he found disturbing indications that perhaps the stratum that he had considered Homeric for all those years might not be Homeric after all . . .

Virchow persuaded Schliemann to bequeath his Trojan collections to Germany. They stayed on exhibition in the Völkerkundemuseum in Berlin until, at the end of the Second World War, much of the material was either destroyed or taken away to the Soviet Union.

A strange fate befell the pottery that Schliemann had found at Troy. It was crated and stored in a castle in East Prussia for safekeeping during the war. Now, a quaint peasant custom in those parts is the *Polterabend*, when men assemble of an evening to get soused on beer and to break a lot of cheap crockery by throwing it against a wall. Some of the natives wanted a *Polterabend* because one of them was getting married. But there was no spare crockery, cheap or otherwise, to be had until somebody remembered the crates in the castle . . . So drunken peasants smashed to smithereens every last piece of the collection of Trojan pottery.

In his last years, Schliemann suffered from fearful recurrent headaches caused by an infection in his ears. Late in 1890 he went to Germany for an operation. Although the operation seemed successful, on his way back to Athens the condition suddenly worsened, and Schliemann died in Naples.

For several years Dörpfeld continued the excavations at Troy, then went on to other sites. In the 1930s an expedition from the University of Cincinnati, under Blegen, reworked the Hisarlık site. The Americans did not do much drastic excavation, but they cleaned up the older diggings and minutely studied their stratigraphy. They subdivided Dörpfeld's nine periods or strata into forty-six sub-periods.

Early in his digging, Schliemann had learned that Troy was a multiple city of superimposed layers, with a much longer history than he had imagined. He distinguished the two oldest and lowest layers, and above these a layer of burned débris, which he called the "Third City" and identified with Homer's Troy. Above this burned layer he detected a Fourth City, a Fifth City, a Sixth City (which he called "Lydian") and a Seventh City of Graeco-Roman times.

At Mykenê, Schliemann had found many pieces of pottery of a distinctive pattern, which archaeologists call "Gray Minyan Ware." It seemed to be characteristic of the greatest period of Mycenaean culture, which Schliemann assumed to be the time of the Trojan War.

In his last campaign at Troy, however, Schliemann found Gray Minyan Ware, not in the layers of the Third City where one would expect it, but in a much later and higher stratum. When Dörpfeld succeeded Schliemann at Troy, he found that Schliemann had missed a couple of layers from the later period. He missed them because, in the central part of the citadel—as Schliemann himself had noted—the whole top of the mound had been planed off by the rebuilders of Hellenistic and Roman times, removing all traces of these later preclassical periods. Fortunately, some fortification walls and building foundations from these periods still survived in the outer, lower parts of the mound. Like Columbus, who set out for Asia and thought to the end of his life he had found it, Schliemann made a great discovery which, however, was not at all what he thought it was.

Therefore Dörpfeld reorganized Schliemann's table of Trojan eras. Later, Blegen and his colleagues made further adjustments, thus:

| Schliemann | Dörpfeld | Blegen |
|---|---|---|
| VII (classical) | IX (Roman) | IX (Hellenistic & Roman) |
|  | VIII (Greek) | VIII (Hellenic) |
|  |  | VIIb-2 |
| VI (Lydian) | VII | VIIb-1 |
|  |  | VIIa (Trojan?) |
|  | VI (Trojan) | VI (Trojan?) |
| V | V | V |
|  | IV | IV |
| IV | III | III |
| III (Trojan) |  |  |
| II | II | II |
| I | I | I |

The Americans were tempted to revise Dörpfeld's scheme further, as by lumping his Troy III, IV, and V together as one city, while splitting his Troy VII into two or three. They decided that this would cause more confusion than it was worth, although they did shift the boundary between VIII and IX from the beginning of the Christian Era back to the time of Alexander the Great.

The archaeological record of Troy, as disclosed by these investigations, tells the following story:

About the year —2900, soon after the Pharaohs of the First Dynasty had united Egypt, some unknown people founded a settlement on Hisarlık. The structures on the mound were not a city but a small castle, like the Pergamos or citadel alluded to by Homer, about 50 yards across. There the chief lived with his retainers, while the peasantry dwelt in huts about the foot of the hill. These people were hardly out of the Stone Age. Although they had some copper pins, needles, and knives, and used lead to mend broken pots, most of their tools and implements were of stone. They had no lamps or swords and of course no iron. Their pots were built up by hand, not turned on a wheel. The walls of the castle and of the roomy houses inside it were probably made of brick and timber, with foundations of plain, unworked stones set in clay on the natural ground surface.

Troy I endured for about three hundred years until, around —2600, a fire destroyed it. (These dates are all uncertain, but radiocarbon dating may one day help to nail them down.) The evidence does not say whether this fire was an accident or the work of an enemy. There does not, however, seem to have been any drastic change in the population. It looks as though the people of Troy I, after their town was burned, resolutely leveled the ruins and built a new city on top of them.

Troy II was a larger stronghold than Troy I—100 yards in diameter—and there are signs of increased trade and prosperity. Wheel-made pottery appears. Schliemann's cauldron of treasure comes from this period, when it was hidden in a recess in the fortification wall. Nothing just like Schliemann's diadems has ever been found elsewhere, but some archaeologists think they were made in central Anatolia.

As for the wall itself, it was built in much the same way as that of Troy I. It had, however, an imposing main gate in the form of a tunnel through a huge tower, 60 feet square. The houses inside the wall were large—the biggest of them over a hundred feet long —but of simple, barnlike shape. Doorways were closed by curtains, since the swinging door was not yet known to the Trojans.

The people of Troy II seem to have been among the world's sloppiest housekeepers. They floored their houses by simply spreading a layer of yellow clay and letting it dry. In time the floor became covered with a litter of shells, bones, potsherds, and other rubbish. When the dwellers were wading ankle-deep in trash and garbage, instead of cleaning house they spread a new layer of clay over the mess. Even when these refloorings raised the level of the floor so high that the people bumped their heads on the ceiling, they did not clean out the floors. Instead, they took off the roof, raised the height of the walls, and put the roof back on. Archaeologists love such squalid ménages because of their beautiful stratigraphy.

After another three centuries, a mighty conflagration destroyed Troy II. Again the evidence does not indicate what caused the fire. But the people of Troy II never even tried to dig into the ruins of their city to recover their valuables. They either fled or were carried away as captives. This is the fire that led Schliemann to class

Troy II (or rather the uppermost level of Troy II, which he called Troy III) as Homer's Troy.

After —2300, people moved back to the site and built Troy III. Troy II had been so thoroughly ruined that the new town did not even follow the street plan of the old. Troy III was smaller than its predecessor, with narrow streets. House walls were of rough construction; but some were of stone instead of brick or a mixture of stone and brick as formerly. Bronze began to appear, although it was still rare. The people made jars with owlish faces and ate much sea food, especially cockles. Some rubbish was still allowed to lie on the floors of houses; but other householders began throwing it out into the street. This was progress of a sort.

Troy III lasted a century or two; so did Troy IV, a slightly larger version of the same. Troy V, founded about —1900, was larger yet, with a substantial wall. The houses were built in a more orderly way and were kept more neatly, with less litter on the floors. Good bronze blades were now common, while stone tools became rare.

About —1800, Troy V yielded to Troy VI. This was a drastic change, indicating that a new people had occupied the citadel. These people brought with them the practice of cremating their dead and putting the ashes in urns. They also brought the horse.

Almost certainly, they were the first wave of the great Aryan expansion. This group of peoples, starting out from a center somewhere on the plains of eastern Europe—perhaps Poland—spread in all directions until they had carried the Indo-European languages from Portugal to India. The horse, which these folk were the first to tame, gave the Aryans—otherwise merely cattle-raising nomadic barbarians of undistinguished culture and uncertain race—an overwhelming if temporary advantage in war. Even the mighty Babylonian Empire fell before them.

Since there is no sign of a violent end to Troy V, it may have fallen in a bloodless conquest. The former inhabitants may have been so terrified of the horsemen that they gave up without a fight. The new rulers probably spoke, if not an ancestral form of Greek, at least a tongue closely related to it.

Troy VI was the largest citadel yet, about 220 yards across. Its massive wall was made in two parts. The lower part was of dressed stones, fairly well fitted. The outer faces of the wall had a strong batter or backward slope, so that an active man could climb the face. On top of this foundation, however, was a vertical wall of brick, probably with a parapet on top. A curious and unexplained feature of this wall is that every 30 feet or so it had an offset or jog of a few inches, like a ledge stood on end. Moreover, the builders of the wall did not dig down to bedrock in laying their foundations, even when they could easily have done so. In fact, they may have deliberately left a cushion of earth below the wall to absorb the shock of earthquakes, which are frequent in that land.

Four gates in this wall are known, and there may have been more on the destroyed northern side. Each gate was protected by a massive square tower set beside it and seems originally to have been a simple opening in the wall, without any doors or movable parts. Later, movable gates were added. In addition, some of the gates had crooked entrances for additional protection. Streets were paved with stone slabs, which became much worn in use; yet there are no signs of wheel ruts.

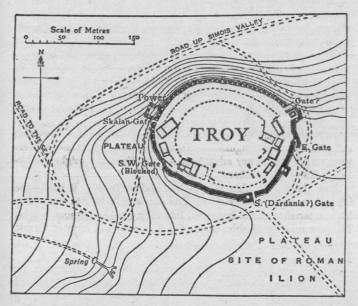

Fig. 8 Plan of Troy VI and VIIa, or Homeric Troy. (After Leaf)

Troy VI had at least one big, thick-walled stone house, about 41 by 91 feet. It was built of dry-wall masonry. Stones of all sizes were fitted together without mortar or plaster, pinned with wooden dowels, and in some places roughly trimmed on the exposed face to make the wall a little smoother. Inside were partition walls and two square central pillars to hold up the roof. It must have been a pretty drafty domicile in windy Troy; perhaps it was a barracks.

Troy VI used Gray Minyan Ware like that of Mykenê. But, although Troy VI imported goods from various places, its culture was decidedly its own. By now bronze had almost entirely taken the place of copper; yet some stone implements persisted. Glass paste and ivory (probably from the extinct Syrian elephant) appear for the first time.

Although few objects of gold or other precious metals have been found in Troy VI, it seems nonetheless to have been a strong and prosperous center for many centuries. Growing population necessitated the rebuilding of the wall to take in more ground. This rebuilding was done a section at a time with better masonry. Before the rebuilding was complete, disaster struck; about —1300 an earthquake overthrew the whole town.

This catastrophe much impoverished the Trojans. Nevertheless, the survivors dug themselves out of the ruins and once more rebuilt their town. They crudely patched the fortification wall and built small, rude houses inside it. The walls of VIIa were a mixture of unworked stones of medium size and large well-dressed stones salvaged from the ruins of Troy VI. The people were still enterprising enough to pave a street, furnish it with a well-built underground storm sewer, and make huge jars called *pithoi* to store their food in. Soon, a growing population again crowded the area inside the walls.

Troy VIIa came to an end about —1260. This time it seems certain that it fell to a foe, who sacked and burned it. Some skeletons have been found in awkward positions, as if the people had been slain during the capture and left where they fell.

Not even this downfall ended the life of the city. People of the same kind reoccupied the site and built Troy VIIb-1. The houses were now more complex, with more rooms than before. But they were set in irregular blocks, leaving narrow, crooked alleys between them.

After Troy VIIb-1 had stood for a few decades, another change took place. The city itself does not seem to have been disturbed; but about −1180 a new people took control, peacefully or otherwise. They used what is called Knobby Ware, and their cultural relationships seem to be with the Danube Valley and other parts of central Europe. This was Troy VIIb-2. The fact that the Knobby Ware Folk gained control of Troy without damage suggests that they did so by some ruse or surprise, of a sort that might give rise to a legend like that of the Trojan Horse.

Troy VIIb-2 lasted until about −1100. Then the town was burned once more, either by accident or by another assailant. After that, the site was deserted. It was abandoned to the lion and the lizard down to about −700, when Aitolian Greeks built another city on the hill.

During this time, people dwelt in the small settlement on Ballı Dağ. Perhaps the surviving Trojans, to escape the marauders who swarmed the shores of the Mediterranean during this Dark Age, or perhaps feeling with some reason that the gods had it in for them, moved to Ballı Dağ and then moved back again when things quieted down. If this be so, then there is truth both in the Hisarlık theory and in the Bunarbashi theory of Troy.

Greek Troy—Troy VIII—early learned to exploit the tourist trade. Since no material traces of Homer's heroes remained, the latter-day Trojans made fake relics, which they showed to visitors. There was a "tomb of Achilles," around which Alexander the Great, visiting Troy at the start of his invasion of the Persian Empire in −334, ran naked thrice "as the ancient custom is."[15] Told that he might see the lyre of Paris, he said it was not worth while, since everybody knew what sort of bedroom hero Paris was; but Achilles' lyre, now, would be something else.

Lysimachos, one of Alexander's successors, ordered the beautification of Troy, which thus became Troy IX. This city throve until, in −85, the Roman politician Gaius Flavius Fimbria, a murderous, ruffianly adventurer, captured the city by treachery and destroyed it once more. Later Roman rulers, believing themselves decendants of Aineias, conferred favors like tax exemption on the town, so that it soon recovered. After Julius Caesar ordered another program of rebuilding, Troy received a couple of theaters, a temple of Athena, and other amenities.

The emperor Constantine I thought of placing his new capital on the site of Troy, but decided instead on Byzantium, which in +330 became Constantinople. Soon thereafter Troy was abandoned again, this time for good.

From Schliemann to Belgen, much has been learned about Troy. But there is still no solid connection between the story of the *Iliad* and the material remains on Hisarlık. For one thing, the Trojans from Troy I to Troy VIIb-2 seem to have been illiterate. Hence they left no inscriptions giving their version of the Trojan War or any other details of their history.

Some feeble, flickering light has been cast upon the affairs of western Asia Minor by the records of Khatti, the Hittite Empire. Until the present century, this onetime world power was practically lost to history. Homer ignores it unless, as some think, Homer's mention of the Trojans' allies the Kêteioi refers to Khatti.[16] But, in the 1880s and 90s, archaeologists began to dig up the remains of Khatti.

Winckler, excavating from 1906 on at the ancient Hittite capital of Hattusas,[17] found ten thousand clay tablets, comprising the Hittite royal archives. Of the eight languages represented in these tablets, the Czech scholar Hrozný learned to read the most important one, Hittite cuneiform. In 1924, Emil Forrer announced that he had found references in the tablets to Homeric heroes and places: Andreus, Alexandros, Ilios, Troy, Eteokles, Atreus, and Achaia. This was largely done by putting the lost digammas back into the Greek names. Thus Eteokles became Etewoklewês, and some scholars believe Etewoklewês to be the man named Tawagalawas, about whom a Hittite king of —1300, the time of the destruction of Troy VI by earthquake, wrote a polite letter of remonstrance to the king of Akhiyawâ.[18]

These identifications have been severely criticized. Nevertheless, the Hittite records tell of an Atarisiyas of Akhiyawâ, and also of an Alaksandus of Wilusas. The resemblance to Atreus of Achaia (father of Agamemnon and Menelaos) and Alexandros of Ilios (earlier Wilios; that is, Paris of Troy) seem too close for coincidence. One or two names could be a matter of luck, but hardly all four. However, even if Forrer's identifications were all correct, it would not follow that the men named in the Hittite records were those on whom Homer's heroes were based. Any personal name may be borne by many different men; the name "King Charles" might refer to any of forty-odd European sovereigns.

Atarisiyas (or Atreus) appears about —1200 in another letter of complaint, from the next to the last of the Hittite emperors.[19] This monarch denounces a certain adventurer[20] who, in collusion with Atarisiyas, seized the throne of Arzawa, a kingdom in southwestern Asia Minor tributary to Khatti.

As for Alaksandus (or Alexandros), he is briefly mentioned as ruler of a northwestern province of Arzawa about —1300, a century before Atarisiyas. Obviously, Alexandros could not have fought against the sons of Atreus (as he does in Homer) if he lived a hundred years before Atreus. Moreover, indications are that his "Wilusas" was not Troy, but at least two hundred miles from Troy. However, it could be that a descendant of the earlier Alexandros, bearing the same name, ruled Troy at a later period and applied to his new kingdom the name of the realm of his forebears. Perhaps that is how Troy came to have two names as different as "Troia" and "Ilios."

Now for Akhiyawâ. Although we speak of "Greeks and Trojans," Homer never uses the term "Greek" and seldom even "Hellene." He usually calls the Trojans' foes Achaioi (in Homer's time, Achaiwoi), less often Argives (in Greek, Argeioi mon of Argolis) and sometimes Danaoi. In historic times Achaia was the northern coastal province of the Peloponnesos, while Argolis was the peninsula jutting out eastward from the Peloponnesos and abutting on Achaia.

On the other hand, one early division of the Greek peoples called themselves "Achaians." These Achaians settled in many places on the eastern side of the Aegean, including the island of Rhodes. From various indications, Professor Page, who has made one of the latest studies of this subject, thinks that the Akhiyawâ of the Hittite records was Rhodes.

According to these records, there were two powerful kingdoms in western Asia Minor: Arzawa in the southwest (corresponding to the Karia of classical times) and Assuwa north of it (corresponding to later Lydia and Mysia). Arzawa was at first friendly to Khatti, then hostile, and at last was reduced to a rebellious province. Assuwa may have had a similar history, although our information is scantier.

There are no Arzawan or Assuwan inscriptions to check against the Hittite records because, like Troy, these kingdoms appear to have been illiterate. However, the name "Assuwa" seems to have evolved, by normal phonetic change, through the stages "Asua" and

"Asüa" into "Asia." By Asia, Homer meant the country later called Lydia, south of Troyland and north of Arzawa.[21] He had not the faintest notion of the immense continent to which the name little by little came to be applied. We cannot tell whether Troy was ever a capital of Assuwa, or on the contrary was ruled by the king of Assuwa, or was wholly independent.

How, then, can we summarize the story of Troy? According to archaeology, after several prehistoric cities had preceded it, Troy VI throve for several centuries until destroyed by an earthquake about —1300. This Troy seems, despite all of Homer's noble imagery, to have been a half-civilized, rustic, illiterate place, backward in the arts and crafts compared with other great cities of its time. Even Schliemann admitted that Homer was indulging in "poetic license"[22] when he credited King Priamos with a great, gorgeous palace of polished stone. Homer's hints that Troy's main products were wool and horses are probably truthful; but his description implies a city of at least 50,000 people, far larger than any of the real towns piled up on Hisarlik.

The earthquake of —1300, which overthrew Troy VI, may be reflected in the legend of Herakles and Laomedon's mares; but the connection would be clearer if Poseidon, the god of earthquakes, had knocked the walls down instead of building them up. At one point in the *Iliad*, however, Poseidon does actually shake Troy by an earthquake, although apparently without much damage.[23] Evidently the quake of —1300 made such an impression that, centuries later, Troy was still known as a place where earth tremors were a constant hazard.

After the earthquake, we have seen that a smaller and meaner Troy VII persisted for another two centuries, undergoing various captures and destructions during this time. Observe that we have *two* Greek legends of the fall of Troy: the more famous one involving Helen, Achilles, Hector, and the Trojan Horse; and the minor legend of Herakles and Laomedon's horses. But we have archaeological records of *four* actual falls of Troy during the period— —1300 to —1100—on which the legends are supposedly based. The four real downfalls are:

1. Troy VI destroyed by an earthquake about —1300.
2. The less imposing Troy VIIa captured, sacked, and burned about —1260.

3. Troy VIIb-1 captured with little or no fighting by the Knobby Ware People about −1180. This date coincides with the date (−1184) that Eratosthenes computed for the fall of King Priamos' Troy. There might be a connection between this capture, probably by a ruse, and the story of the Trojan Horse.

4. Troy VIIb-2 burned about −1100, probably as a result of another capture and sack, and is abandoned for four centuries.

Evidently, there is no simple one-for-one relationship between any of these four real downfalls and either of the two legendary ones. Furthermore, Troy may have been unsuccessfully attacked one or more times during these two centuries, in addition to the attacks that succeeded. The episodes in the legends may be based upon incidents in any or all of these real events.

Comparing Homer's tale with other legend cycles like the medieval German epics of Siegfried and Dietrich, where we know much more about the actual history, we see that we undoubtedly have a conflation. That is, many of Homer's people were real, and some of his incidents were based upon real events. But, whereas in real life the people and events were widely scattered in time and space, the Poet brought them all together in one grand spectacle, like a school pageant that shows Washington crossing the Delaware and, half a minute later, Lincoln freeing the slaves. The same process, using different elements from the several real overthrows of Troy, gave rise to the other fall-of-Troy myth, that of Herakles and Laomedon's mares.

You will note that the more splendid Troy, Troy VI, was destroyed about half a century before the earlier of the two real sacks. Thus the Homeric description fits Troy VI, while the traditional date of the fall of Troy comes closer to fitting twice destroyed Troy VII. Hence there is argument as to whether VI or VII should be deemed Homeric Troy. But this argument is really meaningless. Homer's Troy is not a real place, but a fictional one, based upon a multitude of tales about the several real Troys that rose and fell during −XIII and −XII.

The Hittite records, while a welcome sidelight on Bronze Age Anatolian history, do not much help us to straighten out the Trojan tangle. All through −XIII, judging from Hittite inscriptions, Achaians—probably from Rhodes, but possibly also from mainland Greece —adventured along the west coast of Asia Minor, raiding and conquering when and where they could. In a general way, the Homeric story reflects this movement.

According to the Hittites, Alexandros of Ilios lived about the time of the earthquake that destroyed Troy VI, while Atreus the Achaian lived at the time of the capture of Troy VIIb-1 by the Knobby Ware Folk, who do not seem to have been Achaians. But, if the lives of these real men do not at all fit Homer's timetable, it is still not impossible that one or both of these men, or other men of the same names and families, were involved in some way with the various sieges and destructions of Troy.

No man to spoil a good story for the sake of a few facts, Homer (or his sources) described Troy VI at its most splendid and made it even larger and finer than life, ignoring the dismal fact that the Troy that fell to foes twice or thrice between −1260 and −1100 had declined a long way from its days of glory. Who would listen to an account of the sack of a shabby little town by a boatload of Rhodian pirates, when he could hear a stirring epic about a splendid, tragic war of all the kings of Hellas against the mightiest city of Asia?

Unless, however, we unearth some more inscriptions dealing with the affairs of western Asia Minor during −XIII and −XII, we shall never know exactly what happened at Troy: how many sieges there were; which ones were successful; whether the attackers came from Rhodes, Mykenê, or elsewhere; whether Aineias, or Alexandros, or somebody else was king of Troy VIIb-1 after the sack of −1260; and whether Helen was really a beautiful runaway queen or just another fertility goddess.

# V

# Ma'rib and the
# Queen of Sheba

They say the Lion and the Lizard keep
The Courts where Jamshyd gloried and drank deep:
    And Bahram, that great Hunter—the Wild Ass
Stamps o'er his Head, but cannot break his Sleep.
                                    *Omar Khayyám,*
                                    tr. *Fitzgerald*

A stock figure in the adventure fiction of fifty to a hundred years
ago was the sinister oriental potentate—the fiendish, turbaned despot who plots to get a blue-eyed, golden-haired, Anglo-Saxon heroine into his lecherous clutches, while his diabolical crew of heathen
priests prepares a lingering and humorous doom for her stalwart
Nordic lover.

Of course, in these enlightened days, we no longer dread such
bogies. In fact, some optimists refuse to believe that wicked men
exist. If somebody kills people in a peculiarly gruesome way, they
say that the killer is really a good fellow at heart who suffers from
frustration or insecurity, and in any case that it is all the fault of
Society.

It may surprise you, therefore, to learn that there really were
fiendish oriental potentates. In fact, the species was at one time
quite common and may not yet be extinct. Although the Orient has
no monopoly on cruel tyrants—other parts of the world have suffered from them as well—Asia and North Africa seem peculiarly
prone to this affliction.

Such rulers come into the story of archaeology because archaeologists have often wanted to dig in lands under their control and
have therefore had to deal with these despots. Things become interesting when the potentate—who cares nought for knowledge, is

moved solely by ruthless self-interest, and thinks the archaeologist is on the track of some mountainous hoard of gold or diamonds—plots to let the digger find the treasure and then snatch it from him. If the despot discovers that he cannot carry through his little plan, because no such treasure exists, he becomes pettish and makes things hard for the digger. So, sometimes an archaeological mystery persists, not because the evidence for solving the problem is lacking, but because some ruler will not let the archaeologists at it. This chapter is about one such devilish dynasty of tyrants and the citadel of mystery whose ramparts they long manned.

The sun-baked peninsula of Arabia is shaped like a rough rectangle with its long axis running northwest–southeast. In the southern corner of this rectangle, and along a strip of adjacent southwestern coast, lies the kingdom of Yemen,[1] of all the world's hundred-odd countries the one most resistant to change.

Having a difficult climate, a modest endowment of natural wealth, and an ignorant, bloodthirsty, foreigner-hating populace who still believe with all their hearts that "The swish of the sword of the Lord Allah on the necks of unbelievers is pious and righteous,"[2] Yemen would never have attracted much foreign attention, had it not harbored a wealth of archaeological sites. For, thousands of years ago, there bloomed in South Arabia a group of rich kingdoms, as civilized as any countries of their time: Saba', Ma'in, Qataban, Ausan, Ḥimyar, and Ḥadhramawt. And of these the most ancient, the first to achieve greatness, and the one whose name is most misted in glamour, was Saba'—the Sheba of the Hebrews. You know how the Bible tells:

And when the queen of Sheba heard of the fame of Solomon concerning the name of the Lord, she came to prove him with hard questions. And she came to Jerusalem with a very great train, with camels that bare spices, and very much gold, and precious stones: and when she was come to Solomon, she communed with him of all that was in her heart. And Solomon told her all her questions: there was not any thing hid from the king, which he told her not . . . And she said to the king, It was a true report that I heard in mine own land of thy acts and of thy wisdom. Howbeit I believed not the words, until I came, and mine eyes had seen it: and, behold, the half was not told me: thy wisdom and prosperity exceedeth the fame which I heard . . . And she gave the king an hundred and twenty talents of gold, and of spices very great store, and precious tones: there came no more such abundance of spices as these which the queen of Sheba gave to king Solomon . . . And king Solomon gave unto the queen of Sheba all her desire, whatsoever she asked, beside that which Solomon gave her of his royal bounty. So she turned and went to her own country, she and her servants.[3]

This is absolutely all that is known about the Queen of Sheba, save that the visit must have taken place around —950. The biblical account does not name the lady, nor say how old she was, nor how beautiful, nor state that she and Solomon had any sort of love affair. For aught anybody knows, the queen may have been a tough old beldam like Hatshepsut or Elizabeth I in her later years. And the visit may have been the occasion for a hard-boiled haggle over trade and military alliances.

The imagination of later generations, however, filled out this meager tale with the flesh of romance. The Arabs made their heroine the young and lovely Queen Bilqîs and related the stratagems of King Solomon in adding her to the lengthy list of women he had enjoyed. The Abyssinians pretended that Bilqîs had been an Abyssinian, and that from her amour with Solomon sprang the royal family of Abyssinia.

At least three motion pictures have been made about Bilqîs, the first a silent movie with Theda Bara. Each time, at the climax, a lusciously available queen appeared before Solomon, clad in a few strategically sited beads. Among American adolescents a generation ago there arose a fad for calling swains "sheiks" (after motion pictures that romanticized the Arab shaykh out of all resemblance to the real thing) and their girls "shebas."

Ah well, even if the real Queen of Sheba had the face of a camel and the heart of a pawnbroker, it would be interesting to know more about her and her visit to Solomon. Since historical records of the kingdom of Saba' begin about 150 years after the Queen of Sheba's time, a great deal of archaeological work needs to be done in Yemen. And that is the trouble. For the Arabs of Yemen remember that Ma'rib[4] was once her capital city, and those who dwell in Ma'rib have used this tradition as one more excuse for assaulting foreigners who trod this sacred soil.

The sparkling constellation of kingdoms that arose in South Arabia 3,000 years ago was not called into existence by the *jann* or demons whom, according to legend, King Solomon commanded:

> Giants and the Genii,
> Multiplex of wing and eye,
> Whose strong obedience broke the sky
> When Solomon was king.[5]

Instead, these kingdoms had several good, understandable economic foundations for their prosperity. One reason for their success was the domestication of the camel, which greatly extended men's ability to travel and to move heavy loads about waterless deserts. In —XII, the Assyrian kings began catching wild camels for the royal zoo, and soon afterwards camels came into use for riding over the vast sandy, rocky voids of Iran, Iraq, and Arabia. Sheba's tame camels are among the very first of which there is good historic evidence; for the references to camels in the first five books of the Bible are legend, not history.

The steppe dwellers of Asia tamed the two-humped or Bactrian camel, while the Arabs preferred the one-humped dromedary. Today there are wild Bactrian camels but no wild dromedaries. Zoölogists disagree as to whether the dromedary is descended from a now extinct one-humped wild species, or whether it is a descendant of the wild Bactrian camel modified by selective breeding.

Another reason for Arab prosperity was the trade routes that crossed their lands between India and the West. In the days when merchant ships were little cockleshells with one square sail, which never ventured out of sight of land if they could help it, carriers of trade goods between India and the Mediterranean had but two choices. One was a 3,000-mile, rugged, and chancy land route clear across the Near and Middle East. The other was to travel by sea along the southern coast of Arabia, cutting across the southernmost corner by land when conditions made it more profitable. Although harbor and caravan fees and taxes at each stop raised the price of the goods many times over, they supported the South Arabian kingdoms in style.

Still another factor was the incense trade. The gods of the ancient Mediterranean world liked lots of incense burned at their rites. The priests and worshipers like it, too, because it masked the stench from the spilled blood of sacrificed animals. The best incense, it was found, was the gum of two shrubs from the mountains of South

Arabia: the myrrh tree and the frankincense tree. Soon the Arabs learned to nick the bark of these shrubs and milk them of their gum, somewhat as the sugar maple, chicle, and rubber trees are milked of their sap today. For a thousand years, tons of these gums were sent to the north and northwest to perfume the temples of Ishtar and Isis, Tammuz and Tanith, Nabu and Neptune, Eli and Eros.

The final reason for South Arabian wealth was the development of irrigation systems. Such waterworks had to be something special in a country where, it would seem, the gods opposed the whole idea of agriculture. On a given spot in South Arabia, you are likely to get no rain at all for several years on end. Then, during one summer, you may get one or more terrific thunderstorms, which send furious torrents rushing down the dry *widyân* and sweeping all before them. Then no rain for several years more.

Such irregular desert freshets are called *siyûl*.[6] The South Arabians developed a skilled technique of braking *siyûl* by dams and quickly bleeding off the water into their fields. The purpose of these dams was not to store water, which would have quickly evaporated, but to get it into cultivated ground as soon as possible, so that a crop could grow from that one storm.

North and South Arabia differed in ancient times. The northerners were mostly nomads, while the southerners were mostly sedentary peasants. The northerners were of a fairly pure Mediterranean type, while the southerners had visible admixtures of Negroid and —strangely enough—of apparent Mongoloid ancestry. (Could this seeming Mongoloid strain be a relic of the wave of Malayan migration round the shores of the Indian Ocean, which reached Madagascar and possibly Zimbabwe?)

The South Arabian kingdoms were about as civilized as most ancient realms. The South Arabians had the main ingredients of civilization: writing, metals, and cities. Their cities contained many multi-story houses, veritable skyscrapers, such as still stand in those parts today. Although some were handsomely decorated, all had walls of dried mud. Hence the five-yearly downpours often caused the roof to cave in, or the whole house to collapse. The Arabs, however, cheerfully set about putting their houses back together again while congratulating one another on having received rain at long last.

In +I, King Lisharh ibn Yahsub of Saba' put up a building, which became as famous in Arabia as the Pharos of Alexandria was in the Mediterranean world. This was the castle of Ghumdân,[7] erected near San'a to protect its people against nomadic raids. It stood for several centuries, until it was destroyed in the wars of the Muslim conquests in early +VII. Later writers said it had twenty stories, each ten cubits high, of granite, porphyry, and marble. The roof was made of stone so transparent that a person standing beneath it could tell a crow from a kite overhead. At each corner stood a brazen lion, which roared when the wind blew. Although the size and splendor of this fortress have no doubt been vastly exaggerated, it was certainly no mean structure.

For writing, the South Arabians used an elegant Semitic alphabet, like those of the Phoenicians and the Hebrews. The South Arabians spoke, not Arabic, but a similar Semitic language called Sabaean. They seem to have thought highly of their own literacy, because they set up inscribed tablets on the slightest pretext. Thousands of such inscriptions have been copied and published, and thousands more await further search. Most of our knowledge of South Arabian history comes from these inscriptions.

The religion of the South Arabians was an astronomical polytheism. At the head of the pantheon reigned the moon god, called 'Ilmuqah[8] by the Sabaeans. His wife was the sun goddess, and their son was the planet Venus.

Daily life in an early South Arabian city was probably much like that in pre-industrial Arab cities of today. Drainage from the tall houses was by spouts jutting out from the walls. These spouts emptied household waste into the street below and on passersby not agile enough to dodge. Residences were grouped by families, clans, and tribes, each unit having its own area and looking with suspicion on outsiders who trespassed upon its turf.

There were no policemen. The main deterrent to crime was fear of revenge by the victim's family. The victim of a crime, or his family, complained to the head of his clan, who took the matter up with the head of the offender's clan. The offender hid while the clan chiefs thrashed out the matter of compensation and punishment. If they could not agree, a feud began.

As today, haggling in the market place was the general public amusement. And no doubt the ancient South Arabians, like their modern descendants, banished their cares by chewing the leaves of the narcotic herb qat, *Catha edulis*. The effect is much like that of the Peruvian Indian custom of chewing the cocaine-bearing leaves of the coca plant.

The biblical story of the Queen of Sheba—which there is no good reason to doubt—shows that Saba', her realm, flourished in the early centuries of the first millennium B.C. From −800, when the Assyrian kings began to record payments of tribute from the rulers of Saba', to −450, a line of priest-kings called the Mukarribs ruled this land. After −450, as a result of a change of dynasty, the ruler of Saba' was called simply the king.

If Saba' was the first of the South Arabian kingdoms to make a mark in history, Ma'in, just north of Saba', was next. Ma'in rose to power about −400, soon followed by the kingdom of Qataban, southeast of Saba' with its capital at Timna' . . . But we cannot go into all the details of South Arabian history, because this would take us too far afield from Ma'rib and Queen Bilqis.

Ma'rib was the capital of Saba' in the days of its greatness; and the chief South Arabian technical triumph was the great dam at

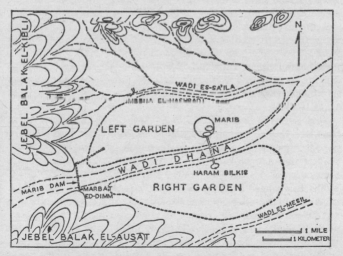

*Fig. 9   Map of the Ma'rib region of Yemen, showing the position of the Ma'-rib Dam. (After Glaser and Brown & Albright)*

Ma'rib. This dam was; in fact, an outstanding engineering feat of the ancient world. Ancient Greek travelers who compiled lists of the Wonders of the World would probably have included the Ma'-rib dam among them, had any of them ventured across the deserts to see it.

This dam, which served the people of Saba' for a thousand years, stretched across the Wâdi Dhana three miles upstream from Ma'-rib. The dam proper was an earthen ridge over a third of a mile long, with both sides sloping up at an angle of 45 degrees. The upstream side was strengthened by a surface layer of small stones set in mortar. The dam was rebuilt several times by piling more earth and laying more masonry on top of the old dam, raising its height. The final rebuilding may have reached a height of over 45 feet.

The dam itself has now practically disappeared. However, at each end, a huge sluice gate was built into the rocky walls of the wâdi. These gates, of carefully fitted ashlar masonry, still stand. The sluices divided the siyûl as they came down the wâdi into two streams, which were distributed about two cultivated areas around Ma'rib. These areas, each several miles long, provided food for the city and made possible the number and wealth of its citizens.

About the dam a number of inscribed stones have been found, on which rulers who repaired or rebuilt the dam recorded their works. The earliest of these stones names an early Mukarrib of Saba', Sumuhu'alay Yanaf.[9] So perhaps Sumuhu'alay was the first builder. At least, his name will do until somebody finds an older inscription. His exact date is not known, but he may have reigned about —VIII.

Such is the violence of the South Arabian siyûl, however, that from time to time the onset of water washed out the dam. Rebuilding was a tremendous task. In the overhaul of +450, twenty thousand workmen were used, some brought from hundreds of miles away.

The Arabs have legends about the final breakdown of the Ma'-rib dam in +VI. They say that God, angered at the Sabaeans, sent a rat to gnaw holes in the dam. They say, moreover, that the breakage of the dam ruined all the South Arabian kingdoms. But this is an exaggeration; there were many dams in South Arabia.

The Qur'ân tells in religious imagery the story of the final breakdown of the dam:

There was indeed a sign for Saba' in their dwelling-place: two gardens on the right hand and on the left (as who should say): Eat of the provision of your Lord and render thanks to Him. A fair land and an indulgent Lord! But they were froward, so We

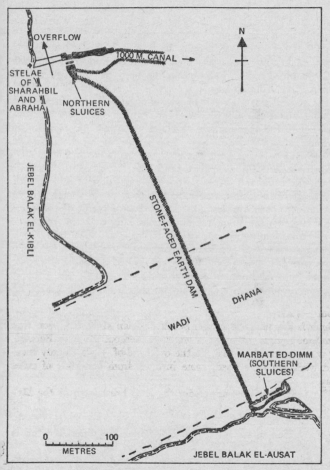

Fig. 10 Map of the Ma'rib Dam. (After Glaser and Bowen & Albright)

sent on them the flood of 'Iram, and in exchange for their two gardens gave them two gardens bearing bitter fruit, the tamarisk and here and there a lote-tree. Thus we awarded them because of their ingratitude. Punish we ever any save ingrates?[10]

Actually, the breakdown of +VI was no different from earlier destructions, except that it came at a time when warfare and anarchy prevented repair. Without the dam, the Ma'rib region could support far fewer people. By the time things had quieted down, Ma'rib no longer harbored its former numerous and energetic populace and so had neither the need for the dam nor the resources to maintain it.

The ruin of the Ma'rib dam was only one of many factors that brought about the decline of South Arabia. First, the land had been conquered successively by North Arabians, Abyssinians, and Persians.

Furthermore, around the beginning of the Christian Era, a Greek mariner named Hippalos discovered that, by using the monsoon winds, one could sail directly from the east coast of Africa to the west coast of India in summer, and back again in winter, without touching at South Arabian ports at all. Soon most of the sea-borne traffic between the Roman Empire and India took this route, depriving the South Arabians of the traders' fees and taxes.

Finally, the rise of Christianity choked off the demand for one of South Arabia's few profitable export crops: incense. Christians, deeming incense a relic of paganism, discouraged its use. Although it was reintroduced into Christian worship later, South Arabia suffered in the meantime.

What with one thing and another, the South Arabians let public utilities like the Ma'rib dam go out of use and forgot some of their highly skilled irrigation techniques. But the decline of civilization in this region was not catastrophic. The populations and areas under cultivation have been estimated as about the same at the height of South Arabian glory as they are now.

Nevertheless, the region stagnated. Life went on with little change, century after century, while other parts of the world made swift advances. So, when Europeans began to pry open these hermit kingdoms in late +XIX, they were startled to find that, except for adding the rifle to their armament, the South Arabians were running their affairs much as they had two thousand years before.

Slavery flourished; law was the ruler's whim; justice was done by whacking off the culprit's hand, foot, or head with a scimitar; and politics was a simple, cutthroat scramble for unlimited power and privilege. Travelers found conditions just as shocking, confusing, and uncomfortable as you would if, like the hero of some science-fiction story, you suddenly found yourself in ancient Rome or Babylon and had to make do with such knowledge and resourcefulness as you possessed.

In +XIX, South Arabia (except for a British protectorate at Aden) formed part of the decaying Turkish Empire. Local rulers, paying tribute to the Sultan, carried on pretty much as they pleased. One of these rulers was the Imâm of Yemen. The title means that the ruler is the spiritual as well as the temporal successor to Muḥammad, since the Imâm is the head of the Zaydi sect of Islam. These priest-kings had ruled Yemen ever since +897. Although in theory each new Imâm was elected by a council of wise men, in practice the reigning Imâm usually managed to have his favorite son succeed him, unless that son were murdered by some rival claimant.

Of all these living fossils of kingdoms, Yemen was the most secluded. On being told that a foreign infidel might enter the country, the ordinary Yemenite would instantly answer: "By God, we'll slay him!" He meant it, too.

Nevertheless, in the 1830s a few Europeans began to brave Yemeni hospitality. In 1843, the Frenchman Joseph Thomas Arnaud made the first notes on Yemeni archaeology. Getting into the country as the private physician of a Turkish general, he made an unauthorized caravan trip to Ma'rib—then a village rising amidst ancient ruins—where his medical skill persuaded the Emir of Ma'rib to protect him. He copied some inscriptions but had to quit when mobs threatened him.

In 1869 another intrepid Frenchman, Joseph Halévy, not only invaded Yemen but traveled widely about the country and brought back copies of 686 inscriptions. Being a Jew, he disguised himself as an oriental Jew and carried letters of recommendation to all the Jewish communities. In early +XX, there were about 45,000 scorned and segregated Jews living in Yemen. Now these have nearly all moved to Israel where, being almost as backward as the other Yemenites, they present an assimilation problem.

Halévy was followed by an Austrian, Eduard Glaser, who made three visits to Yemen in the 1880s and 90s. Glaser not only garnered a treasure of inscriptions, manuscripts, and notes, but even trained a number of Yemenites to collect materials for him. Nevertheless, despite his skill at passing himself off as a Muslim, he had several narrow escapes.

Since Glaser's time, many foreigners have gained access to Yemen on one pretext or other, including such famous oriental travelers as Freya Stark and H. St. John Philby. Few, however, have gotten to Ma'rib. One who did was the Egyptian archaeologist Ahmed Fakhry.

In 1947, Fakhry went to Yemen in hope of visiting Ma'rib. The Yemenites told him it was hopeless; the reigning Imâm never let anyone go thither. He had once permitted a Syrian journalist to go there and had regretted it ever since.

The Imâm, Yahya ibn-Muhammad, was a tough old tyrant who had ruled since 1904 in off-with-his-head style, refused to let himself be photographed, hated the British since he fought against them in the First World War, and sometimes still skirmished with them over Aden. He once said: "I and my people would rather live in poverty and eat grass than allow foreigners to enter the country."[11] A noted pinchpenny, he paid his foreign minister $22.00 a month and made his wives sew uniforms at a low piece rate for the royal army.

In the 1920s a naïvely well-meaning American capitalist, Charles R. Crane, persuaded the Imâm Yahya to let him import $150,000 worth of irrigation machinery and set it up at his own expense. But when the Imâm learned that these devilish contraptions would have to be serviced by foreign infidels, he stifled the whole project.

Despite the Imâm's paranoid suspiciousness, Fakhry unexpectedly got permission to go to Ma'rib. He set out quickly before the Imâm changed his mind.

At Bilqîs' capital, Fakhry had to endure the threats and insults that were the lot of the foreigner in Yemen, even when the stranger was a Muslim and a fellow Arab. He found to his horror that the Yemenites were demolishing the ruins of a dozen structures of ancient Ma'rib in order to cut up the stones and use them in a large, fortresslike governmental building. The local governor said: "He was very proud of his work, and boasted that he was ruining the remains of dead pagans for the welfare of the living Moslems."

When Fakhry protested, the royal officials "could not understand my enthusiasm for the preservation of the remains of the ancient heathen inhabitants, and they told me square to my face, that they could never explain such an attitude from a Moslem like myself. All such remains, they maintain, are the work of non-believers who adored idols, and their memory must be destroyed wherever it occurs. Arguing with people of such a mentality can only complicate matters . . ."[12]

The year after Fakhry's visit, the Imâm's first secretary arranged to have old Yaḥya assassinated. The royal automobile was held up by a roadblock, and the Imâm and those with him were cut down by gunfire. The first secretary's fellow conspirators captured the palace and killed two of Yaḥya's nine sons. For a few days, the first secretary rejoiced in the name of king. But then Crown Prince Aḥmad gathered a following of loyal tribesmen and crushed the revolt, and the first secretary's head adorned a pole in front of the Ministry of Health.

The new Imâm, Aḥmad ibn-Yaḥya, proved a chip off the old block. Nevertheless, in 1951 Wendell Phillips, a young American paleontologist and head of the American Foundation for the Study of Man, called upon him in Ta'izz and urged that his expedition be allowed to work at Ma'rib. To this proposal the Imâm Aḥmad gave a wary consent.

This expedition had been working at Timna', capital of ancient Qataban. There they had been on the friendliest terms with the local ruler, the Sherif of Bayḥân in the Aden protectorates. When Phillips and several of his people went to Ma'rib to look the site over, they were arrested by a mob of ragged soldiers with their faces painted blue. They were soon released, however.

During the summer of 1951, the expedition wound up its dig in Bayḥân and hopefully moved its equipment across the desert to Ma'rib, sixty miles away. Soon they were happily digging away at the ruins of the great temple of 'Ilmuqah, now locally called the Haram or Sacred Inclosure of Bilqîs. The temple proper was a rectangular hall about 66 by 82 feet, with an interior row of square columns, which once supported a roof open to the sky in the center. Behind the temple lay the temenos or sacred precinct, an elliptical area about 250 by 330 feet, surrounded by a thick stone wall 30 feet high.

Phillips went back to the United States to take care of administrative problems, unaware that the Imâm Aḥmad had changed his mind about the expedition. His more xenophobic officials had persuaded the Imâm that these detestable outsiders must be gotten rid of at all costs.

So the Yemeni officials at Ma'rib began a campaign of harassment. They countermanded the orders of expedition members. They demanded duplicates of all rubber squeezes of inscriptions. Although too ignorant to understand the purpose of these records, they saw that the expedition valued them and decided that they must be worth something. They were sure that the expedition was really a treasure hunt, and they meant to be on hand when the hoard of gold and jewels was unearthed. They demanded copies of all inscriptions, with translations. They forbade Yemeni soldiers and workmen to show newly uncovered inscriptions to expedition members. They demanded that the archaeologists inform them in advance of every movement they meant to make and take soldiers with them wherever they went. And so on and so forth.

Learning of these troubles, Phillips returned and tried to no avail to see the Imâm. Meanwhile the game of cat and mouse continued at Ma'rib. The Yemeni officials confiscated all the squeezes and incited the Yemeni soldiers against the expedition. The soldiers kept the archaeologists awake all night by blowing bugles and beating drums. In the daytime they spat at them, insulted them, threatened them, broke the windows of their trucks with rifle butts, and shot the dog of one expedition member. Meanwhile, the government gradually choked off the flow of supplies from the United States, especially gasoline, so that the expedition could not get away with its equipment.

Arriving at the site, Phillips learned that the soldiers planned to provoke an incident that would give them an excuse to kill all the leading members of the expedition—except for the expedition's secretary, a young Frenchwoman, who was to undergo what used to be called a fate worse than death. Then the soldiers would produce a cloud of witnesses to testify that the expedition members had attacked them and forced them to defend themselves.

Back in the bad old days of imperialism, a civilized government whose people were so used would probably have landed the marines and hanged the rascally Imâm from his palace window. But such is not the custom in these progressive times. Knowing he was on his own, Phillips calculated that, by siphoning the gasoline from all his other trucks into two, he would have just enough fuel to enable those two trucks to reach Bayḥân.

Early next morning, all twenty members of the expedition piled aboard the two fully fueled trucks, with guns, notes, and some personal effects. With the usual swarm of officials and soldiers hanging on the trucks, they drove calmly to the temple as if for an ordinary day's work. When they arrived at the temple, the Yemenites jumped down from the trucks, expecting the diggers to do likewise. Instead, the trucks roared off across the desert, leaving the Yemenites too surprised to shoot.

The trucks got stuck on sand dunes and were almost cut off at the border by the Yemeni camel corps. But the expedition won through to Bayḥân and safety. Although they had abandoned $200,000 worth of equipment, they still had some trucks and other materials at Aden. When the story of the escape broke, the Yemeni legations issued fantastic stories, such as the fiction that the expedition had been caught trying to smuggle out a solid gold statue of the Queen of Sheba. Phillips, meanwhile, reorganized his expedition and took them to Oman, where they did some pioneer digging.[18]

The Imâm Aḥmad continued on his accustomed way as a wicked oriental potentate. He survived several attempts at assassination, although ten of his brothers and most of his dozen sons perished in family feuds and palace plots. Life in Yemen made the palaces of Caligula and the Borgias look like health resorts.

In 1955 an army officer, Colonel Thalaya, led a revolt and besieged the Imâm in his palace at Ta'izz. Thalaya meant to make Aḥmad's brother Abdallah, a comparatively enlightened prince, Imâm instead. But Aḥmad's son Badr rallied the tribes. The old Imâm bought off most of the besieging soldiers and then led a counterattack, sword and tommy gun in hand. In the end, Abdallah was secretly executed, while Colonel Thalaya was publicly beheaded.

Soon after, the Imâm went to Italy for medical treatment for his many ailments, including syphilis and bilharziasis. One of his girls ran away and hid in a convent. When the Imâm demanded her back, the Italians smiled and helplessly spread their hands, ignoring the royal screams of rage.

Soon after his return home, a bullet from one of his own bodyguards wounded Aḥmad, who lingered a few months and died. Prince Badr succeeded as Imâm and announced reforms. But another group of army officers revolted, proclaimed a republic, and took the radical step of abolishing slavery. Since then, civil war has raged between the two factions.

If the republicans win and Yemen's stygian night of ignorance lifts, perhaps an expedition can some day go back to Ma'rib and try to close that gap between the mysterious biblical Queen of Sheba and the earliest historical records of Saba'.

# VI

# Zimbabwe and

# King Solomon's Mines

In dreams alone I tread those jungled streets
Where shattered columns, black with bitter age,
Hint of the splendour of some crumbling page
Of history now legended. The seats
Of prehistoric majesty still stand—
The monstrous walls, the cryptic minarets,
—But whose the hand that raised them? Time forgets
Mazed in the darkness of this silent land.

*Carter*

The 1850s and 60s were a time of mighty stir in Africa. In the East, the explorers Burton, Speke, Grant, Baker, and Stanley opened up vast new regions and tracked the Nile and the Congo to their sources. In the West, Baikie, having threaded the Niger for six hundred miles, settled down at Lokaja, deep in the jungle, for five years of collecting and observation. And in the South, Livingstone explored the Zambesi, discovered Victoria Falls, and vainly tried to argue tribal wizards out of their belief that their magical spells made rain.

Europeans had long been settled in sub-Saharan Africa: the Dutch in the South; the Portuguese on the coasts of Angola and Mozambique; other nations in river ports along the palmy shores. Immense areas in the interior were still, however, unknown. Africa was called the Dark Continent, among other reasons, because it remained so long unexplored by literate peoples. A little more than a hundred years ago, the lands of Asia and the Americas were well known. Explorers had struck deep into the flat, arid hinterland of Australia. But much of sub-Saharan Africa was still almost as mysterious as the other side of the moon.

Europeans had often tried to pierce this veil of mystery. Many men had lusted after Africa's ivory, gold, and slaves. Others' curiosity had been aroused to fever pitch by rumors of monstrous beasts and even more monstrous men who dwelt there.

Africa's coasts were early reconnoitered. In —VI, King Niku II of Egypt hired a fleet of Phoenicians to circumnavigate the continent. This they did, clockwise. The task took over two years, because they had to stop from time to time to raise a crop of wheat for bread. During the following four centuries, at least three other explorers tried—or claimed to have tried—to duplicate this feat; one attempt failed, and the outcome of the others is unknown.

During the Roman, Byzantine, and medieval periods, Arab merchants extended their trading posts down the east coast of Africa as far as Tanganyika. Then, in +XV, the Portuguese began exploring the west coast. In 1487, Bartolomeu Diaz reached the Cape of Good Hope, and soon other Portuguese adventurers had skirted the entire coast line. At the same time, other explorers—traders, missionaries, slavers, and adventurers—were probing the continent from all sides. Why did they fail to reach the interior?

They failed because nature had surrounded Negro Africa with barriers as formidable as the Himalayan rampart, which bounds Tibet. Across the North stretched the Sahara Desert, dividing the fertile Mediterranean coast from the rest of Africa. Before men had the domestic camel, it was almost impossible to cross this barrier. Even after the camel reached Africa, probably in the days of the Achaemenid Persian Empire, the journey was still a rugged one.

As for the seacoasts, most of them were flat tidewater plains, made swampy and heavily forested by an abundant rainfall. To hack a way through these insect-swarming, disease-ridden jungles was a task to daunt the mightiest. If a man could win through the low coastal belt to the uplands of the interior, he came upon delightful savannas and parklands; but how to get through?

The problem was aggravated over large areas by the tsetse fly, whose bite is fatal to all beasts of burden. Because of the fly, the traveler had to hire native bearers to carry his gear on their heads. But human bearers, compared with horses, mules, or camels, are very inefficient. An average man can carry only 60 to 70 pounds (the ancient "talent" or man-load) for long distances, compared with 200 to 300 pounds for a horse and 400 to 500 for a camel.

Since the man cannot graze or browse, he must be paid and fed. Hence the safari must either carry its food or buy supplies from the tribes through which it passes. If the tribes are hostile or suffering from famine, food cannot be had. If it is available, it must be bartered for with cheap trade goods, such as beads, which are exceedingly heavy and bulky in proportion to their purchasing power.

So, the coasts of Africa presented the explorer with an almost insuperable problem in logistics. Even if he did not succumb to disease, accident, desertion, or hostile spears, the amount of supplies and trade goods he could carry limited his range to a few score miles inland.

These barriers isolated Negro Africa almost as effectively as the ocean isolated the Australian aborigines, the Pacific Islanders, and the American Indians. Geography cut all these peoples off from the main cultural currents that surged across the Old World from China to Spain and back again. This isolation explains the cultural backwardness of the African Negroes, just as it explains that of the Polynesians and the Amerinds.

There were, however, a few gates or gaps in the barrier. One lay along the bulge of West Africa: the place we call Senegal. Here grassy plains come down to the coast, between the desert to the north and the jungle to the south, so that travel into the interior was feasible. But here lived powerful, warlike, semi-civilized nations, with a fondness for human sacrifice on a large and gory scale. So this gate was not very inviting.

Another gate was south of Egypt, where the Nile winds like a vast blue serpent athwart the desert belt. Here for over a thousand years flourished the ancient kingdom of Kush—the Ethiopia of the Greeks—corresponding to the modern Sudanese Republic. Through Kush, ideas and techniques from the civilized lands to the north slowly trickled through to Negro Africa: among them, for instance, iron smelting and cattle raising.

The third gate yawned in the extreme south, where climate and topography were easy and where the natives, among the world's most primitive people, could offer no serious resistance. This area was in fact overrun by Europeans in +XVIII and +XIX. It was not settled earlier, simply because of its vast distances from Europe and Asia.

Since this chapter has to do with the achievements of the Negroid race, we ought to make sure that we know what we mean by this term. The Negroid race can be subdivided into several types or sub-races, just as the Caucasoid race can be divided into the Alpine, Nordic, and other types. As with the Caucasoids, there are no sharp distinctions among these types. They blend into one another with many intermediate gradations.

When European explorers opened up Africa, they found the Negroid types distributed as follows: In the northeast—the Sudan, Abyssinia, and Somaliland—the prevailing type was one sometimes called "Hamitic." This is an ill-chosen term, because it properly refers to a language family. Some anthropologists speak of this group as the Erythriotic type, from an ancient name for the Red Sea. The Erythriotes are of rather slight build, with features as much like those of Europeans as of Negroes, with hair that is often curly rather than kinky, but with skins of truly Negroid darkness. Whether they are of mixed white-Negro ancestry, or an intermediate type that evolved independently, none can say; in the light of modern genetics the latter seems the more likely.

In the southern Sudan, on the upper White Nile, lived men of another Negroid type: the Nilotes, or Nilotic Negroes, which include such tribes as the Dinka. These are extremely tall, lean blacks, noted for devotion to their cattle and (before the puritanical Muslims of the Sudanese Government began forcing clothes on them) for complete nudity.

In the Ituri Forest of the northeastern Congo dwelt the Pygmies. They are essentially miniature Negroes, averaging under five feet, with slightly lighter skins than most Negroes. The Pygmies are among the world's few remaining hunters and food-gatherers, although they are old hands at smelting and working iron.

The central and western parts of the continent were occupied by Forest Negroes, the people we think of as "typically Negroid." They are of medium to large size and of muscular build, with very broad noses and thick lips. Although they vary from tribe to tribe in physique and in way of life, most are iron-using peasant farmers and herdsmen. Many but not all tribes of Forest Negroes speak languages belonging to the great Bantu family, which has complicated inflections in the form of prefixes. Hence, for example, one Mganda, or two Baganda, live in Uganda and speak Luganda.

In South Africa lived, when the whites arrived, two other groups of brown-skinned people who are classed not as true Negroids but as members of yet another race. One group, widely spread over the interior of South Africa, comprised the Bushmen. These are small yellow-brown folk, a little larger than the Pygmies, with triangular faces, childish features, and hair that grows in little bunches on their heads. Like the Pygmies they are pure hunter-gatherers, save that some of the few surviving Bushmen have in recent decades taken to peasant life. Formerly they inscribed and painted pictures on cave walls, as lively and lifelike as those of the cave artists of western Europe. When discovered by the whites, the Bushmen were still in the Stone Age. As the whites closed in on them from the south, the Negroids overran their lands from the north; between the two the poor Bushmen were nearly extermi-nated.

The other group, found in a narrow strip along the southwestern coast, was the Hottentots. These are much like the Bushmen but taller. When the whites arrived, the Hottentots had graduated from hunting to stock-raising. Some anthropologists think the Hottentots a mixture of Bushman and Erythriote. The Bushmen and the Hot-tentots are the survivors of a once large and varied race of hunting peoples, the "Bushmanoid" race, widely scattered over Africa and having many local sub-races. One such sub-race, which lived in the southeast and is called the Boskop race from the place where one skeleton was found, was of medium height with an unusually large skull and brain.

Thus we come to South Africa of a century ago, when the natural barriers to the interior had finally broken down before the strength and valor of the explorers. Following the explorers came the exploit-ers: missionaries after souls, hunters after game, traders and pros-pectors after gold, settlers after land.

In South Africa, rumors of great, glittering inland cities—cities living or cities dead—ran riot among the encroaching Europeans. The Portuguese, who in +XVI had wrested from the Arabs their holds along the Mozambique coast, had published hearsay reports of imposing inland ruins. They had written of a vast empire be-tween the Zambesi and Limpopo rivers, ruled by a sovereign titled the Monomotapa.[1] This potentate reigned from a capital called Symbaoe, Zimbaoche, or some similar name. John Ogilvie, in 1670, published a geography describing the Monomotapa as dwelling in a palace "covered over with plates of gold."[2]

No matter that the Portuguese had long since reduced the Monomotapa to a powerless puppet. In the uncritical minds of hunters and miners, all these tales swirled together to form a vision of a golden metropolis with gleaming palaces and minarets, where an enterprising man would find a fortune ripe for picking. The same sort of fever sent sixteenth-century Spaniards hiking back and forth across the wilds of South America in search of El Dorado[3] and flooded California with immigrants in 1849.

In the middle of +XVI, several Portuguese historians described these places. Goes told of the "King of Benomotapa" who "keeps great state, and is served on bended knees with reverence."[4] Barros wrote of the principal place in more detail:

> There are other mines in a district called Toroa, which by another name is known as the Kingdom of Butua, which is ruled by a prince called Burrom, a vassal of Benomotapa, which lands adjoin that aforesaid consisting of vast plains, and these mines are the most ancient known in the country, and they are all in the plain, in the midst of which there is a square fortress, of masonry within and without, built of stones of marvelous size, and there appears to be no mortar joining them. The wall is more than twenty-five spans in width, and the height is not so great considering the width. Above the door of this edifice is an inscription, which some Moorish merchants, learned men, who went thither, could not read, neither could they tell what the character might be. This edifice is almost surrounded by hills, upon which are others resembling it in the fashioning of the stone and the absence of mortar, and one of them is a tower more than twelve fathoms high.
>
> The natives of the country call all these edifices Symbaoe, which according to their language signifies court, for every place where Benomotapa may be is so called; and they say that being royal property all the king's other dwellings have this name. It is guarded by a nobleman . . .
>
> When, and by whom, these edifices were raised, as the people of the land are ignorant of the art of writing, there is no record, but they say they are the work of the devil . . .[5]

The Portuguese writers had not actually seen these buildings. Instead, they had heard of them from Arab traders, who plied their commerce on long safaris inland from Sofala.

After Goes and Barros wrote, Portuguese policies ended this Arab trade. The great ambition of the Portuguese, in their invasion of the Indian Ocean, was to set up monopolies so that gold should flow into their purses without their having to work for it. To this end they addressed themselves, like the Spaniards in the Americas, with exemplary courage, resolution, energy, treachery, and cruelty.

Having seized the Arab trading posts on the east coast of Africa —some of which had been flourishing for over a thousand years— the Portuguese arrogated to themselves a monopoly of all African trade, sank Arab ships when they met them, and stopped the Arabs' inland journeys. The Arabs, riven by factiousness, were unable to combine against the Portuguese. Yet the Portuguese themselves were less successful as traders than their predecessors. Most of them would not, like the Arabs, plod patiently into the interior, stopping at each hamlet to fraternize and chaffer. An occasional military foray to show the might of modern arms was more their style. Hence, during +XVI and +XVII, trade dwindled to a trickle over a vast area bordering the Indian Ocean.

In 1871 a man appeared in Mashonaland, the part of Southern Rhodesia that touches southern Mozambique. He was Karl Gottlieb Mauch, a 34-year-old Swabian geologist who had worked his passage to Africa to make his mark as an explorer. Mauch was an arresting figure: broad-shouldered and powerful, with a wide, flat face and a thicket of beard.

From head to foot, Mauch was encased in leather. He wore a leather deerstalker cap, an antelope-hide suit of his own making, and huge hobnailed boots. Sixty pounds of gear, including an enormous umbrella, a double-barreled gun with a spare barrel, two revolvers, a compass, a sextant, a hunting knife, a tin bowl, a blanket, and boxes and bags containing books, writing and painting equipment, and toilet articles dangled here and there from his mighty person.

Mauch had no train of Negroes to carry his kit, no mule or ass for riding, no ox wagon. He walked, usually by himself. For six years, precariously financed by contributions from friends in Germany, he had hiked about South Africa. He had found rich outcrops of gold, dutifully reported them to the British colonial government at Natal, but refused to take part in the gold rush that followed. The glory of exploring and mapping unknown lands was enough for him.

In 1871 Mauch was half starved, at the end of his resources, and threatened with captivity by a local chief named Dumbo, who had poisoned his beer in order to rob him. Just in time, a tall, strong white man turned up in the night and ransomed Mauch. The newcomer was Adam Renders, a German-American trader and ivory hunter. As a result of a scandal, Renders had deserted his family, plunged into the wilds of Mashonaland, and more or less gone native. He got on well with the Negroes, who called him Sa-adama and who liked him because he paid his debts promptly and had married the daughter of a chief named Pika.

Mauch was delighted to discover that Renders spoke German. He confided that, before returning home, he hoped to crown his work by exploring the ruins of the ancient seat of the Monomotapa. He had heard about this ruin from a German missionary named Merensky, who in turn had heard about it from a native chief.

That would be easy, said Renders. He, too, had heard Merensky's tale, and he had actually known the place for two or three years. The village where he lived was less than a dozen miles from it, and he had camped at the ruins during his elephant hunts.

Mauch also learned that an old acquaintance, George Philips, was nearby. Philips was another ivory hunter, from Natal, whose build and temperament had earned him the nickname of the Playful Elephant. A message from Mauch fetched Philips; but the local Negroes, who said they did not know who built the structures, were loath to approach the ruin. Nevertheless, the gift of a gun persuaded one of them to go with the three whites.

For a few days they scrambled about the ancient masonry of Zimbabwe, although the site was too overgrown to enable them to get a very clear picture of it. They were startled by an old man named Babareke,[6] who popped out of the bushes, claiming to be the son of the last high priest of a local cult, which used to sacrifice oxen in the ruins.

Worn down by malaria and prematurely aged by his hardships, Mauch shortly thereafter beat his way to Sena on the coast and home to Germany. There he published a book about his discoveries. From what Babareke had told him, he concluded that the rites the old man's ancestors celebrated were Semitic and that the ruins were—as Portuguese writers had speculated two centuries earlier—nothing less than the Ophir of the Bible, from whose mines King Solomon drew his wealth:

And king Solomon made a navy of ships in Ezion-geber, which is beside Eloth, on the shore of the Red Sea, in the land of Edom. And Hiram sent in the navy his servants, shipmen that had knowledge of the sea, with the servants of Solomon. And they came to Ophir, and fetched from thence gold, four hundred and twenty talents, and brought it to king Solomon . . . Kings' daughters were among thy honourable women: upon thy right hand did stand the queen in gold of Ophir.[7]

In fact, said Mauch, the building on the hill was an imitation of King Solomon's temple on Mount Moriah, while the large elliptical building in the valley was a copy of the palace in which the Queen of Sheba had stayed when she visited Solomon. He even asserted that the ruins had been the residence of the queen herself, who had brought thither skilled Phoenician architects and workmen to erect the buildings. He called the site "Zimbabye," after the place of which the Portuguese had written.

Mauch had been home in Stuttgart but a short time when, in 1875, he died as a result of a fall from a window. Nevertheless, Mauch's discovery got plenty of publicity in Europe and South Africa. Several other writers followed him with books expounding the Ophir theory.

Everywhere, the name "Ophir" conjured up a picture of hidden riches. No matter how leaky Mauch's theory or how slight the chance that any great mass of gold would still lie hidden, the word "treasure" touched off another gold rush. A stream of visitors headed for Zimbabwe: soldiers, explorers, archaeologists, and treasure hunters. The name of the site, after passing through several variants, received its modern form "Zimbabwe"[8] from the hunter Frederick C. Selous. Andrew Lang, the great Scottish mythographer and man of letters—romantic that he was—swallowed the Ophir theory and composed a poem on Zimbabwe:

> Into the darkness whence they came,
>  They passed—their country knoweth none,
> They and their gods without a name
>  Partake the same oblivion . . .[9]

In 1889, Cecil Rhodes organized a British company to settle the countries north of the Dutch-settled Transvaal, and named the new country Rhodesia after himself. Armed settlers and company police poured in, peacefully at first. When the Africans saw they were losing their country, they fought. But all—warlike MaTabele and peaceful MaShona alike—were crushed.

The settlers' methods may be judged from a contemporary complaint in the *Matabele Times*, that the pioneers' current "theory of shooting a nigger on sight" was impractical, as were the practices of "burning kraals because they were native kraals, and firing upon fleeing natives simply because they were black."[10] Natives were forbidden to dig for minerals, as they had been doing for centuries, just as in other parts of Africa they were forbidden to grow cash crops, like coffee, the profits from which the whites were determined to keep to themselves. The natives were heavily taxed, to compel them to work for the whites to earn the money to pay the taxes. If modern African Negroes, in the first throes of independence, sometimes seem insanely hostile towards all whites, their hatred, if foolish, is not incomprehensible.

Among the gold seekers were the brothers Willi and Harry Posselt, who farmed and traded for a time near Zimbabwe. In 1888, Willi Posselt tried to remove one of four carved soapstone birds, which decorated the Acropolis. He quit when a gang of local natives threatened him with guns and spears. Decades later, Posselt had the gall to write a book about his treasure hunt, in which he naïvely expressed chagrin at not finding any loot worth melting up. A few years after Posselt, the archaeologist Bent removed several such stone birds to the Cape Town Museum.

At the height of the gold fever, a group of treasure hunters got a franchise from Dr. Leander Jameson, the adventurer associate of Rhodes, for something called the Ancient Ruins Company. This company obtained the exclusive right to prospect all the ruins in Rhodesia. In the next few years these scoundrels devastated forty-odd sites, especially Zimbabwe. They dug up a few hundred ounces of gold—the equivalent of a few thousand dollars—and in so doing made the job of later archaeologists vastly harder. They not only removed the ancient relics and confused the stratigraphy, but also contaminated the sites with modern objects like liquor bottles and broken umbrellas. Two German scientists, Hans Sauer and Heinrich Schlichter, protested the havoc to Rhodes, who eventually called

Jameson on the carpet and canceled the company's charter; but the damage had been done.

Private exploitation of ruins still continued until, in 1902, Southern Rhodesia's new legislative council passed a law protecting the sites. R. N. Hall, appointed curator of Zimbabwe, spent two years excavating the ruin. He wrote several books, one of which, *Great Zimbabwe*, describes the site in detail.

Hall's attitude was not what we should call objective. He kept remarking on the natives' nudity as if it were something strange and ludicrous. Stone phalli he called "the odious and unmistakeable emblems of nature worship."[11] Nor was his archaeology so meticulous as later standards called for. Therefore Gertrude Caton-Thompson, who dug in the same area in 1929, reproved him. But the very fact that she could take him to task so severely showed how far the science of archaeology had advanced between his time and hers. If nineteenth-century archaeologists had not done their bungling best, their present-day successors could not have improved upon their techniques. And, no doubt, archaeologists of +XXI will note the shortcomings of their predecessors of today.

By Hall's time the town of Victoria had sprung up, seventeen miles northwest of the ruins. A road, over which tourists bounced in buggies and bicycles for a day of sightseeing, was run to Zimbabwe. Today Zimbabwe is one of the main tourist attractions of South Africa, along with Victoria Falls and the game preserves. It has also become one of the world's leading citadels of archaeological mystery.

Zimbabwe lies in the valley of the Mapudzi River, a tributary of the Sabi, which flows into the ocean a little south of Sofala. The valley is broad and gently rolling, broken here and there by hillocks,[12] and rimmed by rugged, distant mountains of sheer cliffs and gloomy gorges. Some of the hillocks are low and gently sloping. Others are abrupt, their tops eroded into fantastic shapes: ledges, cliffs, crags, domes, and skyward-pointing fingers of rock.

This rock is all granite. As the boulders and ledges swell with heat and shrink with cold, their outer surfaces crack off in layers, onionwise. This process, called exfoliation, gave the builders of Zimbabwe readymade building material. A smart blow breaks one of these shells of rock into pieces shaped like square bricks. When they ran out of well-shaped stones, the Zimbabweans could get more from boulders by the use of wedges or fire. For carving their bird totems, they brought soft soapstone from a quarry fifteen miles away; slate, quartz, and other exotic stones were also imported for special purposes.

*Fig. 11  Tribal map of South-east Africa before the Portuguese an British conquests.*

The country has a moderate rainfall with dry winters (from June to August) and wet summers of driving rains and creeping mists. The landscape is typical African parkland. Trees are loosely scattered. Sometimes they occur in clumps, and in places they thicken to jungle density and are festooned with feathery lichens. Between the trees, during the wet season, giant grasses grow to a height of twelve feet.

The trees are African hardwoods of many kinds: the castor-oil tree, the baobab with its thick gray trunk, the Rhodesian teak, eugenias, and flat-topped acacias. Around the ruins occur two distinctive soft-wooded plants: the aloe, which looks like a century plant on top of a stalk, and the euphorbia, resembling a Christmas cactus enlarged to tree size.

In the days of Rendors and Hall, the neighborhood teemed with fauna, from lion and elephant down to the snakes and lizards that swarmed the ruins. Now the animal life is much sparser.

The ruins are located on top of a steep-sided knoll, called Zimbabwe Hill, and spread out over a quarter of a square mile on the valley floor south of this hill. The ruins consist of, first, the so-called Acropolis atop the hill; second, an oval structure, called the Temple or the Elliptical Building, six hundred yards south of the Acropolis; and third, about a dozen smaller structures, called the Valley ruins, north and east of the Elliptical Building. From Zimbabwe Hill the view extends for many miles in all directions, overlooking the parklands and the several native villages scattered about the valley floor.

The largest single structure is the Elliptical Building. (This is a better name than "Temple," because it is not absolutely certain that the structure was in fact a temple.) It consists of a large, massive wall of roughly elliptical shape, about 220 by 280 feet in diameter and 830 feet around. A few small walls lie outside the ellipse, and within it a number of smaller walls run hither and yon among platforms and towers.

All these walls are of dry-wall masonry, made by piling up small blocks of granite laid in courses. There was little shaping of the blocks and no use of mortar, although the early occupants laid floors and plastered lower parts of walls with a simple cement of granite sand and lime. Later occupants spread floors with a red clay called *daga*. Time and weather have disintegrated most of these floorings.

The walls have a pronounced batter. That is, they taper from bottom to top, so that each face leans inwards at an angle of about 10 degrees from the vertical. Battered walls were used by many builders in the early stages of civilization, because they lasted longer. All the walls, also, are more or less curved, which makes them stronger than they would otherwise be. Where the walls end, they are neatly rounded off. Drains at the base of the main wall let rain water out.

Lacking mortar to hold them together, all the walls have suffered from the ravages of time. Trees and other plants have done most of the damage, growing out of the walls themselves and prying them apart, or growing nearby and beating the walls with their branches during windstorms. When a wall collapsed, it sometimes knocked over another in its fall.

The main or outer wall, being the most massively and carefully built, is still in fairly good condition, although several courses of stones have fallen from its top. The slighter interior walls are much more ruinous. One reason for the sinister repute of the site among the local Bantu was that at night, from time to time, an overbalanced stone would fall with a crash, convincing the natives that the ghosts of the ancients haunted the ruins.

The outer wall varies in height from 20 to 33 feet, or less in a few places where it has broken down. This does not count several feet of foundation below the ground surface, and an extra foot or two on top where the topmost courses have fallen off. At its thickest, the wall is about 15 feet wide at the bottom and 10 feet wide at the top.

There are three main entrances to the outer wall, on the north, northwest, and west sides. Similar portals occur in the inside walls. Most are built on a standard pattern. The wall is rounded off on each side of the entrance. At the bottom, the stonework is carried across the entrance to form a series of steps leading up and then down, like a stile. Flanking the entrance are a pair of cylindrical towerlike structures, often with a deep groove that once held some sort of gate or door.

Around the east and south sides of the main wall, a few feet below the top, a course of stones is laid in a zigzag or chevron pattern. Some have sought to read deep symbolism into this strip of decoration; it is probably the "inscription" that Barros heard about from Arab traders. But, as far as anyone can tell, it was intended merely to look pretty. Other ruins of Zimbabwe show other decorations: stones laid in a herringbone pattern, or in a dentelle pattern formed by setting stones so that their corners protrude from the wall, or in alternate courses of pale and dark stones. These forms of decoration are common among the Bantu.

The interior walls form several inclosures and long labyrinthine passages. The longest of these passages, leading to the north entrance, is 220 feet in length.

At the southeast side of the main inclosure, where the long passage opens out, stand a pair of structures that have furnished much food for thought. These are two conical towers of stone. The larger cone is now about 30 feet high. It was about 5 feet higher until Mauch, thinking there might be a crypt inside the tower, climbed to the top and began throwing off stones until he had convinced himself otherwise. Near it stood a much smaller cone, with dimensions less than half those of the large cone. But a tree grew up and pushed the small cone over, so only its stump remains.

The Acropolis is perched atop a 90-foot precipice on the south side of Zimbabwe Hill. It is a congeries of curving walls, like those of the Elliptical Building. The crest of the hill is a mass of outcrops and boulders, which the builders incorporated into their structures. Their purpose seems to have been defense, because access to the Acropolis is by several narrow, winding passages, which could easily be defended. The Acropolis is—or was—decorated with several small conical towers and large elongated stones set upright as monoliths. A cave below the walls of the Acropolis has strange acoustics; a man speaking in his natural voice in the cave can be clearly heard in the Elliptical Building, a quarter of a mile away, but nowhere else in the valley. No doubt the native priests put this phenomenon to good use.

Most of the Valley Ruins are named for the discoverers of Zimbabwe: the Renders Ruins, the Philips Ruins, and so on. They reproduce on a smaller scale the features seen in the two main ruins. Some Valley Ruins are built well and some badly. They may belong to different times. Some have been plundered by treasure hunters, some have been dug by archaeologists, and some await excavation.

Explorers of the Valley Ruins were struck by the fact that the outer walls were not continuous. These walls had been built with more gaps than would be needed for gates, making them useless for defense. To some, this showed that the builders were weak in the head. Miss Caton-Thompson deemed this fact evidence that Zimbabwe was "the product of an infantile mind, a pre-logical mind, a mind which having discovered the way of making or doing a thing goes on childishly repeating the performance regardless of incongruity."[13] Hence, she inferred, the buildings were probably built by the Bantu, whom she assumed to have such minds.

Miss Caton-Thompson made a common mistake. She thought that, because she could not understand an act of some ancient or primitive folk, these folk did not have what seemed to them a good reason for it. A Martian, watching Earthmen playing golf, would find it just as hard to figure out what these organisms were up to. If it occurred to him that they did it for exercise, he would soon be disabused by the sight of some of the creatures riding about the course in electric vehicles. He would probably conclude that it was a magical or religious rite, designed to help the sun along on its course among the stars.

In the case of the interrupted walls, the explanation is simple. Probably the gaps were filled by huts of stud-and-mud construction, which have long since vanished. The huts and the walls between them made adequate rough-and-ready defenses against a rush of hostile spearmen.

Other ruins, less imposing than Zimbabwe, lie scattered about Rhodesia, Mozambique, and Bechuanaland. There are sites called "Little Zimbabwe" and "Clay Zimbabwe." There is Inyanga with its agricultural terraces and "slave pits"—perhaps places for the storage of foodstuffs or corrals for livestock—and a fort, which is a smaller and cruder version of the Acropolis at Zimbabwe. There is Dhlo-Dhlo (a name surely invented by Dunsany or Lovecraft!) with its artistic checkerboard walls, its broken seventeenth-century Chinese bowl, and its Dutch gin bottle of about the same date. There is Mapungubwe with its hoard of little golden objects, including a golden rhinoceros.

As for the present-day people of Mashonaland, it is hard to know by what name to call them.[14] They themselves do not seem to have had any name for the people of the whole region. They went by the names of smaller units—tribes and clans.

The MaShona are rather slender, athletic Negroids speaking one of the many Bantu languages. Opinions differ about their character. Major Willoughby, who dug there briefly in the early 1890s, thought them "thieving, lazy, lying, and cowardly," although he excused these faults on the ground that they had been degraded by the raids, massacres, and oppressions of warlike neighboring tribes.

On the other hand, Hall found the MaShona "readier and more anxious to work . . . more honest and reliable" than most Africans, possessing "taste, tact, courtesy, politeness, neatness," and other attractive qualities; while Bent found them honest, courteous, and diligent, with "cowardice . . . their only vice."[15] This difference of opinion probably rises from the usual difficulty of judging a strange group of people. One's impressions depend on chance encounters with individuals, and on one's luck in hitting it off with them. Doubtless the MaShona vary as much, from man to man, as do other human groups. In +XIX they were adept at building in stone and had many domestic manufactures, such as cloth and iron. But, when Hall wrote, they were losing all these skills because it was easier to buy cheap European trade goods.

If the unmarked stones at Zimbabwe could speak, they could tell us who piled them up, and when, and why; but they cannot. In fact, the whole history of Negro Africa, and of Mashonaland in particular, is vague and sketchy before the coming of the whites. This is what happens where people do not write their history. Oral tradition can carry down memory of happenings for one or two hundred years; perhaps in extreme cases even four or five hundred. After that, events either are completely forgotten or are so transformed into myth that the historical facts are lost forever.

History and anthropology indicate that, before the Christian Era, the Negroid race (save perhaps for the Pygmies) occupied a much smaller part of Africa than now, and that the Forest Negroes were confined to the central and western parts. On the other hand, peoples like the Pygmies, the Bushmen, and the Hottentots were much more widely spread. They were found not only in the areas where they now live but also on the upper Nile, on the upper courses either of the Niger or of the Bahr al-Ghazâl, on the west coast of Africa, and on islands in the Red Sea.

Between −1000 and +1000, the Negroes learned the arts of agriculture, cattle raising, and iron working. These advances enabled them to increase their numbers and to spread out at the expense of the little hunters. Men of the Nilotic sub-race migrated south to become the towering WaTutsi of Rwanda and Burundi. The Erythriotes spread from Abyssinia over East Africa, accounting for the so-called "Semitic features" (a misnomer, but let it go) that early travelers noticed among some Rhodesian natives. And the Forest Negroes, mostly Bantu-speaking, spread all over East and South Africa.

A warmly argued question is: when did the Bantu reach Rhodesia? Some think they did not cross the Zambesi on their way south before +XII, and most agree that they did not arrive before +VI. Obviously, their date of arrival in Mashonaland affects the question of who built Zimbabwe, because they could not have built it if they were not there when it was built.

Before the main Bantu migrations, the Arabs had begun setting up coastal trading posts. The *Periplus of the Erythraean Sea*, written about +60, tells of several such settlements in "Azania"; that is, the East African coast. The last two items on the author's list are "the island Menouthias," probably Zanzibar or some nearby isle, and:

> Two days' sail beyond, there lies the very last market town of the continent of Azania, which is called Rhapta; which has its name from the sewed boats (*rhaptôn ploiariôn*) already mentioned; in which there is ivory in great quantity, and tortoiseshell. Along this coast live men of piratical habits, very great in stature, and under separate chiefs for each place. The Mapharitic chief governs it under some ancient rite that subjects it to the sovereignty of the state that is become first in Arabia. And the people of Mouza in Arabia now hold it under his authority, and send thither many large ships; using Arab captains and agents, who are familiar with the natives and intermarry with them, and who know the whole coast and understand the language.[16]

Rhapta was somewhere on the coast of Tanganyika. Reference to tall pirates implies that Forest Negroes or Nilotics had reached this region.

During the next thousand years, the Arabs extended their posts southward, as far as Sofala. The Arab settlements grew into city-states, some quite wealthy, which viciously feuded and fought among themselves. Kilwa,[17] founded by the Persians in +957, was long the dominant city. Along this coast a new race sprang up, of mixed Arab-African blood. These people spoke a kind of Basic Bantu called Swahili, with a large admixture of Arabic words. Many of the "Arabs" who have played a part in East African history in recent centuries, such as the famous nineteenth-century slaver Tippu Tib, were actually of more Negroid than Arab ancestry.

And what had been happening inland? When the Portuguese arrived in +XVI, they found the Monomotapa ruling a large empire centered in Mashonaland and carrying on a brisk trade in gold, slaves, and other exports with the Arabs. For a thousand years the Arabs fomented the slave trade along this coast and sold the slaves to Romans, Byzantines, Persians, Indians, and other customers. The total number of victims must have been immense, although the trade was never carried on so intensively as it was by Europeans and Americans in West Africa in +XVIII and +XIX.

The Portuguese, marching inland around 1570 from the Arab cities they had conquered, expected to find the ground agleam with gold. When they saw how hard the Bantu miners had to work to get a few tiny flakes from their diggings, they were appalled. On the other hand, these diggings had been intensively worked over a large area for several centuries, so that the total amount of gold extracted was considerable. It has been estimated—on very doubtful grounds—as high as twenty million ounces, which at present prices would mean something like three quarters of a billion dollars. The Bantu also mined copper (the famous copper mines of Katanga had long been worked), iron, tin, and a little silver. But their mining was practically all surface digging, since they had not yet developed the techniques of deep-shaft mining.

As barbaric empires go, the Monomotapa's was a fairly well-organized one. His chief wife or queen had to be one of his sisters, but he was surrounded by thousands of women. He dressed in silk, with ornaments made from sea shells. He went about in high state, preceded by drummers and trailed by his bodyguard. When the bodyguard became bored with having nobody to kill, they set up a cry of "Meat! Meat!" until the Monomotapa pointed out some unlucky subject for them to slay and devour. When the ruler got old and weak, he was forced to poison himself. After he had been buried with suitable human sacrifices, a council of his chief wives chose his successor.

The Monomotapa's power dwindled after the coming of the

Portuguese, who in 1629 forced him to accept their "protection." After that he was just a Portuguese puppet, although a family still claimed the empty title down into +XIX. While the Monomotapa's empire crumbled, the country declined because the intensification of the slave trade disrupted mining and other normal activities, and more barbarous tribes invaded the land from the south.. For a time a rival line of rulers, the Mambos of the BaRozwi tribe, ruled an empire as great as that of the Monomotapas; but they in their turn succumbed to the white man's power.

Mauch's speculations about King Solomon's mines and the Queen of Sheba's palace let loose a flood of theory concerning Zimbabwe. Although few credited his idea that Queen Bilqîs herself had ever resided at Zimbabwe, many subscribed to the general concept that Zimbabwe was an Arab or Asian outpost. In 1891 the archaeologist J. Theodore Bent, who had already explored the past in the Greek islands, Turkey, and Iran, spent two months investigating Zimbabwe. Bent, in *The Ruined Cities of Mashonaland* (1892) concluded that Sabaean Arabs, Phoenicians, or some kindred Semitic folk had originally built Zimbabwe in pre-Christian times, because the soapstone phalli dug up there and the Conical Tower reminded him of certain Semitic religious rites, and the shape of the Elliptical Building recalled that of the Haram of Bilqîs at Ma'rib. Zimbabwe, he thought, had been more or less continuously under Arabian influence from ancient to medieval times. That Zimbabwe was identical with ancient Punt, or Ophir, or both, he regarded as possible but not yet proved. He mentioned a Roman coin of the reign of Antoninus Pius (+138) found in a mine shaft at Umtali, also in Southern Rhodesia; but he did not tell enough about this fascinating find to shed light on how such a thing could have come there.

Then came Dr. Carl Peters, the German explorer, who more or less singlehandedly annexed Tanganyika to the German Empire. A lean, bullet-headed man in professorial pince-nez, with a huge mustache that swept out and up like the tusks of a wart hog, Peters was a colonialist of the old school. He scolded the British colonial government for being too lenient with the "niggers," whom he regarded as "sickly and useless rubbish." This "useless rabble," said he, should either be made to work for the whites by a system of forced labor, like that which the Boers employed and the Portuguese in Africa still practise, or be wiped out.[18] It infuriated Peters to hear of white farmers unable to earn a profit because they were not allowed to make serfs of the local Negroes.

In the 1890s, Peters was ousted as colonial administrator. His hanging of two natives, a man and a woman, for not very grave offenses was too much even for Imperial Germany. Although he did not visit Zimbabwe, in 1899–1900 he explored ruins farther east, along the Rhodesia-Mozambique border, and discovered the "slave pits" at Inyanga. In *The Eldorado of the Ancients* (1902) Peters claimed that Zimbabwe was not only the biblical Ophir, but also the land of Punt, whither in −XV the Egyptian queen, Ḥatshepsut, had sent the famous trading expedition pictured on the walls of her magnificent mortuary temple near Luxor. Thus the Hottentots, Peters thought, were partly of Egyptian descent.

R. N. Hall, the first curator at Zimbabwe, also wrote about the site. Hall concluded that the ruins had first been built in pre-Christian times by sun-worshiping Semites (probably Himyarite Arabs), abandoned, and long afterwards put back into use as a gold-refining and trading center by medieval Arabs.

In 1905, David Randall-MacIver made the first excavations at Zimbabwe that heeded the all-important modern archaeological principle of stratigraphy. Up to this time, all who had written about the ruins had taken it for granted that no rabble of naked, ignorant blacks could have built such imposing structures, and that Zimbabwe's origin should be looked for among civilized Caucasoids.

Randall-MacIver startled the Zimbabwe fans by asserting that all the objects found in the ruins were either typical African products, or trade goods of medieval or later date. These objects included beads, pieces of Persian glass, and fragments of Chinese porcelain. (Similar relics have lately been dug up in the ruins at medieval Kilwa.) Some pieces of glass bore traces of Arabic lettering, but of a type later than Muhammad (+VI). Nothing in the lot could be dated earlier than +XIV or +XV. So, quoth Randall-MacIver, the naked Bantu had built the ruins after all, probably no more than two centuries before the arrival of the Portuguese. He somewhat unfairly attacked Hall, who replied in kind, and an acrimonious debate raged for years.

Randall-MacIver's arguments did not silence the more romantic Zimbabwean fans, who preferred to seek the origin of the ruins long ago and far away. Some found this origin among the Dravidians of southern India. After all, they said, the monsoon winds would have blown these seafarers from India to South Africa and back again with hardly any effort on their part.

Others gave the honor to the Malays. They pointed out that the islanders of nearby Madagascar were of unquestioned Malay origin, and several kinds of plants from southeast Asia grew in Rhodesia. Although this Malay migration must have taken place, there is no historical record of it; therefore, it probably happened before the beginnings of recorded history and much earlier than the other movements of man discussed in this chapter.

Henry Rider Haggard, not yet thirty and a colonial official, added a touch of froth to the whole argument with a famous adventure novel, *King Solomon's Mines* (1895), based on tales of Zimbabwe. Haggard's narrator, the modest but intrepid Allan Quatermain, tells of his expedition with two British companions to unknown Kukuanaland.

On the way they shoot a lot of elephants. In Haggard's world it was deemed a manly and virtuous act to kill wild animals whenever one could, even if the animals were doing no harm and the killer had no pressing need of their meat, hides, or other products. In fact, the less practical use the hunter had for the carcass, the purer a sportsman he was deemed. As Quatermain says: "It went against my conscience to let such a herd as that escape without having a pull at them."[19] On the other hand, Haggard was sympathetic towards the Africans and could always be counted upon to tell a rattling good story.

Haggard's heroes nearly perish of thirst in a desert but finally reach the land of the noble Kukuana, who are ruled by an evil king. They take part in a gory battle between the followers of this king and a rival prince, on whose behalf one of the Britons smites off the head of the wicked monarch. Then they find the caves where King Solomon's miners stored the diamonds they dug. While they are filling their pockets with diamonds, the late king's old sorceress traps them by closing the stone door. But in time's nick they find their way out and return to civilization.

For some years, the question of the age and origin of Zimbabwe simmered gently. In 1929 Gertrude Caton-Thompson excavated Zimbabwe once again. Miss Caton-Thompson came to much the same conclusions as Randall-MacIver: that Zimbabwe had been built by native Africans and was nowhere near so old as the Semitic school had believed. However, considering the trade goods found since Randall-MacIver's dig, she inferred that the ruins were older than Randall-MacIver had thought. They had been built, she said, in +IX or +X.

She also pointed out that, while the ruins might have later been used for gold refining, they could hardly have been built for this purpose. Zimbabwe is not near any gold deposits; nor, in general, are the other Rhodesian ruins. Unfortunately, her sound work was obscured by the publication at that time of the theories of the German ethnologist Leo Frobenius, an enthusiast for locating the lost Atlantis in Africa.

There things rested until 1950, when S. D. Sandes, Warden of Zimbabwe National Park, found a log used as a lintel over a drain in the Elliptical Building. Under carbon-14 tests, samples of this wood gave dates between +591 and +702, with a possible spread from +471 to +794. Although this dating is not so precise as one might wish, it does push back Miss Caton-Thompson's estimates still further. The building may not be quite so old as the wood, which is of a very durable kind and comes from a tree with poisonous sap. Hence the natives use this wood only after it is thoroughly dead. At least we can say that, on one hand, Randall-MacIver assigned much too late a date to Zimbabwe; while, on the other, King Solomon could not possibly have had anything to do with the ruin, because it was built at least fifteen hundred years after his time.

Zimbabwe had the bad luck to get caught up in the great twentieth-century dispute over differences among the races of man. Those who wanted to prove that the white or Caucasoid race is better than others have been eager to show that Zimbabwe was built by whites. South African whites, for instance, have heatedly argued that the Bantu could not have built Zimbabwe, because they were not there when it was built, or because African Negroes have never built anything out of stone, or because they are inherently too stupid and lazy to build such structures.

The first point is doubtful; the second untrue. Even if the Africans never created a Parthenon or an Alhambra, many have known enough to build stone walls around their villages when the building materials were available. When the anti-Bantu writers have been compelled to notice cases where Bantu did build such things, they have taken refuge in a circular argument: Negroes never build in stone or mine for metal. If they did, it only proves that these Negroes must have had a lot of white blood or have come under white influence, because as we know Negroes never build in stone or mine for metal.

As for the third point: many have simply asserted, as a proven fact, that Negroes *could* not erect such buildings or dig such mines because they were "a lot of lazy *canaille*" of "low intellectual capacity," whereas the job required "capacity and intelligence far beyond those of any modern Bantu people," and "it is a well-accepted fact that the negroid brain never could be capable of taking the initiative in work of such intricate nature."[20]

In fact, these reasoners have used a "heads I win, tails you lose" argument. While some have averred that the Bantu could not have built Zimbabwe because Negroes are too stupid, Miss Caton-Thompson said that the queer architecture of Zimbabwe proved that it *was* built by the Bantu, because it was the product of "infantile, pre-logical minds."

On the other hand, Negro writers and those who sympathize with Negroes have been equally eager to overstate their case. They have not only assumed that the Bantu built Zimbabwe, but also that the Bantu were truly civilized before the whites arrived. They write as if the court of the Monomotapa, with its human sacrifices and man-eating bodyguard, were just a sunburnt version of the courts of Elizabeth I or Louis XIV. By all reasonable definitions the South African Bantu were barbarians, albeit no more barbarous than the builders of Troy II—or those of Stonehenge, from whom the majority of my readers are descended.

All prejudices aside, what *do* we know about the intelligence of the different races of man? Not much. That is why people get so heated about the subject; the less they know, the more pugnacious they are.

Intelligence is a vague term meaning mental power, just as "strength" means physical power. We can often say that one man is more intelligent than another, just as we can often say that one man is stronger than another. But it is hard to measure these qualities exactly. You cannot measure a man's over-all "strength" on any one standard scale. You can measure his separate physical powers, such as his ability to run, jump, or lift weights. A man who is good at one of these may be poor at another. So "strength" is not one ability but many, which can be combined in any of an infinite number of ways.

The same with intelligence. One man may be a precise accountant, another a shrewd lawyer, and a third a creative artist. But there is no way to compare John's success as a chess player with William's success as a politician to tell which is the more intelligent.

Intelligence tests measure single mental powers, such as the ability to handle words and numbers and to solve simple puzzles. Such tests are useful when given to people of the same cultural group. But these tests do not work with people of strikingly different backgrounds. We cannot expect a tribesman, however gifted, who has never seen a pencil or paper to score well on a written test. On the other hand, a child from a hunting tribe can beat civilized children all hollow in a test that calls for knowledge of animal footprints.

Language, work habits, aims in life, manners, diet, tradition, and experience all affect the way one thinks: And, when we try to test people of different races, we cannot eliminate all these factors. No test has been found that ignores the effects of environment and measures only a man's inherent mental qualities.

Some people, wishing to prove the Caucasoid race superior to the Negroid, point out the backwardness of African Negroes before the coming of the whites. As we have seen, this cultural backwardness can be explained on grounds other than intelligence. The Sahara Desert isolated the small, thinly spread Negroid population from the currents of Old World culture, just as the oceans isolated the Pacific Islanders. Having no contact with European ideas and techniques during the many centuries when European civilization was arising, the Africans could not be expected to develop in a European manner.

Some people, on the other hand, assert that all races are exactly equal in intelligence. Although this idea is a canonical Marxist dogma and a handy political slogan, it has no scientific basis either.

Few have ever argued that Negroids are inherently more intelligent than Caucasoids. But this concept is just as reasonable as the other two. In fact, one can make out a good *a priori* argument why this might be so: All species are subject to the force of heredity called degenerative mutation pressure. Hence every species tends to deteriorate—that is, to lose organs and abilities. In a wild state, however, selection naturally eliminates these defectives as they appear.

In civilization, however, people with defects, provided the flaws are not too severe, can live and breed along with the rest. Therefore, civilized races tend to degenerate. Thus the peoples who have been civilized the longest, such as the Near Easterners, the Chinese, and the Europeans, have probably degenerated the most; while those who live the most primitive lives, like Pygmies and Papuans, may prove the soundest of mind and body.

This, too, is mere speculation. If anybody ever devises a test that measures inherent mental powers regardless of culture and environment, it might well uncover mental differences among the races. It is anybody's guess as to which race would score best on which test. Perhaps different races would excel in different mental abilities. From such inconclusive evidence as does exist, our own guess, for whatever it may be worth, is that, while racial differences in intelligence may indeed exist, differences among individuals within any one race are much greater than average differences among races. And, given the right circumstances, men of any living race could have built Zimbabwe.

Who *did* build Zimbabwe? The answer is that we don't know. There is, however, a hint in the skeletons dug up, not at Zimbabwe itself, but at other Rhodesian ruins. Whereas some of these skeletons are plainly Negroid, a number show Hottentot (or at least "Bushmanoid") affinities. Unfortunately, bones do not keep well in Rhodesia's acid soil.

We may discard ideas of Ophir and Punt in Rhodesia, because there are better reasons for thinking that Ophir was Eritrea—the home of the modern Afara—and Punt was Somaliland farther south. No pre-Christian relics have been found at Zimbabwe, so it cannot have been so ancient as all that. No inscriptions have been found to link it with the pre-Muslim Arabs, who were a great people for chiseling their records in stone.

What may have happened—combining the results of archaeology with native traditions—is this. About +V or +VI, a migration took place, southward along the East African parkland to Rhodesia. The migrants were Negroid, but just what kind of Negro we cannot tell. They may have been Erythriotes. The tenth-century Arab geographer Mas'ûdi said that a tribe of "Abyssinians" was mining gold in South Africa. Most Abyssinians are of the Erythriotic type, with a touch of Arab; for Arab adventurers once set up a kingdom at

Axum in the northern Abyssinian highlands, and in +IV this power overthrew the ancient kingdom of Kush. So there may be a little something—though not very much—to the "Semitic" theories of Zimbabwe after all.

The migrants settled in Rhodesia among the Hottentots, then still in the hunting and food-gathering stage. They probably fought the Hottentots, mastered them, mixed with them, and taught them their own peasant culture with its stone-walled farmsteads, herds of longhorned cattle, vegetable gardens, cloth, and iron. The resulting mixed people built the first stone structures in Rhodesia, including Zimbabwe. The Elliptical Building was probably a royal compound, divided into compartments for the king's cattle, women, and servants; or a combination of compound and temple. The king lived in a thatched hut like those of his subjects, but larger. The Valley Ruins were the compounds of subordinate chiefs, and the Acropolis was a fortress.

Meanwhile Asian traders—Arabs, Persians, and perhaps Indians—were extending trading posts down the coast. The influence of these settlements on the inland peoples was slight at first. Later, by Mas'ûdi's time, it became strong enough to carry Arab and Persian glassware and Chinese porcelain to the inland centers. Whether the African migrants mined gold right from the start—whether, in fact, they were initially drawn to Rhodesia by its gold—or whether they first learned the value of gold from the oriental traders of the coast, several centuries after their first arrival, is an as yet unsettled question.

Time passed, and the waves of migration from the north continued. One of the last and largest waves, arriving in +XIII and +XIV, came from the Congo to the northwest. Hence the old Hottentot or "Bushmanoid" strain disappeared as a result of slaughter in battle and dilution by interbreeding, and the Bantu-speaking Forest Negro type became dominant in Rhodesia. Perhaps Zimbabwe and other centers were several times abandoned and later reoccupied, during one period by the Monomotapas.

Later occupants rebuilt parts of the structures. Building was active in +XVII, and the last rebuilding at Zimbabwe may have taken place as late as +XVIII. On the whole, the native Rhodesians' building techniques improved during the thousand years or so that they practiced them. About 1830, Zimbabwe was sacked and the last of the BaRozwi Mambos was slain (not at Zimbabwe but at his capital a hundred miles to the northwest) by an invading horde of WaNgoni from Zululand to the south. After that, Zimbabwe was for practical purposes abandoned, although the local tribes made some weak attempts to keep up the religious cult that had centered there, down to the arrival of the whites.

This is about all we can surmise about Zimbabwe. Intensive archaeological research in East Africa, during the next few decades, may clear up many doubtful points about these migrants and migrations. Meanwhile, as Miss Caton-Thompson says: "Zimbabwe is a mystery which lies in the still pulsating heart of native Africa."[21] Its brooding presence testifies that the men of Negro Africa, like those of other regions, could, even before they had attained to writing and cities, rear mighty monuments, which amaze and perplex the peoples of later times.

# VII
# Tintagel and the
# Table Round

O brother, had you known our mighty hall,
Which Merlin built for Arthur long ago!
For all the sacred mount of Camelot,
And all the dim rich city, roof by roof,
Tower after tower, spire beyond spire,
By grove, and garden-lawn, and rushing brook,
Climbs to the mighty hall that Merlin built.
                                    *Tennyson*

From the northern coast of Cornwall—that wedge-shaped peninsula which thrusts out westward from southern England—juts a rocky cape called Tintagel Head. On the narrow saddle of land that joins Tintagel Head to the mainland rise the ruins of Tintagel Castle. The sea has undermined the cliffs on either side, almost sundering the headland from the shore, so that most of the castle is no more. Some rough walls, made of slabs of slate set in mortar and perched above dizzy drops to the sea-washed rocks below, still survive at either end of the saddle. On the landward side stand the remains of a keep, made of more solid stonework.

Despite the hordes of visitors that swarm about Tintagel, braving frequent downpours, it is a site of wildly romantic beauty. The rolling Cornish plateau, covered with grass of emerald green and splotched with purple patches of heather, ends in a cliff, over which a small stream, Valentine's Brook, tumbles in a graceful waterfall. Along the beach, huge sea caves yawn at the foot of the cliffs; while high overhead the ruined castle thrusts jagged walls blackly against the cloud-swarming sky.

This very ruinous ruin is fraught with legend. Local folk used to say that, twice a year, the castle vanished. And, if your imagination be keen enough, you can still hear—over the sigh of the surf, the mutter of the waterfall, and the squealing cries of the gulls—the clang of armor, the blare of trumpets, and the neighing of knightly stallions. For Tintagel Castle, legends say, is the birthplace of King Arthur.

Almost every English-speaking person has heard of King Arthur and his Knights of the Table Round. Hundreds of stories, poems, and plays have been written about them. Motion pictures have been based upon them. Men are still named Arthur, Lancelot, and Percival after them.

For all of that, few could tell you when Arthur lived, or even whether he was a real man. What is the true story of King Arthur and his knights?

If we patch together the many and often inconsistent legends, we have the following fabric of a tale: In early +V, after the Romans withdrew their legions from Britain—at that time one of the Roman Empire's most prosperous provinces—the native Celtic chieftains set themselves up as petty kings. Then Irish from the west, Picts and Scots from the north, and Germans from across the sea assailed the land. The Germans included Saxons from Germany proper, Angles and Jutes from Denmark, and Franks from the Netherlands. Demilitarized by the long Roman peace, the Britons could do little to stop the barbarians.

The British king, Vortigern, invited in the Saxons from Germany, under their chiefs, Hengist and Horsa, to protect the Britons against the other barbarians. Although Vortigern married Hengist's daughter Rowena, strife soon arose between the Britons and the Saxon mercenaries. To provide for his own safety, King Vortigern began to build a tower to which he could flee if things got out of hand. But every night the masonry was swallowed up. To stop this mysterious engulfment, Vortigern's wizards told him:

"You must find a child born without a father, put him to death, and sprinkle with his blood the ground on which the citadel is to be built, or you will never accomplish your purpose."[1]

At Carmarthen in Wales, the king's messengers found a boy, Merlin Ambrosius, whose mother was the daughter of the king of Demetia[2] but whose father was a spirit who had visited the girl in the form of a beautiful man. At Vortigern's court, young Merlin, learning what fate was in store for him, demanded that Vortigern's magicians tell what it was under the foundation that made the stones disappear. When they could not do this, Merlin explained that if the workmen dug down they would discover two stones. Each stone, when broken open, would be found to contain a dragon.

This was done. The dragons awoke, fought, and fled, the white one pursuing the red. Then Merlin uttered a long prophecy, in which he foretold the conquest of the Britons, symbolized by the red dragon, by the Saxons, represented by the white.

Before the distracted Vortigern could decide what to do next, two Celtic chiefs—Aurelius Ambrosius and his brother Uther Pendragon—invaded Britain. They came from Brittany, the northwestern corner of France, which had come to be called "Little Britain" because so many Britons had fled thither from the barbarians. The brothers slew Vortigern. Merlin became adviser, first to Aurelius when he was crowned king; and later to Uther when a Saxon poisoned Aurelius and Uther succeeded to the throne.

One of Uther's vassals was Gorlois, duke of Cornwall. While Gorlois and his wife Igerna[3] were staying at Uther's court, Uther fell in love with the lady. Learning of this, the angry duke took his wife home to Tintagel Castle and defied orders to return.

Not to be denied, Uther followed with his army and besieged Igerna in the castle of Tintagel and Gorlois, at the same time, in another of the duke's strongholds.[4] As the sieges dragged on, Uther impatiently asked Merlin how to approach Igerna. By a magical ointment, Merlin changed Uther's shape to that of Gorlois, and the shapes of one of Uther's men and himself to those of two of Gorlois' retainers. Thus disguised they entered Tintagel, where Uther begat Arthur on the unsuspecting Igerna.

At about the same time, Duke Gorlois was killed in a skirmish with Uther's men. Thereupon Uther wedded Igerna. When their son Arthur was born, Uther placed the infant in Merlin's charge.

After Uther's death, young Arthur attended an assembly of lords of the realm at London. Here in a churchyard had appeared a stone, on which was mounted an anvil wherein a sword was fixed. The inscription on the stone said:

"Whoso pulleth out this sword of this stone and anvil, is rightwise king born of all England."[5]

Arthur handily pulled out the sword, proving himself the rightful king. Such magical swords are commonplace in myths and legends; for instance, the Norse hero Sigurd obtained his sword Gram by pulling it out of the oak Branstock, a feat no other man could do.

After that, Merlin advised Arthur by means of his prophecies and helped him to win his battles by magic. As is usually the case with legendary prophecies, however, nobody ever profited from them, not even the wizard himself. Merlin foretold that he would "die a shameful death and be put in the earth quick [alive],"[6] but that nothing could be done about it. And so it came to pass.

Arthur made his capital at Camelot. He extended his rule over most of Britain and married Guenevere,[7] daughter of a petty British king. This king, Leodegrance, gave Arthur a famous Round Table and a hundred knights. Since the table had room for 150, Arthur appointed fifty more knights to complete the tally of his companions.

Arthur campaigned victoriously against the Scots, the Irish, the Saxons, and the other British kings. When the Roman emperor Lucius Hiberius demanded tribute, Arthur invaded the Continent. Although Lucius led into battle the kings of such places as Libya, Ethiopia, Greece, and Babylon, Arthur slew him. Arthur was marching on Rome itself when news of trouble at home compelled his return to Britain.

After the Roman war, Arthur seems to have been too busy with administrative duties for knight-errantry, for most of the other Arthurian tales deal with the adventures of his knights. Arthur, like Charlemagne in the romances of his paladins, remains in the background as a noble but somewhat pallid figure. The other stories tell of Tristram and Isolt, of Gawain and the Green Knight, of Lancelot's love affair with Queen Guenevere, of the quest of the Holy Grail, and of much else besides.

One of the best-known of these tales—best-known because Wagner made an opera of it—is the story of Tristram and Isolt.[8] In the Arthurian legends, Tristram was the count of Lyonesse, a land west of Cornwall, which like Atlantis sank beneath the sea. Tristram was a vassal of his uncle, King Mark of Cornwall.

After many heroic deeds, Tristram fell in love with his uncle's betrothed, the young Irish princess Isolt, whom he was escorting to Mark's court. Tristram and Isolt eloped. After various twists and turns of plot, Tristram died of a wound he sustained in fighting in Brittany, and Isolt died of a broken heart.

While Arthur's knights were having these stirring adventures, Merlin fell in love with Nimuë,[9] a lady of Arthur's court, sometimes identified with the Lady of the Lake. Although she let Merlin squire her about the country, Nimuë really had no use for elderly egg-heads. "And always Merlin lay about the lady to have her maiden-hood, and she was ever passing weary of him, for she was afeared of him because he was a devil's son . . . And so on a time it hap-pened that Merlin showed her a rock whereas was a great wonder, and wrought by enchantment, that went under a great stone. So by her subtle working she made Merlin to go under the stone to let her wit of the marvels there, but she wrought so there for him that he came never out for all the craft he could do. And so she departed and left Merlin."[10]

At last a young kinsman of Arthur, Modred,[11] rebelled against the "stainless king." In the battle of Camlan, most of the surviving Knights of the Round Table perished. Arthur ran Modred through with a spear; but, before he died, Modred dealt Arthur a ghastly head wound. Arthur either died or was carried away in a boat by three mysterious women to the fairy island of Avalon, whence he will some day return.

Arthur's kinsman Constantine, meanwhile, succeeded him to the British throne and also fought victoriously. Yet by the end of +VII, the Saxons had overcome the British kingdoms and made them-selves lords of the land.

Such is the general outline of the Arthurian legends. However, each account has a different version of the various events. In some versions the infant Arthur, instead of being the son of Uther and Igerna, is cast ashore by the sea at Tintagel Castle and is rescued by Merlin.

Sometimes Modred rebels while Arthur is conquering the Ro-mans; sometimes not until long afterwards, to allow room for tales of knightly derring-do. Sometimes Arthur is neither dead nor con-valescing in Avalon, but instead is sleeping with his knights in a British cave, to awaken some time in the misty future.

Other Arthurian characters show similar variations. Lucius may be, not Roman Emperor, but "Procurator of the Republic." Some-times Merlin, instead of being shut up in a cave by one of his own spells turned against him, has retired to a castle of glass on an island in the sea. Sometimes his mistress, to make sure of always having him available, imprisons him in the forest of Broceliande, Brittany, in a tower magically disguised as a hawthorn bush. Other romancers caused Merlin to visit Julius Caesar, make a pilgrimage to Jerusalem, and study magic under Virgil, whom the storytellers transformed from the gentle poet of Mantua into a mighty wizard.

Spenser told of Merlin's building a brazen wall around his native Carmarthen. The arch-wizard summoned a multitude of demons, set them to work in a nearby cavern, prefabricating the wall, and ordered them not to stop until he gave them leave. Then he went off on his last journey with his *femme fatale*. Nobody has ever told the poor devils to quit, so that if you lay your ear to the ground in that region today,

> . . . such ghastly noyse of yron chaines
> And brasen Caudrons thou shalt rombling heare,
> Which thousand sprights with long enduring paines
> Doe tosse, that it will stonn thy feeble braines . . .[12]

In its day, the Arthurian cycle of legends had enormous influence. The volume of medieval Arthurian romances and of modern scholarly studies about them is staggering. Enough has been written about Arthur and his knights to fill a whole room in a library. Of the earlier writings, most are romances or long narrative poems. They are more like Homer's *Iliad*, Virgil's *Aeneid*, or Longfellow's *Hiawatha* than serious history. These works exist in English, Welsh, Latin, French, German, Italian, and Spanish. They cast such a spell that in +XIV, Edward III of England and Philip VI of France actually began construction of Round Tables of Arthurian dimensions.

Many places in England have been pointed out to tourists as the sites of Arthur's palace, his feats, his death, or his grave. Neolithic dolmens have been named Arthur's Chair, Table, or Stone.

Arthur's Round Table—or at least *a* large round table top—exists at Winchester Castle, which was originally built by William the Conqueror and which has often been altered, partly demolished, and rebuilt since then. The great hall of this castle—almost its only surviving part—is now used as a law court. Inside this building the table top in question, a disk of oaken planks 18 feet in diameter, hangs on the wall at the east end. It is painted in a spoke pattern, with twenty-four alternating bands of white (now darkened to yellow) and green. Around its rim are painted the names of Arthur and his more famous knights.

Furthermore, in 1191 the monks of Glastonbury Abbey, in Somerset, announced that they had discovered the graves and corpses of

Arthur and his queen, which they had reburied with due solemnity. They knew that one of these skeletons was that of Arthur, they said, by its great stature. This discovery helped mightily in gathering funds for rebuilding the Abbey after a great fire in 1184.

Today the Abbey is a group of disconnected pieces of ruined medieval Gothic walling, among which a rectangle is marked off on the velvety greensward as the site of Arthur's final resting place. Recent excavations support the monks' assertion that they had indeed dug up somebody, although their calling the bones "Arthur" seems to have been an act of faith. For aught anyone knows, the remains may have been those of one of Arthur's Saxon foes.

The Arthurian cycle has also been freely used by writers down to the present century. In 1831 the German dramatist K. L. Immermann wrote a celebrated poetic drama, *Merlin—Eine Mythe*. Later in the century, Alfred, Lord Tennyson composed a series of eloquent Arthurian poems, *The Idylls of the King*.

In accordance with the ideals of Tennyson's own time, however, the stories have been much toned down and cleaned up. Tennyson's heroes are much less lustful and violent than those of the earlier versions. No more do knights, in fits of irritation, smite off their ladies' heads. No Victorian gentleman like Tennyson would have thought of such a thing; albeit a real medieval knight, who was often a pretty ruffianly character, might have truly done it.

The Arthur of the earlier versions had the usual royal retinue of mistresses. He cheerfully begat Modred on his own half sister, the wife of King Lot of Orkney (thus combining incest with adultery). But Tennyson's Arthur, on learning of Guenevere's infidelity, plaintively moans: "I was ever virgin save for thee,"[13] a condition as likely in a real sixth-century king—usually a bit of a brigand by our standards as one of the miracles with which the saints' lives of that period are replete.

Later still, Mark Twain composed a burlesque on all chivalric romance, *A Connecticut Yankee at King Arthur's Court* (1889). Twentieth-century writers like John Erskine and T. H. White have also written Arthurian stories, either to entertain or to ride their special hobbies. As Twain used the legends to make fun of the church and of medieval romanticism, so White used them to denounce the modern world.

What facts, if any, underlie all this mass of fiction? For, as you can easily see, the Arthurian stories are mostly fairy tale. Spells like Merlin's do not work in real life, nor can real men perform the feats that Arthur and his knights are said to have done.

For example, in the Welsh versions of the cycle, Arthur's seneschal, Cei or Kay, can hold his breath for nine days and nights under water, stretch himself to the height of the tallest tree, and evaporate rain by his body heat before it touches him. Perhaps Kay is a kind of Celtic Vulcan, shrunken from a pagan god to a mortal in order to avoid the hostility of the Christian Church towards relics of heathen days.

However, as we have seen, there *is* a real Tintagel Castle. And there *was* a real Tristram who lived in Cornwall.

Most of Cornwall is a flattish, gently rolling land, cut up by stone walls into countless irregular green fields, variegated by an occasional patch of woodland. The narrow, winding roads are bordered by stone walls heaped over with earthen banks and covered by brush to a height of six or eight feet, so that the motorist in Cornwall gets the claustrophobic feeling of driving through an endless tunnel.

A mile and a half inland from the southern coast, near Fowey, stands a weathered seven-foot stone pillar. This shaft has been moved from where it was found lying and set up on a plinth in a grassy plot at the crossing of two busy roads, A3802 and B3269. On the north side of the pillar, a cross is rudely sculptured in relief. On the south side, a set of irregularly placed and barely discernible letters make the following sentence, in half-illiterate Latin:

CIRVSTAHS HIC IACIT CVNOWORI FILIVS

or, "Here lies Drustans, son of Cunomorus."

Now, Drustans is one form of the name Tristram.[14] From the life of a Dark Age saint named Paul Aurelius, we learn that there was a king of Cornwall named Marcus Quonomorius. Evidently this Marcus Quonomorius or Cunomorus was the real-life original of the Arthurian King Mark, while his son Drustans was the original of Mark's nephew Tristram.

A couple of miles north of Drustans' gravestone is a set of circular ditches and ramparts, overgrown with trees and brush, called Castle Dôr or Dore. To reach it, you have to set out from Tristram's stone with a British ordnance map and proceed by dead reckoning, because the ruin is not marked in any way. If you persist, you will find, opening on Road B3269, a one-lane dirt road. A few score feet along this track, you pass a gate in the wall. You enter this gate, cross a field (taking care not to damage the wheat) and there is Castle Dôr, thought to have been Cunomorus' capital of Lancien. It fits what we know of the typical fifth-century European "castle," which was merely a stout stone house on a mound, surrounded by a ditch and a stockade. Perhaps the real King Marcus and Drustans did quarrel over a woman; but, if so, it is not likely that we shall ever know the true details.

Furthermore, there were a real Aurelianus Ambrosius in +V and a real King Constantine of Cornwall in +VI. To understand the relationships of these leaders to Arthur, we must go over the surviving records of the period during which these men lived. Very scanty indeed are these records. If we put down all the facts that are definitely known about the political history of Britain during +V and the first half of +VI, they would fill but a few pages.

The earliest account of the Saxon conquest is Gildas' *Destruction and Conquest of Britain*. Gildas, a Breton monk, wrote about at the middle of +VI. The work is a sermon rather than a history, in which Gildas heatedly denounces the British kings of his own time. He castigates them mainly for violating the Christian ideals of sexual morality, which to a Dark Age priest were more important than the fall of empires. Nevertheless, Gildas lived less than a century after the events he told about and may have known people who actually had seen some of them.

According to Gildas, a British king, Guthrigern, invited the Saxons in to fight the other barbarian invaders; but the Saxons turned on their employers and laid waste their country. From Gildas' somewhat vague references to time, scholars agree that he means that the Saxons arrived on or about | 449. At last the Britons,

> . . . that they might not be brought to utter destruction, took arms under the conduct of Ambrosius Aurelianus, a modest man, who of all the Roman nation was then alone in the confusion of this troubled period by chance left alive. His parents, who for their merit were adorned with the purple, had been slain in these same broils, and now his progeny in these our days, although shamefully degenerated from the worthiness of their ancestors, provoke to battle their cruel conquerors, and by the goodness of our Lord obtain the victory.

147

After this, sometimes our countrymen, sometimes the enemy, won the field, to the end that our Lord might in this land try after his accustomed manner these his Israelites, whether they loved him or not, until the year of the siege of Badon Hill, when took place also the last almost, though not the least slaughter of our cruel foes, which was (as I am sure) forty-four years and one month [or: is reckoned the forty-fourth (allowing for one month)] and also the year of my birth.[15]

From various indications—uncertain because of the ambiguities of Gildas' Latin—it has been calculated that he meant that Ambrosius' victory took place about +455 or +456. This was followed by a period of varying fortunes until the Britons gained another great victory at Badon Hill about +500. Nobody knows, although many have guessed, where Badon Hill stood. Gildas says nothing about the Saxon chiefs Hengist and Horsa, or about Arthur, Merlin, Lancelot, Guenevere, or Camelot.

In the first third of +VIII, the English monk Bede[16] penned a *History of the Church of England*. Being English—that is, a descendant of the German barbarians who had conquered Britain—Bede took a poor view of the Britons, holding them to be a sinful and cowardly lot. This is probably unfair. From the scanty evidence, it seems as though the Britons put up a stouter fight against the barbarians than the people of many other parts of the Roman Empire. But they could not win, because they were assailed from all directions at once and cut off from Rome by the barbarian conquest of Gaul.

Anyway, Bede told how the British king "Vurtigern" invited in the Saxons:

The first captains of the strangers are said to have been two brothers, Hengist and Horsa; of the which, Horsa being slain in battle with the Britons was buried in the east part of Kent, where his tomb bearing his name is yet to show. And they were sons of Wictgils, whose father was Witta, whose father was Wecta, whose father was Woden, of whose issue the royal house of many provinces had their original.[17]

Bede quotes Gildas word for word about the recovery of the Britons under Ambrosius Aurelianus and their overthrow of the Saxons at Badon Hill forty-four years later.

1. The Sphinx and the great Pyramid of Cheops

2. Stonehenge, central entrance looking south-west

3. The walls of Troy

4. Zimbabwe ruins

5. Tintagel Castle

6. The Bayon Temple, Angkor

7. A Mayan pyramid at Tikal under reconstruction by the University of Pennsylvania as seen from the pyramid opposite

8. Statues outside the crater of Rano Raraku, Easter Island

Hengist's great-great-grandfather Woden is of course a god, the Teutonic Jupiter. Chiefs like Hengist usually traced their descent from a god, just as Alexander traced his from Thetis and Caesar his from Venus.

So far, we can say that Vortigern and Ambrosius are almost certainly historical, and Hengist and Horsa probably so. Some Arthurian students object that Bede's account of the Saxon conquest fails to jibe with archaeological records. Therefore, they say, he cannot be deemed very trustworthy.

Be that as it may, there is no mention of Arthur until we come to Nennius. About +800, plus or minus a few decades, Nennius wrote, or compiled from older records, a *History of the Britons*. This work is such a mass of miracles and anachronisms that it is hard to take it seriously.

For that matter, Gildas, Bede, and Nennius all leave much to be desired as historians. They are much more interested in affairs of the next world than in those of this. Hence they give far more space to biblical prophecies, denunciations of heresy, and the adventures of St. Germanus on his mission to Britain than they do to the rise and fall of mundane kingdoms.

However, Nennius put into the story several elements that became part of the Arthurian legend cycle. According to Nennius, Britain was first settled by Brutus, a grandson of Aeneas[18] the Trojan hero. Brutus founded a British kingdom just as Aeneas, in Virgil's *Aeneid*, had laid the foundations of Rome. Brutus is an "eponymous hero." That is, he is a fictional character invented to account for the name of the British nation, as Hellēn was said to be the forebear of the Hellenes and Israel of the Israelites.

Although he draws upon Gildas, Nennius also plays fast and loose with his source. He reduces Gildas' Ambrosius Aurelianus to a brief mention of a "King Ambrosius." On the other hand, the victories of Ambrosius over the Saxons are credited to Vortimer, an alleged son of Vortigern, and to St. Germanus, who defeated the savage foe by prayers and hymns alone.

Nennius also tells the story of the crumbling tower. King Vortigern's messengers find the boy Ambrosius, who seems not to be the king of that name, and who reveals an underground pool containing a pair of prophetic serpents.

Finally, Nennius tells us that, after the time of Vortigern, the Saxons increased their pressure. "Then Arthur fought against them in these days, with the kings of the Britons, but he himself was the commander-in-chief." Nennius lists twelve battles, of which "The twelfth was the battle of Mount Badon, in which in one day 940 men fell at one onset of Arthur; and nobody overthrew them but he himself alone, and he stood out as the victor in all battles."[19]

This is the first mention of Arthur in any surviving source. The next addition to the Arthurian cast of characters comes from the *Annales Cambriae* or Welsh Annals, compiled about +995. The *Annales* say:

"Year [+518]. The battle of Badon, wherein Arthur carried the cross of Our Lord Jesus Christ for three days and three nights on his shoulder, and the Britons were victors.

"Year [+539]. The battle of Camlann, wherein Arthur and Medraut perished; and there was death in Britain and Ireland."

Since Medraut—our old acquaintance Modred or Mordred—is not mentioned by any earlier source, we may suppose that the *Annales* got the name from some other document, now lost. The same applies to the battle of Camlann, often identified with Camelford on the Camel River in Cornwall.

The *Anglo-Saxon Chronicles,* which were being collected about the same time, say nothing about Arthur or any other British leader. They do tell about Hengist and Horsa, about Hengist's son Æsc, and the later Saxon chieftains Ælla, Cerdic, and Cynric, who resumed the march of conquest after Ambrosius and the supposed Arthur had checked it.

If we agree that Ambrosius lived, what about Arthur? There are three groups of opinions about Arthur.

One opinion, that of Lord Raglan and some others, is that Arthur is a purely fictional character; there never was any such leader against the Saxons. They say either that the battle of Mount Badon never occurred; or (by a possible alternative translation of Gildas) it happened in the middle of +V, not at the beginning of +VI, and the British commander was not Arthur but Ambrosius Aurelianus.

According to this doctrine, Gildas' Ambrose Aurelian, in later writings, fissioned like an ameba into three literary characters. One is Nennius' "King Ambrosius." One is the prophetic boy Ambrosius. And the third is King Arthur. The warlike deeds of the original Ambrosius Aurelianus were taken away from him, grossly inflated, and foisted upon this fictional character, Arthur, whose presence in Nennius' work is probably an addition to the manuscript by a later hand.

And whence came Arthur? The name is that, not of a mortal man, but of a god. The pre-Christian Celts worshiped a god called Artur by the Irish and Artaius by the Gauls. The name has been variously connected with words for "to plow" (Latin, *arare*), which makes him a god of agriculture; for "bear" (Greek, *arktos*) which makes him a bear god; for "black," which makes him a raven god; and so on. In any case Arthur is, like many other heroes, merely a pagan god transformed into a fictional mortal, with the deeds of some real men attributed to him.

Similar treatment is also accorded other characters in the Arthurian cycle. Thus Gawain is said to be the British version of the Irish Cuchulainn. Modred may be the Irish god Mider. King Lot of Orkney may be the Welsh Lludd, another version of whom is the Irish Nuada of the Silver Hand. Lancelot has been derived from an Irish deity with the awesome name of Lugh Loinnbheimionach. They can all be traced back to assorted Celtic sun gods, war gods, culture heroes, and other supernatural beings.

On the other hand, Arthurian characters can just as easily be traced to Roman origins. Thus Kay may be derived from Gaius, Uther from Eutherius, and so on. This brings us to a second theory: that "Arthur" comes from the Roman clan name Artorius. The Roman writers Juvenal and Tacitus mention this name, although the people they refer to had no connection with Britain.

It is true that there was an eminent Roman soldier of +II, Lucius Artorius Castus. His career is known from two inscriptions found in Dalmatia, whither Castus retired in old age and whence he probably came originally. After serving in various legions and rising to *praefectus* or brigadier, Castus was stationed in Britain. While there, he led an expedition to Gaul to put down a rebellion among the natives of Armorica, the land later called Brittany. This expedition could form the basis for the later legend of Arthur's invasion of the Continent and defeat of the Romans.

The third opinion, held by the largest number of scholars, is that there really was an Arthur, who did fight the Saxons around +500, even though he may have been later credited with the deeds of other heroes and the attributes of gods. Of course, nobody nowadays believes that Arthur slew any 940 foes singlehanded in one grand charge. This argument runs thus: Gildas clearly indicates a victory over the Saxons about +500; some such victory there must have been, or the Saxons would have conquered Britain earlier than they did. The Britons must have had a general at this battle. And there is no good reason why this general could not have been named Arthur or Artorius. Arthur, if not a common Celtic name, was not unknown. If, on the other hand, the name was Artorius, the man could be a member of the same clan as Lucius Artorius Castus and perhaps Castus' descendant.

Like Ambrosius Aurelianus before him, Arthur was not a king at the time of the battle. He was, instead, a *dux bellorum*, a war leader or commander-in-chief, chosen by the jealous, bickering Celtic kinglets in preference to letting one of their own number boss the others.

It is possible that either Ambrosius, or Arthur, or both, seized a throne after their victories. Some scholars have worked out a possible course of events in detail. They infer that Arthur seized the throne of Cornwall from the family of Modred; that, after Arthur and Modred fell at Camlann, Arthur's son Constantine kept the throne; and that Constantine's murder of two princes, for which Gildas denounced the Cornish king, was in fact the murder of Modred's sons.

One scholar, Foord, worked out a pedigree for a family of Aurelii who, he thought, were leaders among the Roman Britons for two centuries, from +380 to +580. By gathering every scrap of evidence and wringing every possible inference out of it, Foord compiled the following chronicle of the fall of Britain:

+343 to +400: Roman troops repulse repeated raids on Britain by Irish, Picts, Saxons, and Franks.

+407: Emperor Constantinus III withdraws troops from Britain for use in a Roman civil war.

+409 to +415: Barbarians raid Britain again. The Britons repulse them. Emperor Honorius sends word that the Britons will have to fend for themselves hereafter.

+417: Emperor Constantius sends a legion to Britain, with whose help the barbarians are again driven off.

+424 to +439: Roman forces are again withdrawn. Barbarian raids continue. Roman forces return to Britain. St. Germanus visits Britain and routs barbarian raiders by leading the Britons in a surprise attack: the so-called "Hallelujah battle," which hagiographers later transform into a miraculous victory. A Romano-British noble named Aurelius raises a regiment of armored cavalry, one of six such regiments.

+440 to +446: Roman forces are withdrawn from Britain for the last time to cope with the Vandals in the Mediterranean. Barbarians raid Britain again. Aurelius dies in this invasion, leaving a son named Aurelius Ambrosius. Both Aurelii probably bear, at one time or another, a Roman title of Comes (Count) or Vicarius of Britain.

+447 to +460: On the Continent, the conquests of Attila the Hun incite more German tribesmen, fleeing from the dreaded Mongolian horse-archers, to migrate to Britain. Vortigern, a Welsh king, comes into conflict with Aurelius Ambrosius. The latter dies about +447, leaving a son named Aurelius Ambrosius but commonly called Ambrosius Aurelianus, and another son named Aurelius Eutherius ("Uther"). Vortigern lets Hengist and Horsa settle their Germans in eastern Kent in return for a promise of military assistance. The Saxons revolt. Vortigern is in Wales, but his sons Vortimer and Categirn drive the Saxons out of Britain. In the fighting, Categirn and Horsa are slain. Vortimer dies, and Hengist comes back with more warriors. Hengist lures Vortigern and his nobles to a parley, massacres the nobles, and captures Vortigern. The latter escapes or is released, flees back to Wales, and dies under obscure circumstances. Thus the Saxons conquer and settle large areas of southern Britain.

+465 to +489: Ambrosius Aurelianus rises to power among the Britons and (probably calling himself by the Roman title of Patrician) drives the Saxons back to the extreme southeast. He dies and is succeeded by his brother Eutherius.

+491 to +500: The Saxons again expand their territories until Artorius ("Arthur"), probably a descendant of Artorius Castus, is appointed British commander-in-chief and defeats the Saxons in several battles. Artorius dies in early +VI.

+542 to +560: After several quiet decades, Aurelius Caninus, a great-grandson of Aurelianus, becomes king of Britain. The Saxons resume their advance.

+565 to +582: A son of Aurelius Caninus, Aurelius Candidianus, now rules Britain. The Saxons defeat the Britons at Bedford, utterly crush them at the battle of Deorham, and occupy all Britain save Cornwall, Wales, and Cumberland.

The Saxons killed many Britons in the areas they settled but did not, in most of these areas, exterminate them, as is shown by the persistence of Roman place names down to modern times. On the other hand, they became more numerous than the Britons in these regions, so that their language replaced both Latin and Celtic.

Roman culture almost completely disappeared. Romanized Britons, who had formed the ruling class in the South and East, fled or turned barbarian in self-defense. The surviving peasantry, who had been reduced to serfdom by the laws of the emperor Diocletianus and his successors, continued their lives of grinding toil and silent poverty, caring little whether their overlords were Romano-Britons or Anglo-Saxons.

Meanwhile, the Celtic chieftains of the West and North, who had never absorbed much Roman culture, continued their old high-spirited, disorderly ways. Although they could fight fiercely, they could not combine against the Germans because of the insensate Celtic spirit of factionalism and jealousy. One of their greatest leaders, Urien of Reged, was murdered in the hour of victory by a jealous kinsman.

These are all intriguing scholarly speculations, but they leave the big questions: How many of these scraps of evidence—casual remarks in scattered Dark Age writings—can we accept as facts? How many of Foord's ingenious inferences are sound? Alas! there seems to be no way to answer these questions. Some of the facts and inferences no doubt are right; others no doubt are wrong. But which is which, or what is the percentage of truth in this mass of myth and legend, tradition and hearsay, gossip and rumor, we cannot tell.

As to the three main theories of Arthur: The differences among them are not really so great as they sound. For nobody nowadays believes the more mythical and magical parts of the Arthurian story; while, on the other hand, all the debaters agree that the Britons must have had leaders in their desperate struggle with the Saxons, and that the deeds of some of these leaders furnished the basis for the story of Arthur in its simple Nennian form. It is a question of degree: how much of the legend—including the name of "Arthur"—is actually based upon real events of about +500?

The identity of Arthur is a fascinating subject for speculation. But you end up with the frustrated feeling that the key piece of the puzzle is missing and likely never to be found. If we only had one good manuscript, letter, or inscription from around +500, telling about the affairs of Britain, or one trustworthy pedigree of the kings of Cornwall . . . But we do not; and, until we do, there is no way to make a final choice among these different ideas of Arthur.

After the Welsh Annals, the story of Arthur soars off into the realms of faërie on the wings of the *History of the Kings of Britain*, by Geoffrey of Monmouth. Geoffrey, like Nennius, told in Latin how Aeneas' grandson Brutus led a band of followers to Britain. Of the twelve books of the *History*, Books VI to XI tell of Vortigern and Vortimer, Hengist and "Horsus," Uther and "Aurelius," Merlin and "Arturus."

Geoffrey claimed to have obtained his information from an old book of chronicles in the ancient British language. Some Arthurians do not think that any such book existed; others, that there was indeed a book of Breton legends on which Geoffrey drew. Some even profess to be able to recognize passages in certain medieval French manuscripts as quotations from this book.

Be that as it may, Geoffrey actually got his materials from many different sources. Besides Nennius, he used English chronicles, French romances, Greek myths, Jewish legends, Welsh traditions, peasant fairy tales, and his own lively imagination. Many of his stories seem to go back ultimately to Irish myths.

The old Celtic sea god Lêr or Llyr became, in Geoffrey's account, the pre-Roman British king Lear, about whom Shakespeare wrote one of his most famous plays. Cunobelin, the Belgic chieftain who ruled southeast Britain at the time of the Roman invasion of +43, became King Cymbeline, whose fictitious career, as told by Shakespeare, is quite unlike that of the real Cunobelin. Perhaps Geoffrey hoped by his writings to persuade the Normans, who in his day ruled and oppressed both the English Saxons and Geoffrey's fellow Welshmen, that the ancient Britons had been a noble and knightly race and that therefore the Welsh, their descendants, merited kind and decent treatment.

Geoffrey it was who added the name "Merlin" to Nennius' "Ambrosius" (the prophetic boy, not the general or king). Welsh poems of about Geoffrey's time mention a legendary Welsh bard named "Myrddin" or "Merdhin." Perhaps Geoffrey got the name from such a source, or perhaps the borrowing was the other way round.

Professor Chambers plausibly suggests that Merlin is the eponym of Carmarthen. In Roman times this town was called Maridunum, "sea fort," the first half of the name being Latin and the second Celtic. The Dark Age Britons called it "Myrddin" and added the Celtic prefix Cær-, "town," making the medieval Welsh form Cærmyrddin. Finally Geoffrey or one of his sources, ignorant of the true origin of the name, assumed that it meant "Myrddin's town" and invented a Myrddin or Merlin to play the role of this supposed local hero. Merlin, too, is a composite character. Part of him is Gildas' heroic Roman-British general, Ambrosius Aurelianus.

Another part comes from Celtic mythology. Besides his *History,* Geoffrey wrote a Latin poem, the *Life of Merlin.* The Merlin in this work is said by the author to be the same as that of the *History;* but he is actually quite different. He is described as a king of Demetia. Going mad when his brothers are slain in battle, Merlin retires to the Caledonian forests, leaving his wife with his sister, who is the wife of King Rydderch[20] of Strathclyde. Rydderch supposedly lived in late +VI, so that Merlin, to have been a contemporary both of Vortigern and of Rydderch, must have survived at least a century and a half:

Be that as it may, in the story, Merlin gradually recovers his senses. Although he sometimes visits the court of his brother-in-law to show off his prophetic powers, he ends his days as a hermit. This tale is one of a whole family of Celtic legends about a prophetic hermit.

Both Nennius and Geoffrey tell the tale of the digging up of two serpents or dragons, and of the prophecy that Merlin bases upon the conflict of these two supernatural reptiles. There is a difference, however. Nennius' Merlin foretells the reconquest of Britain by the Britons, whereas Geoffrey's Merlin foresees their utter defeat. The reason for this change is obvious. In Nennius' time the Britons were still holding out in the West—in Cornwall, Cambria, and Cumberland—so that one could plausibly imagine their making a comeback. But by the time of Geoffrey it was plain to be seen that the Saxons—not to mention their Norman overlords—were there to stay.

In the centuries following Geoffrey, many people took his work seriously as history; he was even cited in legal arguments. Eventually the English historian Ranulph Higden (+XIV) had the wit to ask how it was that the Roman, Saxon, and French historians knew nothing of their peoples' having been conquered by Arthur and his Britons?

In these centuries, also, several new Arthurian stories were composed, such as the *Brut* ("Brutus") of the Norman poet Wace (who invented the Table Round), the *Brut* of the English priest Layamon, and the *Merlin* of the French romancer Robert de Boron. After these writers came the huge mass of French and other Continental medieval Arthurian romances of which we have spoken.

The Arthurian cycle took the form we know today about three hundred years after Geoffrey, in Sir Thomas Malory's *Le Morte d'Arthur*. Malory was a country gentleman of Warwickshire, in central England. Besides his literary gifts he was a first-class rascal and ruffian who spent much of his life in jail for assaulting and robbing his neighbors and raping their wives. In the 1460s, while doing time for one of these offenses, he lightened the tedium of prison by combining several French versions of the Arthurian story and translating the result into English. In 1485, fourteen years after Sir Thomas' death, Caxton, the first printer in England, published the *Morte d'Arthur*.

It is hardly necessary to argue that the additions to the narrative by Malory and other medieval romancers are fictions. Much of Tristram's story is lifted from the myths of the ancient Greek hero Theseus, the legendary founder of Athens. There never was any such Roman emperor as the Lucius Hiberius slain by Arthur; he may be derived from the Celtic god Lug or Llwch.[21] The real Tintagel Castle was first built in +XIII by Reginald, Earl of Cornwall, on the foundations of an ancient Celtic monastery, whose ruins can be seen today strung out along the northern side of Tintagel Head.

The site of Camelot is unknown. Malory said it was Winchester, where the so-called "Round Table" hangs, near the great southern port of Southampton. But others have located Camelot in Cornwall, in Somerset, or in Wales.

As for the Round Table at Winchester, it is no older than +XII, and it was first painted in its present pattern about 1520; Henry VIII had it painted with the Tudor colors in order to show it to Emperor Charles V when the solemn Habsburg came to visit. So the Round Table is a fake antique, but so old a fake as to have become a valued antiquity in its own right.

An actual Round Table to seat 150—as legend says Arthur's table did—must needs be at least 125 feet in diameter. This would be a most impractical piece of furniture. It would seem that Edward III and Philip VI found this out, because they never completed either their Round Tables or the halls to contain them.

Our own suspicion is that Camelot is derived from Camulodunum, King Cunobelin's capital in +43. Camulodunum means "fort of Camulos," a Celtic war god. Perhaps the real Camulodunum furnished the basis for the fictional Camelot, just as the real L. Artorius Castus may have given us the fictional Arthur. And, if Castus' expedition against the Armoricans is the prototype of Arthur's invasion of the Continent, it is hard not to suspect that the war of Cunobelin (or his sons, for Cunobelin died at about that time) against the Roman invaders has become confused in the legends with the later British resistance to the Saxons.

True, Cunobelin's capital was at modern Colchester, at the extreme eastern end of southern Britain, whereas Arthur is supposed to have ruled in the southwest, in Cornwall and Devon. But there was at least one other Camulodunum in Britain, and the geography of legends can become quite scrambled in a few centuries. Witness the Irish legends of how the Emerald Isle was settled by such unlikely invaders as the Scythians of Greece and the Scots of Egypt. The names of Camulodunum, Camelot, Camlan, and the Camel River may all derive from the god Camulos, although the precise histories of these terms may never be known.

In Geoffrey and all the later medieval versions of the Arthurian story, fifth-century Britain is rife with dukes and counts, pages and squires, centuries before the feudal system came into being. King Arthur keeps a body of knights six hundred years before knighthood was invented. Statues, paintings, and movies show these knights as clattering about in steel plate armor, topped off by crested helms with movable visors, eight hundred years before armor of this kind was worn. In the real +V and +VI, western European warriors wore very little armor. What they had consisted of simple steel caps and shirts of chain or scale mail.

Crediting Arthurian Britain with feudalism, knighthood, and plate armor is like describing Geoffrey's contemporary, King Richard the Lion-Hearted, as having himself psychoanalyzed, holding a press conference, and then setting out on the Third Crusade with tanks and aircraft. After all, Richard is but little farther from us in time than Arthur was from Geoffrey.

All in all, the Arthurian legends do have some basis in history. There may even have been a real Arthur (or Artorius) who commanded the British hosts at Mount Badon, between +500 and +518. This question, however, cannot be settled with the evidence now at hand.

Once Nennius began to add legendary details to the plain statements of his sources, the Arthurian story attracted more and more fictional anecdotes and episodes, as a magnet draws iron filings. The process went on until the few facts became almost lost in the fiction. Hence the Arthurian romances of Malory and Tennyson have as much to do with history as would a story in which Napoleon, with the help of Santa Claus, crossed the Delaware to beat the Japanese at the battle of New Orleans, invented the automobile, and finally married Queen Victoria.

In fine, Arthurian Britain is not a real world at all. It is a mighty province of the continent of Imagination. But, realizing this, we can enjoy these lovely legends just as we can any other masterpiece of storytelling.

# VIII
# Angkor and the
# Golden Window

On every hand rose the grim relics of another, forgotten age:
huge broken pillars, thrusting up their jagged pinnacles into the
sky; long wavering lines of crumbling walls; fallen cyclopean
blocks of stone; shattered images, whose horrific features the
corroding winds and dust-storms had half erased. From horizon
to horizon no sign of life: only the sheer breath-taking sweep of
the desert, bisected by the wandering line of a long-dry river-
course; in the midst of that vastness the glimmering fangs of
the ruins, the columns standing up like broken masts of sunken
ships—all dominated by the towering ivory dome before which
Shevatas stood trembling.

*Howard*

On a day in February, 1860, a traveler issued from New Angkor in
the province of Battambang in the kingdom of Siam. Having set out
some weeks before from the town of Battambang, he had traveled
down the Battambang River to the place where several streams join
together to form the Tonle Sap, the second river of Cambodia.

Thirty-odd miles down the Tonle Sap, the river widens out into
an immense, shallow lake, coated with lily pads, lined with rattan
palms and the bone-white trunks of fromager trees, and called by
the same name as the river. In the summer wet season, excess water
from the Mekong River backs up into the lake, which expands to
cover an area larger than that of Lake Ontario. But this was the dry
season. Therefore the lake had shrunk to about the size of Great
Salt Lake, leaving huge expanses of dried, cracked mud.

After crossing the shrunken lake, the traveler ascended a small
tributary for a few miles, then traveled over a causeway to the
village of New Angkor. Somewhere along the way he had heard
rumors of vast ruined cities in the jungles north of the Tonle Sap.

There might be nothing to it, but the traveler meant to find out. So, as soon as he was up to it, he set out on the sandy path which, the local people said, led to the ruins.

The traveler was Henri Mouhot, a naturalist especially interested in tropical butterflies. A French Protestant from Montbéliard, near the Swiss border, married to an Englishwoman, he had been sent by the British Geographic and Zoological societies to brave swarms of mosquitoes and leeches on a scientific reconnaissance of Indo-China.

Mouhot does not tell us how he heard these rumors or how he felt about them. We may doubt that he showed much excitement. He seems to have been a competent, methodical, rather unimaginative man. While he got along with the Indo-Chinese well enough, his attitude towards them was the conventional one of a European of his time. He deplored the fact that they had "little idea of modesty. The men and women bathe together without any clothing." He was eager to see France, then waging a colonialist war in Cochin-China, extend its imperial rule over all these countries, to develop their resources and to impose upon them belief in the "true God" in place of their "false divinities."[1]

Picture him, then, striding along this dusty path in sweat-stained white jacket and trousers: an active, powerfully built man in his mid-thirties, bearded like an Assyrian grandee. When he pushed back his wide-brimmed hat to mop his face, he revealed a high-domed forehead with receding hair. Behind him trailed a French missionary in flapping robe and a gaggle of small, flat-faced, yellow-brown Indo-Chinese in loincloths. The two Frenchmen towered over their native attendants.

On all sides rose a dense, scrubby forest, spreading out across the wide, flat plain. When the men could see beyond the jungle, they noticed a low mountain range breaking the horizon to northward. Gorgeous butterflies flapped through the air, but for once Mouhot was not thinking of butterflies. Little yellow lizards scuttled out of the path. Gibbons and monkeys chattered in the treetops; flocks of parakeets rushed by, screeching. Vultures hung in the sky.

The path followed the course of the small stream, the Siemreap, on which stood New Angkor. The serpentine bed of the river crossed and recrossed the path many times. Perhaps the party saw the tracks of tiger or elephant; both beasts then abounded in the region and are not unknown there today.

After a two-hour hike, signs of tumbledown, man-made masonry began to appear among the tree trunks. Towers of sandstone blocks, intricately carved, loomed over the greenery. Mouhot arrived

> . . . at an esplanade about 9 metres wide by 27 long, parallel to the building. At each angle, at the extremity of the two longer sides, are two enormous lions, sculptured out of the rock, and forming, with the pedestals, only a single block. Four large flights of steps lead to the platform.
>
> From the north staircase, which faces the principal entrance, you skirt, in order to reach the latter, a causeway 230 metres in length by 9 in width, covered or paved with large slabs of stone, and supported by walls of great thickness. This causeway crosses a ditch 220 metres wide, which surrounds the building; the revetment, 3 metres high by 1 metre wide, is formed of ferruginous stone, with the exception of the top row, which is of free-stone, each block being of the same thickness as the wall . . .[2]

As far as Mouhot's eager eye could reach into the shadowy, silvan distances, there stretched megalithic walls bedight with sculptured reliefs in riotous profusion. Endless galleries bounded vast overgrown courtyards. Inside these galleries, clusters of bats hung from the tottering roofs. They squeaked angrily at the intruders before whirring away into deeper darkness.

Even a man of Mouhot's rather stolid temperament could not fail to feel the excitement of his discovery. The sight, he wrote, made the traveler "forget all the fatigues of the journey, filling him with admiration and delight, such as would be experienced on finding a verdant oasis in the desert. Suddenly, and as if by enchantment, he seems to be transported from barbarism to civilization, from profound darkness to light."[3]

Mouhot asked the Indo-Chinese about the city but got no trustworthy reply. "It is the work of giants," they told him. "It built itself." "It is the work of Pra-Eun, the king of the angels."[4]

Others said the buildings were the work of an ancient Cambodian king who contracted leprosy when the blood of a giant snake he was fighting sprayed on his skin. The king cured his affliction by a pilgrimage to India. They even pointed out the statue of the leper king.

For three weeks Mouhot lingered at "Ongcor" (as he spelled it), conscientiously sketching, measuring, and writing notes. The great temple on which he had stumbled, he learned, was but one of a vast congeries of ruins, spreading out into the jungle for miles in all directions.

Then Mouhot returned to Bangkok and set out northward into Laos. He had almost reached Luang Prabang, near the Chinese border, when "jungle fever" (malignant malaria) struck him down. In a few days, despite his stalwart frame, his abstemious habits, and his faith in his Calvinist God, he was dead. His brother assembled his journal and letters into a rather dry narrative of his travels.

Mouhot was not the first European to learn of Angkor. In 1604 a Portuguese priest, Quiroga de San Antonio, told about a brace of hunters who had seen such ruins in the jungle thirty-odd years before. In 1672 a French missionary, Chevreuil, spoke of such a place named "Onco."

Then for nearly two centuries Angkor lay deserted, save for the prowling leopard and the wandering native hunter, until Mouhot rediscovered it. His posthumous report sent other French explorers along his track: De Lagrée, Garnier, and in 1871 Delaporte, who came with a fully equipped expedition.

These visitors and others carried away many statues, stelae, and other parts of the ruins for private collections and European museums. The plundering continued until checked at the end of +XIX by the newly formed École Française d'Extrême-Orient.

This institution could not, however, fully protect the ruins so long as they lay in Siamese territory. For centuries the Thais of Siam and the Khmers[5] of Cambodia—the dominant ethnic groups in these two countries—had been warring, and the Thais had had the better of it. Therefore, the land around Angkor, once Cambodian, was now Siamese. As a result of these wars, this once densely peopled region had become almost uninhabited. The rancor engendered by these wars still smolders today and nullifies Western efforts to unite these countries against the aggression of Communist China.

Throughout +XIX, the Siamese watched with growing alarm as the British conquered Burma to the west and the French seized control of Tongking, Annam, and Cochin-China to the east. In the 1860s, the French used Cambodian fear of their ancient Siamese foes to persuade the king of Cambodia to accept a French protectorate. By every dodge and shift, the Siamese managed to avoid being altogether engulfed by their two mighty imperial neighbors. However, they had to yield parts of the Malay Peninsula to the British and several border provinces to the French.

In 1907, a new treaty restored to Siam some of the French-occupied territory in exchange for the province of Battambang, which included Angkor and which was ceded to Cambodia. Given a free hand at last, French archaeologists swarmed over the ruins, hacking away the jungle, putting fallen stones back in place ("anastylosis," archaeologists call the process), studying the many inscriptions, and so, little by little, solving the mystery of Angkor. But plenty of work remains to be done; merely keeping the jungle out of cleared sites is a Sisyphean task.

By the end of the First World War, the ruins had been cleared and restored to the point where they could become a tourist attraction. Since then a small but steady stream of tourists has trickled through the site. During the 1920s several rather gushy popular travel books were written about Angkor. Now, with the rise of world-wide air travel, only distance, warfare, and political instability hinder Angkor from becoming a tourist goal to rank with Pompeii and the Pyramids.

For decades, men wondered who built Angkor. The ruin looked like Cambodian work. But, when the French gained control of Cambodia, the Cambodians were not building any such vast stone structures. Nor did their own history say who built Angkor. The Chronicles of Cambodia, which had disappeared during the wars of +XVIII, were rewritten from memory early in +XIX. But these Chronicles began only in +XV, and their beginning is full of myth.

According to this myth, an Indian hero named Kambu Svayambhuva[6] wandered into a desert. There the Nagas, a race of genii in the form of seven-headed cobras, befriended him. Kambu wedded the Nagaraja's daughter, who considerately took human form for the occasion. The serpent king was so pleased by Kambu's description of his native India that he cast a magical spell, which turned his land, too, into a well-watered country. From Kambu and his serpent princess sprang the ruling house of the land, called Kambuja or Kambujadesa. "Cambodia" is merely a modern Latinized form of "Kambuja." Being immortal, the serpent princess never died. She made herself the permanent first wife of the Kambujan kings, who visited her nightly in the tower of the temple called the Phimeanakas.

Legends of heroes who mate with serpent princesses to found royal houses are widespread in Asia. Obviously, only a hero would undertake such a task. In this case, the legend conceals a grain of fact: that, long before the beginning of the Chronicles, Indians—adventurers, traders, and missionaries—came to Cambodia. They came by sea, because mountain chains made the country very hard to reach from the landward side. They gained control of the still barbarous Cambodians and imposed upon them a veneer of Indian civilization. Hence, from earliest times, the kings of Cambodia bore Indian names and put up inscriptions in the classical Indian Sanskrit language, while the common people continued to speak Khmer, a very different language remotely related to the many Malayan, Melanesian, and Polynesian tongues.

The early years of this century saw a lot of speculation and mystification about the builders of Angkor. Why had they walked out of their capital en masse, leaving it to the jungle? What became of them? Had they simply disappeared, or were the modern Cambodians their descendants? In the latter case, what had caused the downfall of the civilization these ruins mutely proclaim? Sir Osbert Sitwell suggested that the Angkorians' prosperity was based on the export of kingfisher plumes to China, and the kingdom fell when Chinese fashions changed. Others surmised that the proletariat had revolted, slain their overlords, and gone back to simple village life.

There has been a good deal of nonsense written about Angkor. The people of Angkor once built a number of temples in the form of a step pyramid with a shrine on top. These pyramid temples resembled the ziggurats of ancient Babylonia and, even more, the pyramid temples of the Mayas of Central America. Moreover, the Angkorians used a peculiar architectural feature also found among the Mayas: an ornamental wall, called a roof comb or ridge crest, placed on top of a building to carry sculpture and other ornamentation.

In the 1920s a group of amateur anthropologists, who came to be called Diffusionists, set forth the extreme view that human inventiveness is so rare that no invention could have independently been made twice over. They stated that all inventions and therefore all civilization must have developed from a single center.

The leading Diffusionist, the anatomist Sir Grafton Elliot Smith, traced all civilization back to Egypt, whence it was carried—said he and his followers—all over the world by sun-worshiping, gold-seeking Egyptians. Other Diffusionists preferred to find the source of enlightenment in India, Brazil, the Ohio Valley, the Arctic, or Atlantis. According to Smith, the Heliolithic Egyptians, spreading out from Egypt, first came to Mesopotamia, where they built or taught the natives to build ziggurats in imitation of their own pyramids. Later they repeated the performance in Cambodia, and finally in Central America, where they founded the Aztec and Mayan civilizations.

However, as the chronology of the Khmers and the Mayas became better known, it turned out that the Cambodian pyramids had all been built in a period of two centuries, from middle $+$X to middle $+$XII. The Mayas, on the other hand, began building temple pyramids about $+$V, several centuries *before* the earliest Cambodian pyramids. Therefore the Mayas could not, as the Diffusionists alleged, have built pyramids in imitation of those of Cambodia; for these did not yet exist.

Present informed opinion does not take the Diffusionist claims seriously. Instead, it holds that, while there has been a lot of diffusion of culture traits, there has also been a good deal of independent invention in different cultures. For example, whereas the American Indians adopted a few Old World inventions, like the bow (which diffused over from Asia about the beginning of the Christian Era), they themselves invented most of the distinctive traits of their native cultures.

While camping at Angkor in 1860, Mouhot, too, pondered these matters. He thought that the buildings might be as much as two thousand years old. But the stolid, sensible Henri was no mystifier. He said:

Knowledge of Sanscrit, of "Pali," and of some modern languages of Hindostan and Indo-China, would be the only means of arriving at the origin of the ancient people of Cambodia who have left all traces of their civilization, and that of their successors, who appear only to have known how to destroy, never to reconstruct. Until some learned archaeologist shall devote himself to this subject, it is not probable that aught but contradictory speculations will be promulgated. Some day, however, the truth will surely appear and put them all to flight.[7]

During the century since Mouhot wrote, many eminent French archaeologists, such as George Coedès, have applied themselves to this task. Little by little the history of the Khmer Empire of Angkor has come to light. There was no one big breakthrough, comparable to the decipherment of cuneiform writing. Instead, there has been a patient, unspectacular piling of fact on fact, and a correction of previous errors.

For example, one striking sight of Angkor is the Bayon: a square structure containing a great cluster of square towers, each having four huge faces, one on each side. Mouhot assumed that all such sculptures were representations of the Buddha. Later, the opinion prevailed that they depicted the Hindu god Shiva[8]; a popular book of the twenties on Angkor was called *Four Faces of Siva*. Later still it was thought that the faces were those of Vishnu, another member of the Hindu trinity. Now it seems that the faces represent the Buddhist divinity Lokeshvara.[9] The features, however, may be actually those of Jaya-Varman VII,[10] the king who built the temple about 1200 and who fancied himself a Living Buddha.

Whence came the information about this and other Khmer kings? Mostly from the inscriptions, in Sanskrit and Khmer, on hundreds of monuments in Cambodia. Nearly a thousand such inscriptions are on record, and most of them have been translated into French. In addition, many passages in Chinese, Hindu, and Muslim history shed light on the shape of things in Indo-China. China and India had long been civilized when the Indo-Chinese emerged from barbarism early in the Christian Era. Hence Indo-China became a cultural sink—that is, an area that received cultural influence from both of its mighty neighbors, but that never got far enough ahead of them to be able to radiate much culture back to them in its turn.

Although there are still many gaps in Khmer history and many doubtful points—especially during the earlier centuries—the outlines have now been well established. In sooth, there never was much real mystery about Angkor. There was only a problem, which could be solved and which to a large extent has been solved.

Let us survey the actual ruins of Angkor. The road first leads us to Angkor Wat, the funerary temple of Surya-Varman II, built in early +XII. This temple, connected with the worship of the Hindu god Vishnu, has been called "the largest religious edifice ever built by man,"[11] with the possible exception of another Cambodian temple, Banteay Chhmar, still in ruins. Angkor Wat covers an area of just under one square mile.

Next we see Angkor Thom,[12] a capital city in the form of a square about two miles on a side, which lies half a mile north of Angkor Wat, and which was built by Jaya-Varman VII in late +XII. It was the fifth capital city situated on this same site. The earlier cities had been built and then abandoned, leaving some of their temples of brick and stone to remain after the palaces and private houses of wood and bamboo had crumbled away. In Khmer days, Angkor Thom was called Yashodharapura; that is, King Yasho's City, after Yasho-Varman I, who built the first of these five capitals in late +XI.[13]

Then we come upon the Bayon, a great Buddhist temple, also built by Jaya-Varman VII, at the center of Angkor Thom. Although much smaller than Angkor Wat (nearly square like the other structures and about 650 yards around) it is the second largest building in the area. Crowded into its 56 acres were 54 great four-faced towers, many of which still stand. Like much late Khmer construction, it was built in a hasty and slipshod manner; hence, although decades younger than Angkor Wat, it is more dilapidated.

Returning to Angkor Wat, we traverse a thousand-foot causeway on the west side, the railings of which are a pair of endless sculptured nagas, or seven-headed cobras, rearing up to a height of 13 feet. We pass over a moat and under a great wall to find ourselves in an enormous square inclosure. Actually there are three concentric main structures, each in the form of a hollow square. The Khmers, loving squares and straight lines, shaped their public buildings into hollow squares, sometimes divided into four smaller squares by cruciform structures. These squares and sub-squares are made up of long galleries whose walls are covered with reliefs.

The builders erected towers at the center and on each corner of the large hollow squares. Each inclosure is terraced, so that each inner square is higher than the one surrounding it, giving the whole a slightly pyramidal form.

The towers of Angkor Wat take the form of lotus buds. The central and tallest tower—over 200 feet high—and the four towers of the innermost square are still in good shape. The towers at the corners of the intermediate square have lost their tapering, conical tops, while those of the outer square have practically disappeared.

The five central towers are said to symbolize the mythical Mount Meru (the Hindu Olympos) and its foothills.

Where the causeway enters the outer square through an ornate gateway, a vestibule of the same square-and-cross shape fills the space between the outer and intermediate squares. There were special entrances for chariots and elephants. Dignitaries dismounting from their elephants stepped off on a raised platform, as we do in getting off a train in a large railroad station.

As you walk around the galleries, disturbing the bats and the lizards, you have to step over two-foot-high stone door sills. These sills did not bother the Khmers, who walked on heavy teakwood floors, now vanished. Stairs are steep. Arches and vaults are of the corbeled type, made by overlapping each course of masonry over the course below until the stones meet at the top. Southeast Asia knew not the true or voussoir arch and vault until Muslims and Europeans brought them thither.

Reliefs are everywhere. Bare-breasted dancing girls cavort, kings review their soldiers, armies clash on land and sea, and the gods of Hinduism enact their immemorial myths.

On the east side, for instance, is shown the legend of the Churning of the Sea of Milk. Once the Three Worlds went into decline because of a curse. At Vishnu's advice, the gods and the demons formed an alliance. Using Mount Mandara as a churnstick and Vâsuki, the king of snakes and god of the waters, as the churn rope, they churned the Sea of Milk until it turned into the nectar of immortality, the goddess of wine, the Tree of Paradise, the moon, and many other delightful things . . .

I could go on at length about the wonders of Angkor: the three-headed elephants, which guard the gates of Angkor Thom; the thousand-foot terraces; the balustrades in the form of seven-headed serpents carried by rows of 8-foot squatting stone giants; the remains of earlier temples and cities in the area; the two rectangular reservoirs five miles long, called the East Baray and West Baray, which once flanked the city; the other canals, moats, and reservoirs. The immense waterworks, which irrigated rice fields for miles around, were actually a greater and more costly achievement than all the temples. It was customary to build a temple in connection with each reservoir. But you would soon become saturated and confused with detail. Possessing all these splendid structures, how came the Khmer empire to fall?

The first accounts of civilized life in Indo-China come from the Chinese. According to Chinese accounts, a kingdom they called Funan arose in +I, south of the Great Lake and in the Mekong Delta. Chinese writers tell of an enterprising young Hindu named Hun Tien—the Kauṇḍinya of Indian legends—who took ship for Funan, then ruled by a queen named Lyou Ye[14] or Willow Leaf. When Willow Leaf approached Kauṇḍinya's ship to attack it, Kauṇḍinya shot an arrow, which pierced Willow Leaf's war canoe from side to side. Having thus shown that he was a man to be reckoned with, Kauṇḍinya married Willow Leaf and became king of Funan.

At that time, the Funanese went completely naked, a custom which in that climate is not a bad idea. The scandalized Kauṇḍinya, however, insisted that his wife wear *something*. Thus the women of Funan took to wearing a strip of cloth around the middle. It took a command from a later king to make the men do likewise. Through the time of the Khmer Empire, however, men and women, high and low, went bare above the waist. Women's costume was a skimpy skirt; men's, a G-string. Not until modern times did the example of Siamese and Europeans persuade Cambodians to cover the upper body.

The Chinese found many Funanese customs barbarous. Trial was by ordeal. The accused had to carry a piece of red-hot metal, or pick something out of a boiling cauldron. If he was burned, he was presumed guilty and thrown to the crocodiles awaiting him in the moats of the cities and palaces.

On the other hand, women had a comparatively high position. The Indo-Chinese, like the Polynesians, took a permissive attitude towards sex. This has remained unchanged over the millennia. An eighteenth-century English diplomat posted to Indo-China complained that he could not enjoy a stroll in the evening because of the "horrible fornications" he was compelled to witness.

From the Funanese period a few small stone buildings, some statues, and the names of a few kings survive, although the history of the period is largely mythological. A faraway event brought prosperity to Funan. This was the rise of Malay piracy, which made the sea route from India to China so dangerous that most of the traffic shifted to a land route through Funan. In +120 a band of Greek and Roman acrobats and musicians passed over this route on their way to China; and in +160 a Roman embassy did likewise.

In +VI, the vassal state of Chenla revolted from Funanese rule and conquered its former masters. Now contemporary inscriptions appear. The names of kings are largely garnered from the genealogies that the later kings of Kambuja inscribed on their monuments. But, like many other pedigrees, these are probably as much fiction as fact; the more so because several kings were usurpers trying to legitimatize their rule. The kings of Chenla worshiped Shiva and persecuted rival sects. They also built sizable buildings, some of which still exist.

During +VIII, Chenla became divided into two kingdoms and then into smaller units. At the same time, a powerful empire arose among the Malays. Its leaders, as in Indo-China, were colonists and adventurers from India. The Indians claim this penetration of Indo-China and Indonesia was entirely peaceful. Well, maybe; but we have our doubts. Under the Shailendra[15] dynasty, the Malay Empire dominated Lower Chenla as a vassal. The ruler of this empire, called the King of the Mountain, reigned from Java.

One rash young king[16] of Lower Chenla, or Khmer as it was coming to be called, in a fit of jealous irritation told his minister: "I wish to see before me, on a plate, the head of the Maharaja, King of Zabag [Java]."

The minister nervously tried to shush his ruler, saying: "I do not wish, O King, that my sovereign should express such a desire. The people of Khmer and Zabag have never manifested hatred toward each other, either in words or in acts. Zabag has never done us any harm. It is a distant land . . . What the King has said should not be repeated."

Angrier than ever, the king raised his voice and repeated his wish for all the court to hear. The story soon came to the ears of the King of the Mountain, who told his minister:

"After the statement which this fool has made public, wishing to see my head on a plate because he is young and light, after the divulgation of his statement, it is necessary for me to act. To disregard his insults would be to harm myself, to debase myself and lower myself before him."

By a surprise attack, the King of the Mountain captured the Khmer capital and its king. When the prisoner was brought before him, the King of the Mountain said:

"You have manifested the desire to see before you my head on a plate; but if you had also wished to seize my country and my kingdom or only to ravage a part of it, I would have done the same to Khmer. As you have expressed only the first of these desires, I am going to apply to you the treatment you wished to apply to me and I will then return to my country, without taking anything belonging to Khmer . . . My victory will serve as a lesson to your successors; no one will be again tempted to undertake a task above his power nor desire more than the share given to him by destiny; one will consider himself fortunate to have health when he can enjoy it."[17]

So the King of the Mountain had the Khmer king's head cut off. Then he called the Khmer minister, praised him for having tried to moderate his king's conduct, and advised him to convene the royal council and choose a more sensible king.

The next ruler of Khmer was Jaya-Varman II, an able and long-lived king who in +802 declared his independence from Java. Thus began the Kambujan or Angkorian period of Cambodian history. From then on, Khmer kings were deified. Although Shaivism (worship of Shiva) was the state religion, Vaishnavism (worship of Vishnu), Buddhism, ancestor worship, and the veneration of a horde of petty godlets and demons also flourished under a rule of toleration. The state cult of Shaivism kept its place throughout the Angkor period, even though some later kings were personally Vaishnavites or Buddhists. As in ancient Egypt and Mesopotamia, much of the king's waking time was spent in religious rituals, wherein he urged and begged his fellow gods to favor the kingdom.

Each king built a special temple to house his linga,[18] the symbol of his authority. A linga is a pillar carved in the likeness of an erect phallus—conventionalized and decorated with reliefs but nonetheless perfectly recognizable. The record lingas, at Prasat Phnom Bok and Chok Gargyar, were about 14 feet tall. An inscription tells of a hundred-footer put up by Jaya-Varman IV in +X, but the object itself has vanished.

The linga is one of the forms under which Shiva is worshiped. Now that the kings were divine, the devout subject could worship both king and god at once in the fine frenzy of theological confusion dear to the Hinduist mind. One can imagine how horrified Henri Mouhot would have been to learn of this practice.

Yasho-Varman I, who reigned from +889 to +900, built the first of the cities named Yashodharapura, at the site now called Angkor Thom. He also dug the East Baray and built a temple, the Phnom

Bakheng, atop a nearby hill. In later times, Buddhists largely destroyed this temple to make room for a colossal statue of the reclining Buddha. For a time, Yasho-Varman I was credited with having also built Angkor Wat and the Bayon. This was a mistake, caused by the fact that some of Yasho-Varman's boastful inscriptions were among the first to be discovered and translated.

We need not list all the kings who ruled Kambuja during the next five centuries, or catalogue the temples they built. By our standards the government of this faery kingdom would seem intolerably cruel, corrupt, and despotic; but that is the kind of government that most Asians had to put up with before modern times. Nineteenth-century European imperialists were not being entirely hypocritical when they insisted that they were conquering the Asian and African natives for the natives' own good.

Nor need we tell of the Khmer kings' endless wars with the Chams of Champa to the east, who worshiped a rat god and whose warriors wore flower-shaped helmets. The Khmer armies, besides the usual pikemen, archers, horsemen, and chariots, included elephants with catapults mounted on their backs.

Surya-Varman I (reigned 1006 to 1050) dug the West Baray and rebuilt Yashodharapura. Surya-Varman II (reigned 1113 to 1150) built Angkor Wat and battled the Chams. As far as is known, there is no basis for the legend that the temple was built by a leper king.

The Khmer king who made the biggest mark was Jaya-Varman VII (reigned 1181 to after 1215). A Buddhist, he renounced the kingship rather than wage civil war against a brother or cousin who, though not next in line, had nevertheless preëmpted the throne. Jaya-Varman remained in exile through his kinsman's reign and that of a usurper following it. Then a king of Champa, employing the novel idea of mounted crossbowmen, invaded Kambuja and sacked the capital. Jaya-Varman rallied the scattered Khmer armies, drove out the Chams, and became king at last.

Although already in his fifties, Jaya-Varman VII reigned for about forty years more. His empire eventually included most of Indo-China. Its fame spread far and wide over Farther Asia. Rumor said that in Kambuja there was a statue of Buddha so crusted with emeralds that it seemed to have been carved from one gigantic emerald. This Emerald Buddha glowed with a green light so fierce that only the faithful could gaze upon it.

Jaya-Varman VII was the greatest Khmer builder. Besides once more rebuilding Yashodharapura, he erected a vast number of temples in other parts of the kingdom. Much concerned with his subjects' welfare, he also constructed roads, hospitals, and healing shrines. In fact, obsessed with his own divinity, he overdid the whole thing. Since ancient public works were usually performed by forced labor, the amount of forced labor needed for the vast projects of this Living Buddha impoverished the masses and wore them out.

After Jaya-Varman VII, the Khmers relaxed. Construction of public works practically ceased, not only because of public opposition, but also because the outlying parts of Jaya-Varman's empire, one by one, revolted and broke away. The weaker kings who followed him had neither the force of character nor the resources to stop the crumbling of the empire, and the loss of these provinces further reduced the revenues, resources, and supplies of slaves that these kings could command.

Although much shrunken, Kambuja was still a prosperous land of gleaming, gold-plated temple towers when Jou Da-gwan[19] visited it as the commercial attaché of a Chinese embassy in the 1290s. His report, found in Chinese archives in 1819, gives the most detailed picture we have of life in medieval Kambuja. Besides lengthy descriptions of buildings and sculptures, crops and animals, parades and rituals, he tells about the breech-clouted Khmers themselves, with their perfumes and golden bangles and their customs of birth, marriage, illness, and death. All the more prosperous citizens owned slaves, who were captives from the barbarous hill tribes of the kingdom. He noted the troops of homosexuals who wandered about, begging. "It is vile!" he exclaimed.[20]

Women controlled most of the trade. Trial was still by ordeal—but so it was in some cases in Europe at that time. Convicted malefactors were usually punished by cutting off toes, fingers, noses, ears, hands, or arms. Capital punishment was by burial alive.

The king gave audience to his people while standing at a palace window with a golden frame. When he left the palace, riding the royal elephant and grasping the sacred sword, he went clad in iron armor against assassins and surrounded by troops of his soldiers, war elephants, and women. On the New Year's festival, the Khmers set off rockets and huge firecrackers whose explosions shook the city. Other festivals featured national dancing tournaments, boxing matches, cockfights, or combats of elephants.

Chinese immigrants found life easy, since wants were few, and food and women were easy for an industrious son of Han to come by. But the Khmers laughed at the Chinese for using toilet paper.

The end of Angkor, however, was nearing. Pushed on by the growth of the great Mongol Empire, another Mongoloid people, the Thais, had swarmed down from hilly Yunan, in southern China, into the valley of the Menam River west of Kambuja. While this power was rising on their borders, the Khmers were being weakened as a military power by the spread of Hinâyânian Buddhism, brought by missionaries from Ceylon. The earlier Buddhism of Kambuja had been the Mahâyâna, a high-church variety of the religion centering in Tibet. In the Mahâyâna, the austere, non-theistic, moralistic teachings of the Buddha had been fancied up with a host of heavens, hells, multiple Buddhas, graduate Buddhas, and apprentice Buddhas. The Hinâyâna, or low-church Buddhism, was much simpler, more modest in its demands on the people, and nearer to the original doctrine. It was also less magical and ritualistic, more altruistic and pacifistic. And pacifism did not prove an effective way of coping with the loot-hungry Thais.

In 1431 a Thai ruler, King Paramarâja of Ayuthia, invaded Kambuja and, after a seven-month siege, took and sacked Angkor Thom. An enormous booty was carried off, including the Khmer king's own royal troupe of dancing girls and as many of the Indian-descended intelligentsia as the Thais could catch. Rumors still waft about of treasure hidden from the invaders in a crypt beneath the Bayon. Like most buried-treasure yarns, this is probably a case of wishful thinking.

The Thai king put his own son on the Kambujan throne. The Khmer crown prince had this puppet king murdered and himself crowned king. Finding Angkor still uncomfortably close to the lands of the dreaded Thais, he moved the capital to its present site at Phnom Penh. The Angkor region, now a border province exposed to raids, was largely abandoned.

The shrinkage of the realm and the direct loss of wealth, brains, and power to the Siamese invasion caused a decline in Cambodian culture. It was not a catastrophic fall. Life went on at the new capital much as before, until Europeans began to appear from +XVI on. But the Cambodians indulged in no more frenzies of building huge stone temples. They had been all through that, and what had it profited them? The Shaivite priesthood had become enormously rich and powerful; and the maintenance of the temples of this and other sects had become a burdensome task, which everyone outside of the priesthoods was glad to shirk.

During the four centuries following the abandonment of Angkor, what with the perishability of palm-leaf paper and the frequency of wars with neighboring states, the historical records of the Angkor period became garbled and largely disappeared. Much of the information still existed in the form of inscriptions, but the Cambodians were living too much in the present to send expeditions to jungle-lost ruins to copy the carvings on ancient stelae. That task remained for the French.

So, thanks to French archaeologists, Cambodia recovered its past. It has now recovered its independence, too, under its brilliant, versatile, temperamental, erratic—and currently anti-American— leader, Prince Norodom Sihanouk, who abdicated the kingship in order to play a more active part in politics. In 1954 the jovial British diplomat Malcolm MacDonald went water skiing with the prince on the West Baray. MacDonald managed well enough until he tried to outdo the prince by gliding on one ski, whereupon he took a header. One wonders what the ghosts of the Jaya-Varmans and the Surya-Varmans must have thought.

# IX
# Tikal and the
# Feathered Elephants

A time-black tower against dim banks of cloud;
Around its base the pathless, pressing wood.
Shadow and silence, moss and mould, enshroud
Grey, age-felled slabs that once as cromlechs stood.
*Lovecraft*

As you fly north from Guatemala City, the country changes. The hulking mountain ranges with their sparse scrub forest of pines and palmettos, the towering volcanic cones, the broad valleys checkered with farms roll out into a wide plain covered by dense tropical jungle. For the Petén, the northernmost province of Guatemala, lies in the Central American rain-forest area. Here a heavy rainfall, in places over seventy-five inches a year, fosters a dense jungle. They speak of a dry season and a wet; but a "wet" season and a "wetter" would better fit the facts. Mild in winter, the climate is hot and humid in summer.

You cross the twenty-mile Lake Flores,[1] find a hole in the clouds, and come down on the landing strip at Tikal. A few minutes, by car or afoot, brings you to Posada la Selva, the "Forest Dwelling" put up for tourists.

All around looms the forest: huge, dark, sinister. At first glance it does not look too unlike the temperate-zone hardwood forests of the northeastern United States, such as you see in Pennsylvania or New York State. But you soon observe differences.

The local kings of the plant world are huge deciduous hardwoods, towering one to two hundred feet. There are the *caoba* or mahogany; the *cedro* or Spanish cedar, which is not a cedar or even an evergreen but a relative of the mahogany; the *ceiba* or kapok tree; the *chico* or *sapodilla*, whose sap is made into chewing gum;

the rubber tree; and many smaller species, including several kinds of palms peculiar to the region. Have a care in reaching out for limbs or trunks; you may grab the *lancetilla* with its myriads of needle-sharp spines.

Lianas—including the vanilla vine—hang everywhere, like the clotheslines of a tribe of sluttish dryads. Orchids and other epiphytes bloom on the trunks and boughs of the hardwoods. Vines with nasty barbs droop over the trails to tangle the hair of lady visitors.

The big hardwoods are braced by buttress roots standing out from their trunks near the ground. You might think that such a forest would grow on deep, fertile soil; but this is not the case. The warmth and wet speed up bacterial action, so that humus is destroyed as fast as it is formed. Hence in many places you can with one blow drive a pick through the soil into the limestone hardpan. Therefore the trees, unable to send their roots down very far, send them outward instead and need buttresses to keep from being blown over during hurricanes.

Birds swarm: big, noisy green parrots, toucans with grotesque, great bills, large woodpeckers, and many smaller fry. The woods resound with bird calls and the chatter of squirrels. There are monkeys, too—howlers and spiders—but a recent epidemic of yellow fever has killed off most of them.

Larger mammals abound. Jaguars and pumas sometimes lair in the rooms of ruined palaces; you catch the distinctive smell of cat when you enter these rooms. There are also ocelots, deer, tapirs, peccaries, armadillos, and agoutis—the last a rabbit-sized relative of the guinea pig. But you are not likely to see any of them. They see, hear, or smell you and flee long before you observe them. Some archaeologists have worked for years on the site without glimpsing any of these creatures.

There are lizards, snakes, and turtles, too. The snakes include several venomous tropical cousins of the rattlesnake, but these are seldom seen. In one of the pools across the road from the Posada lives a crocodile—the true American crocodile, not the alligator. On sunny days this five-footer floats lazily on the surface. At other times he lurks around the shore, hoping that one of the Indians' chickens will stray within snapping distance.

There are two settlements of Indians at Tikal: one living in a group of houses around the pools; the other in a village nearby.

Both groups farm and work for the archaeologists. They are short, dark brown people of Mayan origin who, unlike many Central American Indians, have dropped their native language for Spanish. Their features are typical of the unmixed Central American Indians, as shown on Mayan monuments: broad skulls, very wide cheekbones, slightly hooked noses, and retreating foreheads and chins. Their behavior—quiet, subdued, polite, poker-faced—is also typical.

People who have lived with the Mayas describe them as exceptionally honest, good-natured, industrious, orderly, self-controlled, stoical towards pain and hardship, and as intelligent as most people; but conservative, unambitious, and full of supernaturalism. Not long ago, Indians destroyed a set of fine murals in British Honduras in the belief that ancient statues and paintings harbor evil spirits. The Mayan behavior pattern contrasts with that of the charming, mercurial, individualistic, sensual, hedonistic, capricious Hispano-American who, four centuries after the Conquest, still rules the roost in most Central American nations.

Except for a few Indian villages, the Petén is practically uninhabited. In Mayan days it harbored a dense population; diseases brought in by Europeans—malaria, yellow fever, and hookworm—probably caused the change. Small groups of Guatemalans called *chicleros* (chicle-hunters) roam the forest, hacking at *chico* trees with their machetes to make the sap run. Chicleros have found many ruined Mayan cities. They have also destroyed not a few relics of this ancient civilization. Any group of ignorant men, deprived of the normal human amusements of sex, drink, gambling, and sadism, are apt to start smashing things up to relieve their boredom.

The ancient Mayan city of Tikal does not stand alone. Only eleven miles north is Uaxactún[2], about as old as Tikal. Scores of other ruined cities lie scattered around the province. There are ruins enough in the jungles of Petén to keep all the world's archaeologists busy for centuries. Tikal has become a tourist attraction because it is one of the largest and oldest of all Mayan cities and because, like Copán to the southwest in Honduras, and Uxmal and Chichén Itzá[3] to the north in Yucatán, it has been partly cleared, excavated, and restored.

As you move about the roads and trails at Tikal, you glimpse, through the aisles of the forest, steep-sided mounds or hills rising abruptly from the plain, sometimes to a height of over a hundred feet. Although they are as densely overgrown as the flatlands, their shape suggests that they are man-made, not natural knolls. And so it transpires. Beneath the groping fingers of tree roots lie thousands of dressed and carven blocks of stone, sometimes forming a recognizable wall. So perfectly does Lovecraft's poem, quoted at the head of this chapter, describe many of the ruins at Tikal that, when one of the authors saw them, he could not help reciting it aloud to the parrots.

Enough excavating has been done so that you can glimpse with your mind's eye the Tikal of twelve hundred years ago. The center of the city was a one-acre plaza, completely paved, and surrounded on all sides by towering Mayan buildings. While the main public edifices were massed around the central plaza, other stone structures were spread out for two or three miles in all directions. Wide streets led from building to building; raised paved roads or causeways ran between the Mayan cities.

Although the huts of the common folk, made of wood and thatch, have long since disappeared, you can still see the remains of temples, palaces, astronomical observatories, ball courts, dance platforms, vapor baths, reviewing stands, stadiums, and pyramids. In all there must have been forty large and two hundred smaller public buildings.

The temples were the most striking of the Mayan edifices. They were small, chambered structures perched on lofty stepped pyramids, which towered over the jungle, as high as a modern fifteen- or twenty-story building. The sides of the pyramids rose steeply. Monumental staircases with narrow treads and high risers made a breath-takingly steep climb of over a hundred steps to the temple. Inside the temple were only a few small rooms; for the thick stone walls occupied much of the available space. Above the chambered building rose an ornamental wall, called a roof comb, carved with reliefs.

At the base of the temple pyramids the Mayas placed rows of inscribed stone slabs: some like gravestones, meant to stand upright, which we call stelae; others drum-shaped and meant to lie flat, called altars. Some altars have, carved in relief, a sculpture of a sacrificial victim with his limbs bound, stretched out on a similar altar in order to have his heart cut out and offered to the gods. Were the drum-shaped stones used for that sanguinary purpose? Perhaps, although nobody can say for sure.

After the Spaniards conquered the Aztecs around 1520, the Incas around 1530, and the Mayas around 1540, the aboriginal civilizations of the Americas were practically forgotten. The Spaniards razed many native temples and palaces and used the stone to build their churches and other houses. The Amerind cities that they occupied were replanned on a grid or checkerboard street pattern. The other cities were abandoned to the jungle.

In 1695 began the rediscovery of the Mayan civilization. Father Andrés Avendaño, with two other Franciscan monks and some Indians, journeyed from Mérida in Yucatán deep into the Petén jungle. They hoped to bring Christianity to the Itzá Indians around Lake Flores, who still maintained their independence and practiced their own gory religion. Learning that some of the Itzás planned to kill them, Avendaño and his party fled from the lake, got lost in the jungle, nearly starved to death, and stumbled upon the ruins of Tikal.

Tikal had long been uninhabited. The reason for its abandonment is one of the enigmas of the Mayas. The Spaniards soon afterwards conquered the Itzás; Father Avendaño's report was filed away; and Tikal was again forgotten for a century and a half.

In fact, during +XVIII the opinion prevailed that Cortés, Pizarro, and the Montejos had merely conquered barbarous tribes. The Scottish historian Robertson asserted: "Neither the Mexicans nor the Peruvians were entitled to rank with those nations which merit the name of civilized," because "it seems altogether incredible that in a period so short, every vestige of this boasted elegance should have disappeared."[4] Tales of Amerind empires, cities, palaces, and temples must be wild exaggerations.

Even as Robertson wrote, the second rediscovery of Mayan civilization was under way. In 1773, Indians told a priest about the ruins of Palenque, a Mayan city they had discovered in Yucatán. The priest composed a report, which incited several expeditions. One explorer, Captain Antonio del Río, visited the site, ruthlessly battered down walls that stood in his way, and wrote a book on the ruin. In 1822 an English translation of del Río's book appeared, illustrated by Jean Frédéric, Count de Waldeck.

The colorful Waldeck (1766–1875) was a soldier, artist, explorer, courtier, revolutionist, adventurer, and archaeologist; but it is doubtful if he was a real count. At nineteen he went with Le Vaillant's expedition into the unknown interior of Africa. Later he became an adventurer in the French Revolution, then a soldier and a naval officer under Napoleon. He took an active part in Spanish and Latin-American revolutions. In 1821 his imagination was fired by the sight of Mayan ruins in Guatemala, and on his return to London he illustrated del Río's book.

This book came to the attention of Edward King, Viscount Kingsborough. This gently mad young Anglo-Irish peer was convinced that the American Indians were the Lost Ten Tribes of Israel. To confirm his theory, he got Waldeck a job in Central America as a mining engineer and dispatched him to draw pictures of American antiquities and look for evidence of the Lost Ten Tribes.

For several years Waldeck, now in his sixties, scrambled over jungle-matted ruins. Alas! he had none of the literal accuracy so important in archaeology; his beautiful drawings showed the ruins not as they were but as he thought they should have been. Not satisfied with inserting his young mestiza mistress *sans* clothes into many of the pictures, he added details that were never there at all, such as four statues of men in Phoenician headdress holding up the front of the Temple of the Magicians at Uxmal. Waldeck also put nonexistent elephant heads into some of the Mayan glyphs he drew, thus starting a cycle of speculation about Mayan elephants and Chinese Indians.

Here, on the left, is one of Waldeck's drawings, with an accurate drawing of the same glyph made some years later by Catherwood:

*Fig. 12 Drawings of the same Mayan glyph by Waldeck (left) and Catherwood (right).*

The myth that elephants existed in Central America during historic times drew additional strength from a book by a writer named John Ranking, titled: *Historical Researches on the Conquest of Peru, Mexico, Bogota, Natchez and Talomeco in the Thirteenth Century by the Mongols, Accompanied with Elephants.* Ranking had evidently read about the fossil remains of mammoths and mastodons, which once abounded in the Americas and were still living when the first men arrived in the New World ten or twenty thousand years ago. Although these animals died out long before the rise of the Mayas, Ranking assumed that their remains were those of tame elephants of the modern species.

Another source of this elephant myth is a monument called Stela B, in the Mayan city of Copán. On top of this stela are carved two creatures, which do look somewhat like elephants with mahouts on their backs. When the British archeologist Alfred P. Maudslay, who explored Mayan ruins in the 1880s, reported the existence of this monument, he furnished more ammunition to the believers in Mayan elephants. However, if you look closely at Maudslay's drawing (Fig. 13) you will see that the "elephants" have nostrils, not at the ends of their "trunks," as elephants should, but in front at the roots of these organs. Furthermore, they have large, round eyes surrounded by feathers. Feathered elephants, as you know, are extremely rare; these are probably conventionalized macaws.

*Fig. 13   The top of Stela B at Copán, as drawn by Sir Alfred P. Maudslay.*

For all its shortcomings, Waldeck's first book, *Voyage pittoresque et archéologique dans la province de Yucatan* (1838) won him a medal and a pension from the French Government. He went on to marry, at 84, a 17-year-old girl by whom he had a son, to publish his second book at 100, and finally to drop dead at 109 just after turning to look at a pretty girl on the boulevards of Paris.

Meanwhile, Lord Kingsborough had spent his entire fortune of £40,000 on the publication of *The Antiquities of Mexico* (1848), a monumental work in nine immense volumes containing reproductions of Aztec picture writings and art objects, and voluminous notes expounding the Jewish-Indian theory. Poor Kingsborough's obsession landed him in the debtor's prison in Dublin for nonpayment of his printer's bill, and there he expired.

Although Waldeck's books were scientifically worthless, his *Voyage pittoresque* came to the notice of John Lloyd Stephens (1805–52). Stephens, a successful American lawyer, had already traveled widely. A short, lively, voluble bachelor with bushy red side whiskers and a way with the ladies, Stephens had visited Paris, Rome, Greece, Russia, and Poland. He made a perilous journey to the ruins of Petra in Arabia, traveling from Cairo disguised as a Muslim merchant and guided by a shaykh who enlivened the journey by demanding more money at every step.

In London, Stephens became friends with Frederick Catherwood, an English architectural draftsman who had likewise been traveling about the East in disguise, sketching old monuments at the risk of his life. Catherwood—a tall, calm, solid Briton—was lucky not to have been murdered by pious Muslims for violating the Second Commandment.

When he returned to the United States, Stephens wrote a book on his Arabian journey. Praised by Edgar Allen Poe, the book became a best-seller and inspired John William Burgon to compose his poem *Petra*, with its one immortal line:

A rose-red city half as old as time.

Fascinated by contradictory reports about the Central American ruins, Stephens arranged with Catherwood to visit the Mayan country and examine them. Stephens got himself appointed United States Minister to the Federation of Central America, and the pair set forth in 1839.

The young federation was racked by strife. The Federalists, under the idealistic, anticlerical Honduranean liberal Morazán, were losing the struggle to a young Guatemalan bandit, Carrera. The latter, supported by the clergy and the landowners, campaigned under the slogan: "Hurray for religion and death to foreigners!"[5] He led a horde of Indians whom the priests had roused to a fanatical frenzy by telling them that a recent cholera epidemic had been caused by foreigners' poisoning their wells. Seeking to break up the federation and restore Guatemala to the rule of the Church and the squirearchy, Carrera massacred prisoners by the hundreds, chopping down many with his own saber.

Thus things were when Stephens and Catherwood sailed to British Honduras and beat their way overland. On muleback they wallowed through bottomless quagmires and jogged over hair-raising precipices. They narrowly escaped being shot by suspicious soldiers at Comatán before they reached the ruins of Copán. To the astonishment of the landowner, to whom it was a useless patch of jungle, Stephens bought the whole site of Copán for fifty dollars. As Catherwood settled down to draw, his friend described the scene:

> Standing with his feet in the mud, he was drawing with his gloves on to protect his hands from the mosquitoes. As we feared, the designs were so intricate and complicated, the subjects so entirely new and unintelligible that he was having great difficulty in drawing. He had made several attempts both with the camera lucida and without, but failed to satisfy himself or even me, who was less severe in criticism. The idol seemed to defy his art; two monkeys on a tree on one side appeared to be laughing at him . . .[6]

To take care of his diplomatic chores, Stephens went off to find the central government. He was eaten alive by mosquitoes, fleas, and ticks. He shivered and sweltered in the throes of malaria, while perfecting his Spanish by reading *Gil Blas* and *Don Quixote* in the original. He was drenched by tropical thunderstorms, shaken by an earthquake, and singed by a forest fire. He peered into the craters of erupting volcanoes, narrowly escaped an ambush by bandits, and helped to subdue an American sea captain taken with a fit.

Rejoined by Catherwood in Guatemala City, Stephens finally caught up with Morazán just as the latter, beaten at last by Carrera's hordes, was about to flee into exile. Morazán, who had the misfortune to be the only honest and intelligent man in a milieu of knaves, fools, fanatics, and paranoid egotists, tried a comeback in 1842 but was caught by Carrera and executed.

Seeing that the federation was dead, Stephens packed the American Embassy's effects and went back to archaeology. He and Catherwood made their way to Palenque in Yucatán over a terrifying trail, winding up and down the sides of cliffs. At Palenque they sweated to clear away trees and sketch the ruins until both were felled by disease and insect bites. Later, Stephens sent a man back to Palenque to make plaster-of-Paris molds of the sculptures. But a local "patriots' committee" seized the molds, demanded several thousand dollars' ransom, and broke the molds when this was not forthcoming.

After a visit to Uxmal, which ended in another physical collapse for Catherwood, they returned to New York. Safely home, Stephens wrote his most successful book: *Incidents of Travel in Central America, Chiapas, and Yucatan* (1841), which sold even better than his previous one. In fact, it is one of the greatest travel tales of all time, more exciting than most novels. On the origin of the Amerinds he said:

> Volumes without number have been written to account for the first peopling of the Americas. By some, the inhabitants of these continents have been regarded as a separate race . . . Others have considered them the most ancient race of people upon the earth, ascribing their origin to some remnant of the antediluvian inhabitants of the earth who survived the deluge which swept away the greatest part of the human species in the days of Noah. Under the broad range allowed by a descent from these sons of Noah, many peoples have had ascribed to them the honor of peopling the Americas: the Jews, the Canaanites, the Phoenicians, the Carthaginians, the Greeks, and the Scythians in ancient times; the Chinese, the Swedes, the Norwegians, the Welsh, and the Spaniards in modern times. North and South America have been joined together and rent asunder by the shock of an earthquake; the fabled island of Atlantis has been lifted out of the ocean; and, not to be left behind, an enterprising American has turned the tables on the Old World and planted the ark itself within the state of New York.[7]

Instead, asserted Stephens, all the Mayan cities belonged to one culture. They were built, not by Egyptians or other exotic visitors,

188

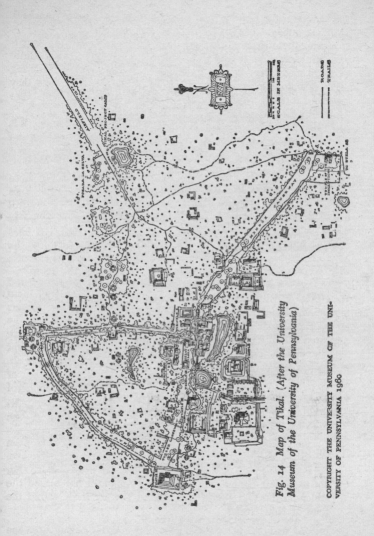

Fig. 14 Map of Tikal. (After the University Museum of the University of Pennsylvania)

COPYRIGHT THE UNIVERSITY MUSEUM OF THE UNIVERSITY OF PENNSYLVANIA 1960 but by the same small, brown, slant-eyed folk who still farmed the featureless plain of Yucatán. Time has vindicated Stephens.

On another journey to Yucatán, Stephens and Catherwood visited Uxmal, Chichén Itzá, and more than a dozen other Mayan sites. They discovered the Mayan road system, comparable on a smaller scale to that of Rome. After more books and further travel, both worked at railroading in Latin America until, in middle age, Stephens succumbed to malaria and Catherwood perished in a shipwreck.

Tikal shared in the general rediscovery of the land of the Mayas. In 1848 some Indians described the colossal ruin to their priest, who wrote an account of it. This report stimulated several expeditions. Colonel Modesto Méndez, who led one of these, published a description, which was translated into German and so got into general archaeological literature.

Other travelers and scientists followed Stephens and Méndez. In 1877 a Swiss botanist, Bernouilli, visited Tikal and removed several of the carved wooden lintels over the doorways of the temples. These lintels rest today in the Museum of Archaeology in Basel. In the 1880s, Sir Alfred Maudslay made casts of the carvings on Mayan monuments for the Victoria and Albert Museum. Teobert Maler, an Austrian working for the Peabody Museum of Harvard, dug and measured at Tikal in 1895 and 1904. Maler's neat graffito, along with those of hundreds of less eminent visitors, is seen today in the plaster of the palace named after him. As a result of a quarrel between Maler and his museum, his report was left unfinished until Alfred M. Tozzer completed it in 1910.

During the last hundred years, a vast amount of archaeological research has been done on the Mayan civilization, so that today it is fairly well understood. However, many problems about the Mayas remain to be solved.

After the Second World War, archaeologists of the University Museum of the University of Pennsylvania laid plans for a long-range program of clearing, excavation, and restoration of Tikal. The Guatemalan Government declared the area a national park and furnished the archaeologists with free air freight service between the site and Guatemala City. Money for the work came from a number of sources, including the American Philosophical Society, the

Rockefeller Foundation, and the Carnegie Foundation of Washington. The splendid result is the Tikal of today.

The future of Tikal is in doubt. The University Museum does not plan to go on indefinitely. The Guatemalan Government has been urged to furnish enough park personnel to prevent vandalism and to keep the place up. For, if a trail in Petén is neglected, it soon becomes so overgrown that one must hack one's way through with a machete. But the Guatemalan Government has been in sore financial straits.

Moreover, appreciation of archaeology is not widespread in Guatemala. Building contractors around Guatemala City—ancient Kaminaljuyú—order their bulldozer operators, when they unearth Mayan relics, to destroy or bury them, lest archaeologists hear of the find and delay the contractors' operations. (The same sort of thing happens in the United States.) Although all such finds are supposed to go to the excellent museum in Guatemala City, only about one fifth of them arrive there. The rest either are destroyed or pass into private hands.

Most of the work of excavation and restoration at Tikal has been done in the center of the city, about the one-acre Plaza Mayor, but much more remains to be done. The large buildings at Tikal fall into two classes. We call them "temples" and "palaces" for convenience, although we cannot tell exactly how they were used. The six largest "temples" are steep-sided pyramids, roughly 100 to 200 feet tall, with small chambered structures containing one or more dark, narrow little rooms on top. The sides of these pyramids rise at angles between 60 and 70 degrees. The heights of the five tallest "temples" —pyramid, chambered building, roof comb, and all—range from 143 feet for Temple II to 229 feet for Temple IV.

Temples I and II stand at the east and west ends of the Plaza, facing each other across the court. Temple I—the Temple of the Giant Jaguar—has been largely cleared of plants and partly restored. A brave traveler can climb the steep stairway to the top of the pyramid and enter the chambered building. Since the treads of the steps are narrow and partly worn away, an iron chain is secured at the top of the stairs to help climbers haul themselves up the fifteen-story height and let themselves down again backwards.

When one of the authors was at Tikal, the party included an energetic young physician with an urge to excel. Spurning the chain, he trotted down the hundred steps facing forward as if it were an ordinary stairway, while those watching him shuddered. If you will look at Plate XX, you will see why they did so.

Temple II, the Temple of the Masks, is now being excavated. Temple III rises from the jungle about 200 yards west of the plaza. An able-bodied tourist can climb it by pulling himself up by tree roots and trunks. Temple IV, largest of all, rises 450 yards still farther west; it is a longer climb, but less arduous than III, and affords the best vista. Temple V, south of the Plaza, is so steep that its ascent had better be left to experienced mountaineers. The smaller Temple VI, the Temple of the Inscriptions, stands alone, half a mile southeast of the Plaza.

Besides these large "temples" there are about a score of smaller stepped, truncated pyramids, sometimes with a structure on top, sometimes without. On the north side of the Plaza rises a cluster of nine of these lesser buildings, forming the North Acropolis. Here the diggers are trying to unravel the complicated architectural history of the group. When the original builders decided to erect a new pyramid, they had no compunction about tearing down an old one that stood in the way, or covering it with stone and incorporating it into the new building.

The "palaces" are groups of structures surrounding courtyards, as if they had been intended as dwelling places. About a dozen such complexes can be recognized. Their inner chambers have been cleared, but the buildings themselves have not been restored. They are called by such names as the Palace of the Nobles (south of the Plaza), the Palace of the Bats (after its present tenants), and the Palace of the Inner Chambers.

Other structures include causeways joining the various groups of buildings and the remains of a ball court south of Temple I. There the Mayas played a game combining features of soccer and basketball. Since the rubber tree is native to this region, the Mayas invented the bouncing rubber game ball.

The buildings are largely made of local limestone, so soft and chalky that you can dig your thumbnail into it. They were plastered over with stucco, inside and out, although the plaster has now mostly disappeared from the outside of the buildings.

Scattered around the Plaza and among the buildings are stelae, probably commemorating events like the dedication of temples. For stelae and other works meant to be durable, the Mayas imported harder stone from other parts of Mayaland. However, in contrast to the stelae from other Mayan sites, some of those at Tikal are blank. Perhaps they, too, were once coated with plaster, which has since disappeared, and the inscriptions were carved in this plaster coating.

Our energetic young doctor, not satisfied with climbing two hundred feet up Temple IV as the rest of us did, undertook in addition to climb the remaining thirty feet to the top of the roof comb. This meant going up a sheer wall and past an overhang, by digging fingertips and toes into the cracks that time had eroded between the courses of soft limestone. He gave up only when we pointed out that, while he might get to the top, there was no conceivable way by which he could get down again.

The next day, in climbing over a log, the doctor sprained an ankle and limped back to camp on a stick. At dinner that night in the dimly lit dining room of the rest house, he suddenly gave a strangled shout, kicked out with his injured leg, and shoved his chair back. People asked him what was the matter.

"Something was crawling up my leg!" he said.

We got up. Sure enough, up the wall wriggled a foot-long, dark brown lizard.[8] We grabbed the lizard and the lizard grabbed us. For a little fellow he had a punishing bite. We said: "Ouch! Does anybody want to look at him? Ouch!"

When the lizard had been shown around and tossed into outer darkness, we turned to see the doctor lying on his back on the floor. Seeing our surprise, he explained: "I just realized I was going to faint; so I did what I tell my patients to do."

The shock of reaching down in the dimness to grasp a wriggling reptile, added to the pain in his injured ankle, had been too much for him.

You can fill a book with eccentric theories about the origin of the American Indians and their culture. In fact, it has been done.[9] But to tell the full tale of the Jewish Indians, Egyptian Indians, Welsh Indians, Polynesian Indians, Norse Indians, Sumerian Indians, Mormon Indians, and Atlantean Indians would carry us too far afield.

Suffice it to say that the evidence firmly supports the present "orthodox" theory: that the Amerinds are a branch of the Mongoloid race, which includes the Eskimos, the Chinese, and the Malays; and that they came from Asia via Alaska in a trickle of migrations beginning ten to twenty thousand years ago. These migrations brought the ancestors of the Mayas, along with others, to the New World.

When we speak of the Mayan civilization, we really mean two cultures: the so-called Old Empire in Guatemala and Honduras and the New Empire in Yucatán. The word "Empire" is misleading, because nowhere in Middle America, so far as we know, was there any strong, centralized government of the European type. Cortés' foe, the Aztec "emperor" Montezuma II, was no hereditary despot of the European kind, but an elected tribal chief, of limited powers, whose tribe had established a precarious rule over some of their neighbors. One reason for the speed of the Spanish Conquest in Central America was the fact that some of the tribes joined the invaders in order to settle accounts with their local enemies, heedless of the fact that they were helping the Spaniards to reduce to serfdom all Central Americans, including themselves.

The New Empire Mayas were divided into several small tribal states, something like the city-states of ancient Greece and medieval Italy. The Mayan city-states were ruled by dominant clans. Sometimes these states joined in a confederacy and sometimes they fought one another. It is a plausible guess that the Old Empire Mayas were organized along similar lines.

The so-called Old Empire arose around the beginning of the Christian Era and flourished for a thousand years. We know this from the dates on Mayan monuments. The Mayas put an enormous amount of effort—physical and mental—into keeping track of dates, a task more difficult for them than for us. They seem to have been obsessed by the mysteries of time. Each day was deemed a god and was worshiped as such.

On their monuments the Mayas chiseled the date, not in one calendar only, but in three. They recognized a period of 260 days, the *tzolkin*, divided up into shorter periods. Then they had a 365-day period, the *haab*, divided into eighteen periods of twenty days each, with five extra days to make it almost equal to the true solar year.

By writing the date of a given day according to both the tzolkin-calendar and the haab-calendar, the Mayas recorded a combination that repeated itself only once in fifty-two haabs. Then, to make sure there was no mistake, they also wrote the date in the "long count" calendar. This was a system of recording the number of days elapsed since the date 4 *Ahau* 8 *Cumhu,* which on our calendar would be about −3113. This probably represents some event in Mayan mythology, like the creation of the world; just as the Orthodox Jewish calendar starts from the Creation in −3761. Unfortunately, under the New Empire the Mayas stopped using the "long count" several centuries before the Conquest. Hence we can only roughly correlate Old Empire dates with our own.

Between +700 and +1000, the Mayas of Guatemala ceased to erect monuments. Most Mayologists think they abandoned their cities at that time. So abruptly did they leave that some new public buildings stand unfinished in the jungle beside the overgrown squares, temples, and highways. Why? This is the main Mayan mystery.

The Old Empire was a purely Neolithic culture. No trace of metals has been found in its ruins save those dating from the end of the period. If we define "civilization" as meaning possession of cities, writing, and metals, the Old Empire Mayas had the first two of these but not the third. The Incas, by contrast, had cities and metal but no writing; so in a way both peoples were on the borderline between barbarism and full civilization.

The rise of the Old Empire cannot be sharply dated, because civilizations do not appear overnight. One of the earliest Mayan dates has been found on the monument called Stela 9 at Uaxactún. According to the most generally accepted system of correlation of Mayan dates, Stela 9 was carved in +328.

Another early date appears on the Leyden Plate, found on the Gulf Coast of Guatemala. This pendantlike piece of carved jade 8.5 inches long displays a date corresponding to +320. From the art work on this plate, the late Sylvanus G. Morley, in his day one of the foremost Mayologists, believed that it was originally carved at Tikal.

Hence we may suppose that Mayan civilization arose in Petén around the beginning of the Christian Era. For, if these dates were cut in stone and jade in +IV, we can be sure that they were carved in perishable wood some centuries earlier. Moreover, charcoal from a grave recently discovered at Tikal gives a carbon-14 date of early +I. Presumably Tikal and Uaxactún grew up at about the same time, and (contrary to a former belief) civilization can arise in a tropical rain forest.

Dates apparently earlier than those of Stela 9 and the Leyden Plate exist. The Tuxtla Statuette is dated +162 and the La Venta Stone —31. However, it is uncertain whether these dates are based upon the same system as the later Mayan dates. Some Mayologists think that Mayan civilization got its first impulse from a still earlier culture that grew up around Vera Cruz on the Gulf of Mexico; but this question is unsettled. The Mexican civilization of the Toltecs and Aztecs arose around +500, long after the beginning of the Mayan Old Empire. Besides the Aztecs and the Mayas, several lesser-known Central American peoples, such as the Kichés of Guatemala, had achieved a fair degree of semi-civilization by the time of the Conquest.

Were these early Mayan cities true cities or merely ceremonial centers, like Stonehenge and Angkor Wat, where people gathered from afar for religious rites? Recent excavations at the New Empire city of Mayapan indicate that it was a real city, covering two and a half square miles and having ten to twenty thousand inhabitants. The huts of the common people, however, were made of perishable materials of which only slight traces remain. Possibly the same was true of Tikal and other Old Empire cities. The population of Tikal has been estimated as high as 200,000, which would class it with ancient Babylon, Nineveh, Athens, Syracuse, and Carthage; but this is an unsettled question.

It was also believed a few decades ago that the Old Empire was a peaceful culture, without war or human sacrifice. But brilliantly colored murals discovered at Bonampak in 1946 showed the Old Empire Mayas engaging with gusto in both practices. All the civilized Amerinds were, in fact, extremely warlike. When Hernández de Córdoba and his party landed at Catoche in 1517, the Mayas ambushed and attacked them without provocation, and only the Spaniards' guns and armor saved them from destruction.

Mayan art and architecture were highly original, with remarkable achievements and even more striking limitations. Mayan art, growing up in isolation, shows no Old World influence. This fact made it hard for Westerners like Waldeck and Catherwood to grasp.

Mayan architecture, like that of Egypt three thousand years earlier, began by developing stone structures in imitation of existing

wooden houses. Mayan architects evolved a style of massive ceremonial buildings and chiefs' houses, with stucco-faced stone and
concrete walls, so thick that there was little room left inside. Like
the Khmers, not knowing the true arch and vault, they used the
false or corbeled arch and vault. Not until the New Empire did
they learn to build houses with large rooms by supporting a series
of parallel vaults on colonnades.

Mayan public buildings were of many kinds. However, the
pyramids of the Mayas and Aztecs had nothing to do with the
pyramids of Egypt and the ziggurats of Mesopotamia, which they
superficially resemble. Egyptian pyramids were simply oversized
tombs. In Mesopotamia, ziggurats were towers whose height, the
priests hoped, would bring them near enough to heaven so that
their prayers would be clearly heard by the gods. New World
pyramids, built thousands of years after those of the Old World,
evolved from temple platforms, although the Mayas sometimes
buried high priests and other eminent people in them as well.

The Mayas based their agriculture on maize, eked out with a
host of other plants like beans, tomatoes, and peppers. They domes-
ticated dogs, turkeys, deer, and bees. When their maize was thriv-
ing, it gave them plenty of leisure for their great construction projects, religious ceremonials, and art.

They began to use gold, silver, and copper about the time of
the rise of the New Empire. At first they employed metals only for
ornaments, although later they learned to make copper knives and
axes. All their metal was imported, because Mayaland has none to
speak of. Like the Aztecs, however, the priests continued to open
up their victims with knives of obsidian (volcanic glass) since the
gods are conservative in such matters.

Mayan religion was much like that of other early agricultural
societies, with a multitude of departmental gods and an elaborate
calendar of observances. Among their chief gods were the sky god
Itzamná, and the rain god Chac. Chac was more or less the same
as the storm god Kukulcán, the equivalent of the Aztec Quetzalcoatl.[10]

The gloomy Mayan religion involved a good deal of human
sacrifice, albeit not on the grisly scale of the Aztecs, who killed as
many as 20,000 people in dedicating one temple. The Mayas, like
the Aztecs, ripped open victims and tore out their hearts; they
threw virgins down sacred wells, shot other captives with arrows,

mounted severed heads on skull racks next to their temples, and ate selected victims at ceremonial feasts. Mayan religion was closely connected with the elaborate Mayan calendar and with Mayan astrology, which made much of the revolutions of the planet Venus.

Because (aside from Bishop de Landa's blundering "Mayan alphabet") no Rosetta Stone for deciphering Mayan writing has ever been found, Mayalogists have had to interpret written Mayan by the laborious process of trial and error. During the last century they have learned to read the numerals and calendric signs, the names of many gods, and some common nouns.

Mayan writing was mainly ideographic—one conventionalized picture for each word. It is also claimed that there were some phonetic elements, standing for syllables. A Mayan glyph might include two or three of these picture elements intricately entangled. Each glyph took several radically different forms having only certain "essential elements" in common. The Mayas could hardly have made their system more cryptic if they had deliberately set out to do so.

The surviving Mayan literature consists of many inscriptions on temples and monuments and the three original Mayan books that escaped burning by Bishop de Landa. The three codices are all religious, calendric, or astrological; the Dresden Codex is a prophecy covering 34,000 years to the end of the world.

The Spanish missionaries in Yucatán adapted their own alphabet to the native languages so that they could print prayers and hymns for their converts. The Indians found this system so much easier than their own writing that they soon dropped the latter. They wrote, in their own languages but using the Spanish alphabet, a number of village chronicles called the *Books of Chilan Balaam*.[11] "Chilan Balaam" means "interpreter jaguar," the title of an order of soothsayers in the Mayan priesthood. These books consist of brief notices, in obscure language, of plagues, tribal wars, the deaths of chiefs, and similar happenings.

Recently several Russian scholars have undertaken to solve more of the Mayan writing system by the use of statistical methods and computers. They determine how often certain words occur in Mayan texts that are written with the Spanish alphabet and therefore can be read. They also determine the frequency with which word-signs occur in Mayan hieroglyphic writing. Some American Mayalogists think that the Russians are on the right track but that they are still some way from complete success.

From the point of view of preserving Amerind history, the Spanish Conquest took place at the worst possible time. Two or three centuries earlier, European military superiority would not have been so overwhelming; and the native states might have held their own, at least for a while. Two or three centuries later, the decline of Christian fanaticism and the rise of antiquarianism would have encouraged the conquerors to cherish the native records instead of destroying them.

Nevertheless, by piecing together the statements of the *Books of Chilan Balaam* and the accounts of Spanish clerics, we can get a pretty good idea of New Empire history. We learn about the dominance of the three strongest clans—the Xiu[12] or Tutulxiu, the Cocom, and the Chel—and about their union under the League of Mayapan. The League broke up about 1194, when the Cocom chief[13] brought in Mexican mercenary soldiers to attack the other clans. Thereafter fierce warfare raged among the clans until the arrival of the Spaniards, and even afterwards, making the Conquest easier than it would otherwise have been.

There is, however, no history of the Old Empire. All we know is that, from +IV to +VIII, the Mayas put up stelae in ever increasing numbers to commemorate the dates of such events as the completion of buildings. After +800, however, the number of new stelae dropped off sharply. By +900 practically no monuments were being erected. There is some evidence that great cities like Tikal were not abandoned overnight, but that people continued to dwell there even after they had stopped carving these date stones. Nevertheless, most of the cities were deserted by +1000.

What happened? That is the greatest Mayan mystery of all. Many theories have been advanced to explain the collapse of this busy urbanized civilization. These explanations include: earthquakes, change of climate, disease, foreign conquest, civil war, decadence, and agricultural exhaustion.

Geology opposes the idea of earthquakes, since Petén is free of these catastrophes. It also casts doubt on the idea that the climate could have changed enough to matter during the life of the Old Empire. Medical specialists think that the most devastating diseases of the region—hookworm, malaria, and yellow fever—did not exist in the Americas before the Spaniards and their Negro slaves brought them in.

There is no record of foreign conquest, and "decadence" is one of those words that people apply to things they do not understand. When a nation is conquered, we sometimes explain its defeat by saying the people were decadent—that is, their morals were not what we approve of. But there is no necessary connection between the two. The only cause of their downfall that we can really be sure of is that at the critical moment they were weaker than their foes on the battlefield. This might happen to anybody. When the Romans were at their most "decadent" they conquered the Mediterranean world; when they became more moral and virtuous and adopted Christianity, the barbarians overcame them.

Morley favored the theory of agricultural exhaustion. His argument ran thus: The Mayas have always farmed by cutting and burning a few acres of jungle to plant maize. While this system produces an easy living for a few years, the yield then drops off sharply, forcing the farmer to slash and burn a new patch. The old patch, instead of reverting at once to jungle, is covered by tough grasses with which the Mayas, lacking plows, draft animals, or even digging tools, could not cope.

Thus in time the Mayas converted the lands around their cities into great grassy plains, until each farmer had to go so far to reach his plot that life in the city was no longer practical. Eventually the jungle returned and the cycle began again; but meanwhile the Old Empire Mayas, perhaps egged on by priests convinced that they had offended the gods, migrated north and built a whole new constellation of cities in Yucatán.

For a while Morley's theory was popular. Then new findings cast doubt upon it. J. Eric S. Thompson,[14] for instance, asserted that abandoned lands in the Petén return at once to jungle without passing through a grassy stage. Moreover, some northern Mayan cities in Yucatán were found to have flourished during the Old Empire and to have fallen into disuse at the same time as the cities of Petén.

So the picture changed. Instead of a wholesale migration from south to north, we suppose a general collapse of Mayan civilization, in the North as well as in the South. This was followed by a révival centering in the North rather than in the South, although the areas of the Old and New Empires overlapped.

Now archaeologists seem to be coming around to Thompson's view that the collapse was brought about by revolution and civil war. The priestly caste, they say, may have exacted more and more labor from the peasantry for building ever more magnificent temples. At last the common Indians revolted, slaughtered their oppressors, and went back to their easygoing life of earlier times. Ancient damage done to Old Empire monuments supports this theory.

As for the revival in Yucatán, it is thought that this was stimulated in +X by the arrival of foreigners from Mexico. It has been suggested that these invaders were Toltecs, fleeing the overthrow of their Mexican realm by the more barbarous Aztecs.

This may well turn out to be the case. But let us not commit ourselves wholeheartedly to any one view just yet; Morley's theory looked good, too, for a while. In a few decades, as more of those scores of ruined cities in Petén are excavated, much hidden Mayan history will surely come to light.

One more Mayan mystery. Several statues and reliefs from Petén, dating from the early Old Empire, show men and gods, such as the sky god, Itzamná, wearing full, bushy beards. Some of these beards look false, but others are undoubtedly meant to be real.

Everybody knows that Mongoloid men have scanty beards or none at all. Most Amerinds pulled out their few facial hairs with tweezers made from clam or other shells. So where did these early Mayas, bewhiskered like Karl Marx, come from?

We can discard romantic notions of noble Nordics from northern Europe, sailing down the American coast and founding Mayan civilization. For one thing, the statues are nearly a thousand years earlier than the age of Norse exploration. For another, the faces of the bearded men that we have seen are not Caucasoid; they seem to be Mongoloid like those of other Amerinds.

Now, among all mankind, only two of the main races have thick beards: the Caucasoid or white race and the Australoid race of Australia. Yet in Hokkaido, the northernmost of Japan's main islands, live a people called the Ainu, who combine Australoid and Caucasoid characters. Their bearded features are somewhat Australoid, but their skins are pale. Although they are called the "Hairy"

Ainu, they are hairy only in comparison with the Mongoloids around them. In all probability, peoples of the Ainu type were once widely spread around eastern Asia until driven into their present corner or absorbed by the expanding Mongoloids.

Of the many ancient skulls dug up in the Americas, most are of standard Amerind type. Some anthropologists, however, claim to recognize Australoid traits in some of them. We must not take this too seriously, because the skulls of different races look much more alike than the men themselves. Racial differences lie mainly in skin color, texture and distribution of hair, and shape of the nose and lips; human skulls display no such marked variation.

Still, those Old Empire beards refuse to fit into our picture. Could it be that one of the early migrations from Asia to North America consisted, not of Mongoloids, but of an Ainu-like folk who spread widely, had the Americas to themselves for a while, and survived as small but distinct groups, beards and all, down to the beginnings of the Mayan Old Empire? This is only a wild surmise; yet perhaps worth looking into.

In any event, even if all these mysteries are some day solved, the towering ruins of Tikal will long provide those who see them with food for thought:

> About us looms the forest of Petén,
>> Immense, and dark, and threatening. All around
>> Colossal buttress-rooted trees, liana-wound,
> Rise orchid-laden from the humid fen.
> Beneath the jungle's blindly groping touch
>> Lie scattered and askew the works of man,
>> To raucous parrot and grotesque toucan
> Abandoned, in the forest's subtle clutch.
>
> Obeying *Señor Profesor*'s command,
>> José the Mayan, swart and slant of eye,
>> Pecks gently at his forebears' temples. Why?
> He nothing knows of when they ruled this land.
> Shall our descendants, for a stranger's coin,
> Peck likewise at the ruins of Des Moines?[15]

# X

# Machu Picchu and the Unwalled Fortress

... Between the walls of mighty mountains crowned
  With Cyclopean piles, whose turrets proud,
The homes of the departed, dimly frowned
O'er the bright waves which girt their dark founda-
  tions round.

*Shelley*

On the morning of July 24, 1911, three men emerged from a forested trail on the banks of the Urubamba River in Peru. A cold drizzle pattered down from the overcast. Around them rose one of the most dramatic landscapes in the world: "great snow peaks looming above the clouds more than two miles overhead; gigantic precipices of many-colored granite rising sheer thousands of feet above the foaming, glistening, roaring rapids."[1] Far above, glaciers shimmered through the clouds. Below the peaks, dense tropical jungle covered the slopes. Rain dripped from tree ferns, and orchids bloomed on towering trunks and far-spreading branches.

The three men were a local farmer hired as guide, a Peruvian soldier, and a handsome young professor from Yale named Hiram Bingham. Born in 1875 in Hawaii of two generations of missionary forebears, Bingham had chosen the academic life, specializing in Latin American studies. On this Yale Peruvian Expedition, Bingham had already climbed the 21,703-foot peak of Mount Coropuna in southern Peru and identified Vitcos,[2] the last Inca capital.

Nervously the explorers inched their way across a flimsy bridge of poles lashed together with vines, which spanned the gaps between the boulders. These boulders protruded from rapids, where the Urubamba roared past on its long journey to join the mighty Amazon. Safely across the chasm, they attacked the steep slope.

Sweating, slipping, creeping on all fours, and scaling tree trunks placed against the slope, they climbed for an hour and twenty minutes. At last they came upon a couple of grass huts built by two friendly Indian farmers who assured them that there were ruins higher up.

Guided by an Indian boy, Bingham and the soldier struggled up the rest of the slope. Here they found a long flight of ancient terraces, which the Indians had cleared of jungle and put back into agricultural use. Above these they found themselves "in a maze of beautiful granite houses"[8] made of pale, ponderous blocks, fitted and keyed with the meticulous care of the best Inca stonework.

Half hidden by vegetation, the ruin stood on a saddle between two enormous peaks, both rising over 9,000 feet above sea level: Huayna Picchu to the north and the even higher Machu Picchu (10,300 feet) to the south. Four thousand feet below, the Urubamba curled snakelike above the foot of Huayna Picchu. Outlying works were built on the slopes of the two peaks; some of these, on Machu Picchu, overhung a 3,000-foot vertical precipice.

This extraordinary citadel had no known name. None of the Spanish chroniclers mentioned it. It had come to be locally known as Machu Picchu, after the taller of the two guardian peaks.

Next year, Bingham was back at the ruin with a larger expedition, under the auspices of Yale and of the National Geographic Society. They cleared the site and explored the old Inca roads in the region. In one place, the road leading to the citadel itself burrowed through the cliffs by means of a tunnel. They mapped the buildings and the agricultural terraces by which the vanished dwellers supported themselves.

During this work, the surveyor Kenneth Heald had a close call. In trying to reach the top of Huayna Picchu, he hacked his way with a machete through a growth of spiny mesquite, until

. . . about 3 P.M., I had almost gained the top of the lowest part of the ridge, which runs along like the back-plates of some spined dinosaur. The trees had given way to grass or bare rock, the face of the rock being practically vertical. A cliff some two hundred feet high stood in my way. By going out to the end of the ridge I thought I could look almost straight down to the river, which looked more like a trout brook than a river at that distance, though its roar in the rapids came up distinctly. I was just climbing out on the top of the lowest "back plate" when the grass and soil under my feet let go and I dropped. For about twenty feet was a slope of about seventy degrees and then a jump of about two hundred feet, after which it would be bump and repeat down to the river. As I shot down the sloping surface I reached out and with my right hand grasped a *mesquite* bush that was growing in a crack about five feet above the jump-off. I was going so fast that it jerked my arm up and, as my body was turning, pulled me from my side to my face; also, the jerk broke the ligaments holding the outer ends of clavicle and scapula together. The strength left the arm with the tearing loose of the ligaments but I had checked enough to give me a chance to get hold of a branch with my left hand. After hanging for a moment or two, so as to look everything over and be sure that I did nothing wrong, I started to work back up. The hardest part was to get my feet on the trunk of the little tree to which I was holding on . . . It was distressingly slow work, but after about half an hour I had gotten back to comparatively safe footing. As my right arm was almost useless, I at once made my way down, getting back to camp about 5:30 . . .

A few days later, despite his injured arm, Heald—a determined man—got to the top of Huayna Picchu.

Bingham led further expeditions thither in 1914 and 1915. Then he went on to a full and colorful career. In the First World War, Bingham—at forty-two—learned to fly and served as an officer in the U. S. Army Air Service. Already active in Republican politics, he held a series of public offices and in 1924 was elected United States Senator from Connecticut. He wrote many books about his South American travels, especially about Machu Picchu, and led an active and varied career in many different fields up to his death in 1956. His reputation was marred, however, when he was officially censured by the Senate, in 1927, for bringing a lobbyist—a representative of the Connecticut Manufacturers' Association—into a closed session of a committee on tariffs.

The fact that Machu Picchu was unknown for so long, the appalling site on which it stood, and the silence of the chronicles about it all wrapped it in mystery. August Derleth brought Machu Picchu into the "Cthulhu mythos," the fictional cosmogony originally invented by the fantasy writer H. P. Lovecraft. According to one of

Derleth's stories, the octopus-god Cthulhu was worshiped near Machu Picchu. Cthulhu is one of the Ancient Ones, a race of malevolent deities long ago put under supernatural restraint but now and then let loose by rash mortals with frightful results.[5]

Nowadays, to visit Machu Picchu, you take a train along the Urubamba Valley and transfer to a bus, which snakes you up a terrifying switchback road to a tourist hotel perched amid the crags. Thence it is but a short walk to the ruins.

The city of Machu Picchu—whatever its inhabitants called it—straggles for seven hundred yards along the saddle between the two peaks. The southern end of the settlement, towards the peak for which it has been named, consists of more than fifty agricultural terraces and a few stone buildings. A single massive stone wall bounds the terraced area on the southeast side.

The northern end of the settlement, separated from the southern by a long straight ditch and a pair of walls that run athwart the saddle, consists of stone houses, with only a few terraces. The houses are divided into distinct groups, as if they were meant to be inhabited by separate clans. People in the first stages of urban civilization often divide up their cities in this way. Most of the lower walls of the houses are of massive cyclopean masonry, while the upper parts are made of smaller stones. Some of the upper walls are of crude stonework, using stones of random size set in clay; others are composed of regular courses of well-cut ashlars.

The houses were crowded together, but the many narrow streets and rock-hewn stairways made it easy to get about the settlement. Where possible, houses had little garden plots. Machu Picchu was furnished with over a hundred stairways, some having as many as 150 steps. In some cases an entire flight of six to ten steps was cut from a single ledge or boulder; we can imagine what a laborious task that must have been.

Was Machu Picchu a fortress, a walled city in the usual sense of the term? Some archaeologists call it walled and some unwalled. It depends on what one means by "wall." Machu Picchu had plenty of walls bounding agricultural terraces; but it had no single continuous defensive wall encircling the whole structure, as ordinary fortresses have.

When people build a walled farming terrace and the terrace is later neglected, the earth behind the wall often washes out, leaving the wall standing by itself. So, in lands where such terracing is usual, stone walls are sometimes described as the remains of ancient fortresses or palaces when they are nothing but terrace walls whose terraces have eroded away.

At Machu Picchu, there is some sign of fortification where the trail up the mountain enters the main city through a gate. Otherwise, it is hard to ascertain whether any of the massive stonework was meant as a defense rather than as a house wall or the retaining wall of a terrace. You see, the city occupied such a lofty, inaccessible site, surrounded by such hair-raising precipices, that it did not need defensive walls of the usual kind. Against the wild Chunchos, the terrace walls furnished adequate platforms from which to drop stones on the heads of the foe.

Bingham formed his own explanation of Machu Picchu. He insisted to the end of his days that it was the Tampu Tocco mentioned by Fernando Montesinos, a seventeenth-century priest who wrote a history of pre-Conquest Peru.

According to Father Montesinos, long before the Incas a mighty dynasty called the Amautas ruled the Andean region. In the reign of the sixty-second Amauta, Pachacuti VI, barbarian hordes overran the empire. About +800, the Amauta was slain in battle. Some of his soldiers took his body to a place of refuge called Tampu Tocco, buried it, and chose a new king.

The little kingdom flourished for several centuries, until pressure of increasing population caused its rulers to look abroad. About 1300 King Manco Capac[6] marched out, seized the ancient Amauta capital of Cuzco, and founded the Inca Empire.

Bingham matched various details of this story with things he had observed in his Peruvian travels. These resemblances, he argued, were good reasons for taking the story of Manco Capac seriously and for identifying Tampu Tocco with Machu Picchu. For example, Father Montesinos said that Manco Capac had caused a wall with three windows to be built at Tampu Tocco, and Bingham found such a wall at Machu Picchu.

Most students of Andean history, however, disagree with Bingham. In the first place, they do not consider Montesinos a historian of much critical worth when he deals with early events. He labored long, for instance, to prove that the Peruvians were descended from Noah's great-grandson Ophir.

Nor do they admit that Manco Capac was a real man. More

likely, they say, he is a culture hero. Many peoples invent culture heroes—legendary demigods to whom they attribute the founding of their nation and the discovery of the useful arts. Perhaps Manco Capac represents, not a single real ruler, but a whole dynasty of pre-Inca chiefs in the Cuzco region.

Even if we assume that Manco Capac was a real man, the legends say that he came to Cuzco from the south. Some tales locate Tampu Tocco in the province of Paruro, south of Cuzco; others have Manco Capac coming from Tiahuanaco, another ruined city with a mysterious prehistoric past.

Now, Tiahuanaco lies at the southeastern end of the 139-mile-long Lake Titicaca in the Peruvian highlands, several hundred miles southeast of Cuzco. With an altitude of 12,644 feet, it is the highest navigable lake in the world. A ship on Lake Titicaca is said to be the only place where you can suffer from seasickness and mountain sickness at the same time.

But Machu Picchu stands northwest of Cuzco, in the opposite direction from Tiahuanaco. Nor does Bingham's chronology agree with that which has been worked out by comparing the narratives of the Spanish historians with the findings of archaeology. So, for all of Bingham's ingenious arguments, Americanists today tend to brush aside his Tampu Tocco theory as an amateurish guess, whose author let it become an *idée fixe*. Nevertheless, Bingham belongs in the front rank of those who, like Stephens, Catherwood, and Maudslay, rediscovered the native civilizations of the Americas.

If Machu Picchu was not the capital of a pre-Inca ruler, what was it? Well, the Incas did not fortify whole cities. Instead, near each city, they built a hilltop fortress—like the Pergamos of Troy and the Acropolis of Zimbabwe—which was called a *pucará*, and to which the citizens could flee. The enormous fortress of Sacsahuamán, surrounded by sixty-foot walls made of stones weighing up to two hundred tons, was the pucará for the Inca capital of Cuzco. And Machu Picchu was a pucará for the villages along the Urubamba Valley. Philip A. Means thinks it was probably built in early +XV against raids by the primitive warriors of the Amazonian jungles to the east.

This somewhat prosaic solution of the mystery of Machu Picchu does not, however, clear up all the enigmas of the Andes. Far from it. For it leaves unsolved the far greater mystery of the vanished

Tiahuanaco Empire, which preceded the Inca hegemony. For this, however, we shall have to see what is really known about pre-Conquest Peru.

About the year 1526 on our calendar, the only Inca, Huayna Capac—the living god, the Son of the Sun, the lord of Tahuantinsuyu (the Four Quarters of the Earth)—heard rumors that strange, palefaced men in ships of unheard-of size and outlandish form had been seen off the northern coasts of his empire. It happened at an unfortunate time. Huayna Capac, plagued by dynastic troubles, was in bad health and soon to die. There were two claimants to the throne of the Son of the Sun: by a concubine, the Inca's oldest and favorite son, Atahuallpa; and by one of the legitimate wives, a younger son, Huáscar.[7] Before he died in 1529, Huayna Capac divided Tahuantinsuyu between the two: Atahuallpa to have the smaller northern part, with his capital at Quito; and Huáscar the remainder, with his capital at Cuzco.

As might be expected, the brothers soon fell out and fought. After several battles, Atahuallpa prevailed. Huáscar was captured and imprisoned. Atahuallpa had hardly finished killing off those of his relatives who might contest his right to the throne when, in 1532, Francisco Pizarro landed on the coast of Ecuador and began his march south through the Inca Empire.

Pizarro told the Indians that his party was an embassy from the mighty Emperor Charles V. In view of the size of the party, this seemed plausible. When he neared Cajamarca,[8] where Atahuallpa lay with his army, Pizarro's party consisted of only 168 men. They had sixty-seven horses, three arquebuses, two small cannon, and a few crossbows. Otherwise the Spaniards were armed simply with pikes and swords. Atahuallpa, who had good intelligence reports, was not unduly alarmed, even by accounts of the arquebus. The reports indicated that the weapon was but a superior kind of sling. Despite its terrifying noise and smoke, it felled only one man at a blow and took a long time to reload after each discharge. The Inca's Andean soldiers bore slings and bronze-headed spears, maces, and axes. Light armor of wood, leather, wicker, and quilted cotton protected them.

The Spaniards arrived at Cajamarca, presented their respects to Atahuallpa, and invited him to their camp for dinner. The Inca came with an unarmed escort. What had he to fear from such a handful, who knew that they were surrounded by his tens of thousands of well-trained warriors?

When Atahuallpa arrived, a monk approached him and informed him that he was now a subject of Emperor Charles V, to whom the Pope had given North and South America. Astonished, the divine Inca retorted that the Pope "must be crazy to talk of giving away countries that do not belong to him!"[9]

Pizarro gave his signal. The Spaniards rushed from hiding, seized the god-king, fell upon the escort with a cry of "Santiago and at them!" and slaughtered several thousand. The rest, once their ruler was captured, offered no resistance and tamely returned to their homes when dismissed by Pizarro. Thus, by the most daring, brilliant, and successful act of brigandage in all history, Pizarro became master of an empire that compared in size, population, and power with that of the early Pharaohs.

Atahuallpa offered Pizarro a roomful of gold for his release. When most of the gold had been collected, the Spaniards executed Atahuallpa on trumped-up charges of treason. Since Atahuallpa had earlier sent out word to kill Huáscar, the Andeans had no real leader left.

For several years the Spaniards ruled through puppet Incas, while more colonists—including Pizarro's numerous brothers—came from Spain to loot the country, to enserf the people, and to betray and murder each other. One puppet, Manco, ran away and raised a rebellion. He laid siege to Cuzco and might have captured it; but the planting season came around, and not even the threat of conquest and enslavement could keep the Andean peasants away from their farms at that time.

When his army melted away, Manco fled to the mountains northwest of Cuzco, around Machu Picchu. From the village of Vitcos, Manco, not at all mollified by Pizarro's having his favorite wife tortured to death, carried on a guerrilla against the Spaniards. At length, forgetting that the only good Spaniard was a dead Spaniard, he allowed survivors of a defeated Spanish faction to take refuge with him. They soon turned on him and killed him.

After that, the land was governed as a viceroyalty of the Spanish crown. In 1543, Emperor Charles V issued a decree guaranteeing various rights to the natives. But Peru was a long way from Spain, and the Spanish colonials paid no more attention to these restrictions than they had to.

After the conquest of Tahuantinsuyu, as the Incas called their empire, there was no burning of native books by Spanish priests, as had happened in Yucatán, because the Andeans had had no writing. They did have a mnemonic device called a *quipu:* a fringe-like arrangement of colored strings. By their colors, knots, and arrangement, these strings preserved records of population and resources throughout the empire. The priests burned some of these; but this had little effect on our knowledge of Andean history, because the quipus were no good without those trained to interpret them.[10]

On the contrary, in the years following the conquest, a number of Spaniards—priests, soldiers, and Garcilaso de la Vega who was half Inca himself—wrote down such historical traditions of the Inca Empire as they could gather. Some of these chroniclers were able historians. So there exists quite a large literature on the history of pre-Conquest Peru. The chroniclers listed the following Incas:

> Manco Capac, to 1105
> Sinchi Roca,[11] 1105–40
> Lloque Yupanqui, 1140–95
> Mayta Capac, 1195–1230
> Capac Yupanqui, 1230–50
> Inca Roca, 1250–1315
> Yahuar Huaccac, 1315–47
> Inca Viracocha,[12] 1347–1400
> Pachacuti,[13] 1400–48
> Tupac Yupanqui, 1448–82
> Huayna Capac, 1482–1529
> Atahuallpa and Huáscar, 1529–33

Of these rulers, Manco Capac was probably mythical. The Incas between Manco Capac and Inca Viracocha are doubtful. Most are probably real men, but the stories about them are full of contradictions and mythical elements. Inca Viracocha and those who followed him were real emperors, and the history of the empire during their two centuries is well known.

Before 1350, Tahuantinsuyu was a realm of modest size, limited to a piece of southern Peru and western Bolivia. Under Viracocha, Pachacuti, and Tupac Yupanqui, it expanded to take in all of Peru, much of Ecuador and Bolivia, and half of Chile.

"Inca" is not the name of a nation. The Incas were a leading clan of the Quechua tribe. This clan came to rule the tribe, and the tribe in turn ruled the empire. The head of the clan, who became the emperor, was called Sapa Inca, "the only Inca"; but all his fellow clansmen were called Incas, too. As the empire grew, the Sapa Inca found that he did not have enough relatives to occupy all the offices in the empire. Hence he promoted promising men to be honorary Incas so that they could hold offices or command armies. Thus there came to be a ruling caste of Incas.

The Inca Empire is the most successful example of benevolent despotism that the world has seen. The theory of benevolent despotism was set forth in +XVIII to flatter rulers like Frederick the Great of Prussia and Catherine the Great of Russia. More recently it has been revived by the Communists, who demand unlimited power for the Communist Party (which in practice means for the head of the Party) and who substitute a committee for a hereditary despot.

The theory of benevolent despotism is, roughly: give all power to the best-qualified ruler and trust him to do what is best for the people. Trouble arises, of course, in deciding who is best qualified and in choosing his successor. Moreover, how can one be sure that the despot, once he gains power, will not prove, like most men, to be motivated mainly by self-interest? Then he will use his power, not to benefit his subjects, but solely to secure his own position, augment his own wealth, and expand his own glory. That, of course, is what usually happens, whether the head man be called a king or a commissar.

It must be said for the Incas that, for at least a couple of centuries, they ran as efficient, well-organized, and benign a despotism as men have ever achieved. Their rule was the nearest thing yet to a practical communism.

Every peasant family, clan, and tribe had certain lands assigned to it. The assignments were revised from time to time to make sure that each family had enough land to support itself. Cultivation was coöperative. Along with their own plots, the Andeans had to cultivate those of the church and the state. The produce of the church lands supported the priesthood. The state religion was sun worship, but the gods of conquered peoples were also welcomed into the pantheon. Inca religion entailed some human sacrifice, but much less than among the Central American nations.

The lands of the state not only supported the Inca and his

212

officials and soldiers, but also filled storehouses all over the empire. These storehouses furnished food for the aged and crippled. They could also be drawn upon by individuals in case of crop failure or other misfortune.

Most Inca laws were severe, death being the usual penalty. But the law concerning theft had a curious quirk. If the thief had been driven to theft by hunger, he was punished lightly; while the official responsible for his welfare was punished more severely.

Since the empire had no money, taxation took the form of labor, called *mit'a*. Every year, each able-bodied man had to put in a certain number of days at such labor, constructing roads, public buildings, and so forth. Mining was by forced labor, as it was in most ancient empires and kingdoms; but men were made to work as miners for short periods only, lest their health be impaired. Men in their fifties were assigned to light work or retired on pensions.

When the Inca went forth to conquer, he commanded his soldiers: "We must spare our enemies, or it will be our loss, since they and all that belong to them must soon be ours."[14] Captured chiefs and their sons were brought to Cuzco, given an intensive indoctrination in Inca ways, and integrated into the bureaucracy. To discourage revolt, newly conquered populations were often deported to other parts of the empire; however, care was taken to see that they were placed in familiar surroundings—highlanders in highlands and lowlanders in lowlands.

For the lands of the empire varied enormously, from the "Rainless Coast" of Peru to the high, bleak *altiplano* and the steaming jungles of the upper Amazon. The Andean highlands lie at such a high altitude that the native Indians have evolved special bodily features to enable them to live and breed in the thin air. They are very short men with abnormally large chests; large, powerful hearts; and a blood supply so abundant that it gives them a purplish complexion. Because of the dehydrating effect of high altitude, they are the world's greatest soup eaters. They are also addicted to chewing the leaves of the coca plant, whence comes cocaine.

Inca rule was a triumph of common sense and enlightened self-interest. Given the technological level of the Andeans, their lack of writing, and the impracticability of large-scale self-government in such a culture, it is hard to see how the Incas could have done much better than they did.

Still, Inca rule had its shortcomings. Even if he never starved,

213

the ordinary Andean peasant lived (as many still do) in frightful squalor. His hut was a mere kennel, the floor of which was covered with guinea-pig droppings and alive with fleas and other vermin. The guinea pigs, which ran at large in the houses, furnished their owners with a small taste of meat. But then, the Indians were used to such an existence; in fact, even the ruling classes among the civilized Amerinds lived in surroundings that would seem to us very uncomfortable.

Finally, the Inca peasant led a very restricted life. He might not move, or change his occupation, or travel on the splendid roads without special permission. In fact, he was so strictly regimented that, when the Spaniards overthrew the Incas, he obeyed his new masters with the same docility he had shown the old.

Under the Spaniards, however, he soon found himself much worse off. The Spaniards discarded the Incas' elaborate welfare-state machinery and exploited the peasant more harshly than the god-kings ever had. When in 1780 the long-suffering Indians revolted under Tupac Amaru, a descendant of the Incas, the revolt was crushed; and the Indians' lot became more miserable than ever.

Like all despotic states, Tahuantinsuyu was plagued by wars of succession. The war between Huáscar and Atahuallpa doubtless helped the Spaniards to overthrow the empire. However, the Incas would have succumbed sooner or later, even if they had been united. European military techniques were so far ahead of those of the Amerinds that any small but resolute band of European adventurers could have overthrown any of the native American states. This in fact happened with Cortés in Mexico, Alvarado in Guatemala, and the Montejos in Yucatán. Whether the Amerinds fought fiercely or temporized, whether they were united or riven by local feuds, the final result was always the same. If Pizarro and his band had been wiped out at Cajamarca, other invaders would soon have followed in their footsteps.

Furthermore, the vast majority of human beings are so much prisoners of childhood beliefs and long-established habits that they are helpless to save themselves in the face of some new and unfamiliar danger. They go on reacting in their accustomed ways, even though to do so may cost them their lives. It was this factor that doomed the American Indians as much as their technical inferiority to the invaders. To save themselves, they would have had to change their ways and their technics as much in a few years as most people do in centuries; and this, not surprisingly, they failed to do. We need not belabor the parallels between the plight of the Amerinds and the position of all mankind under present international conditions and the state of the military art.

The traditional histories of the Inca Empire, which members of the Inca caste passed on to the Spanish chroniclers, gave the impression that all the lands of Tahuantinsuyu were sunk in the blackest barbarism before the great enlightener, the first Inca, Manco Capac. This, however, was artful propaganda. The Incas wanted credit, not only for what their ancestors had done, but also for the achievements of the pre-Inca rulers, whose memories they tried to blot out.

They did not quite succeed in this deception. Some Spaniards recorded the semi-legendary histories of other kingdoms, and archaeology has revealed still more. One early civilized kingdom was Chimú, whose capital lay at Chan-Chan on the northern Peruvian coast. The Chimu kingdom flourished from about +1000 until its conquest by Pachacuti in early +XV. The ruins at Chan-Chan, once quite impressive, have been largely obliterated by treasure hunters and by the heavy rains of 1925. On the Rainless Coast, even a light shower can devastate buildings not made to withstand it.

Five hundred miles southeast of Chan-Chan, on the southern Peruvian coast, another culture flourished even earlier than the Chimú kingdom. On the desert plains through which the tributaries of the Nazca River wind their way, the people of Nazca traced in sand and gravel an extraordinary series of "lines." These lines depict, on a colossal scale, geometrical figures and pictures of birds, spiders, whales, and other creatures. Some of the lines are as much as four miles long. Perhaps the Nazcans were trying to signal the gods.

Earlier still, from −1200 to −400, the Chavín culture flowered in the northern highlands, leaving behind art work full of fierce-looking puma-gods and nightmarish centipede-demons. The shovels of archaeologists have also turned up other prehistoric cultures. Some of these peoples built colossal pyramids and fortresses of adobe bricks. There is some fossil evidence that mastodons roamed the valleys of Ecuador down to the early centuries of the Christian

Era, and so the Chavín people and their successors presumably knew about them; but it has not yet been proved that they hunted them or used their ivory.

The most striking of these prehistoric cultures was that of Tiahuanaco,[15] the remains of which lie at the southeast end of Lake Titicaca. If we can judge from the spread of its artistic styles, Tiahuanaco was once the center of an empire comparable in grandeur to the Inca Empire itself. Located on the bleak altiplano 13,000 feet above sea level—too high for intensive agriculture—Tiahuanaco hardly seems a promising site for the capital of an empire. The ruins, scattered over a sixth of a square mile, include large truncated pyramids or artificial hills, a terraced pyramid 50 feet high, rows of monoliths, platforms, inclosures, and underground chambers.

There are also monolithic gateways, in which the two upright supports and the lintel are carved out of one solid piece of stone. The largest of these, called the "Gateway of the Sun," was chiseled from a single block of andesite, a very hard rock. It is 10 feet high, 12.5 feet wide, and weighs about 10 tons. Above the doorway is carved a feline-looking god, probably the same as the creator-god Wiraqochan of the Incas. This sculpture is flanked by forty-eight small, rectangular, birdlike figures, running towards the center.

Since Tiahuanaco is as improbable a place as Machu Picchu, it drew the attention, half a century ago, of the German pseudo-scientific cult of Hörbigerism. Hörbigerites like Hans Bellamy and Arthur Posnansky "proved" that Tiahuanaco was 250,000 years old. Its extraordinary altitude was explained very simply: when it was built, it was near sea level; convulsions of nature raised it to its present height.

Hans Hörbiger was an Austrian inventor, a gadgeteer who bragged that he never calculated anything. When people questioned his extreme statements he would shout:

"Instead of trusting me you trust equations! How long will you need to learn that mathematics is valueless and deceptive?"[16]

Hörbiger said that as a boy, while looking through a telescope at the moon and the planets, he suddenly realized that they were made of ice. When he was a young engineer, the sight of water-logged soil exploding with puffs of steam as molten iron ran over it gave him the clue for constructing a private cosmos almost as colorful as Mme. Blavatsky's and even more alarming. This became known as the Cosmic Ice Theory.

The universe, it seems, is a kind of cosmic steam engine. Interstellar space is full of rarefied hydrogen and water vapor (partly true). When a small star, moving through this damp mixture, loses its heat, it picks up ice. When a larger star draws the small one into itself, the small star remains buried in the large one, a vast ball of ice, for millions of years while the ice melts. Finally the small star turns to steam. The resulting explosion throws pieces of star material into space. These pieces condense into planets, while the oxygen of the giant star, also blown out, unites with the hydrogen of space to make a ring of ice particles, called "bolides," outside the planets.

As the hydrogen of space slows them up, these bodies all spiral in towards the sun. Because the smaller particles are retarded the most, they spiral in the most rapidly, passing the larger ones. So, as the ice blocks of the solar system fall towards the sun, most of them are picked up by the gravitational fields of the outer planets. Therefore the latter have acquired thick coats of ice.

When an ice block reaches the sun, it causes another explosion, which fills the space around the sun with fine particles of ice. The inner planets Venus and Mercury, moving through these, have also become sheathed in ice; the earth is luckily just far enough from the sun to avoid icing. Large planets catch smaller ones spiraling past them and make satellites of them, eventually drawing them into themselves.

The capture of a satellite and its later fall to the surface of a planet impose great stresses upon the planet. The gravitational pull of the satellite causes floods and earthquakes until the moon settles into a stable orbit. Then all is quiet until the satellite, retarded by the hydrogen of space, nears its primary, and the gravity of the satellite draws the oceans into a belt or bulge around the equator, drowning the equatorial regions but leaving the polar lands high and dry.

When the satellite approaches within a few thousand miles, gravitational forces break it up. The fragments shower down upon the planet. The oceans, released from the satellite's pull, flow back towards the poles, exposing tropical lands and submerging polar territories. All human catastrophe myths can be fitted into this

217

scheme, be they the biblical Flood, Atlantis, the Revelation of St. John, or the Norse Ragnarök.

At least six satellites before the present moon have been captured and destroyed by our earth in various geological eras. Since man was civilized in the Cenozoic or Tertiary Era, he remembers the fall of the Cenozoic moon, whose approach submerged all the tropical lands save a few highlands like Peru and Ethiopia 250,000 years ago. The capture of the present moon, the ex-planet Luna, inundated Atlantis and Lemuria. The breakup and fall of Luna will probably end all life on earth.

Although the First World War interrupted the progress of this cult, Hörbiger reappeared after the war with a high-powered publicity machine, which flooded Europe with books, pamphlets, and threatening letters. Soon Hörbiger's followers numbered millions, some of whom interrupted meetings of learned societies by yelling:

"Out with astronomical orthodoxy! Give us Hörbiger!"

Although Hörbiger died in 1931, his movement continued active for years. With the rise of Hitler, the Hörbigerites identified themselves with the Nazi racial philosophy: "Our Nordic ancestors grew strong in ice and snow; belief in the World Ice is consequently the natural heritage of Nordic Man."

Practically every one of Hörbiger's assertions is dead wrong. For example, the planet Venus, far from being coated with ice, has been shown by the measurements of the space craft Mariner II to have a surface above the melting point of lead and almost at a dull red heat. But then, Hörbiger's theories are no more ridiculous than those of Immanuel Velikovsky, the comet-collision man, whose works attained an equal if transient vogue in the United States in the 1950s.

What do we really know about the lost empire of Tiahuanaco? There were two stages of culture there. The earlier and simpler, Tiahuanaco I, appeared before the Christian Era. The later, imperial Tiahuanaco II arose between +500 and +1000, spread its rule far and wide for several centuries, and fell before the coming of the Incas. When the Incas conquered the region around Lake Titicaca, they found Tiahuanaco already deserted; at least that is what they told the Spanish chroniclers. The people of the region were the Aymara Indians, a dour, silent folk who still grow potatoes and herd llamas on the bleak plateau with its glaring suns and frigid nights. The Incas, however, copied at least the megalithic stonework of the Tiahuanaco people.

Legends collected by the chroniclers do contain hints of the Tiahuanaco Empire. There is an allusion to "the kings of Vilcas, Huaitara, and Tiahuanaco."[17] Perhaps some of the legends of Manco Capac and of the pre-Inca empire of the Amautas are connected with real events in the history of Tiahuanaco. But how? We cannot tell, any more than we can reconstruct the history of Minoan Crete from the legend of King Minos, Daidalos, the Minotaur, Theseus, and Ariadnê.

Since the Tiahuanaco people, like the other semi-civilized South American nations, had no writing, there are no inscriptions waiting to be deciphered; no way to recover the lost story of Tiahuanaco. If history is not written down, it vanishes forever when those who remember it die off. Short of a time machine, there is no way to recover it.

The archaeologist can unearth many details of a forgotten people's lives and material equipment. He can infer much about their costumes and customs, their beasts and buildings, their social and economic systems. But to preserve details of names and pedigrees, reigns and battles, plots and rebellions, sects and philosophies, people need writing. And without it, both the history of the Inca stronghold at Machu Picchu and the enigma of the lost empire of Tiahuanaco are likely to remain forever hidden in the mists that swirl about the towering peaks of the Andes.

# XI
# Nan Matol and the Sacred Turtle

And there, in sombre splendour by the shore
Of Hali dark, an ancient city stood;
Black monolithic domes and towers loom
Stark, gigantic in the starless gloom
Like druid menhirs in a haunted wood.

*Carter*

From the blue tropical waters of the western Pacific, the steep green peaks of a mountainous, jungled island rise more than half a mile into the sky. Around the 164 square miles of this island lies a necklace of coral reefs and small islets. This is Ponapé, the largest of the Carolines.

A broad bay gapes in the southeastern coast of Ponapé. Scattered about this bay are scores of small islands, many of which come and go like the Cheshire cat's grin as the tides rise and fall. The largest of these isles is called Temuen. At high tide, the eastern end of Temuen is sea-washed into nearly a hundred low-lying islets, on which stand a vast array of huge, dark, strange, silent ruins of deep blue stone. Such is Nan Matol.

Nan Matol is an awesome ruin in spite of damage from hurricanes, treasure hunters, and the prying action of tropical vegetation. Most of the islets are bounded by enormous walls, up to thirty feet high. These walls are built of long columnar pieces of dark rock laid crisscross, like the logs of a log cabin, and revetted on the inner sides by masses of coral piled against them. Several canals, swarming with sharks and rays, lap at these walls even at low tide. At high tide the walled islets, covering eleven square miles, float on the waves like the ruins of some primeval Venice.

Even today, when tourists buzz about the world by the millions, few come to Ponapé; for there is no easy access to Nan Matol. No road leads through the jungle. There is no nearby airstrip. The only way to reach the ruin is by a bouncing, bruising, drenching, fifteen-mile motorboat ride along the coast. So, for the most part, the ruin remains silent save for the sound of wind and wave, the calls of birds, and perhaps the faint echoes of the long-ago voices of the men who built it.

Lying in the equatorial rain belt, a few degrees north of the equator, Ponapé is warm and dank, with frequent rains and occasional hurricanes. Like other Micronesian islands, it harbors birds and insects but no land mammals save those, like pigs and rats, brought in by man. This fact alone proves that the island could never have formed part of a continent, as some have claimed.

Because the high interior is covered with tropical rain forest, nearly all the inhabitants live along the coast, in villages clustered about the six good harbors. There are six or seven thousand of them today—small, wiry, brown folk with straight or wavy black hair and flat Mongoloid features.

White men first saw Ponapé on the evening of December 23, 1595. Captain Alvaro de Mendaña had set out from Peru with four ships to hunt for Terra Australis, the Unknown Southland, which in his day was thought to fill most of the Southern Hemisphere. Mendaña had found the Solomon Islands and died there. Now the one surviving ship of his squadron, the *San Jeronimo*, under Pedro Fernández de Quiros, was trying to reach Manila.

When Quiros anchored inside the reef to renew his supplies, grass-skirted natives came out in canoes. After the natives decided that the visitors were not ghosts, there was some friendly trade by sign language, although the Ponapeans later boasted of having stolen one of Quiros' cannon. After eleven days, Quiros sailed on to Guam, in time got back to Peru, and recorded his visit to Ponapé.

During the following centuries, other ships showed up off the coasts of the island but did not land; or, if they did, there is no record of their coming. The next visitor to Ponapé was an Irish sailor, James O'Connell, who in 1826 arrived with a few fellow survivors from a shipwreck. O'Connell made a hit by dancing an Irish jig and by his fortitude in letting himself be tattooed all over. The Ponapeans rewarded him by marrying him to the fourteen-year-old daughter of the king of Net[1] before ever he knew what was happening. He stayed on the island for eleven years until a passing ship offered him a chance to return to civilization.

At this time the island was divided into five warring kingdoms: Jokaz in the north, U in the northeast, Metalanim[2] in the southeast, Net in the south, and Kiti in the west. The island of Temuen and its ruins lie in the harbor of the district of Metalanim. O'Connell, who was paddled to the island by a frightened Ponapean, described the ruins as he saw them:

But, the most wonderful adventure during the excursion, the relation of which will put my credit to a severer test than any other fact detailed, was the discovery of a large uninhabited island, upon which were the most stupendous ruins of a character of architecture differing altogether from the present style of the islanders, and of an extent truly astonishing. At the extreme eastern extremity of the cluster is a large flat island, which at high tides seems to be divided into thirty or forty small ones by the water which rises and runs over it. It differs from the other islands in its surface, which appears to be placed there by nature. Upon some parts of it fruit grows, ripens and decays unmolested; as the natives can by no persuasion be induced to gather or touch it. My companions at the time of discovering this island were George and a nigurt; the latter having directed our attention to it, promising us a surprise—and a surprise indeed it proved. At a little distance the ruins appeared like some of the fantastic heapings of nature, but upon a nearer approach, George and myself were astonished at the evident traces of the hand of man in their creation. The tide appeared to be high, our canoe was paddled into a narrow creek; so narrow that in places a canoe could hardly have passed us, while in others, owing to the inequality of the ground, it swelled to a basin. At the entrance we passed for many yards through two walls, so near each other that, without changing the boat from side to side, we could have touched either of them with a paddle. They were about ten feet high; in some places dilapidated, and in others in very good preservation. Over the tops of the wall, cocoanut trees, and occasionally a bread fruit spread their branches, making a deeper and refreshing shade. It was a deep solitude, not a living thing, except a few birds being discernible. At the first convenient landing, where the walls left the edge of the creek, we landed; but the poor nigurt, who seemed struck dumb with fear, could not be induced to leave the boat. The walls inclosed circular areas, into one of which we entered, but found nothing inside but shrubs and trees. Except for the wall, there was no perceptible trace of the footsteps of man, no token that he had ever visited the spot. We examined the masonry, and found the walls to be composed of stones, varying in size from two to ten feet in length, and from one to eight in breadth, carefully propped in the interstices and cracks with smaller fragments. They were built of the blue stone which abounds upon the inhabited islands, and is, as before stated, of a slatose formation, and were evidently split and adapted for the purpose to which they were applied. In many places the walls had so fallen down that we climbed over them with ease. Returning to our canoe we plied our nigur with questions; but the only answer we obtained was "Animan!" He could give no account of the origin of these piles, of their use, or of their age. Himself satisfied that they were the work of *Animan*, he desired no further information, and dared make no inspection, as he believed them the residence of spirits. We returned to the island of Kitti, where we announced our intention to inspect the ruins on the next morning. It was with difficulty we got away from the islanders, who declared that our lives would be forfeited for our temerity. Arriving a second time at this deserted Venice of the Pacific, we prepared for deliberate survey. We paid several visits to the ruins, but could find no hieroglyphics or other traces of literature.[8]

The "blue stone" whereof O'Connell wrote is prismatic basalt which, crystallizing slowly from lava deep in the earth, forms large six-sided (or sometimes five or eight-sided) prisms. The best-known formation of this kind is the Giant's Causeway in Ireland. The island of Jokaz, off the northern coast of Ponapé, is made of prismatic basalt and has an exposed cliff of these rocks, with heaps of broken prisms at its foot. The builders of Nan Matol must have hauled these prisms down to the shore, put them on rafts, and towed them fifteen miles around the northeast side of Ponapé to Nan Matol. Clusters of prisms scattered on the sea bottom along the coast show where some of these rafts came to grief on the way. Other stones were brought from various spots on the coasts of Ponapé.

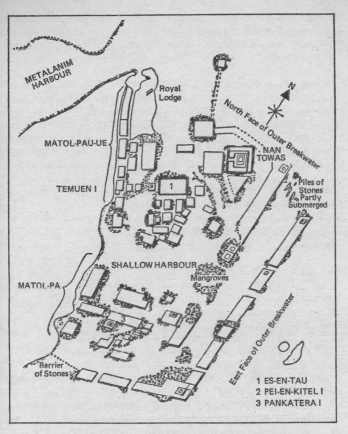

Fig. 15  Map of Nan Matol. (*After Christian*)

The walls of Nan Matol look from a distance as if they were made of black logs, with courses piled alternately parallel to the axis of the wall and then at right angles to it. The "logs," however, are six-sided columns of basalt. In spite of all that has been written about the wonderful stonework of Nan Matol, it is really very crude, with holes the size of your head. The stone was not dressed or trimmed at all. The builders simply hunted through the talus on Jokaz until they found prisms of the right size; or, if they failed to find them, they split some prisms off from the cliff by building fires against it.

While O'Connell was living on Ponapé and fathering two children by his native wife, the Russian bark *Senyavin,* under Lütke, touched at Ponapé in 1828. Lütke had a fight with the Ponapeans when he tried to send a longboat into Kiti harbor. In the following years, more and more whites came to Ponapé. Whalers stopped there; deserters and beachcombers settled. The Ponapeans massacred a British crew, and the British Navy massacred them in return. In 1865 the Confederate raider *Shenandoah* destroyed a group of Yankee whaling ships anchored in the lagoon at Ponapé. American and Spanish missionaries came.

Of the many overthrows of native cultures that occurred during the period of European expansion in +XIX, that of the Pacific Islanders was the most complete and catastrophic. Scattered about on their thousands of islands, these peoples were utterly exposed to the onslaughts of traders, slavers, missionaries, and the armed forces of European powers. Because of the small size of most of their islands, the natives could neither fight nor flee effectively. The traders sold them liquor and stirred up intertribal wars to provide a steady market for guns and ammunition. The slavers, called "blackbirders," kidnaped them to work on Australian plantations.

Meanwhile the missionaries did all they could to undermine the native cultures in order to replace the natives' beliefs with their own. They stopped such simple fun as singing and dancing and forced their own clothing customs and tabus on tropical peoples to whom clothes merely brought dirt and disease. Protestant missionaries encouraged their converts to war upon Catholic natives and vice versa. When the natives rebelled against mission tyranny, the missionaries summoned their nations' navies to chastise the ungrateful savages.

Furthermore, the whites helped to depopulate the islands by spreading European diseases among folk with no resistance to them. As a result of all these forces, the native population of the Marquesas, for example, dwindled from 120,000 in 1790 to 1500 in 1920. (In recent decades, as a result of modern medicine, the islanders have begun to repopulate their territories.)

In 1886, during the last great scramble for colonies, Spain annexed Ponapé. But the Spaniards never controlled much of the island, and the warlike Ponapeans rose several times against them. The islanders had a stern, Spartan culture, which went in for self-mutilation as a sign of bravery. Before missionaries, traders, and adventurers demoralized them, they were also said to be a notably cheerful and honest people, albeit a formal folk, with a caste system and a passion for titles.

During the past century, the Ponapeans have been handed about among the great powers. In the Spanish-American War, the United States seized the Carolines but gave them back to Spain after the war. Spain then sold them to Germany. When the Ponapeans rebelled against German rule in 1910–11, the Germans crushed the revolt with a bombardment from the famous cruiser *Emden* and hanged the leaders. In the First World War, the Japanese seized the Carolines and kept them under an ill-observed League of Nations mandate. Today the United States governs them under a United Nations trusteeship.

Ever since its discovery, Nan Matol has been a subject of mystified speculation. Some said it was a fortified base built by Spanish pirates; others, that it was the capital of a once-great Pacific empire; still others, that it is a relic of a lost continent.

Abraham Merritt, the learned newspaper editor and fantasy writer, laid one of the best-known of his colorful novels, *The Moon Pool* (1919), in Nan Matol. At Nan Matol, the narrator and his companions find the entrance to an underground world. Here the leaders of an advanced civilization, locked in civil strife, wield fantastic occult weapons against each other.

The occultists—especially the Theosophists—have put the mysteries of Nan Matol to the most dramatic use of all. According to the occultists, Nan Matol is a relic of Lemuria, a former continent in the Pacific, which sank much as they thought Atlantis had sunk in the Atlantic.

Curiously enough, the idea of Lemuria started out a century ago as a sober and reasonable scientific hypothesis. After the Darwinian revolution in science, the latter half of +XIX witnessed a great surge in the advance of biology and geology. In the 1860s and 70s, several British geologists noted resemblances between certain rock formations in India and in South Africa. William T. Blandford,

227

especially, pointed out the likeness of the Permian beds in these two places. The deposit in India occurs in a tract called Gondwana, meaning "Land of the Gonds." The Gonds are a forest tribe who once had the unpleasant custom of slowly torturing people to death in magical rituals to make their crops grow.

Blandford inferred that a land bridge had once connected India with South Africa by way of Madagascar and the Seychelles Islands. These observations came to the notice of the German biologist Ernst Heinrich Haeckel. Haeckel seized upon this land bridge to explain the distribution of lemurs, primitive primates that look like a cross between a monkey and a squirrel. Lemurs abound in Madagascar and are found here and there in Africa and tropical Asia. Haeckel supposed that the land bridge might have endured from the Permian Period (over 180,000,000 years ago by modern reckoning) down to the Cenozoic Era or Age of Mammals, which began about 70,000,000 years ago.

Then the English zoölogist Philip L. Sclater suggested the name "Lemuria" for this bridge. Other geologists thought that Lemuria was a remnant of a much larger and earlier continent, which they called "Gondwanaland." They supposed that Gondwanaland had once extended three quarters of the way around the earth in the Southern Hemisphere, with a gap in the Pacific.

These hypothetical continents, however, have no bearing on human civilization. Even if they existed—which seems more and more unlikely in the light of modern geological research—they subsided many millions of years before men evolved.[4] Nevertheless, the occultists have found the idea of primeval continents, peopled by strange races, grist to their mill.

The greatest of modern occultists was Helena P. Blavatsky, the founder of Theosophy. In the 1870s she was a fat, middle-aged Russian adventuress living in New York City. The estranged wife of a Russian general, she had been the mistress successively of a Slovenian singer, an English businessman, a Russian baron, and a merchant from the Caucasus living in Philadelphia. In her younger and slimmer days she had made her living as a circus bareback rider. Later she had worked as a professional pianist, a businesswoman, a sweat-shop worker, and a spiritualist medium. Although H.P.B., as her followers called her, had enjoyed a pretty lively career as it was, she painted the lily by inventing an even more remarkable past. She claimed to be a persecuted virgin who had traveled the world in search of occult wisdom and had visited the world-ruling Mahatmas in Tibet.

Mme. Blavatsky took as her partner Henry Steel Olcott, an American lawyer who left his wife and sons to live with her. Theosophy really got started when the pair moved to India. Here Mme. Blavatsky combined her knowledge of western magic and occultism with a wide and inaccurate smattering of East Indian philosophy and mythology.

In 1882 she was dazzling a pair of well-connected Anglo-Indian dupes, Sinnett and Hume, by delivering letters which she said were written by her "Master" Koot Hoomi, but which, as handwriting analysis later showed, she wrote herself. In these letters she was feeling her way to the grand occult cosmogony that she later advanced, with seven planes of existence, sevenfold cycles through which everything evolves, seven Root Races of mankind, the seven bodies that each individual possesses, and the Brotherhood of Mahatmas who run the world from Tibet by sending out streams of occult force.

Mme. Blavatsky had picked up the Lemuria theory in the course of her reading and incorporated it, along with Atlantis, into her own gaudy cosmos. Her doctrines took final if wildly confused form in her chef d'oeuvre, *The Secret Doctrine*. She wrote this huge, multi-volume work in Europe after a pair of accomplices who had assisted in producing her magical feats betrayed her and compelled her to leave India.

This book, she said, was based upon an Atlantean treatise, *The Book of Dzyan*. Her Mahatmas showed her a manuscript copy of this ancient work in the trances by which they visited her in their astral bodies. *The Secret Doctrine* consists of quotations from the imaginary *Dzyan* and Mme. Blavatsky's commentaries thereon, interspersed with passages of occult gibberish and diatribes against "materialistic" science and "dogmatic" religion. *The Stanzas of Dzyan* begin:

1. The Eternal Parent, wrapped in her Ever-invisible Robes, had slumbered once again for Seven Eternities.

2. Time was not, for it lay asleep in the Infinite Bosom of Duration.

3. Universal Mind was not, for there were no Ah-hi to contain it.

4. The Seven Ways of Bliss were not . . .

Presently the Universe begins to awaken: "The last Vibration of the Seventh Eternity thrills through Infinitude. The Mother swells, expanding from without, like the Bud of the Lotus . . ."

After various cosmic events described in this iridescent language, life appears: "After great throes she cast off her old Three and put on her new Seven Skins, and stood in her first one . . . The Wheel whirled for thirty crores more. It constructed Rupas; soft stones that hardened, hard Plants that softened. Visible from invisible, Insects and small Lives . . . The Watermen, terrible and bad, she herself created from the remains of others . . . The great Chohans called the Lords of the Moon, of the Airy Bodies: 'Bring forth Men, Men of your nature . . .' Animals with bones, dragons of the deep, flying Sarpas were added to the creeping things . . ."[5]

Without going into the elaborate Theosophical world-plan of multiple planes of existence and chains of planets, we are told that life on earth is evolving through seven cycles or Rounds. During this time, mankind develops through seven Root Races, each comprising seven Sub-Races. The Theosophical concept of evolution, however, is utterly different from Darwin's.

The First Root Race, we learn, was a kind of astral jellyfish, invisible to ordinary human eyes, who lived in the polar Imperishable Sacred Land. The Second Root Race, a little more substantial, dwelt in the arctic continent of Hyperborea (derived, like Atlantis, from Greek myths and geographical speculations). As the continent of Hyperborea broke up by the sinking of its various parts, that of Lemuria formed, occupying most of the Southern Hemisphere. The Third Root Race were the giant, apelike, hermaphroditic Lemurians, some with four arms and some with eyes in the backs of their heads. Their downfall was caused by their discovery of sex. (Mme. Blavatsky took a dim view of sex after she reached the age when she herself was no longer interested in it.)

Then Lemuria, like Hyperborea before it, subsided and broke up into smaller land masses, while Atlantis took shape in the North Atlantic. The Fourth Root Race were the highly civilized Atlanteans. As Atlantis in turn sank, as a result of a long series of catastrophes, islands in other parts of the world grew into the present continents. We of today are the Fifth Root Race, and the Sixth will soon evolve from the present-day Americans. In the distant future, South America will give birth to the Seventh and last Root Race.

*The Secret Doctrine*, alas, is neither so ancient, so erudite, nor so authentic as it pretends to be. When it appeared, an elderly Californian scholar named William Emmette Coleman, outraged by Mme. Blavatsky's false pretensions to oriental learning, made an exegesis of her works. He showed that her main sources were H. H. Wilson's translation of the ancient Indian *Vishnu Purana;* Alexander Winchell's *World Life; or, Comparative Geology;* Donnelly's *Atlantis;* and other contemporary scientific, pseudo-scientific, and occult works, plagiarized without credit and used in a blundering manner that showed but skin-deep acquaintance with the matters discussed. Most of the *Stanzas of Dzyan* were cribbed from the *Hymn of Creation* in the ancient Sanskrit *Rig-Veda,* as a comparison of the two works readily shows.

Mme. Blavatsky's followers, however, were not to be daunted by a few mere facts. She kept control of a sizable body of believers even after she had been exposed in many chicaneries.

After H.P.B. died in 1891, her following, as often happens, broke up into several quarreling sects. Rival leaders and other Theosophists wrote books in which they clothed Mme. Blavatsky's skeletal account of the history of mankind with the flesh of lush and colorful detail. William Scott-Elliott, a scholarly English merchant-banker fascinated by the then novel study of comparative religion, composed (before he got fed up with occultist trickery) the most readable Theosophical account of Lemuria and Atlantis. In this you can read about twelve-foot, skin-clad Lemurians leading pet plesiosaurs on leashes; about the adepts from Venus who guided the evolution of these sub-men into the wholly human Atlanteans; about the sorcerer-kings who ruled Atlantis from the City of the Golden Gates; and about other wizardly wonders.

The Theosophical accounts of Lemuria and Atlantis were put to practical use by a novice adventure-story writer, Edgar Rice Burroughs, the creator of Tarzan. In 1912 Burroughs published a serial, *Under the Moons of Mars,*[6] in *All-Story Weekly*. Five years later the same story appeared as a book under the title *A Princess of Mars* and became the first of ten novels of this series.

Burroughs' Martians were essentially Theosophical Atlanteans and Lemurians, removed to a Mars based upon the then popular theories of the astronomer Percival Lowell. According to Lowell, the faint streaks on the surface of the planet were canals built by intelligent Martians to conserve the scanty water supplies of this "dying" planet. Astronomers no longer believe Lowell's theory, although they have not yet agreed on the true nature of the streaks.

We have not been able to learn just how and when Burroughs acquired his knowledge of Theosophical Atlantism. He was never much of a reader, and we are told that his library contained no Theosophical books. But some contact there must have been, for the resemblances are too many for mere chance. For example, Burroughs' noble Red Martians are derived from the Theosophical Toltecs, one of the Atlantean races. They use flying machines much like those of Theosophical Atlantis. His gigantic, four-armed, pop-eyed, egg-laying Green Martians are nothing but H.P.B.'s Lemurians transplanted.[7]

Other occultists moved Lemuria from the Indian Ocean, where Mme. Blavatsky at least had the grace to leave it, several thousand miles to the central Pacific, where for geological reasons we can be quite sure there never has been a continent and, furthermore, that there never will be one. Members of the occult societies calling themselves Rosicrucians wrote voluminously, borrowing Mme. Blavatsky's lost-continent doctrines.

In 1898, Frederick Spencer Oliver published a tedious occult novel, *A Dweller on Two Planets*, which started a rumor of Lemurians in long white robes performing mystic rites on Mount Shasta, in northern California. Occult societies eagerly added the Shasta Lemurians to their credos. In 1932 a hoax article in the Los Angeles *Sunday Times*, telling of transcendental fireworks still to be seen on the mountain, gave a new lease on life to the legend. Churchward's lost continent of Mu followed the general description of the occultists' Pacific Lemuria.

Again and again, in writing of this lost land, the occultists cited, as irrefutable evidence, the weird statues on Easter Island and the ruined city of Nan Matol on the island of Ponapé. But the mysteries of Nan Matol turn out to be mostly man-made. The unwritten facts of its design and use were simply forgotten as those who knew them died off. First, the missionaries tried to blot out "heathen" native traditions. Then the island was long ruled by the Germans and the Japanese, neither of whom encouraged nosy foreigners, scientific or otherwise.

Much information about Ponapé was gathered by a German Pole, Johann Stanislaus Kubary, who settled in the Carolines in late +XIX. Kubary took four native wives, whom he kept on different islands, and killed himself when one of his wives eloped with another man. His manuscript passed into the hands of a native Ponapean family, who kept it as an heirloom until it was accidentally burned in the 1930s.

The history of Ponapé, nevertheless, did not perish entirely with this manuscript. In 1908–10 the Thilenius expedition set out from Germany to study Micronesia. One of this team of scientists, Dr. Paul Hambruch, made Ponapé his target. The results of his visit were published in three large volumes in 1932–36. Because this work is in German, its information has only slowly seeped into the English-speaking world. Hence Lemurian speculations about Ponapé have continued to flourish.

Hambruch devoted the first volume of his treatise to the history of Ponapé; his second to the anthropology of the Ponapeans; and his third to Nan Matol and the native myths and legends. One of his most helpful informants was Nalaim of Metalanim, a hereditary high priest and tradition bearer.

The story that Hambruch heard about the building of Nan Matol tells how two young wizards, Olo-Sipe and Olo-Sopa,[8] set out from Jokaz to build a great cult center to the gods, demons, and ghosts. They tried several places on the coasts of Ponapé, but each time the wind and the surf destroyed their handiwork. At last they found their ideal site at Temuen. A mighty spell made the basaltic prisms on Jokaz fly through the air and settle down in the right positions to form Nan Matol.

More plausible are the traditions of the conquest of Ponapé by the king of Kusae, an island several hundred miles to the east. Once, said the Ponapeans, their island was ruled by a single king, whose title was the Satalur.[9] One version says that the Satalur demanded tribute from the king of Kusae, who replied by conquering Ponapé. The invader, Iso-Kalakal,[10] started a new dynasty with the title of Nan-Marki.[11] The Nan-Markis failed to keep control of the whole island, which split into five kingdoms. The Nan-Markis ruled Metalanim, while other dynasties ruled the other kingdoms.

A mythical version of the conquest runs as follows: In the days of the last Satalur, the thunder god Nan-Japue came to Ponapé. There he seduced the wife of the Satalur. When the king found this out, he trapped Nan-Japue in one of the buildings of Nan Matol and blocked him up. The god would have died of hunger and thirst had not his screams drawn another man, who turned him loose. Nan-Japue went to Kusae, riding on a fish. He sprinkled an old woman with lemon juice so that she became pregnant and bore Iso-Kalakal.

One day Iso-Kalakal was out fishing when he sighted Ponapé. Back home he built a great war canoe. With 333 followers he sailed to Ponapé, landing at Nan Molusei near Nan Matol. The Satalur received him warily but hospitably.

However, a quarrel soon arose between one of Iso-Kalakal's followers and the nobleman in charge of feeding the visitors. War began. After victories on both sides, the Kusaeans prevailed. The Satalur fled and turned himself into a fish, leaving Iso-Kalakal to reign in Metalanim.

Iso-Kalakal reigned for many years. One day he looked at his image in a pool and saw that his hair was white. Ashamed of his age, he killed himself in a gruesome manner.

The Kusaeans also have a legend about their conquest of Ponapé. Although this tale differs from the Ponapean version, there is little doubt that the conquest took place.

Hambruch inferred that Nan Matol was built by one of the early Satalurs. Although such a task would not take the manpower of a vast empire, it would require the united efforts of all the Ponapeans.

Hambruch's informants thought that there had been twelve Satalurs. Then came Iso-Kalakal, followed by seventeen Nan-Markis. Hambruch estimated that these two dynasties covered about five hundred years. No better estimates are yet available. Carbon-14 dates show that the Micronesian Islands have been occupied by men since about —1500, but these dates have not yet shed much light on the details of Ponapean history.

Once Nan Matol was made up of several different groups of structures. The main center is Matol-Pa, the lower city, where dwelt the king. The upper city, Matol-Pau-Ue, includes the tallest building in Nan Matol: Nan Towas, "the Place of the High Walls," where the Satalurs were buried. It also includes Es-En-Tau, the house of the high priests, and Pei-En-Kitel, supposedly the burial place of Iso-Kalakal. The third section consists mainly of sea walls, canal borders, and other retaining walls. Near the south end of the ruins is Pan Katera, the sacred governmental center including a palace and altars for offerings.

The crudity of the stonework of Nan Matol and the lack of any writing or relics of urban civilization (although there are some petroglyphs or rock carvings three miles inland) rule out the idea that Nan Matol was built by men of an advanced culture. Everything indicates that it was a religious or cult center rather than a true city. Other Micronesians built similar centers, although never on so vast a scale. They probably did not duplicate Nan Matol because they did not have, for building material, a mountain of prismatic basalt, ready to be broken into pieces of convenient size.

Nanpei of Metalanim told Hambruch that until recent times Nan Matol was used as a center for the worship of the turtle god Nanusunsap. Whenever the Ponapeans caught a sea turtle, they brought it to Nan Matol and kept it in one of the buildings. When the tribe was assembled, the priests anointed the turtle with coconut oil and hung it with ornaments. The priests loaded the turtle into a boat and paddled about the canals of Nan Matol, while one priest stared at the turtle and blinked his eyes every time the turtle blinked. When they arrived at Pan Katera, where a fire had been lit, a priest killed the turtle by breaking its shell with a club. The turtle was cut up, cooked, and served to the priests and the king, with prayers and ritual.

In the reign of the Nan-Marki Luk-En-Mueiu, about 1800, the ritual was brought to an end in a ridiculous fashion. At one ceremony, a priest got no roast turtle. He walked out in a rage, howling curses, and went off to live by himself on a sand bank and eat eels. The Metalanimians feared that he had so profaned the ceremony that they could no longer hold it.

The Ponapeans also had myths about a dragon or giant lizard. In one version, the dragon lived in Jokaz and gave birth to two girls. When the girls grew up, they married the reigning Satalur and asked their husband to let their mother come to live in Nan Matol. When he assented, the dragon moved into one of the buildings, excavating the canals of Nan Matol in the process.

235

Next morning, when the Satalur brought some food for his mother-in-law, he saw the dragon for the first time. In terror he burned up the house and the dragon. His wives jumped into the fire and burned themselves up, too; and in grief the Satalur did likewise. The likeliest explanation for the dragon myth is that Ponapé was once visited by the New Guinean crocodile, a large man-eating species often found swimming in the open sea, where one would never expect to see a crocodile.

Sifting fact from legend, what can we say about this once teeming sacred center, now a silent ruin? We know that about 1400 after many migrations and conquests, the population of Ponapé was much as it is now. At this time, when the Renaissance was in full flower in Italy and Chaucer was finishing his Canterbury Tales in England, a single chief made himself high king of all Ponapé with the title of Satalur. He or one of his successors started Nan Matol as a cult center. Successive kings added new buildings to take care of more cults.

About 1600, when Shakespeare was writing, the Satalur demanded tribute from King Iso-Kalakal of Kusae. Instead of sending tribute, Iso-Kalakal came with his warriors and conquered Ponapé. His successors ruled as the Nan-Markis of Metalanim. Although they lived, not at Nan Matol, but on the island of Nanue-Zu Taman, they continued to use Nan Matol as a cult center; perhaps they even added to its frowning walls. There were probably several cults, but the turtle cult is the only one we know about.

Because the Nan-Markis did not long rule the whole island, but only one of the five kingdoms, Nan Matol was no longer the religious center for all of Ponapé. It therefore declined in importance. The other kingdoms built their own smaller cult centers, whose ruins still exist. The last active cult of Nan Matol, the Nan-Markis personal cult of the sacred turtle, disappeared, probably in the early 1800s, after the hot-tempered priest profaned its ceremonies.

Then came the missionaries; and Nan Matol was left forlorn, to be covered with mangroves and to mock later visitors with its dark silent walls and empty, overgrown courts. And that is the true tale of the Isle of the Sacred Turtle. If there are no four-armed Lemurian giants in it, I am sorry; but then, the story of the turtle cult and its bizarre ending is almost as curious as anything devised by the sorcerer-kings of the Theosophical Atlantis.

# XII
# Rapa Nui and the
# Eyeless Watchers

How many weary centuries have flown
  Since strange-eyed beings walked this ancient shore,
  Hearing, as we, the green Pacific's roar,
Hewing fantastic gods from sullen stone!

*Howard*

One of the loneliest places on earth is Easter Island. Its nearest
neighbor is Sala-y-Gomez, 210 miles eastward across the South
Pacific; but Sala-y-Gomez is a mere jut of barren rock, three
quarters of a mile long and useful only to sea birds. You must travel
two thousand miles farther to reach the South American coast; or,
in the other direction, 1,200 miles into the sunset to find Pitcairn
Island. The desolate isolation of Easter Island makes its ruins all
the more astonishing.

From the sea the island appears as a green, grassy land, rolling
away behind tall black cliffs and guarded by the black fangs of
deadly reefs. It is roughly triangular. The hypotenuse, facing
southeast, is about fifteen miles long; the circumference measures
about thirty-five miles; and the total area is forty-five square miles.

Near the points of the triangle rise the cones of three extinct
volcanoes: Rano Raraku in the east, Rano Kao in the southwest,
and Rano Aroi in the northwest, each cradling a fresh-water lake
in its crater. Similar cones rise here and there over the rest of the
island. In addition, the remains of a large ditch, the Poike Ditch,
runs across the easternmost point, sundering it from the rest of the
island. Although this ditch is referred to as a fortification in the
native legend of the Long-ears, some archaeologists believe that it
was, not a fortification at all, but an agricultural work. The climate

is mild and windy, with gusty rains. There are no native mammals, but the insects are bothersome.

The Dutch admiral Jaakob Roggeveen[1] made a landfall there on Easter Sunday, 1722, and named the place Paasch Eyland or Easter Island. The natives do not seem to have had any name for their island; so isolated were they that they needed no special word to distinguish their land from any other. When the first Tahitians arrived in the 1870s, they called the island Rapa Nui, "Great Rapa," because it looked like little Rapa Iti in the Tubuai Islands. And Rapa Nui it has remained in the speech of the Pascuans or Easter Islanders.

Rapa Nui is volcanic, with a soil of decomposed lava. Despite the bleak look of the land, this soil is fertile. It is also porous. Hence the island has no rivers and only a few springs. The Pascuans had to work hard to clear stones from the rough surfaces of their fields and to carry water for irrigation in order to raise their simple crops, mainly sweet potatoes.

Rapa Nui is known far and wide for its huge-headed statues. Although many have fallen into the sea, or have been used for building material, or have been taken away to museums, there are still over six hundred of them. Completed statues range from 3 to 36 feet in height. Some larger ones, up to 66 feet long, were begun in the quarries of Rano Raraku. There they lie unfinished, along with a multitude of chisels and other tools of stone, which were used to shape them.

These sculptures, although often called "heads" or "busts," are for the most part complete statues. However, the size of the heads is so exaggerated in proportion to the squat bodies that the latter pass unnoticed. Moreover, the statues that are mounted on the slopes of Rano Raraku—the only ones remaining upright in large numbers—are buried to the neck by wind-blown soil and débris from the quarry, leaving the heads alone to gaze sternly across that treeless land.

Who are the people of Rapa Nui? They are Polynesians: big, rather handsome folk with brown skins and straight or wavy black hair. They speak a dialect of the Marquesan language, although nowadays they also know Spanish.

The Pascuans farm and fish, much as they always did, and work on the sheep ranch run by the Chilean Government. They wear castoff western-style clothing, some of it stolen from visitors; for they are known as the world's most accomplished and persistent thieves. They have also become expert at forging antiquities. They carve little statues of stone or wood in the ancient style to pass off on visitors as relics of the pagan past. When regular air service begins, this forgery will doubtless become big business.

The question of how and when these people came to Easter Island has long puzzled civilized men. Scientists, adventurers, and cultists have all tried to solve the problem. In this welter of opinion and speculation, the general public cannot easily tell fact from fiction, reasoned inference from wild guess. So let us look at some of the surmises about the origin of the Pascuans and their great stone heads.

In late +XIX and early +XX, some scientists tried to account for the migration of men, animals, and plants across the Pacific by means of prehistoric land bridges. About the same time, Easter Island was swept into the current of lost-continent doctrine. Mme. Blavatsky averred that the Pascuan statues were life-size. Therefore, she said, the ancient Lemurians, who carved them, must have been a race of giants. Later, Churchward made Easter Island a southeastern bastion of his Pacific continent of Mu.

It is plain, said the cultists, that these statues could not have been carved and erected by simple Polynesians. They must be relics of an advanced civilization, commanding large resources of manpower and advanced techniques. Why, the avenues built by the ancient Lemurians not only lead across Easter Island but on down into the sea, where they can be traced under water . . .

As for the fate of the sunken land, Churchward laid its disappearance to the collapse of his "gas belts." On the other hand, Hörbiger and his followers ascribed it to the worldwide disturbances that attended the capture of the moon by the earth. For a while, in the winter of 1922–23, it looked as if these ideas might have a basis of fact, when a ship reported that Easter Island itself had sunk beneath the sea. But time proved that Easter Island was all right; it was the ship's navigator who was wrong.

In 1932 Owen Rutter based an amusing adventure novel, *The Monster of Mu*, on the lost-continent theories of Rapa Nui. A party of treasure hunters, including a girl, find, near Easter Island, another land where white priests of Mu rule the last remnant of their continent. Little brown men do the work on the island. All these

Muvians are immortal; but, since women are forbidden, the priests tie the heroine to rocks to sacrifice her, like Laomedon's daughter Hesionê, to a monster resembling a blind plesiosaur. After much lively action, the island conveniently sinks; the hero and heroine alone escape.

In recent decades, however, the progress of geology has put all the Pacific sunken-continent theories on the shelf. There is no sign of a submerged continent in the eastern or central Pacific. The water is all deep—mostly one to three miles—save where volcanic islands like Rapa Nui thrust up to the surface.

We can make these statements because of the nature of the rocks that are found in the Pacific. Continents have rocks of a distinctive type: light silicon-aluminum rocks like granite. East of a line running through New Zealand, Fiji, and the Melanesian islands, called the Andesite Line, no rocks of continental type have been found in the Pacific. From other indications, such as the speed of earthquake waves across the sea bottom, geologists are sure that no such rocks exist in this vast area, even under water. So no thousand-mile land bridges, no sunken continents are possible in this area. The submerged causeways built by the wise Lemurians simply do not exist.

If there were no land bridges to hike across, how did the natives of Rapa Nui get to their distant island? Of the many fanciful speculations on this subject, none has aroused more public interest in recent years than the ideas of Thor Heyerdahl, organizer of the Kon-Tiki expedition.

In the spring of 1947, Heyerdahl and five other stalwart Scandinavians sailed a raft of balsa logs from Callao, Peru, 4,300 miles across the Pacific to the Tuamotu Archipelago. By this trip, Heyerdahl proposed to prove his theory about the settlement of the Pacific islands. He believed that Nordics from northern Europe had brought culture to Peru and founded the Andean civilization. Then, having been civilized by these white enlighteners, the ancient Peruvians set forth about +500 in balsa rafts. They sailed westward over the trackless Pacific until they found the Polynesian islands. Around 1100, another wave of migrants, this time from the northwest coast of North America, sailed to Hawaii and thence to the other Polynesian islands, where they mingled with the previous Peruvian migrants to engender the Polynesians of historic times.

To buttress his argument, Heyerdahl called attention to Peruvian legends of white-skinned, bearded enlighteners who had founded the early civilizations of that land and hinted that these were probably noble Nordics from his native Norway.

The pseudo-scientific Nordic cult is based upon the idea that all advances in civilization stem from the white race and in particular from tall, blond, blue-eyed, pale-skinned northern Europeans. All the great men of antiquity are asserted to have been Nordics; and the superiority of the Nordic race in turn is demonstrated by the achievements of these men. By this circular logic, even Julius Caesar (who in fact had dark brown eyes) and Jesus of Nazareth (about whose appearance nothing is known) are "proved" to have been Nordics.

This cult, propagated some decades ago by writers like Madison Grant, is a twin to the Aryan cult. In fact, many of the cultists assumed that Nordics and Aryans were one and the same. At least a Nordic sub-race or type does exist, whereas the race of the original Indo-European-speaking Aryans is not known. The British writer Hilaire Belloc had fun with the Nordic cult in his verse:

> Behold, my child, the Nordic man
> And be as like him as you can;
> His legs are long, his mind is slow,
> His hair is lank and made of tow.[2]

While the Nordic and Aryan cults flourished, it was common to make much of native legends about light-skinned civilizers. Since Europeans then regarded themselves as the only leaders of civilization, it seemed plausible that backward peoples should have received illumination from a European source. The American Indians had many myths of pale culture heroes, although it is hard to be sure whether the legends refer to white-skinned, white-painted, or white-clad enlighteners.

Certainly, these alleged civilizers could not have been the Norsemen who visited North America around +1000, because when these explorers arrived they found the legend already afloat. Thorfinn Karlsevni's men captured two Amerind boys who, when they learned Norse, said they had heard that across the sea lay a land "where people went about in white clothes, uttered loud cries, and carried poles with banners fastened to them."[3]

There is a simple explanation for this recurring theme of pale rulers over dark subjects. This reason has nothing to do with ancient conquests, explorations, or racial talents. Everybody knows that sunlight causes the human skin to darken. This effect is especially strong among people of medium hue—neither so pale as a Nordic nor so black as a Negro—that is to say, among people like Mediterraneans, Arabs, Polynesians, and Amerinds.

Now, in a pre-industrial society, most people are farmers and other outdoor workers. Hence a dark skin becomes the stigma of a proletarian, who is much exposed to the sun. On the other hand, a pale skin is the sign of an aristocrat. Hence many barbarous peoples like the Pascuans, as their daughters neared marriageable age, imprisoned the girls in huts until they had bleached to an aristocratic pallor.

After his voyage, Heyerdahl wrote the best-selling *Kon-Tiki*—certainly a splendid adventure story. Having become famous, he organized a serious archaeological expedition, which spent over half a year on Rapa Nui and visited other Pacific islands.

Heyerdahl's theory sounds persuasive to people who know nothing of the subject. For instance, he noted resemblances between the culture of Easter and other Polynesian islands and those of South America. The Polynesian Adam was called Tiki; the Peruvian creator-god was also called Tiki; so, he said, the myths of these two peoples must have had a common origin. But when we look into this "Tiki" matter, it turns out to be merely another case of a casual resemblance between two words in unrelated languages, proving nothing about ancient migrations.[4]

Heyerdahl did what most enthusiasts with an *idée fixe* do. He diligently searched for evidence to back his theory and resolutely ignored any that confuted it. Thus he tells about a legend which indicates that the Pascuans' ancestors came from the east; but he does not tell the whole story. This legend came from Alexander P. Salmon, a half-Tahitian who bossed Rapa Nui from 1877 to 1888 as a kind of benevolent dictator and who collected antique lore. Salmon told one visitor that the islanders had come from the west; four years later he told another that they had come from the east. Some, he said, thought they had come from the Galápagos to the north. Evidently the Pascuans of Salmon's time had no clear idea of their original homeland.

Furthermore, Heyerdahl pointed out that a statue his men dug up on Rapa Nui proved to have the same kneeling pose as certain statues of Peru. Actually, sculptures in this pose have been carved in many parts of the world. For instance, there is a kneeling statue of King Amenhotep II of Egypt. Kneeling statues prove only that this is one of the postures that people the world over take to rest their feet.

Heyerdahl also made much of a Pascuan legend of the war between the Long-ears, who practiced distention of their ear lobes, and the Short-ears, who did not. In the legend the Short-ears, some time in late +XVII, almost exterminated the Long-ears. According to Heyerdahl, the Long-ears were a Peruvian aristocracy and the Short-ears a Polynesian proletariat who, arriving later, were compelled by the Long-ears to work at building statues and other structures until they revolted.

Although the legend may refer to a real battle, neither the legend nor Heyerdahl's interpretation of it fits all the facts. For one thing, the early white explorers who touched at Rapa Nui found the Pascuans freely stretching their ear lobes long after the alleged battle, so there was no general disappearance of Long-ears. The story is probably an elaboration of one of the many fierce inter-tribal wars that happened at that time, padded out with fictional and mythological elements "to give artistic verisimilitude to an otherwise bald and unconvincing narrative."

Although nearly all professional students of Pacific archaeology and anthropology rejected Heyerdahl's theories, the general public went right on buying the adventurer's books. As one of Heyerdahl's critics remarked:

"If there is anything that an avid adventure-reader hates it is an egghead scholar who primly pours a test tube of cold water on an already brine-soaked blond Viking hero who conquered the roaring Pacific to demonstrate his faith in a dramatic theory, when the spectacled scientists had said it couldn't be done."[5]

Sober scientists have also searched for the truth about the settlement of Easter Island. They are now convinced that the Polynesians anciently lived along the southeast coasts of Asia—in South China, Indo-China, or Malaya. The rise of a powerful Chinese Empire in the second millennium B.C. touched off a general movement of peoples. Each tribe on the fringes of Chinese civilization, fleeing from advancing Chinese imperialism, crowded its neighbors outward. Because the Polynesians were already spread along the coast, they could go nowhere but across the sea. Probably their flight was speeded by the fact that they were still in the Stone Age when their enemies, the Mongoloid peoples, had metal weapons.

Whether the Polynesians settled first in Indonesia, or the Philippines, or the Melanesian islands are fine subjects for argument. In the coming decades we may learn more about their exact route, because serious stratigraphic study has only recently been started in the Pacific islands.

The Polynesians are a fairly uniform race, combining Caucasoid, Mongoloid, and Negroid traits. In addition, they often have a jawbone of distinctive shape, called "rocker jaw." Except for their large size they might pass for "average" human beings—the sort of people who would inhabit the earth if all mankind freely interbred for several generations.

As with the Hamitic-speaking people of northeast Africa, we cannot tell whether the mixed physical characteristics of the Polynesians are the result of actual racial interbreeding or whether they evolved as a distinct intermediate type. Their neighbors to the southwest are the Australoids, also a distinct race. To the west live the Melanesians or Oceanic Negroes, who differ from African Negroes in their hooked noses and curly (rather than kinky) hair. Northwest are the Micronesians, an offshoot of the Mongoloid race, whose teeming millions fill eastern Asia. It is hard to make categorical statements about the Polynesian race because, as a result of their genial sexual hospitality to visitors, most of them today are of more or less mixed blood.

Their languages form a family whose different members—Hawaiian, Maori, Samoan, and so forth—differ among themselves no more than Italian differs from Spanish. The Polynesian languages in turn are related to the languages of the Malayan group and, more remotely, to some languages of the Asian mainland, such as Thai. From the point of view of language, culture, and archaeology, there is little doubt that the Pascuans came from the Marquesas Islands, one of the most easterly of the Polynesian groups, possibly stopping off at Pitcairn Island on their way. In any case, there is no chance at all that the short, copper-skinned, straight-haired Peruvian Indians evolved in a few centuries into the tall, muscular, brown-skinned, wavy-haired Polynesians.

It is not unlikely that Polynesians, the greatest of all barbarian seafarers, occasionally reached the coast of South America. But it is less likely—though not impossible—that any Peruvian Indians ever got to Polynesia. Despite their balsa rafts, these people were essentially landlubbers; they made little use of the sea and paid it little attention. The geography of western South America, with its harborless coasts, its terrific surf, and its dearth of offshore islands explains this attitude. It is not even certain that the Peruvians had a true sail. The Spaniards found them stretching a piece of cloth against the wind on a balsa raft; but the purpose of this rig may have been, not to propel the craft, but to stabilize it and thus make it easier to paddle.

Many people have argued about possible unrecorded trans-oceanic voyages. They wonder, for instance, whether the Phoenicians or the Chinese ever reached North America, or whether any seafaring Amerinds ever reached the Old World. Even before ocean-going ships were developed, such voyages may have some-times taken place under unusual conditions of wind and weather. Of such expeditions, the great majority—let's say nine tenths—must have perished on the way. Of those who did make land on the far side, most of the voyagers must soon have died. They were slain by disease, snakebite, or hostile natives, like the Spanish castaways who landed in Yucatán in 1511 and who were promptly sacrificed and eaten by the Mayas.[6]

Of those who did survive, nine tenths must have grown old and died without leaving any record of their adventure. For a few years, a tribe might remember "that funny-looking stranger who lived with us but who could never speak our language correctly and seemed ignorant of the simplest things . . ." Then all memory of the exile would fade away. Moreover, even in those rare instances where the far voyagers survived the journey and were hospitably received by the natives, everything we know about the transmission of culture makes it wildly improbable that the culture of the natives would be visibly changed by such an isolated visit. Most people are much too stubbornly attached to their own traditional ways.

We know of the Phoenicians' voyage around Africa only because of a paragraph in Herodotos; we know of Miguel Cortereal's fate only because he scratched his name on Dighton Rock. How many other far voyagers perished without leaving even so slight a record? However, it is one thing to admit that such voyages *may* have taken place, and quite another to assert, without positive evidence, that any particular voyage *did* take place. And there is no such hard evidence of contacts between the South American Indians and the Pacific islanders. True, there are many remarkable parallels between artifacts made in the New World and in the Old, which have led some reputable archaeologists to suppose that such contacts occurred before Leif Ericsson. Such contacts *could* have happened; we might even say they *may* have happened. But we do not think that the evidence now known makes it right to say they *did* happen.

What do the people of Rapa Nui themselves say of their past? Early in +XX Juan Tepano, a Pascuan with a reputation for collecting tribal lore, told the following tradition of his people:·

The land of our fathers was a great island to the west called Marae Ranga. The climate was warm and many trees grew there, of which our ancestors made large boats or gathered together to build themselves houses. In spite of the shade, people were sometimes killed by the heat.

Hotu Matu'a was a chief of this island, but he was forced to leave it after a quarrel with his brother Te Ira-ka-tea. We do not know the cause of this dispute, which provoked a war between the two chiefs. Another story is also told. Hotu Matu'a's brother was in love with a woman whom the *ariki* [nobleman] Oroi wished to marry. The young woman, hesitating between the two, promised Oroi she would be his if he walked round the island without stopping to rest or sleep. Oroi submitted to this test, but meanwhile the girl ran away with Hotu Matu'a's brother. There was war between the tribe of Oroi and the tribe of Hotu Matu'a. Oroi being the stronger, Hotu Matu'a was obliged to set out in search of new lands in order to escape death or dishonor.

There was in the island a certain Hau Maka, who had tattooed King Hotu Matu'a. Hau Maka had a dream: his soul journeyed across the sea to an island where there were holes [craters] and fine beaches. Six men had landed there at the same time.

Hotu Matu'a understood that Hau Maka's dream was a promise. He chose six men, gave them a canoe, and told them to sail straight ahead until they reached the land Hau Maka's soul had seen. As they moved away from the shore, the king called after them: "Go and look for a fine beach where the king can settle."

The pioneers found Rapa Nui. Hotu Matu'a followed close behind them:

The same day, all the people who had come in the canoes disembarked. They unloaded the plants and animals they had with them. These plants were taros, yams, sugar canes, bananas, *ti*, and then all the trees that have disappeared—such as hibiscus and *toro-miro*. As for the animals, only the chickens and the [edible] rats had survived. Hotu Matu'a had set out with several other species, but these did not come to the island until the white men brought them later.[7]

Oroi, thirsting for revenge, had stowed away in one of the ships. For a while he lurked about Rapa Nui, trying to catch Hotu Matu'a at a disadvantage and kill him. He did succeed in killing two of Hotu Matu'a's sons. Eventually Hotu Matu'a killed Oroi but refrained from eating him out of deference to his rank. At last Hotu Matu'a grew old, divided the island amongst his sons, and died.

For a defeated chief to gather his supporters and set out to try to find new land was the usual procedure in Polynesia; otherwise he was liable to be eaten by the victors. While most such expeditions perished at sea, some succeeded. In this way, the more distant habitable islands were populated. The Polynesians had a vast fund of sea lore and some navigating instruments and charts of their own invention. The term "canoe" for their great sailing catamarans gives a false impression. These ships were up to 150 feet long—larger than a classical trireme—and carried as many as four hundred persons. By traveling in line abreast, several miles apart, and communicating by smoke signals, a fleet of such vessels could cover thousands of square miles and discover all the islands in the area.

Assuming that Rapa Nui was actually settled in some such fashion, students of Pacific migrations, working from the genealogies and the lists of kings furnished by the Pascuans, calculated that Hotu Matu'a's voyage must have taken place about the year 1200.

However, radiocarbon testing of charcoal samples collected by the Heyerdahl Easter Island expedition indicates human habitation ranging back to about +480 (plus or minus a hundred years). Some think this date too early to be credible (a slight contamination of a radiocarbon sample can throw the date far off in either direction), but it is not inconsistent with radiocarbon dates from other Pacific islands. At any rate, the second oldest radiocarbon date from Rapa Nui is +857. These dates, together with such indications as rate of change of languages, imply that the settlement of the westernmost Polynesian islands had begun as early as −500, and that Rapa Nui, the farthest east of all the Polynesian islands, was occupied at the latest by +IX.

In the thousand years following the settlement of Rapa Nui, the Pascuans farmed, fished, fought tribal wars, carved hundreds of awesome statues, and finally saw their culture crushed by the all-conquering white man.

In 1576, the Spanish seaman Juan Fernández reported a land of continental size about where Rapa Nui lies, with "the mouths of very large rivers . . . the people so white and so well clad"[8] that he was amazed. If he had sighted Rapa Nui—which is doubtful—it must have taken an imagination worthy of an adman to have described it as he did.

Juan had achieved notoriety some years before by sailing wide of the South American coast in order to take advantage of the winds. He later made the voyage from Callao to Chile in such good time (thirty days) that upon his arrival he was seized by the Inquisition on suspicion of witchcraft. Having convinced the Holy Office that he had not sold his soul to the Devil for seamanship, he planned to go back for another look at his continent, but died without fulfilling his dream.

The next to cruise those empty seas was an English buccaneer, Edward Davis, who sighted land in 1687 but did not come ashore. The account later published by one of his men is either a very bad description of Rapa Nui or a fairly good one of Timoe and Mangareva, 1,600 miles to the west.

In 1722 came Admiral Roggeveen. Some naked natives came aboard bearing food. When they had presented their gifts, they stole whatever they could get their hands on, including several sailors' caps and the admiral's tablecloth, and dived overboard.

When Roggeveen sent a party ashore, hundreds of Pascuans gathered on the beach. Some made friendly gestures; others threatened the visitors. Two natives pounced upon a sailor to rob him; other Dutchmen came to their comrade's rescue; the natives picked up stones to throw. A volley of musketry littered the sand with a dozen dead Polynesians and several wounded. The Pascuans scattered but soon returned with servile gestures. A few hours later, Roggeveen sailed away.

Half a century passed. In 1770, a Spanish expedition under Felipe González, looking for the equivocal "Davis Land," touched at Rapa Nui. The Spaniards, although a little shocked by the willingness of the women, kept on friendly terms with the natives.

Soon afterwards, in 1774, Captain Cook arrived. To him the Pascuans seemed few, poor, and miserable. The probable reason is that the Pascuans had been engaging in terrific intertribal wars. Survivors of a losing side hid in their underground storerooms, hoping to avoid being roasted for a victory dinner. A favorite Pascuan taunt was: "Your flesh has stuck between my teeth," meaning: "I have eaten your kinsmen!"

When in 1786 a French expedition under Comte J. F. C. de la Pérouse landed for a one-day visit, things were better. La Pérouse, full of eighteenth-century notions about the Noble Savage, kept his men under strict control and laughed at the Pascuans' incessant thieving. He reported:

> The physique of many of these women was pleasing. They offered their favors to anyone who would make them a present. The Indians pressed us to take them . . . and pending the importunities of the women they stole the hats from our heads and the kerchiefs from our pockets. All appeared to be accomplices in these thefts; for no sooner had one been committed than, like a bird flight, they all fled at the same instant. But seeing that we did not resort to our fire arms they returned some minutes afterward. They renewed their caresses and waited opportunity for new larceny. This trickery went on throughout the morning. As we were going away that night and had so short a time in which to undertake their education, we played the part of being amused by the ruses which the islanders employed to rob us.[9]

In early +XIX, foreign pressure on the Pascuans rose. American whalers stopped to kidnap natives for slaves or to shoot a few for target practice. As a result, the Pascuans became increasingly hostile towards strangers, and their hostility caused further clashes. A group of French missionaries who landed in 1843 were massacred.

Even without modern weapons, the Pascuans presented a formidable sight. Like other Polynesians, they were a tall, powerful, heavily built race, the men being notably taller than the women.

Many went entirely naked, although some men wore a G-string and many women a grass skirt, and they all donned bark-cloth cloaks against the chilling winds.

The men were bearded, tied up their hair in topknots, and wore large wooden plugs in their ear lobes. They tattooed themselves all over. In addition, the men were painted over the tattooing in gaudy patterns of red and black. When a visitor arrived, they crowded down to the beach, capering, dancing, talking, and yelling at the tops of their voices. Many would be friendly, but others at the least provocation would start throwing stones with alarming accuracy.

Of all the Noble Savages popularized by the literature of late +XVIII and early +XIX, none was deemed nobler than the Polynesian. White visitors often liked these friendly, charming, jolly, volatile, high-spirited, generous, lazy, gallant, and artistic folk. They preferred them to the black Melanesians, despite—or perhaps because of—the fact that many Melanesians displayed traits we think of as typically Caucasoid, being practical, industrious, crafty, determined, and ambitious.

Actually, Polynesian life was not so ideal as romanticists of the Noble Savage school had thought. A disillusioning picture of Polynesian home life was given by the recent archaeological excavation of the floor of a rock shelter in the Marquesas:

> The living floors were covered by a litter of basalt flakes, shell fragments, leaves, wood chips, pieces of broken wooden tools, unnumbered scraps of braided cocoanut fiber, fecal matter, broken water gourds, animal and fish bones, dead insects, fragments of desiccated lizards, scraps of old discarded tapa loincloths, charcoal, and ashes. Along the wall of one of the shelters was a dirty heap of shredded banyan fiber upon which the inhabitants slept. In the other shelter, close by, an oven contained the remains of a young child who had been cooked and partially eaten. The skull and hand bones had been scattered over the cave floor during the feast, but the torso had been dumped back into the oven, after which life had gone on as usual, as signalized by an accumulation of several inches of undisturbed trash over the surface of the oven and its pathetic contents.[10]

Some whites even mistook the Polynesians' permissive attitude towards sex as evidence of a kind of primitive "democracy." The

Polynesians were certainly liberal about sex. One of their institutions was a joint family wherein each man was the husband of all the women and each woman the wife of all the men.

But in other respects they were very rigid. A Polynesian was subject to as many rules of living as an Orthodox Jew or a high-caste Hindu; it is not for nothing that the word *tabu* is Polynesian. A chief's head, for instance, was sacred; to touch one earned instant death.

Moreover, their social organization was anything but democratic. Their societies were divided vertically into clans, organized somewhat like the clans of Scotland, as well as horizontally into castes of kings, noble warriors, commoners, and slaves. Their main amusements, apart from sex, were genealogy, war, and water sports. Although extremely friendly and amiable towards those they liked, they could also be extremely fierce, cruel, and callous. War was deadly and cannibalism rampant. Unwanted girl babies and feeble old people were often killed out of hand.

The whites taxed the Polynesians with thievishness largely because they did not understand the Polynesian attitude towards property. A Polynesian divided property into two kinds. Possessions that the owner deemed important, such as farmland, he placed under *tabu*, a kind of spell or curse laid upon anybody who should disturb the property.

The spell had to be cast by a chief, priest, or other qualified person. Thieves were warned away by a keep off sign in the form of an arrangement of sticks or stones. Since everybody believed that the property had become charged with *mana* or spirit force, fatal to all but the owner, tabus were seldom broken.

On the other hand, less important property, such as a man might carry with him, was looked upon as more or less communally owned. If a man saw something he wanted in another's possession, he took it. The owner, instead of getting angry, took the theft as a joke and laid plans to steal the object back.

The culture of Rapa Nui received its fatal blow in 1862. One day, several Peruvian ships anchored off the the island, attacked the islanders, killed some, and rounded up about a thousand others, whom they carried off as slaves to work on the guano islands. After Bishop Tepano Jaussen of Tahiti protested, the Peruvian Government ordered the victims returned. By this time nine tenths of them had perished. Of the remaining hundred, all but fifteen died of smallpox on their way back home, and the survivors spread the disease among those who had remained on the island. Consequently, the total population, which had been several thousand, fell to a few hundred. Although the survivors caught and ate some Peruvian sailors, this did not restore their losses.

Those who had died included King Kamakoi, his son, and nearly all the priests and nobles. Since these were the people who had kept the records and knew the procedures, the culture fell to pieces. Then French Catholic missionaries landed and took up their work, made easier by the disappearance of native leaders and the decay of traditions.

In 1870 a French adventurer, Dutroux-Bornier, set himself up as a sheep rancher. He plotted with a trader in Tahiti to remove all but a handful of Pascuans and resettle them in Tahiti. The pair planned to kill two birds with one stone: to clear Rapa Nui of natives who might interfere with sheep-raising and to furnish labor for the trader's plantation. By enlisting some of the Pascuans, attacking the rest, and repeatedly destroying their crops, Dutroux-Bornier drove most of the natives from Easter Island to Tahiti, where their descendants dwell today. His victory profited him little, though; the few who remained on Rapa Nui soon murdered him.

The population, down to 111 in 1877, slowly recovered. Efforts to teach the Pascuans to grow fruit trees and grapevines failed because the people, with characteristic improvidence, chopped up the trees and vines for firewood whenever the whim so moved them.

In 1888, Chile annexed the island and leased it to a Scottish sheep-raising firm, Wiliamson and Balfour Company. (Nobody asked the Pascuans' permission, for "natives" were not considered to have any rights.) The Scots ran the enterprise according to their own dour notions of rectitude. They detested the Pascuans for their hedonistic, mercurial, light-fingered ways. To discourage the stealing of sheep, they herded all the natives into a single village, Hanga Roa, surrounded by barbed wire. The Pascuans hated the Scots in turn and now and then murdered a company man who made too much fuss over their theft of livestock.

The modern ideal of benevolence towards the backward, however, at length made its way to Chile. In 1954 the Chilean Government refused to renew the sheep company's lease, bought up the property, and began to operate the ranch for the benefit of the Pascuans. Although poor by western standards and bereft of most of their ancient culture, the Pascuans of today seem healthy and reasonably happy. In 1955 there were 842 of them. They are increasing in numbers, and their young men are eager to get to the mainland and learn a trade.

If the Pascuans were just one more cannibal tribe, the story of their downfall would not concern us. But, despite their isolation, they developed a complex culture with remarkable achievements. Besides painting and tattooing themselves and sculpturing their famous statues, they carved pictures on rocks. Like other Polynesians they were given to such active sports as surfboard riding and games like cat's cradle.

Moreover, they observed complicated religious ceremonials. We have the details of only one of these rites. Every July, a number of chiefs gathered at Orongo, at the southwest tip of Rapa Nui, for the bird-man ceremony. This was a contest to see who could collect the first egg of the season laid by a sooty tern on the rocky offshore islet of Moto Nui.

The chiefs did not, however, obtain the eggs in person. Each chief sent a servant paddling across on a reed float, and a second servant in case the first was eaten by sharks or smashed against the rocks. While the chiefs relaxed in rock shelters decorated with paintings and petroglyphs of the bird-man, the servants camped out on Moto Nui, for weeks if necessary, until the egg had been gathered. The chief whose servant seized the egg and brought it back to his master became an incarnation of the god Makemake and was treated as a divine being for the following year.

More importantly, the Pascuans had a system of writing, which made them unique among the Polynesians. They incised lines of characters on wooden boards. The lines ran *boustrophedon* ("oxpath"); that is, the words of one line were written from left to right and those of the next from right to left. A special class of reciters, called *tangata rongorongo*, kept the boards and read them when required.

With the destruction of the ruling class by the great slave raid of 1862, this system of writing was almost forgotten. By the 1870s, when scholars began to take an interest in their writing, the Pascuans were using the last of their rongorongo boards for firewood or for building canoes. They said the missionaries had encouraged them to burn the tablets as relics of paganism. A few men claimed to be able to read the tablets; but some at least were bluffing. When shown a tablet, they went through the motions of reading and intoned a chant; but next day they would utter a different chant from the same board, or the same chant from a different board.

In the absence of solid knowledge, far-fetched speculations were advanced about the rongorongo boards. In 1932 a Hungarian, Hevesy, proclaimed that this system of writing was related to that of the pre-Aryan Indus Valley people, despite the gap of thousands of miles and thousands of years between the two cultures. Others thought it descended from the earliest Chinese scripts. All were guessing wildly.

It is easy to be misled by superficial resemblances between a few signs. If two peoples independently create simple symbols to represent various sounds or words, some resemblances are bound to occur. For example, the ancient Numidians had an alphabet, several of whose letters resemble letters of our own Latin alphabet. But the meanings assigned to the symbols by the Numidians were entirely different from ours.

Many efforts have been made during the last century to decipher the Pascuan writing. Bishop Jaussen, who tried to rescue the Pascuans from Chilean slavery, persuaded Metoro Tauara, a Pascuan living in Tahiti, to read a collection of talking boards. Metoro's knowledge was imperfect; moreover, Jaussen's original notes disappeared after his death.

In the 1950s a German scholar, Thomas Barthel, rounded up all the existing information on the rongorongo tablets. He obtained copies of the two dozen surviving boards, as well as of a staff and several breastplates. These relics, all covered with ciphers, lie scattered in museums around the world. After a world-wide search, Barthel even ferreted out Bishop Jaussen's notes, which had been gathering dust in an Italian monastery.

With this material and modern cryptographic techniques, Barthel began to decipher the writing. Some students believe that he has succeeded, at least in part, and that soon the script of Rapa Nui will be as legible as it is ever likely to be. Furthermore, they surmise that this form of writing may once have existed in other parts of

Fig. 16 The writing on a Puacuan rongorongo board.

Polynesia, but that the other Polynesians abandoned it before the coming of the whites.

The writing was made up of 120 pictograms, which could be combined in over a thousand ways. Each picture represented a word. Since many grammatical particles were omitted, it was a rudimentary system, halfway between the notched sticks and knotted strings used as memory aids by some Polynesians and a fully developed system of writing. The material seems to be all ritualistic. Barthel's translation of one hymn reads:

> Blow the shell trumpet and beat the drum
> For the precious ornament
> For the first-born son of the earth
> For the prop of heaven
> For Tane.[11]

Although the writing of Rapa Nui represents a worthy achievement, so far as we know these records shed no light upon the stern stone faces and the men who carved them. Howard, from whose sonnet I quoted, wondered about these vanished sculptors:

> What dreams had they, that shaped these uncouth things?
> Before these gods what victims bled and died?
> What purple galleys swept along the strand
> That bore the tribute of what dim sea-kings?
> But now they reign o'er a forgotten land
> Gazing forever out beyond the tide.

Stirring though the poet's lines may be, we know today that no purple galleys plied between Rapa Nui and distant lands. Neither did the statues, as the poem implies, stand in rows facing the boundless sea.

The Pascuans built sacred inclosures, which they used as burial platforms. These platforms, called *ahu*, varied widely in shape—rectangular, ship-shaped, pyramidal. Some were as much as 300 feet long, the size of a small city block. While some were made of neatly fitted blocks of volcanic rock, others were mere heaps of rubble. Around each platform the Pascuans erected statues, facing inward like diners at a banquet table. Altogether, the ahu probably represented more work on the part of the Pascuans than the statues, impressive though the latter are. When a Pascuan died, his kin wrapped his body in bark cloth and placed it on a scaffold on the ahu, where it remained exposed for months or years before being buried.

The Pascuan ahu with their statues were used for religious rites as well as for burial grounds. Admiral Roggeveen in 1722 described the scene: ". . . they kindle fire in front of certain remarkably tall stone figures they set up; and, thereafter squatting on their heels with heads bowed down, they bring the palms of their hands together and alternately raise and lower them."[12] Perhaps the Pascuans believed that during these rites the spirits of their ancestors entered into the statues. We cannot be sure that this was the purpose of these statues, for primitive peoples have erected such monuments for many different reasons.

Competition for prestige led each chief to build bigger and bigger statues. Megalithic building was not confined to Rapa Nui. In many parts of Polynesia, chiefs used it as a way to gain honor. They paid their workers with huge quantities of surplus food. Thus Tonga acquired its famous trilithon, consisting of two uprights of coral rock weighing thirty-odd tons each, supporting a lintel of the same material. The Tongans say these masses were hauled up ramps with ropes and levers and tipped into place, much as the Egyptians raised their obelisks.

On Rapa Nui there were once about 260 ahu, with one to sixteen statues each; some ahu, however, had no statues at all. Many ahu were demolished during the past century by the Scottish sheepranchers, who built walls of the stones to protect their animals.

Other Polynesian peoples also built sacred inclosures[13] and carved gigantic statues. They used wood when it was plentiful, as in New Zealand; otherwise they used stone. In the Tubuai Islands the stone statues reach a height of nine feet. But in Necker, a now uninhabited island of the Hawaiian group, one sacred inclosure was surrounded by rows of stone statues only about a foot tall.

All the Pascuan stone statues are made of volcanic tufa from one quarry, in the crater of Rano Raraku. This rock had the advantage of being soft and easy to work with stone tools and, at the same time, more resistant to weather than some harder rocks.

Everything we have learned about the Pascuan statues indicates that they were made, not by men of Lemuria or some other vanished civilization, nor yet by Peruvian explorers, but by the ancestors of the present Pascuans. They are a typical Polynesian product, albeit more impressive than similar sculptures in other parts of Polynesia. Although there is no exact way to date the individual statues, it seems likely that the custom of erecting them lasted down to +XVIII or early +XIX.

Early visitors to Rapa Nui wondered how such primitive people could ever have set up such colossal sculptures. The method remained doubtful until Heyerdahl persuaded Pedro Atan, the "mayor" of Hanga Roa, to raise a fallen statue. Atan and five of his relatives accomplished this feat in eighteen days. They pried up one end of the statue with timbers and shoved some stones under it; then they pried it up a little more, and so on until it lay at a slant against a heap of stones. The final erection was done with ropes. When Heyerdahl asked Atan why he had not told earlier inquirers how this feat was accomplished, he replied simply:

"No one asked *me!*"[14]

Aside from the nearly two hundred unfinished statues in the quarries of Rano Raraku, and a few scattered along the roads from the quarries to the ahu along the coast, the statues on the island of Rapa Nui fall into two groups. One group comprises the statues surrounding the ahu. Another group—between 250 and 300—were erected on the slopes of the volcano Rano Raraku itself, some inside and some outside the crater.

These groups differ in several ways. Whereas the ahu statues have the orbits of the eyes sculptured all the way round, the volcano statues have no distinct eyes. The planes of the cheeks are carried right up to the eyebrow ridges, the shadows of which give the illusion of eyes. This difference of style suggests that the two groups were made at different periods.

Moreover, the ahu statues were once provided with cylindrical "hats" of red volcanic rock from the crater of Mount Punapau. These headpieces represented the topknot of the male Pascuan. The volcano statues lacked topknots. Finally, the ahu statues have flat bases for standing on the stone pavement of the platform, while the volcano statues end in a tapering stone peg, designed to extend down into soft volcanic soil to support the statue.

During the ferocious inter-tribal wars between 1722 and 1840, when the island had become overpopulated and the whites were making their first contacts, all the ahu statues (with the exception of one, which was already badly weathered and partly buried) were thrown down. Along with burning their houses and destroying their exposed corpses, each warring tribe overthrew the statues of its enemies further to insult them. Today, every ahu statue lies flat on the ruins of its platform, save for the weathered one and the one that Pedro Atan reërected in 1956.

The volcano statues, however, were not vandalized. Although many have been upset and buried by landslides, more than half of them still stand, frowning forever across the rolling land and the boundless sea. These are the statues you see in photographs. Whether the volcano statues were made before or after the ahu statues, why they were set up on Rano Raraku, why they were not toppled along with the others, when and why the Pascuans abruptly stopped making statues altogether—these questions may never be answered.

One theory has it that the volcano statues are simply unfinished ahu statues. They were erected on the slopes of the volcano in order easily to finish the carving on their backs. Then they were hauled to their sites, where their pegs were cut off so that they could be set up on their ahu. The Pascuans showed Heyerdahl how easily 180 men could haul a twelve-ton statue with simple ropes. When a statue had been finally erected, the carving around its eyes was completed so that the statue could see at last.

You may wonder why the Pascuans went about everything in such a frantic manner, whether they were erecting huge statues, welcoming visitors, or butchering and eating each other in their relentless wars. The reason is not hard to see. Consider their lot. Having settled on their little island, they could not leave, because the island lacked timber for shipbuilding.

Wood was precious on Rapa Nui. The Pascuans had to depend upon driftwood and upon a dwarf tree or shrub, the *toro-miro*—now, thanks to the white man's goats, practically extinct. The bread-fruit and coconut trees they brought with them found the climate too cool and died out.

The island gave its people a good living—at least until they became too numerous—but it afforded almost no variety. There were only the grassy fields and volcanic knolls, and beyond them the sounding sea. There were no wild animals to hunt or be hunted by; no neighboring tribes to fight or trade with; no other lands they could reach with their flimsy little canoes, patched together from pieces of driftwood; no traders to stop by with trinkets and news. They were as isolated as people can be.

So they got bored. To relieve the tedium they went in for games and sports, for fantastic rites and ceremonies, for bizarre forms of personal adornment, for megalithic construction projects, and finally for ferocious warfare. Anything was better than simply eating sweet potatoes day after day and listening to the boom of the surf.

This isolation is the key to the mystery of Easter Island. And perhaps the islanders can teach us a lesson. Many people want to improve the world, and it certainly could stand improvement. But these philanthropists often assume that if people are furnished with a high standard of living, pleasant surroundings, and security, they will become virtuous, industrious, law-abiding, public-spirited citizens, who do their duty and, in their spare time, read good books and listen to classical music.

Well, maybe; but we doubt it. We suspect that, with most of the risks and injustices removed from life, many would begin to yearn, not for more social justice or self-improvement, but for more change and excitement. And then their conduct would not much resemble that of the inhabitants of a paper Utopia. Instead, they would behave more like those delightful thieves, killers, and cannibals of Easter Island.

We have now explored our twelve citadels of mystery. We have dispelled some of the mystery and cleared up some misunderstandings; but, in doing so, we have uncovered new and even more perplexing puzzles. Whereas some of these problems may be solved by further archaeological research, others will remain forever enigmatic, because the facts we need to solve them have vanished forever into the ravenous maw of time.

We have also learned a few lessons from the behavior of people who lived long ago and far away—people quite as human as we, with the same unstable mixture of faults and virtues, even though they lived in very different surroundings and under different traditions.

We have learned that ancient or primitive men, without any modern tools or machines, could nevertheless move huge weights and build enormous structures—pyramids, towers, temples, castles, waterworks, and statues—if they had among them gifted minds to plan the project, and an effective organization to carry it out, and the motivation to keep them toiling away until the task was done.

We have seen that men of all the main human races can accomplish these feats, regardless of color or reputed mental level.

We have discovered that, when a people has no written records, its memories of preceding ages become telescoped together. After a few centuries we can no longer disentangle fact from fiction. In any body of myth there are probably embedded scraps of historical fact; but, in the absence of independent written records, there is no way to filter them out.

We have learned that, while the main Old World civilizations all arose in the broad valleys of great rivers, people can achieve the basic elements of civilization in very different surroundings—in a tropical rain forest, or in a nearly waterless desert, or on a bleak and inhospitable high plateau. And, if civilizations can arise under varying conditions, they can also be snuffed out by a chance, unforseen combination of factors, none fatal in itself but all together overwhelming.

We have learned that, when the foe is at the gate, virtue and good will cannot take the place of physical force. We have also learned that unity in the face of danger, although a seemingly simple lesson, is one of the hardest for men to learn—as the Roman Britons, the East African Arabs, and the Mayas all found to their cost.

We have seen that, when a people in peril can save themselves only at the cost of a quick and drastic change in their habits and beliefs, they usually prefer to perish.

We have learned that the boredom arising from secure monotony can be as deadly an enemy of peaceful, orderly life as privation and injustice.

We have learned that, no matter how fantastic or absurd a theory is, you can always find somebody eager to embrace it.

Finally we have had, let us hope, some fun in pushing out the boundaries of our knowledge, by looking over the shoulders of historians and archaeologists as they recover the lost records of forgotten folk and probe the twilight zone between the known and the unknown. In the process we have enlarged our own selves, by realizing our kinship to men of every nation and all ages. As the archaeologist Petrie said: "The man who knows and dwells in history adds a new dimension to his existence; he no longer lives in the one plane of present ways and thoughts, he lives in the whole space of life, past, present, and dimly future."[15]

# Postscript

Since this book was first written, more light has been shed on the sources of Atlantis by discoveries in the Aegean. Sixty miles north of Crete lies the small, crescent-shaped island of Thera (also known by its Italian name of Santorin). Several smaller islets lie on the concave side of the crescent. The group is volcanic; at least six eruptions have taken place among the smaller islets during the last two millennia.

For several decades, evidence has been accumulating that Thera is the ruin of a major volcano and that this volcano once blew up in a cataclysmic eruption, like that of Krakatoa in 1883. This eruption left a blanket of volcanic ash, the "Santorin tephra," over an oval area about 150 by 200 miles in extent, taking in most of Crete and most of the Aegean Sea.

In 1939, a Greek archaeologist, Spyridon Marinatos, surmised that this eruption caused the downfall of Minoan Crete, by drowning the people of the coastal cities with a tsunami or earthquake wave and smothering the inland farms under ash. With the development of radio-carbon dating, it transpired that this eruption took place in –XV. (There is also evidence for an even bigger eruption about 25,000 years ago, but that concerns us not.)

In the 1960s, a Greek seismologist, Angelos Galanopoulos, connected the eruption of Thera with Plato's Atlantis. The discrepancies between the time and the dimensions of Atlantis and the actual Thera could be explained, he said, by assuming that, in the transmission of the tale, somebody garbled the numbers by a factor of ten. This mistake made Plato's Atlantis ten times as big and ten times as old as Minoan Thera. In 1967,

Greek and American archaeologists found the well-preserved remains of a –XV Minoan city on Thera, under a blanket of tephra at the site of the modern village of Akrotiri. Excavations are still going on.

The Atlantis-in-Thera theory seems to fit the facts better than most. If it is true, there might even be something to Plato's account of Solon's having heard the Atlantis tale in Egypt. To say that Thera "is" Atlantis, however, involves a semantic confusion. Plato's Atlantis is still a fictional concept, bedight with gods, mythical heroes, and miraculous happenings. The eruption of Thera may well be one of the main factual sources on which Plato drew in composing his fiction, along with Tartessos, the earthquake at Atalantê, and the other possibilities that we have discussed. Just how Plato got his information, and the relative importance of his various sources, we shall probably never know.

More information has been uncovered concerning Stonehenge. In the early 1960s, a British-born astronomer, Dr. Gerald S. Hawkins of Boston University, ran the positions of the stones of Stonehenge through the Smithsonian-Harvard computer for comparison with known astronomical directions. He then announced that the monument was a more elaborate astronomical instrument than had been thought. It was used, he said, not only to keep track of the summer and winter solstices but also to predict lunar eclipses. Dr. Hawkins's theory aroused some controversy, but most of the scientists concerned seemed to favour it.

A recent revaluation of the radio-carbon dating method indicates that all the Stone Age megalithic monuments of western Europe, including Stonehenge and the Breton menhirs, are several centuries older than had been previously calculated. This implies that these monuments owed more to native western European ingenuity and less to civilising influences from the East than had been widely supposed.

# Notes

INTRODUCTION

1. Robert E. Howard: *Conan the Conqueror* (N.Y.: 1950), p. 2; Gilbert & Colette Charles-Picard: *Daily Life in Carthage* (N.Y.: 1961), p. 253. The allusions are to the Theosophical writings about Atlantis (for which see Chap. XI); Howard's series of adventure-fantasy stories, published as the five Conan books; and Gustave Flaubert's novel *Salammbô*.

2. Percy Bysshe Shelley: *Lines Written Among the Euganean Hills*.

3. Clark Ashton Smith: *Revenant*.


CHAPTER I

1. Göran Schildt: *In the Wake of Ulysses* (N.Y.: 1953), p. 103.

2. His real name was Aristokles, son of Ariston. *Platón*, from *platys*, "broad," was a nickname.

3. Landa, pp. 16f.

4. Brasseur de Bourbourg, I, p. 151.

5. Donnelly: *ten, siao, tien, na, nugo*; Standard North Chinese: *tou, ye, ya, gên, wo*.

6. Pronounced "chetch."

7. Mayan *x*=English *sh*. There is another set of Japanese numerals borrowed from Chinese: *ichi, ni, san, &c.*

8. 1 Kings x:22.

9. Or Turdetani. Southwestern Spain was called Tartessis, Turdetania, or Hispania Baetica.

10. The ancient Tartessis or Baetis.

11. Plato: *Timaios*, 26C-D.


CHAPTER II

1. Variously called the City of the White Wall (from its limestone fortifications); the Abode of the Soul of Ptah (He-Ku-Ptah, whence Greek Aigyptos and modern Egypt); and Men-nofer (whence the Greek and modern Memphis). The letter ḥ denotes a guttural sound between ordinary *h* and *kh* (the *ch* of German *ach*).

2. Also spelled Djoser, Zoser, or Zeser.

3. Or Aiemhetp, Yemhatpe, &c.

4. Arabic: *maṣṭaba*, "bench."

5. Modern Ṭura.

6. "Sax Rohmer" (pseud. of Arthur Sarsfield Ward): *Brood of the Witch Queen* (Garden City, N.Y.: 1924), reprinted in *Famous Fantastic Mysteries*,

Jan. 1951. "Harry Houdini" (pseud. of Ehrich Weiss) & H. P. Lovecraft: *Imprisoned With the Pharaohs*, in *Weird Tales*, May–June–July 1924; reprinted in *Weird Tales*, July 1939; and in H. P. Lovecraft: *Marginalia* (Sauk City, Wis.: 1944).

7. Greek: Mykerinos; Latin: Mycerinus.

8. Some archaeologists believe that this pyramid had been robbed long before, about −XXIII, and that the mummy that fell victim to al-Ma'mûn's greed was not Khufu's but that of a later intruder.

9. Herodotos, II, 125.

10. Or Tehutihotep, Jehutihetep, &c.


## CHAPTER III

1. Geoffrey, VII, x, xi.

2. John Evelyn: *Diary*, 22 July, 1654.

3. Samuel Pepys: *Pepys' Diary*, 11 June, 1668.

4. Rhymes with "bayberry," or even with "débris."

5. Caesar: *The Gallic War*, VI, xvi.

6. Tacitus: *Annals*, XIV, 30.

7. Strabon, IV, v, 4 (C201).

8. Owen, p. 16a.

9. Florence Teets: "Stonehenge Visit," in the New York *Sunday Times*, 6 June 1954, p. X–15.

10. Or the Presely Mountains. "Mynydd" rhyms with "another" without the *-er*.

11. Singular: *dyss*.

12. Egyptian: *hiku-khasut*, "desert princes."


## CHAPTER IV

1. Greek: Achilleus.

2. *Iliad*, III, 164f.

3. Greek: Ilias.

4. *Iliad*, XXI, 166f.

5. Latin: Ulysses.

6. *Iliad*, XX, 307f.

7. Greek: *Odysseia*.

8. Pausanias, I, xxiii, 8.

9. *Iliad*, VI, 117f; X, 263f; XI, 485; XV, 645f; XVII, 138.

10. The Turkish letter ı represents a sound something like the vowels in the words *tick*, *tuck*, and *took*, but not exactly like any of them. The pronunciation "hee-sar-LICK" is close enough.

11. The identity of Odysseus' Ithaka is another subject of controversy. Although it is usually taken to be modern Thiaki, some German Homerists have asserted that it was, instead, the larger island of Lefkas (ancient Leukas or Leukadia) north of Thiaki, or even Corfu (Greek: Kerkyra) farther north yet.

12. *Iliad*, XXI, 350f.

13. *Ibid.*, V, 773f.

14. Payne, p. 138.

15. Plutarch: *Alexander*, XV, 4.

16. *Odyssey*, XI, 519ff.

17. Modern Boğazkale, Turkey; formerly Boğazköy.

18. Spelled (like the rest of these names) in many different ways: Ahhijawa, Ahhijjawâ, Akhkhiyavâ, &c.

19. Arnuwandas IV.

20. Maduwatas.

21. Homer uses the name only once, when he speaks of the "Asian meadows" of the Kaystros River in Lydia (*Iliad*, II, 461).

22. Schliemann, p. 326.

23. *Iliad*, XX, 59f.; XXI, 446f.


CHAPTER V

1. More correctly spelled Yaman; rhymes with "salmon."

2. Achmed Abdullah: *The Cat Had Nine Lives* (N.Y.: 1933), p. 22.

3. 1 Kings x:1–13. 2 Chron. ix:1–12 contains the same account, almost verbatim.

4. In modern colloquial Arabic, Mârib.

5. G. K. Chesterton: *Lepanto*.

6. Singular: *sayl*.

7. Or Ghamdân.

8. Or 'Ilumquh.

9. Son of Dhimri'alay; or Sumuhu'alay Yanuf, son of Dhamar'alay. Like other Semitic written languages, Sabaean ignored most vowels, so that we have to guess what many of them were.

10. Qur'ân, Surah xxxiv, 15ff.

11. *Time*, 1 Mar. 1948, p. 27.

12. Fakhry (1952) I, pp. 11, 89.

13. Since the Yemeni version of the dispute is an obvious tissue of lies, we have followed Phillips' version. We should warn you, however, that some American archaeologists are severely critical in private of Phillips' methods of handling the Yemenites and of his ideas of proper archaeological procedures.


CHAPTER VI

1. Of several derivations of this name, the most plausible is *mwana-matapa*, "owner of the mines."

2. Quoted in Paver, p. 87.

3. For an account of this search, see de Camp & Ley, Chap. IX.

4. Damião de Goes, in *Records of South-Eastern Africa* (Cape Colony, 1898–1903, 9 vols., edited by G. M. Theal), III, p. 129; quoted by Caton-Thompson, p. 86, & Davidson, p. 244.

5. João de Barros, in *ibid.*, VI, pp. 267f; quoted by Caton-Thompson, p. 87, & Wieschhoff, pp. 8f.

6. So spelled by Paver; Wieschhoff gives it as "Bebereke."

7. 1 Kings ix, 26ff; Ps. xlv, 9.

8. Writers of the time thought this name meant "stone houses" (Chikalanga *zimba*, "houses," + *bwe*, "stone"). Later scholars learned that the natives call the ruins by quite different names, and that "Zimbabwe" is at best pidgin-Bantu. Probably nobody will ever know what the original name, spelled by the Portuguese "Symbaoe" and applied to any large village or chief's kraal, really meant.

9. Andrew Lang: *Zimbabwe*, in *Poetical Works* (Lon.: 1923), III, p. 42.

10. Quoted in Paver, pp. 251f. A kraal is a fenced native village compound or farmstead.

11. Hall (1905) p. 4.

12. In Africa and in books about Africa, such a hillock is often called by the Afrikaans name *kopje* ("little head," pronounced "copy").

13. Caton-Thompson, p. 103.

14. The usual names applied by outsiders are MaShona, MaKalanga, Ma-Karanga, or MaKalaka.

15. Willoughby, p. 37; Hall (1905), p. 89f; Bent, p. 56.

16. *Periplus*, 16 (Schoff, p. 28). "Moûza" is probably the city of Mocha or Mukha.

17. Portuguese: Quiloa.

18. Hall (1909) pp. 15, 247; Peters, p. 252.

19. H. Rider Haggard: *King Solomon's Mines* (N.Y.: 1961), p. 56.

20. Hall (1909), pp. 15, 247; Peters, p. 252; Bent, p. xiv.

21. Caton-Thompson, p. 199.


CHAPTER VII

1. Nennius, xl (Giles, p. 402).

2. Or Dyfed, modern Pembrokeshire.

3. These names are spelled in various ways: e.g., Igerne, Iguerne, Igraine, Ygerne, &c.

4. Called Dimilioc or Terrabil.

5. Malory, I, v.

6. *Ibid.*, I, xx.

7. Or Guinever, Jennifer, Gwenhwyfar, Guenièvre, Vanora, Gonore, Wander, &c.

8. Or Isolde, Isold, Isoud, Isoude, Iseult, Yseult, Yseut, Essylt, &c.

9. Or Nyneue, Nyene, Niniane, Niniene, Nimenne, Viviane, Vivienne, Vivien, &c.; possibly derived from the Welsh goddess Rhiannon.

10. Malory, IV, i.

11. Or Mordred, Medraut, Medrawt, Medraud.

12. Edmund Spenser: *The Faerie Queene*, III, iii, 9.

13. Tennyson: *Guenevere*, l. 554.

14. Or Tristan, Trystan, Drystan. Some read the DRVSTANS of the inscription as DRVSTAGNI.
15. Gildas, II, xxv, xxvi (Giles, pp. 312f).
16. Or Beda, Bæda.
17. Bede, I, xv.
18. Greek: Aineias; I use the Latin spelling here because Virgil does.
19. Nennius, l.
20. Or Rodarch.
21. Pron. about as "hlookh."

CHAPTER VIII

1. Mouhot, II, p. 272; I, p. 118.
2. *Ibid.*, I, p. 285.
3. *Ibid.*, I, p. 282.
4. *Ibid.*, I, p. 279.
5. Pron. "tie" and "kuh-MAIR" (or in modern Khmer, "kuh-MEH").
6. Called Kaundinya in the Indian version of the legend and Hun Tien in the Chinese version.
7. Mouhot, II, p. 20.
8. Or Śiva, Çiva.
9. Or Lokeśvara, Avalokiteśvara.
10. Often spelled as one word, Jayavarman; I have divided it to make it easier. All Khmer kings bore throne names ending in -*varman*, literally "armor" but here meaning "protector" or "protegé." Hence Jaya-Varman means "protegé of victory"; Indra-Varman, "protegé of Indra," &c.
11. Briggs, p. 196.
12. *Angkor* is a Khmer corruption of the Sanskrit *nagara*, "capital." *Wat* (or *vat*, from Sanskrit *vaṭa*) means "temple." *Thom* (pron. "tawm") means "great." So Angkor Wat and Angkor Thom are simply "Capital Temple" and "Great Capital" respectively.
13. Or Yaśodharapura, Yaśovarman, Yaço.
14. Or Liu-yeh.
15. Or Śailendra.
16. Probably Mahipati-Varman.
17. Briggs, pp. 67f.
18. Or *lingam.*
19. Or Chou Ta-kuan; the oft-seen French spelling is Tcheou-Ta-Kouan.
20. Briggs, p. 247.

CHAPTER IX

1. Or Lake Petén Itzá.
2. Pron. "wah-shahk-TOON."
3. Pron. "oosh-MAHL," "chee-CHEN eet-SAH."
4. William Robertson: *The History of America* (1777), III, Book vii, pp. 152, 191ff; quoted by von Hagen (1948) p. 76.

5. *"¡Viva la religión y muerte a los extranjeros!"*

6. Stephens, I, p. 92.

7. *Ibid.*, I, pp. 73f. The final clause refers to Joseph Smith's *Book of Mormon.*

8. Genus *Gerrhonotus.*

9. Wauchope; see also de Camp, Chap. VI.

10. Pron. "kayt-sahl-QUATL'." Both names mean "feathered serpent."

11. Or *Chilam Balam* or *Balan*, depending upon the dialect.

12. Pron. "she-YOO."

13. Hunac Ceel (pron. "hoo-NAHK KAYL") of Mayapan.

14. A leading contemporary Mayologist, not to be confused with Edward H. Thompson (1856–1935), a pioneer investigator of the Yucatecan Mayas.

15. L. Sprague de Camp: *Tikal.*


CHAPTER X

1. Bingham (1922), p. 314.

2. Or Uitioos. The Spaniards represented the common *w*-sound of many Amerind languages variously by *v, o, u, hu,* and *gu.*

3. Bingham, *op. cit.*, p. 320.

4. Bingham (1930), pp. 8f.

5. Ch. I, "The House on Curwen Street," in *The Trail of Cthulhu,* by August Derleth (Sauk City: 1962).

6. Or Ccapac; in modern phoneticized Quechua (or Keshwa), Manku Qhapaq.

7. Pron. "ah-tah-WILE-pah," "WAH-skar."

8. Or Caxamarca, Caxamalca.

9. Prescott, p. 940.

10. Montesinos said the Andeans once had a system of writing, but that an early Inca abolished it on the advice of his soothsayers. As no traces of such writing have been found, this story is not believed by modern Americanists.

11. Quechua: Zinchi Roq'a. These names are all titles glorifying the ruler, assumed at the time of accession.

12. Quechua: Wira Qocha.

13. Or Pachacutec.

14. Prescott, p. 765.

15. Pron. "tee-ah-wah-NAH-ko."

16. Ley (1947), p. 95.

17. An earlier name for Tiahuanaco is said to have been Taypicala.


CHAPTER XI

1. Or Not.

2. Or Matolenim. The strange Micronesian names have many spellings; Jokaz appears also as Jokesh, Jokaj, Chokach, Dschokadsch, Chocoich, &c., depending on the dialect of the native speaker and the orthography used by the hearer.

3. O'Connell, pp. 31f.

4. The recent revival of Alfred L. Wegener's theory of continental drift—according to which the present continents once formed a single land mass, which broke into parts, which drifted about the earth's surface until they reached their present positions—likewise has no bearing on human cultural history, because the drift, if it occurred, happened much too long ago.

5. Blavatsky, I, pp. 91f; III, pp. 28f.

6. The magazine version was published under the pseudonym "Norman Bean"; the book version, under Burroughs' own name.

7. For a further account of these derivations, see Fritz Leiber: "John Carter: Sword of Theosophy," in *Amra* (a fan magazine), II, 6 (Sep. 1959) pp. 3–9. Burroughs also borrowed ideas from Edwin Lester Arnold's Martian novel, *Lieut. Gulliver Jones: His Vocation* (Lon.: 1905).

8. Or Shipe and Shaupa.

9. Or Shau-telur.

10. Or Isho-kalakal.

11. Or Nanamáriki.

CHAPTER XII

1. Also spelled "Roggeween."

2. Hilaire Belloc: *Short Talks with the Dead*, in *An Anthology of his Prose and Verse* (Lon.: 1951), p. 253; also in *Short Talks with the Dead and Others* (Lon.: 1926), p. 96.

3. Haugen, p. 76.

4. The Peruvian creator-god had a number of names or titles, among which was Teqzi Wiraqochan, meaning "fundamental, respected god." *Teqzi*, which means simply "fundamental" or "basic," was picked up by the Spaniards and spelled "Tici" or "Ticci"; hence the confusion with Tiki.

5. Wauchopé, p. 104. See also the review of Heyerdahl & Ferdon by Kenneth P. Emory in *Science*, CXXXVIII (23 Nov. 1963) pp. 884f.

6. To be exact, five perished thus; two others were being fattened for a similar fate when they escaped.

7. Metraux, pp. 208f. (Slightly edited.)

8. Lewis Spence (1925) p. 181.

9. J. F. C. de la Pérouse: *Voyage de la Pérouse autour du Monde*, quoted by Casey (1931) p. 319.

10. Suggs, p. 122.

11. Barthel, p. 66.

12. Heyerdahl & Ferdon, pp. 45f.

13. The commonest Polynesian name for these inclosures is *marae*.

14. Heyerdahl (1958–60) p. 126.

15. W. M. Flinders Petrie: *Methods and Aims in Archaeology* (1904), p. 193.

# Bibliography

Abbreviations: LC—Loeb Classical Library (London & Cambridge, Mass.);
PB—Pelican-Penguin Books (Harmondsworth, England).

ANDERSEN, JOHANNES C.: *Myths and Legends of the Polynesians*, N.Y.: Farrar & Rinehart, 1928.

ARRIBAS, ANTONIO: *The Iberians*, Lon.: Thames & Hudson, 1963.

ATKINSON, R. J. C.: *Stonehenge*, N.Y.: Macmillan Co., 1956; & PB, 1960.

ATKINSON, R. J. C.: *Stonehenge and Avebury (and Neighbouring Monuments)*, Lon.: H. M. Stationery Off., 1959.

BABCOCK, WILLIAM H.: *Legendary Islands of the Atlantic: A Study in Medieval Geography*, N.Y.: Amer. Geographical Soc., 1922.

BACON, EDWARD (ed.): *Vanished Civilizations of the Ancient World*, Lon.: Mc-Graw-Hill Book Co., Inc., 1963.

BAEDEKER, KARL: *Egypt and the Sûdân*, Leipzig: Karl Baedeker, 1929.

BARNARD, F. A. P.: *The Imaginary Metrological System of the Great Pyramid of Gizeh*, from *Proc. of the Amer. Metrological Soc.*, N.Y.: John Wiley & Sons, 1884.

BARTHEL, THOMAS S.: "The 'Talking Boards' of Easter Island," in *Scientific American*, CXCVIII, 6 (June 1958) pp. 61–68.

BAUDIN, LOUIS: *Daily Life in Peru (Under the Last Incas)*, N.Y.: Macmillan Co., 1962.

BECHOFER-ROBERTS, C. E., *The Mysterious Madame: Helena Petrovna Blavatsky*, N.Y.: Brewer & Warren, 1931.

BEDE: *The History of the Church of England*, LC, 1930.

BEERSKY, P. JEANNERAT DE: *Angkor: Ruins in Cambodia*, Boston: Houghton Mifflin Co., 1924.

BELLAMY, HANS SCHINDLER: *Built Before the Flood (The Problem of the Tiahuanaco Ruins)*, Lon.: Faber & Faber, 1943.

BENT, J. THEODORE: *The Ruined Cities of Mashonaland* (*Being a Record of Excavation and Exploration in 1891*), Lon.: Longmans, Green & Co., 1892–96.

BESANT, ANNIE: *The Ancient Wisdom* (*An Outline of Theosophical Teachings*), Adyar, India: Theosophical Pub. House, 1897–1939.

———: *The Pedigree of Man*, Benares: Theosophical Pub. Soc., 1908.

BESSMERTNY, ALEXANDRE: *L'Atlantide* (*Exposé des hypothèses relatives à l'énigme de l'Atlantide*), Paris: Payot, 1935.

BIBBY, GEOFFREY: *The Testimony of the Spade*, N.Y.: Alfred A. Knopf, 1956.

BINGHAM, HIRAM: *Inca Land*, Boston: Houghton Mifflin Co., 1922.

———: *Lost City of the Incas* (*The Story of Machu Picchu and its Builders*), N.Y.: Duell, Sloan & Pearce, 1948.

———: *Machu Picchu* (*A Citadel of the Incas*), New Haven: Yale Un. Pr. for the Nat. Geographic Soc., 1930.

BJÖRKMAN, EDWIN: *The Search for Atlantis*, N.Y.: Alfred A. Knopf, 1927.

BLAVATSKY, HELENA PETROVNA: *The Secret Doctrine* (*The Synthesis of Science, Religion and Philosophy*), Adyar, India: Theosophical Pub. House, 1888, 6 vols.

BLEGEN, CARL W.: *Troy and the Trojans*, Lon.: Thames & Hudson, 1963.

BLEGEN, CARL W., *et al.*: *Troy*, Princeton: Princeton Un. Pr., 1950, 4 vols.

BONWICK, JAMES: *Pyramid Facts and Fancies*, Lon.: Kegan Paul & Co., 1877.

BORCHARDT, LUDWIG: *Gegen die Zahlenmystik an der grossen Pyramide bei Gize*, Berlin: Verlag von Behrend & Co., 1922.

BOWEN, RICHARD LE BARON, JR., & ALBRIGHT, FRANK P.: *Archaeological Discoveries in South Arabia*, Baltimore: Johns Hopkins Pr., 1958.

BRACHINE, A.: *The Shadow of Atlantis*, N.Y.: E. P. Dutton & Co., 1940.

BRAMWELL, JAMES: *Lost Atlantis*, N.Y.: Harper & Bros., 1938.

BRANDT, JOHN H.: "Nan Matol: Ancient Venice of Micronesia," in *Archaeology*, XV, 2 (June 1962) pp. 99–107.

# BIBLIOGRAPHY

BRASSEUR DE BOURBOURG, CHARLES-ÉTIENNE: *Manuscrit Troano: Études sur le Système et Langue des Mayas*, Paris: Imprimerie Impériale, 1869, 2 vols.

BRIGGS, LAWRENCE PALMER: *The Ancient Khmer Empire*, in *Transactions of the Amer. Philosophical Soc.*, New Ser., XLI, Part 1; Phila.: Amer. Philosophical Soc., 1951.

BRODEUR, ARTHUR G.: *Arthur, Dux Bellorum*, in *Univ. of Calif. Pubs. in English*, III, 7 (1939).

BUSHNELL, G. H. S.: *Peru*, Lon.: Thames & Hudson, 1956.

CAESAR, GAIUS JULIUS: *The Gallic War*, LC.

CANDEE, HELEN CHURCHILL: *Angkor the Magnificent (The Wonder City of Ancient Cambodia)*, N.Y.: Frederick A. Stokes Co., 1924.

CARRIAZO, JUAN DE M.: "Gold of Tarshish? . . ." in *The Illustrated London News*, CCXXXIV, 6243 (31 Jan. 1959), pp. 191ff.

CASEY, ROBERT J.: *Easter Island (Home of the Scornful Gods)*, N.Y.: Blue Ribbon Books, 1931.

————: *Four Faces of Siva (The Detective Story of a Vanished Race)*, Indianapolis: Bobbs-Merrill Co., 1929.

CATON-THOMPSON, GERTRUDE: *The Zimbabwe Culture (Ruins and Reactions)*, Oxf.: Clarendon Pr., 1931.

CERVÉ, WISHAR S.: *Lemuria, the Lost Continent of the Pacific*, San Jose, Calif.: Rosicrucian Pr., 1931.

CHADWICK, H. MUNRO: *The Heroic Age*, Cambridge.: Camb. Un. Pr., 1912.

CHAMBERS, E. K.: *Arthur of Britain*, Lon.: Sidgwick & Jackson, 1927.

CHILDE, V. GORDON: "Dates of Stonehenge," in *The Scientific Monthly*, LXXX, 5 (May 1955) pp. 281–85.

————: *The Dawn of European Civilization*, N.Y.: Alfred A. Knopf, 1948.

CHITTICK, NEVILLE: "The Medieval Arab Empire on the Coast of Tanganyika: Excavations in the Ancient Metropolis of Kilwa," in *The Illustrated London News*, CCXLIII, 6472 (17 Aug. 1963), pp. 234–37.

CHRISTIAN, F. W.: *The Caroline Islands*, 1899.

CHURCHWARD, JAMES: *The Children of Mu*, N.Y.: Ives Washburn, 1931–45.

———: *The Lost Continent of Mu*, N.Y.: Ives Washburn, 1933–63.

———: *The Sacred Symbols of Mu*, N.Y.: Ives Washburn, 1933–45.

CLARK, J. DESMOND: *The Prehistory of Southern Africa*, PB, 1959.

COE, WILLIAM R., & MCGINN, JOHN J.: "Tikal: The North Acropolis and a Early Tomb," in *Expedition*, V, 2 (Winter 1963), pp. 24–32.

COHEN, DANIEL: "Heinrich Schliemann, Archaeologist Extraordinary," in *Science Digest*, LIII, 3 (Mar. 1963), pp. 79–86.

COOPER, GORDON: *Dead Cities and Forgotten Tribes*, N.Y.: Philosophical Lib. 1952.

CORBIN, BRUCE: *The Great Pyramid (God's Witness in Stone)*, Guthrie, Okla. Truth Pub. Co., 1935.

COUPLAND, R.: *East Africa and its Invaders (from the Earliest Times to the Death of Seyyid Sultan in 1856)*, Oxf.: Clarendon Pr., 1938.

DANIEL, GLYN: *The Megalith Builders of Western Europe*, PB, 1958–63.

DAVIDSON, BASIL: *The Lost Cities of Africa*, Boston: Little, Brown & Co., 1959

DAVIDSON, DAVID, & ALDERSMITH, HERBERT: *The Great Pyramid: Its Divine Message*, Lon.: Williams & Norgate, 1924.

DE CAMP, L. SPRAGUE: *Lost Continents (The Atlantis Theme in History Science, and Literature)*, N.Y.: Gnome Pr., 1954.

DE CAMP, L. SPRAGUE, & LEY, WILLY: *Lands Beyond*, N.Y.: Rinehart & Co., 1952.

DELABARRE, EDMUND BURKE: *Dighton Rock (A Study of the Written Rock of New Engand)*, N.Y.: Neale, 1928.

DONNELLY, IGNATIUS: *Atlantis: The Antediluvian World*, N.Y.: 1882–1949

EDGAR, MORTON: *The Great Pyramid; Its Time Features*, Glasgow: Bone & Hulley, 1924.

## BIBLIOGRAPHY

EDWARDS, FREDERICK A.: "The Mystery of Zimbabwe," in *The Imperial and Asiatic Quarterly Review*, 3d Ser., XXXII, 63 & 64 (Jul.–Oct. 1911) pp. 110–21.

EDWARDS, I. E. S.: *The Pyramids of Egypt*, PB, 1947–52.

FAKHRY, AHMED: *An Archaeological Journey to Yemen (March–May 1947)*, Cairo: Govt. Pr., 1952.

——: *The Pyramids*, Chi.: Un. of Chicago, Pr., 1961.

FOORD, EDWARD: *The Last Age of Roman Britain*, Lon.: Geo. Harrap & Co., 1925.

GALLENKAMP, CHARLES: *Maya (The Riddle and Rediscovery of a Lost Civilization)*, N.Y.: Pyramid Pubs., 1959–62.

GANN, THOMAS, & THOMPSON, J. ERIC: *The History of the Maya (from the Earliest Times to the Present Day)*, N.Y.: Chas. Scribner's Sons, 1931.

GARDNER, HARRY J.: *1940 What's Next*, L.A.: priv. pub., 1939.

GASTER, M.: "The Legend of Merlin," in *Folk-Lore*, XVI, 4 (Dec. 1905), pp. 407–26.

GATTEFOSSÉ, JEAN, & ROUX, CLAUDIUS: *Bibliographie de l'Atlantide et des questions connexes . . .*, Lyon: Bosc & Riou, 1926.

GEDDES, WILLIAM D.: *The Problem of the Homeric Poems*, Lon.: Macmillan Co., 1878.

GEOFFREY OF MONMOUTH: *History of the Kings of Britain*, N.Y.: E. P. Dutton & Co., 1958.

GILES, J. A. (ed.): *Six Old English Chronicles*, Lon.: Henry G. Bohn, 1848.

GIOT, P. R.: *Brittany*, Lon.: Thames & Hudson, 1960.

——: *Menhirs et Dolmens (Monuments Mégalithiques de Bretagne)*, Chateaulin: Jos Le Doare, 1957.

GROSLIER, BERNARD, & ARTHAUD, JACQUES: *The Arts and Civilization of Angkor*, N.Y.: Frederick A. Praeger, 1957.

*Guia del Museo Nacional de Arqueologia y Etnologia*, Guatemala, n.d.

GURNEY, O. R.: *The Hittites*, PB, 1952.

HALL, R. N.: *Great Zimbabwe, Mashonaland, Rhodesia (An Account of Two Years' Examination Work . . .)*, Lon.: Methuen & Co., 1905.

———: *Pre-Historic Rhodesia (An Examination of the Historical, Ethnological and Archaeological Evidences as to the Origin and Age of the Rock Mines and Stone Buildings . . .)*, Lon.: T. Fisher Unwin, 1909.

HAMBRUCH, PAUL: *Ponape*, Hamburg: Friedrichsen, de Gruyter & Co., 1932–36, 3 vols.

HAUGEN, EINAR: *Voyages to Vinland: the First American Saga*, N.Y.: Alfred A. Knopf, 1942.

HAWKES, CHRISTOPHER, & HAWKES, JACQUETTA: *Prehistoric Britain*, PB, 1944–58.

HAWKES, JACQUETTA: "Stonehenge," in *Scientific American*, CLXXXVIII, 6 (June 1953) pp. 25–31.

HELFRITZ, HANS: *Land Without Shade*, N.Y.: Robert McBridge & Co., 1936.

HERODOTUS: *History*, in *The Greek Historians*, N.Y.: Random House, 1942; & LC.

HEYERDAHL, THOR: *Aku-Aku*, N.Y.: Rand McNally, 1958; Pocket Books, 1960.

———: *Kon-Tiki (Across the Pacific by Raft)*, N.Y.: Rand McNally, 1950; Permabooks, 1953–62.

HEYERDAHL, THOR, & FERDON, EDWIN N., JR.: *Archaeology of Easter Island*, N.Y.: Rand McNally, 1961.

HITTI, PHILIP K.: *History of the Arabs (From the Earliest Times to the Present)*, Lon.: Macmillan Co., 1937–53.

HOMER: *The Iliad of Homer*, Lon.: Macmillan Co., 1921; & LC.

JAKEMAN, M. WELLS: *The Origin and History of the Mayas (A General Reconstruction, in the Light of Basic Documentary Sources and Latest Archaeological Discoveries)*, L.A.: Research Pub. Co., 1945, 3 vols.

JERABEK, CARLOS: *Tikal*, Guatemala: 1959.

# BIBLIOGRAPHY

JOHNSON, J. P.: *The Pre-Historic Period in South Africa*, Lon.: Longmans, Green & Co., 1912.

JUSTIN, CORNELIUS NEPOS, AND EUTROPIUS, Lon.: Henry G. Bohn, 1853.

KINGSBOROUGH, LORD: *Antiquities of Mexico, Comprising Fac-Similes of Ancient Mexican Paintings and Hieroglyphics . . . ,* Lon.: Henry G. Bohn, 1848, 9 vols.

KNIGHT, CHARLES S.: *The Mystery and Prophecy of the Great Pyramid*, San Jose, Calif.: Rosicrucian Pr., 1928–33.

LANDA, DIEGO DE: *Landa's Relación de las Cosas de Yucatan*, Cambridge, Mass.: Peabody Museum, 1941.

LEAF, WALTER: *Homer and History*, Lon.: Macmillan & Co., 1915.

——: *Troy: A Study in Homeric Geography*, Lon.: Macmillan Co., 1912.

LE PLONGEON, AUGUSTUS: *Queen Móo and the Egyptian Sphinx*, Lon.: Kegan Paul, Trench, Trubner & Co., 1896.

——: *Sacred Mysteries Among the Mayas and Quiches 11,500 Years Ago (Their Relation to the Sacred Mysteries of Egypt, Greece, Chaldea, and India . . .)*, N.Y.: Macoy, 1886.

LEWIS, H. SPENCER: *The Symbolic Prophecy of the Great Pyramid*, San Jose, Calif.: Amorc, 1936.

LEY, WILLY: "The Island of the Stone Heads," in *Galaxy Science Fiction*, XV, 6 (Apr. 1958) pp. 41–55.

——: "Pseudoscience in Naziland," in *Astounding Science Fiction*, XXXIX, 3 (May 1947) pp. 90–98. See also DE CAMP.

LLOYD, SETON: *Early Anatolia (The Archaeology of Asia Minor Before the Greeks)*, PB, 1956.

——: "A Forgotten Nation in Turkey," in *Scientific American*, CXCIII, 1 (Jul. 1955) pp. 42–46.

LOOMIS, ROGER SHERMAN: *Celtic Myth and Arthurian Romance*, N.Y.: Columbia Un. Pr., 1927.

LORCH, F. B.: "Zimbabwe," in *Africana Notes and News*, VIII, 4 (Sep. 1951) pp. 107–18.

LORIMER, H. L.: *Homer and the Monuments,* Lon.: Macmillan & Co., 1950.

LOUGH, JAMES P.: *In the Beginning God Created the Heaven and the Earth,* N.Y.: Erudite Book Distributing Co., 1936.

MACBAIN, ALEXANDER: *Celtic Mythology and Religion,* N.Y.: E. P. Dutton & Co., 1917.

MACDONALD, MALCOLM: *Angkor,* N.Y.: Frederick A. Praeger, 1959.

MACKAY, L. A.: *The Wrath of Homer,* Toronto: Un. of Toronto Pr., 1948.

MAGOFFIN, R. V. D., & DAVIS, EMILY C.: *The Romance of Archaeology,* Garden City, N.Y.: Garden City Pub. Co., 1929.

MALONE, KEMP: "The Historicity of Arthur," in *Jour. of English & Germanic Philology,* XXIII (1924) pp. 463–91.

MALORY, SIR THOMAS: *Le Morte d'Arthur,* N.Y.: E. P. Dutton & Co., 1906–47.

MARSHALL, DONALD STANLEY: "The Settlement of Polynesia," in *Scientific American,* CXCV, 2 (Aug. 1956) pp. 58–72.

MASON, J. ALDEN: *The Ancient Civilizations of Peru,* PB, 1957.

MEANS, PHILIP AINSWORTH: *Ancient Civilizations of the Andes,* N.Y.: Chas. Scribner's Sons, 1936.

MÉTRAUX, ALFRED: *Easter Island (A Stone-Age Civilization of the Pacific),* N.Y.: Oxford Un. Pr., 1957.

MORLEY, SYLVANUS GRISWOLD: *The Ancient Maya,* Stanford, Calif.: Stanford Un. Pr., 1946.

——: *An Introduction to the Study of the Maya Hieroglyphs,* Washington: Govt. Printing Off., 1915.

MOUHOT, HENRI: *Travels in the Central Parts of Indo-China (Siam), Cambodia, and Laos . . . ,* Lon.: John Murray, 1864, 2 vols.

MURRAY, GILBERT: *The Rise of the Greek Epic,* Oxf.: Clarendon Pr., 1924.

MYRES, SIR JOHN L.: *Homer and his Critics,* Lon.: Routledge & Kegan Paul, 1958.

## BIBLIOGRAPHY

NASH, W. D.: *Merlin the Enchanter, and Merlin the Bard*, priv. pub. in Gt. Brit., 1865.

NYLANDER, CARL: "The Fall of Troy," in *Antiquity*, XXXVII (1963), pp. 6–11.

O'CONNELL, JAMES F.: *The Life of James F. O'Connell, the Pacific Adventurer*, N.Y.: 1853.

OWEN, A. L.: *The Famous Druids (A Survey of Three Centuries of English Literature on the Druids)*, Oxf.: Clarendon Pr., 1962.

OWNBEY, E. SYDNOR: *Merlin and Arthur*, Birmingham, Ala.: Birmingham-Southern College Bulletin, XXVI, 1 (Jan. 1933).

PAGE, DENYS L.: *History and the Homeric Iliad*, Berkeley, Calif.: Un. of Calif. Pr., 1959.

PARRY, JOHN JAY: "The *Vita Merlini*," in Un. of Ill. *Studies in Language and Literature*, X, 3 (Aug. 1925), Urbana, Ill.: Un. of Ill. Pr.

PAUSANIAS: *Description of Greece*, Lon.: Geo. Bell & Sons, 1886; & LC.

PAVER, B. C.: *Zimbabwe Cavalcade (Rhodesia's Romance)*, Lon.: Cassell & Co., 1957.

PAYNE, ROBERT: *The Gold of Troy*, N.Y.: Funk & Wagnalls Co., 1959; Paperback Lib., 1961.

PETERS, CARL: *The Eldorado of the Ancients*, Lon.: C. Arthur Pearson, 1903.

PETRIE, SIR W. M. FLINDERS: *Seventy Years in Archaeology*, Lon.: Sampson Low, Marston & Co., 1931.

PHILLIPS, WENDELL: *Qataban and Sheba*, N.Y.: Harcourt, Brace & Co., 1955.

PIGGOTT, STUART: *The Neolithic Cultures of the British Isles (A Study of the Stone-Using Agricultural Communities of Britain in the Second Millennium B.C.)*, Cambridge: Cambr. Un. Pr., 1954.

PLATO: *Timaeus & Critias*, in *The Works of Plato*, N.Y.: Tudor Pub. Co., n.d.; & LC.

PLUTARCH (PLOUTARCHOS): *Lives of the Noble Grecians and Romans*, N.Y.: Modern Lib., n.d.; & LC.

PORTAL, SIR WILLIAM W.: *The Great Hall of Winchester Castle*, Winchester: Hampshire County Council, 1916–61.

PRESCOTT, WILLIAM H.: *History of the Conquest of Mexico and History of the Conquest of Peru*, N.Y.: Modern Library, n.d.

RAGLAN, LORD: *The Hero (A Study in Tradition, Myth, and Drama)*, Lon.: Methuen & Co., 1936.

RIVET, PAUL: *Maya Cities*, Lon.: Elek Books, 1954–60.

ROUTLEDGE, KATHERINE PEASE (MRS. SCORESBY ROUTLEDGE): *The Mystery of Easter Island (The Story of an Expedition)*, Lon.: Sifton, Praed & Co., 1919–20.

SCHIFFERS, HEINRICH: *The Quest of Africa (Two Thousand Years of Exploration)*, N.Y.: G. P. Putnam's Sons, 1957.

SCHLIEMANN, HENRY (HEINRICH): *Ilios: The City and Country of the Trojans*, N.Y.: Harper & Bros., 1881.

SCHOFF, WILFRED H. (transl.): *The Periplus of the Erythraean Sea (Travel and Trade in the Indian Ocean . . . )*, N.Y.: Longmans, Green & Co., 1912.

SCHREIBER, HERMANN, & SCHREIBER, GEORG: *Vanished Cities*, N.Y.: Alfred A. Knopf, 1957.

SCHUCHHARDT, C.: *Schliemann's Excavations (An Archaeological and Historical Study)*, Lon.: Macmillan Co., 1891.

SCOTT-ELLIOT, W.: *The Story of Atlantis and The Lost Lemuria*, Lon.: Theosophical Pub. House, 1896–1930.

SMYTH, C. PIAZZI: *Life and Work at the Great Pyramid . . . ,* Edinburgh: Edmonston & Douglas, 1867, 3 vols.

———: *Our Inheritance in the Great Pyramid*, Lon.: Daldy, Isbiter, 1877.

SOMMER, H. OSKAR: *Le Roman de Merlin, or the Early History of King Arthur*, Lon.: priv. pub., 1894.

SPENCE, LEWIS: *Atlantis in America*, N.Y.: Brentano's, 1925.

———: *The History of Atlantis*, Lon.: Rider & Co., 1926.

———: *The Problem of Atlantis*, N.Y.: Brentano's, 1924–25.

# BIBLIOGRAPHY

———: *The Problem of Lemuria* (*The Sunken Continent of the Pacific*), Phila.: David McKay Co., 1933.

STEINER, RUDOLF: *Atlantis and Lemuria*, Lon.: Anthroposophical Pub. Co., 1923.

STEPHENS, JOHN L.: *Incidents of Travel in Central America, Chiapas, and Yucatan*, New Brunswick: Rutgers Un. Pr., 1949, 2 vols.

STONE, J. F. S.: *Wessex Before the Celts*, Lon.: Thames & Hudson, 1958.

STRABO: *Geography*, Lon.: Henry G. Bohn, 1854–57; Lon.: Geo. Bell & Sons, 1881; & LC.

SUGGS, ROBERT C.: *The Island Civilizations of Polynesia*, N.Y.: New Amer. Libr., 1960.

SYMONDS, JOHN: *The Lady with the Magic Eyes* (*Madame Blavatsky—Medium and Magician*), N.Y.: Thos. Yoseloff, 1960.

TACITUS, CORNELIUS: *Annals*, N.Y.: Modern Lib., 1942; & LC.

THÉVENIN, RENÉ: *Les Pays Légendaires* (*Devant la Science*), Paris: Presses Universitaires de France, 1946.

THOMPSON, EDWARD HERBERT: *People of the Serpent* (*Life and Adventure Among the Mayas*), Boston: Houghton Mifflin Co., 1932.

THOMPSON, J. ERIC S.: *The Rise and Fall of Maya Civilization*, Norman, Okla.: Un. of Okla. Pr., 1954. See also GANN.

TOLMAN, HERBERT CUSHING, & SCOGGIN, GILBERT CAMPBELL: *Mycenaean Troy*, N.Y.: Amer. Book Co., 1903.

VON HAGEN, VICTOR WOLFGANG: "Hiram Bingham and his Lost Cities," in *Archaeology*, II, 1 (Spring 1949) pp. 42–46.

———: *Maya Explorer* (*John Lloyd Stephens and the Lost Cities of Central America and Yucatán*), Norman, Okla.: Un. of Okla. Pr., 1948.

———: *Realm of the Incas*, N.Y.: Mentor Books, 1957–61.

———: "Waldeck," in *Natural History*, LVI, 10 (Dec. 1946) pp. 45off.

———: *World of the Maya*, N.Y.: Mentor Books, 1960–62.

BIBLIOGRAPHY

WAUCHOPE, ROBERT: *Lost Tribes and Sunken Continents (Myth and Method in the Study of American Indians)*, Chi.: Un. of Chicago Pr., 1962.

WIESCHHOFF, H. A.: *The Zimbabwe-Monomotapa Culture in Southeast Africa*, Menasha, Wis.: Geo. Banta Pub. Co., 1941.

WILLIAMS, GERTRUDE MARVIN: *Priestess of the Occult: Madame Blavatsky*, N.Y.: Alfred A. Knopf, 1946.

WILLOUGHBY, SIR JOHN C.: *Further Excavations at Zimbabye (Mashonaland)*, Lon.: Geo. Philip & Son, 1893.

# Index

(Italic numerals refer to illustrations in the text.)

Aac, 8, 13

Achaia & Achaians or Achaioi, 67–70, 90–93

Achilles, 67–71, 74, 78, 92; tomb of, 89

Acropolis, North, 192; Zimbabwean, 122, 123–26, 137, 208

Aden, 105 ff

Ælla, 150

Aeneas (see Aineias)

Aeneid, 144, 149

Æsc, 150

Afara, 136

Agamemnon, 67, 80, 82, 90

Ahmad ibn-Yahya, 107 ff

ahu, 256 ff

Aineias or Aeneas, 70, 89, 94, 149, 155

Ainu, 201 f

Akhiyawâ, 90 f

Alaksandus or Alexandros (see Paris)

Alexander the Great, 84, 89, 149

Alexandria, 72, 100

Aliseda, 23

Alkinoös, 24

All-Story Weekly, 231

altiplano, 213, 216

Amautas, 207, 219

Amazon River, 203, 213

Amazons, 69

Ambrosius (boy), 140, 149 f, 155; Aurelianus or Aurelius, 45, 65, 141, 147–56 (see also Merlin); King, 149 f

Amenhotep II, 243

America, 7, 117, 208; archaeology of, 108, 191

Aminds or American Indians, 101, 113, 167, 180 f, 184, 201 f; cities of, 183, 195; civilization of, 17, 183, 195, 208, 214; color of, 242; downfall of, 214 f; migrations of, 202; myths & legends of, 241; origin of, 7–11, 19,

193 f; palaces of, 183; temples of, 183; voyages by, 245

Amesbury, 44, 64

Ancient Order of Druids, 49, 51

Andesite Line, 240

Angkor, abandonment of, 177; builders of, 165 f; discovery of, 163 f; empire of, 168; fall of, 2, 176; mystery of, 166 ff; records of, 177; Thom, 169 f, 173, 176; Wat, 168 ff, 174, 196

Anglo-Saxon Chronicles, 150

Annales Cambriae or Welsh Annals, 150, 155

Antiquities of Mexico, The, 186

Aphroditè, 67 (see also Venus)

Arganthonios, 21

Argives or Argeioi & Argolis, 91

Argonautika, 74

Aristarchos, 72

Aristotle (Aristoteles), 6, 29, 72

Ark, 29

Armorica (see Brittany)

Arnaud, Joseph Thomas, 105

Artaius (see Artur)

Artemis, 31

Arthur (general), 152 f; King, 44, 140–59

Artorius Castus, L., 151 ff, 158 f

Artur or Artaius, 151

Aryans, 15, 23, 63, 86

Arzawa, 16, 20, 91 f

Ascending Corridor, 37

Assyria, 98, 101

Aswân (see Swenet)

Atahuallpa, 209 ff, 214

Atalantè, 19 f

Atan, Pedro, 258 f

Atarisiyas, 90 f

Athanase, Prince, 1

Athena, 4, 67 f; temple of, 80, 89

Athens, 4, 19, 25, 157, 196

Atkinson, R. J. C., 52, 62
*Atlántida, La*, 3
Atlantis & Atlanteans, 51, 188, 218, 227 ff; ceremonies of, 6, 19; city of, 5, 20; civilization of, 11, 17, 167; continent of, 3, 19; destruction of, 7, 15, 17, 22–25, 142, 262-3; empire of, 4; kings of, 6, 14, 231, 236; location of, 7, 20, 133; map of, *12*; palaces of, 5; queen of, 13; temples of, 5; Theosophical, 230ff, 236
*Atlantis: The Antediluvian World*, 11, *12*, 231
*Atlantis: die Urheimat der Arier*, 15
Atlantism, 10 f
Atlas, 4, 20
Atreus, 90 f
Aubignac, Abbé, d', 72
Aubrey, John, 46–49
Aubrey Holes, 47, 51, *53*, 54–59, 62
Aurelianus or Aurelius Ambrosius (*see* Ambrosius)
Aurelius Candidianus, 153; Caninus, 153; Eutherius, 153
Avalon, 143
Avebury, 47, 57 f, 64
Avendaño, Andrés, 183
Axum, 137
Ayuthia, 176
Azania, 128
Aztecs, 167, 183, 194, 196, 201; priests of, 197; pyramids of, 197; writing of, 185

Ba'albakk or Baalbek, 44
Babylon & Babylonia, 46, 60, 86, 105, 166, 196; kings of, 142
Bacon, Francis, 7, 11
Badon Hill or Mt. Badon, 148, 150, 159
Baghdad, 4
Baikie, William B., 111
Baker, Samuel W., 111
Ballı Dağ, 75–78, 89
Bank, the, 52, *53*, 54 f, 59, 62
Banteay Chhmar, 169
Bantu, 114, 124–29, 133 f, 137
Bara, Theda, 97
Barays, 170, 173, 177
Barnard, F. A. P., 31
BaRozwi, 130, 137
Barros, João de, 116 f, *124*
barrows, *53*, 54–57, 82
Barthel, Thomas, 254, 256
*Barzaz-Breiz*, 50
Battambang, 161, 165
Battle-ax People, 63, 65
Bayhân, 107, 109
Bayon, 168 f, 174, 176

Beaker Folk, 21 f, 60 ff
Bede or Bæda, 148 f
Bedford, 153
Bel, 14
Belgae, 64 f
Bellamy, Hans, 216
Belloc, Hilaire, 241
Benomotapa, 116
Bent, J. Theodore, 120, 130
Bentley, Richard, 72
Bernoulli, Gustav, 190
Bible, 11, 96, 119, 218
Bilqîs, 97, 106 f, 130 (*see also* Sheba, queen of)
Bingham, Hiram, 203–8
Blandford, William T., 227 f
Blavatsky, Helena P., 217, 228–32, 239
Blegen, Carl W., 83 f, 90
Bolton, Edmund, 45
Bonampak, 196
*Book of Dzyan, The*, 229 f
*Books of Chilan Balaam*, 198 f
Borchardt, Ludwig, 31
Boron, Robert de, 157
Boskop, 115
Botta, Paul-Émile, 75
Boudicca, 45
Brasseur de Bourbourg, C.-É., 9, *10*, 11, 13
Brittany or Armorica & Bretons, 58, 141 ff, 147, 151 155, 158
Broceliande, 143
*Brood of the Witch Queen*, 38
*Brut*, 157
Brutus, 149, 155, 157
Buddha & Buddhism, 168, 173–76; statues of, 174; temples of, 14, 169
Bunarbashi, 75–78, 89
Burroughs, Edgar Rice, 231 f

Cádiz, 2, 24
Caesar, C. Julius, 44, 48, 64, 89, 144, 149, 241
Cairo, 27, 32–35
Cajamarca, 209, 214
Calvert brothers, 76, 79 f
Camel River, 150, 158
Camelot, 142, 148, 157 f
Camlan or Camlann, 143, 150, 152, 158
Camulos & Camulodunum, 158
Capac Yupanqui, 211
Carambolo, El, 23
Carmarthen, 140, 144, 156
Carnac, 58
Caroline Islands, 221, 227
Carrera, Rafael, 186 ff
Carthage & Carthaginians, 24, 188, 196
*Catalogue of Ships*, 73

Categirn, 153
Catherwood, Frederick, *184*, 186–90, 196, 208
Catoche, 196
Caton-Thompson, Gertrude, 121, *122*, 126, 132 ff, 138
Causeway, the 54 ff, 59; Cambodian, 159, 163, 170; Mayan, 182
Cei (see Kay)
Celts, 21, 48 f, 63 ff, 140 f, 151–54; myths & legends of, 156
Cerdic, 150
Chac, 197
Chaldea, 14, 46
Champa & Chams, 174
Chan-Chan, 215
Charles V, 157, 209 f
Chavín 215 f
Chel, 199
Chenla, 172
Cheops (see Khufu)
Chephren (see Khafra)
Chevreuil, 164
Chichén Itzá, 13, 181, 190
Chimú, 215
Chok Gargyar, 173
Chubb, Cecil, 51
Churchward, James, 14 f, 232, 239
Chyndonax, 48
Cicero, M. Tullius, 72
City of the Dead, 2; of the Golden Gates, 231
Claudius (emperor), 64
Clay Zimbabwe, 126
Cochin-China, 162, 164
Cocom, 199
Coedès, George, 168
Coh, 13
Colchester, 158
Coleman, William E., 231
Columbus, Christopher, 6, 22, 81, 83
Connecticut Yankee at King Arthur's Court, A, 145
Constantine I (emperor), 89 f; king, 45, 143, 147, 152
Constantinople or Istanbul, 79 f, 90
Constantinus III, 152
Constantius, 152
Cook, James, 249
Copán, 181, *185*, 187
Córdoba, Hernández de, 196
Cornwall, 139, 146 f, 150, 153–58; duke of, 141; earl of, 157; kings of, 142, 146 f, 152, 155
Coropuna, Mt., 203
Cortereal, Miguel, 19, 245
Cortés, Hernán, 183, 194, 214
Crane, Charles R., 106

Crete, 20, 62, 82, 219, 262
cromlechs, 58
Cronos, King, 14
Crustumius, 2
Cthulhu, 205 f
Cunnington, William, 51
Cunobelin or Cymbeline, 155, 158
Cunomorus or Quonomorius, Marcus, 146 f
Cursus, 57, 61
Cuzco, 207–10, 213
Cynric, 150
*Cypria*, 74

Daidalos, 219
Damascus, 2
Danaoi, 91
Davidoon, David, 31
Davis, Edward, 248
Days of Ignorance, 39, 79
Dedefra, 37
Delabarre, E. B., 19
Delaporte, L., 164
del Río, Antonio, 183 f
Demetia, 140, 156
Deorham, 153
Derleth, August, 205 f
*Destruction and Conquest of Britain*, 147 f
Dhlo-Dhlo, 126
Díaz, Bartolomeu, 112
Diffusionists & Diffusionism, 166 f
Dighton Rock, 19, 245
Dinka, 114
Diogenes Laërtius, 48
Diomedes, 69
Ditch, the, 52, *53*, 54 f, 59
Donnelly, Ignatius, 10 f, *12*, 14 f, 231
*Don Quixote*, 187
Dôr or Dore, Castle, 146 f
Dorado, El, 116
Dörpfeld, Wilhelm, 77 f, 83 f
Dravidians, 131
Druids & Druidism, 19, 46–51, 56, 63
Drustans (see Tristram)
Dunsany, Lord, 126
Dutroux-Bornier, 252
*Dweller on Two Planets, A*, 232

Easter Island or Rapa Nui, 232, 237; annexation of, 252; ceremonies of, 253; culture of, 242, 248, 251 ff; discovery of, 238, 249; mystery of, 260; settlement of, 239 f, 243 f, 247; writing of, 253 f, *255*, 256 (see also Pascuans)
École Française d'Extrême-Orient, 164
Edward III, 144, 158

*Eldorado of the Ancients, The*, 131
Elizabeth I, 97, 134
Elliptical Building, *122*, 123 ff, 130, 133, 137
*Emden*, 227
Engastromenos, Sophia (Frau Schliemann), 77–80
Eratosthenes, 72, 93
Ericsson, Leif, 246
Erskine, John, 145
Erythriotes or Hamites, 114 f, 128, 136
Escorial, 2
Es-En-Tau, *225*, 235
Eteokles or Etewoklewês, 90
Evelyn, John, 46

Fakhry, Ahmed, 106 f
Fernández, Juan, 248
Fimbria, C. Flavius, 89
Flood, the, 17, 218
Flores, Lake, 179, 183
Foord, Edward, 152, 154
Forrer, Emil, 90
*Four Faces of Siva*, 168
Fox, A. H. Lane (*see* Pitt-Rivers)
Frobenius, Leo, 133
Funan, 171 f

Gades (*see* Cádiz)
Galápagos Islands, 242
Gallipoli, 70, 78
Gargaris, 20
Garnier, M. J. F., 164
Gateway of the Sun, 216
Gaul & Gauls, 23, 151
Gawain, 142, 251
Geoffrey of Monmouth, 44 f, 65, 155–58
George III, 51
George V, 51
Germanus, St., 149, 152
Ghumdân, 100
Giant's Causeway, 224
Giants' Dance, 45, 65
*Gil Blas*, 187
Gildas, 147–52, 156
Giza, 27
Glaser, Eduard, 106
Glastonbury Abbey, 144 f
Gloucester, Bishop of, 45
Goes, Damião de, 116 f
Gonds, Gondwana, & Gondwanaland, 228
González, Felipe, 249
Gorlois, 141
Gowland, William, 51
Grand Gallery, 31, *35*, 36 f
Grant, James A., 111
Grant, Madison, 241

Gray Minyan Ware, 83, 88
*Great Cryptogram, The*, 11
Great Zimbabwe, 121
Greece & Greeks or Hellenes, 21, 78, 89, 91, 149, 171, 188, 194; gods of, 25, 67 ff, 73, 92; government of, 80; kings of, 67–70, 94, 142; myths & legends of, 19, 50, 69 f, 92, 155; queens of, 94
Guadalquivir River, 20–23
Guenevere, 142, 145, 148
Guthrigern, 147 (*see also* Vortigern)

Habis, 20
Hadhramawt, 96
Hadrian's Villa, 2
Haeckel, Ernest Heinrich, 228
Haggard, H. Rider, 132
Hahn, J. G. von, 76
Halévy, Joseph, 105 f
Hall, R. N., 121, 123, 127, 131
Hambruch, Paul, 233 ff
Hanga Roa, 252, 258
Haram of Bilqîs, 107, 130
Harappâ, 16
Hatshepsut, 97, 131
Hattusas, 90
Hawley, William, 51
Heald, Kenneth, 204 f
Hector, 67 ff, 74, 78, 92
Heid, 15
Helen of Troy, 67–70, 92, 94
Hellên, 149
Hellenes (*see* Greeks)
Hellespont, 70, 78
Hemniunu, 35
Hengist, 44 f, 140, 148 ff, 153, 155
Henry VIII, 157
Henry of Huntington, 44
Hephaistos, 68
Hera, 67 f
*Herakleia*, 74
Herakles, 74, 92; Pillars of, 4
Herodotos, 34, 37–40, 245
Hesionê, 70, 240
Hévesy, Guillaume de, 254
Heyerdahl, Thor, 240–43, 258
*Hiawatha*, 144
Hiberius, Lucius, 142 f, 157
Higden, Ranulph, 156
Hippalos, 104
Hiram, King, 21
Hisarlik, 75–81, 84, 89 ff
*Historical Researches on the Conquest of Peru* . . . , 184
*History of the Britons*, 149
*History of the Church of England*, 148
*History of the English*, 44

*History of the Kings of Britain*, 44, 155 f
Hittites & Khatti, 90–94
Holes, Aubrey, 47, 51 f, 53, 54–59, 62; Q & R, 52–55, 61; Y & Z, 51, 53, 54 f, 62, 64
Holy Grail, 142
*Homecomings*, 74
Homer (Homēros), 24, 44, 67–72, 75, 77, 84, 90–94, 144
Homeric Age, 75, 81
Honorius, 152
Hörbiger, Hans, & Hörbigerism, 216 ff, 239
Horsa, 140, 149 ff, 153, 155
Hottentots, 18, 115, 127, 131, 136 f
Hotu Matu'a, 246 f
Houdini, Harry (Ehrich Weiss), 38
*How I Discovered Atlantis*, 13
Howard, Robert E., 256
Hrozný, Bedřich, 90
Huáscar, 209 ff, 214
Huayna Capac, 209, 211
Huayna Picchu, 204 f
Hume, Allan Octavian, 229
Hun Tien, 171
Hyksôs, 60
*Hymn of Creation*, 231
Hyperborea & Hyperboreans, 50, 230

Iamboulos, 7
Igerna, 141, 143
Île-Melon, 58
*Iliad*, 69–74, 80, 82, 90, 92, 144
Ilion or Ilios (*see* Troy)
'Ilmuqah, 100, 107
Imâm, 105–9
Imhotep, 32 f
Immermann, K. L., 145
*Imprisoned with the Pharaohs*, 38
Inca Roca, 211; Viracocha, 211
Incas, 183, 207–19; roads of, 204, 214
*Incidents of Travel in Central America . . .*, 188
Indians (American), Atlantean, 188, 193; Aymara, 218; Chinese, 184, 188; Egyptian, 188, 193; Itzá, 183; Jewish, 7, 9, 184, 186, 188, 193; Mayan, 8, 180 f; Mormon, 188, 193; Narragansett, 19; Norse, 193; Otomi, 11; Peruvian, 101, 204, 213, 244 ff; Phoenician, 184, 188; Polynesian, 193; Sumerian, 193; Welsh, 7, 188, 193 (*see also* Amerinds)
Inyanga, 126, 131
Ireland & Irish, 7, 45, 49, 65, 140, 142, 150, 152; gods of, 151; myths & legends of, 48, 155, 158; tombs of, 59
Isis, 13, 99

Iso-Kalakal, 233–36
Isolt, 142
Israel (nation), 105; Lost Ten Tribes of, 7, 184, 186; (patriarch), 149 (*see also* Jews)
Istanbul (*see* Constantinople)
*It Can't Happen Here*, 17
Ithaka or Thiaki, 24, 69, 76
Ituri Forest, 114
Itzamná, 197, 201
Itzás, 183

James I, 45
Jameson, Leander, 120 f
Jason, 74
Jaussen, Tepano, 251, 254
Java-Varman II, 173; IV, 173; VII, 168 f, 174 f
Jericho, 2, 96, 144
Jesus Christ, 30 f, 241
Jews, Hebrews, or Israelites, 19, 100, 105, 149, 188, 251; myths & legends of, 155
Jokaz, 223–26, 233, 235
Jones, Inigo, 45 ff
Joser, 32 f
Jou Da-gwan or Chou Ta-Kuan, 175
Justinus, M. Junianius, 20
Juvenal (D. Iunius Iuvenalis), 151

Kafr-es-Sammân, 28, 34, 36
Kamakoi, 252
Kambu Svayambhuva, 165
Kamimaljuyú, 191
Karia & Karians, 20, 23 f, 91
Karlsevni, Thorfinn, 241
Kaundinya, 171
Kay or Cei, 146, 151
Kêteioi, 90
Khafra or Chephren, 37 f, 42
Khufu or Cheops, 27–30, 35–39, 42
Khuit-Khufu, 34
Kichés, 196
Killaraus or Kildare, 45
Kilwa, 128, 131
Kingsborough, Viscount, 184, 186
King's Chamber, 35, 36 f
*King Solomon's Mines*, 132
Kiti, 223–26
Kleito, 4
Knobby Ware Folk, 89, 93
Knossos, 2, 82
Kolaios, 21
*Kon-Tiki*, 242
*Kritias*, 3 f, 5, 19, 24 f
Kubary, Johann S., 233
Kukulcán, 197

Kusae, 233–36

Lady of the Lake, 143
Lagrée, E. M. L. D. de, 164
Lancelot, 140, 142, 148, 151
Lancien, 147
Landa, Diego de, 7 f, 9 f, 11, 13, 198
Lang, Andrew, 119
Laomedon, 70, 92 f, 240
La Pérouse, J. F. C. de, 249
La Vega, Garcilaso de, 211
La Venta Stone, 196
La Villemarqué, Hersart de, 50
Layamon, 157
Layard, Austen, 75
Lear, King, 155
Lemuria & Lemurians, 14, 218, 227–33, 236, 239 f, 257
Leodegrance, 142
Le Plongeon, Augustus, 10, 13 ff
Lêr or Llyr, 155
Lewis, H. Sinclair, 17
Leyden Plate, 195 f
Libby, W. F., 56
Life of Merlin, 156
Limpopo River, 115
Little Zimbabwe, 126
Livingstone, David, 111
Lloque Yupanqui, 211
Lludd, 151
Lockyer, Norman, 56 f
Locmaricquer, 58
Lokeshvara, 168
Long-ears, 237, 243
Longfellow, Henry W., 144
López de Gómara, Francisco, 9
Lost Continent of Mu, The, 14
Lot, King, 145, 151
Lovecraft, H. P., 38, 126, 182, 205
Lowell, Percival, 232
Lug or Llwch, 157
Lugh Loinnbheimionach, 151
Luk-En-Mueiu, 235
Lütke, Feodor P., 226
Luxor, 2, 131
Lydia, 91 f
Lyonesse, 142
Lyou Ye, 171
Lysimachos, 89

Macchu Pichu, 204–7, 219
MacDonald, Malcolm, 177
Macpherson, James, 50
Madoc, Prince, 7
Ma'în, 96, 101
Malays, 99, 132, 165, 171
Maler, Teobert, 190
Malory, Thomas, 157, 159

Mambo, 130, 137 f
Ma'mûn, al-, 39
Manco, 210; Capac, 207 f, 211, 215, 219
Mandara, Mt., 170
Manetho, 31, 34
Mansûr, al-, 4
Mapungubwe, 126
Ma'rib, 97, 101, 103, 104–10, 130
Maridunum, 156
Mariette, Auguste, 75
Marismas, Las, 22
Mark, King, 142, 146 f (see also Cunomorus)
Marlborough Downs, 52, 55, 61
Marquesas Islands, 226, 244, 250
MaShona & Mashonaland, 117–20, 126–29
Mas'ûdi, 136 f
MaTabele, 120
Matabele Times, 130
Matol-Pa, 234
Matol-Pau-Ue, 225, 234
Mauch, Karl Gottlieb, 117 ff, 125, 130
Maudslay, Alfred P., 185, 208
Mayapan, League of, 199
Mayas, 166, 261; alphabet of, 8, 9 f, 11, 13, 198; architecture of, 196 f; art of, 196; bearded, 201 f; calendar of, 194 f; character of, 181; chiefs of, 197, 199; cities of, 181 f, 188, 196, 199f; civilization of, 17, 167, 183, 190, 194, 196, 200 f; conquest of, 183; customs of, 13, 245; empires of, 194–202; gods of, 197–201; history of, 167, 185, 199; inscriptions of, 198; migrations of, 200; monuments of, 181, 198; mysteries of, 199–202; myths & legends of, 195; origin of, 13, 193 f; palaces of, 182, 191 f; pyramids of, 167, 182, 191 f, 197; religion of, 197 f; roads of, 190; temples of, 166, 182, 190–93, 198; writing of, 3, 8, 9 f, 11, 195, 198 f
Mayta Capac, 211
Means, Philip A., 208
Medraut (see Modred)
Mekong River, 161, 171
Melanesia & Melanesians, 240, 244, 250
Memnon, 69
Memphis, 32 f
Mendaña, Alvaro de, 222
Méndez, Modesto, 190
Menelaos, 67, 70, 90
Menkaura or Mycerinus, 29, 38
Menzies, Robert, 31
Merensky, 118
Mérida, 183
Merlin, 45, 65, 140–48, 155 f
Merlin, 157

*Merlin—Eine Mythe*, 145
Merritt, Abraham, 227
Meru, Mt., 170
Mesopotamia, 167, 197
Metalanim, 223, 225, 233 ff
Micronesia & Micronesians, 233 ff, 244
Milford Haven, 55, 61
Minos & Minotaur, 219
mit'a, 213
Modred or Mordred, 143, 145, 150 ff
Mona, 49
Monomotapa, 115–18, 129 f, 134, 137
*Monster of Mu, The*, 239 f
Montejo, Francisco de, 183, 214
Montesinos, Fernando, 207
Montezuma (Moctezuma) II, 194
Móo, 13
*Moon Pool, The*, 227
Morazán, Francisco, 186 ff
More, Thomas, 7
Morganwg, Iolo, 50
Morley, Sylvanus G., 195, 201
*Morte d'Arthur, Le*, 157
*Most Notable Antiquity of Great Britain, The*, 46
Moto Nui, 253
Mouhot, Henri, 161–64, 167 f, 173
Mu & Muvians, 10, 13 f, 232, 239 f
Muḥammad, 39, 105, 131
Mukarribs, 101 f
Mundy, Talbot, 49
Mycerinus or Mykerinos (*see* Menkaura)
Mykenē or Mycenae, 62, 67, 80–83, 88 94
Mynydd Prescelly, 52
Myrddin, 155 f (*see also* Merlin)

Nabataeans, 2
Nabuna'id or Nabonidus, 46
Nagas, 165, 169
Nalaim, 233
Nan-Japue, 234
Nan-Marki, 233–36
Nan Matol, abandonment of, 236; builders of, 224, 233 f; discovery of, 223; map of, 225; myths & legends of, 233; ruins of, 221 f, 232; speculation about, 227; walls of, 225, 235
Nan Molusei, 234
Nanpei, 235
Nan-Towas, 225, 235
Nanue-Zu-Taman, 236
Nanusunsap, 235
Napoleon Bonaparte, 159, 184
Nazca, 215
Necker Island, 257
Nekhebu, 40
Nennius, 149 ff, 154 ff

Net, 222 f
New Angkor, 161 f
*New Atlantis, The*, 7
Newfoundland, 7
New Grange, 59
New Guinea, 236
Newhall, R. S., 51
Niger River, 111, 127
Niku II, 112
Nile River, 27, 32, 41, 111–14
Nilotes, 114, 128
Nimuë, 142 f
Nineveh, 2, 196
Nisbet, Captain, 7
Noah, 29, 50, 188, 207
Nuada, 151

O'Connell, James, 222–26
*Odyssey* & Odysseus, 24, 69–74
Olcott, Henry Steel, 229
Oliver, Frederick Spencer, 232
Olo-Sipe & Olo-Sopa, 223
Oman, 109
Ophir (patriarch), 207; (place), 119, 130 f, 136
Orkney, 145, 151
Oroi, 246 f, 253
Otomie, 11
*Our Inheritance in the Great Pyramid*, 29

Pachacuti, 211; VI, 207
Page, Denys L., 91
Palenque, 183, 188
Pan Katera, 225, 235
Paramarāja, 176
Paris, Alexandros, or Alaksandus, 67, 69, 89 ff, 94
Paruro, 208
Pascuans, appearance of, 249 f; boredom of, 259 f; ceremonies of, 253, 257, 260; condition of, 253; culture of, 242, 248, 251 ff; customs of, 242, 259; discovery of, 248; gods of, 253; history of, 246; kings of, 247; myths & legends of, 237; origin of, 242, 244; wars of, 248 f, 258, 260; writing of, 253 f, 255, 256 (*see also* Easter Island)
Patroklos, 68
Pausanias, 71
Pei-En-Kitel, 235
Peisistratos, 72 f
Penn, William, 9
Penthesilea, 69
Pepys, Samuel, 46
Pergamos, 84, 208
*Periplus of the Erythraean Sea*, 128
Persepolis, 2

Petén, 179–83, 195, 199–202
Peters, Carl, 130 f
Petra, 2, 186
Petrie, W. M. Flinders, 31, 261
Phaiakes or Phaeacians, 24
Philip VI, 144, 158
Philips, George, 118
Phillips, Wendell, 107 ff
Phimeanakas, 166
Phnom Bakheng, 173 f
Phnom Penh, 176
Phoenicians, 19 f, 51, 112, 119, 130, 184, 188, 245
Phokaia & Phokaians, 21
Picts, 140, 152
Piggott, Stuart, 52
Pitcairn Island, 237, 244
Pitt-Rivers, A. H. L. F., 81 f
Pizarro, Francisco, 183, 209 f, 214
Plato, 3–7, 14–20, 24 f, 262-3
Plaza Mayor, 191 f
Plinius Secundus, C., or Pliny the Elder, 6, 48
Poike Ditch, 237
Polterabend, 82
Polynesia & Polynesians, 113, 238–45, 248, 257; chiefs of, 246 f, 251; customs of, 171, 247, 251; myths & legends of, 242; writing of, 256
Ponapé & Ponapeans, 221–24, 232; culture of, 227; Europeans in, 226; gods of, 233 ff; history of, 233–36; mysteries of, 232; myths & legends of, 233–36; palaces of, 235; writing of, 235
Poseidon, 4 f, 70, 92
Posnansky, Arthur, 216
Posselt brothers, 120
Pra-Eun, 163
Prasat Phnom Bok, 173
*Pravda*, 4
Priamos or Priam, 67–70, 80, 92
*Princess of Mars, A*, 231
Proklos, 6
Punapau, Mt., 258
Punt, 130 f, 136
Pygmies, 114 f, 127, 136
Pyramid Hill, 27 f, 34
Pyramidology, 29 ff
pyramids, Aztec, 197; Bent, 34; Cambodian, 167; construction of, 39–42; Dahshûr, 33 f; Dedefra's, 37; Egyptian, 27–44, 57, 165, 197; Great or Khufu's, 27–34, 35, 36–40, 57; Joser's, 32 f; Khafra's, 37–40; Mayan, 167, 182, 191 f, 197; Maydûm, 33 f; Menkaura's, 29, 38; Peruvian, 215 f, 260; step, 33, 166; temple, 167, 182

Qataban, 96, 101, 107
Quatermain, Allan, 132
Quechuas, 212
Queen's Chamber, 35, 36
Quetzalcoatl, 197
Quiros, Pedro Fernández de, 222
Qur'ân or Koran, 102

Ra, 14
Raglan, Lord, 150
Rainless Coast, 213, 215
Randall-MacIver, David, 131 ff
Ranking, John, 184 f
Rano Raraku, 237 f, 257 ff
Rapa Nui (*see* Easter Island)
Red Sea, 114, 119, 127
Reginald of Cornwall, 157
*Relación de las Cosas de Yucatán*, 8, 9, 10
Renders, Adam, 118, 123
*Republic, The*, 4, 24 f
Rhind, Alexander H., 75
Rhodes, Cecil, 120
Rhodesia, 117, 120, 126–31, 136 f
Rich, Claudius James, 75
*Rig-Veda*, 231
Robertson, William, 183
Robinson, Tom, 64
Roggeveen, Jaakob, 238, 248 f, 257
Rome & Romans, 51, 65, 105, 129, 142 f; army of, 44, 150, 152 f; decadence of, 200; defeat of, 151; empire of, 6, 104, 142 f, 157; founding of, 70, 149; in Britain, 140, 158; in Indo-China, 171; roads of, 190; temples of, 44, 46
Romer, Sax (Arthur S. Ward), 38
Romulus & Remus, 15
Rosicrucians, 232
Round Table, 44, 140–44, 157 f
Rowena, 140
Royal Society, 29
*Ruined Cities of Mashonaland, The*, 130
Rutter, Owen, 239
Rydderch or Rodarch, 156

Saba', Sabaea, or Sheba, & Sabaeans, 96 f, 100, 101, 102, 103, 110; palace of, 119, 130
*Sack of Ilion*, 74
Sacsahuamán, 208
Sahara, 20, 112
Saïs, 4
Sala-y-Gomez, 237
Salmon, Alexander P., 242
Samians, 21
San Antonio, Quiroga de, 164
*San Jeronimo*, 222

Sandes, S. D., 133
Sanlúcar de Barrameda, 22
Saqqâra, 33
Satalur, 233–36
Sauer, Hans, 120
Savfet Pasha, 79 f
Saxons, 44 f, 51, 65, 140–56
Schlichter, Heinrich, 120
Schliemann, Heinrich, 13 f, 74–85, 90
   92
Schliemann, Paul, 13 ff
Schulten, Adolf, 22
Sclater, Philip L., 228
Scott-Elliot, William, 231
Scythians, 158, 188
Sea of Milk, 170
Secondary Neolithic People, 60
*Secret Doctrine, The*, 229 ff
Selous, Frederick C., 119
Semites, 100, 119, 130–33
Seneferu, 34
*Senyavin*, 226
Seven Wonders of the World, 27, 102
Seville or Hispalis, 22 f
Seychelles Islands, 228
Shailendra, 172
Shakespeare, William, 11, 46, 155, 236
Shasta, Mt., 232
Sheba, queen of, 96 ff, 101, 109 f, 119,
   130 (*see also* Saba'; Bilqîs)
Shelley, Percy Bysshe, 1
*Shenandoah*, 226
Shiva & Shaivism, 168, 172 f
Short-ears, 243
Siegfried or Sigurd, 93, 141
Sihanouk, Norodom, 177
Sijilmassa, 2
Silbury Hill, 58
Simoeis River, 78
Sinchi Roca, 211
Sinnett, Alfred P., 229
Sinon, 69
Sitwell, Osbert, 166
Skamandros River, 78
Smith, G. Elliot, 166; John, 50
Smyth, Charles Piazzi, 29 ff
Sofala, 117, 121, 128
Sokrates, 3
Solomon Islands, 222; King, 21, 96 ff,
   119, 130, 133
Solon, 4
Speke, John H., 111
Sphinx, 28, 37 f
Stamatakes, 80
Stanley, Henry M., 111
*Stanzas of Dzyan, The*, 229 ff
Stasinos, 74
Stephens, John Lloyd, 75, 186–90, 208

Stone Age, 60, 84, 115, 244
Stonehenge, 44, 196; Baronet of, 51;
   builders of, 52, 57, 134; date of, 56 f;
   history of, 59 f; investigation of, 51,
   263; Mediterranean influence on, 62;
   mystery of, 65; origin of, 45 f, 65; plan
   of, *53*; rites at, 2, 50; site of, 61; stones
   of, *52*, *53*, 55–58
Stone, J. F. S., 52
Strabon, 6, 72
Stukeley, William, 47 ff, 57, 64
Styx, River, 69
Suetonius Paulinus, C., 49
Sumerians, 30, 193
Sumuhu'alay Yanaf, 102
Surya-Varman I, 174; II, 168, 174
Swenet or Aswân, 40 f

Table, Arthur's, 144; Round (*see* Round
   Table)
Tacitus, P. Cornelius, 48, 151
Tadmor (Palmyra), 2
Tahiti & Tahitians, 238, 251–54
Tahuantinsuyu, 209, 211, 214 f
Tampu Tocco, 207 f
Tarshish, 20 f
Tartessos, 20 f, *22*, 23 f
Tauara, Metoro, 254
Tawagalawas, 90
Taylor, John, 29
Temuen, 221, 223, *225*, 233
Tennyson, Alfred, 145, 159
Theosophy & Theosophists, 227–32, 236
Thera, 262–3
Theseus, 157, 219
Thetis, 68, 149
Thiaki (*see* Ithaka)
Thomas, H. H., 52
Thompson, J. E. S., 200 f
Thothmes IV, 38
Tiahuanaco, 208, 216–19
Tikal, 179 ff; abandonment of, 183, 199;
   discovery of, 183, 190; founding of,
   195 f; map of, *189*; restoration of, 191;
   ruins of, 202; stelae, 193
Tiki, 242
Timaios, 3 f, 19, 24
Timna', 101, 107
Tintagel, 139–43, 146, 157
Tippu Tib, 129
Titicaca, Lake, 216, 218
Toland, John, 49
Toltecs, 196, 201, 232
Tonga, 257
Tonle Sap, 161
Tozzer, Alfred M., 190
Tristram or Drustans, 142, 146 f, 157

Troano Codex, 9, *10*, 13 f
Troy & Trojans, abandonment of, 90;
   bronze at, 86, 88; builders of, 134;
   chiefs of, 84; chronology of, 84; citadel
   of, 84, 208: excavations at, 78 ff, 83;
   fall of, 70, 85, 88–94; gates of, 70, 87;
   gold of, 80, 88; Greek, 89; Homeric,
   83 f, *87*, 90–93; house of, 85, 88;
   kings of, 70, 91 f; palaces of, 80, 92;
   plain of, 68, 71; plan of, *87*; siege of,
   67–71, 74, 94; site of, 74–78; treasure
   of, 79 f, 85; walls of, 68–71, 84, 86, *87*,
   88
Troyu, 33, 40
Tuamotu Islands, 240
Tubuai Islands, 238, 257
Tupac Amaru, 214; Yupanqui, 211
Turduli, 21–24
Tuxtla Statuette, 196
Twain, Mark (Samuel L. Clemens), 145
Tyre, 2, 21

U, 223
Uaxactún, 181, 195
Umtali, 130
*Under the Moons of Mars*, 231
Urien of Reged, 154
Urubamba River & Valley, 203–8
Uther Pendragon, 45, 141, 143, 151–
   55
*Utopia* & utopias, 3, 7, 25, 260
Uxmal, 181, 184, 188, 190

Valentine's Brook, 139
Vasco da Gama, 6
Vâsuki, 170
Velikovsky, Immanuel, 11, 15, 218
Verdaguer, Jacinto, 3
Victoria (town), 121; Falls, 111, 121
Vikings, 59, 243
Virchow, Rudolf, 77 f, 82
Virgil (P. Vergilius Maro), 44, 144, 149
Vishnu & Vaishnavism, 168, 170, 173
*Vishnu Purana*, 231
Vitcos, 203
Vortigern or Vurtigern, 45, 140 f, 148 f,
   153–56
Vortimer, 149, 153, 155
*Voyage pittoresque et archéologique . . . ,*
   185 f
Vyse, Howard, 29

Wace, 157
Wâdi Dhana, *101*, 102
Wagner, Richard, 142
Waldeck, Count de, 183, *184*, 185 f, 196
Wales or Cambria & Welsh, 52, 55, 61,
   65, 140, 150, 156, 188; Camelot in,
   157; kings of, 153; myths & legends
   of, 48, 146
WaNgoni, 138
WaTutsi, 128
Welsh Annals, 150, 155
Wepemnofret, 35
White, T. H., 145
Wilios or Wilusas, 90 f
William the Conqueror, 144
Williams, Edward, 50
Williamson & Balfour Co., 252
Willoughby, John C., 127
Willow Leaf, 171
Wilson, H. H., 231
Winchell, Alexander, 231
Winchester Castle, 144, 157
Winckler, Hugo, 90
Windmill Hill People, 60
Wiraqochan or Viracocha, 216
Woden or Wotan, 15, 148 f
Wolf, Friedrich August, 73
Woodhenge, 58, 63
*World Life*, 231

Xiu or Tutulxiu, 199

Yahuar Huaccac, 211
Yahya ibn-Muḥammad, 106 f
Yashodharapura, 169, 173 ff
Yasho-Varman I, 169, 173 f
Yggdrasil, 15
Yucatán, 13, 181, 183, 188, 190, 194,
   200 f, 211, 245; bishop of, 8; conquest
   of, 214

Zambesi River, 111, 115, 128
Zeus, 6, 15
Zimbabwe, 99; abandonment of, 138;
   Acropolis of, *122*, 123–26, 208;
   builders of, 128 130, 136 ff; discovery
   of, 118, 125; exploitation of, 119 ff;
   origin of, 131 ff; ruins of, 125;
   temple of, 123; theories of, 118 f
   130–33, 137; walls of, *122*, 123–26
Zschaetzsch, Karl Georg, 15